FABIAN CHUNG

PILLARS

JetFable

Cover Design by Shum Wing Yan

ISBN: 978-0-578-00891-2

Published by: JetFable

Visit our Website at www.JetFable.com

To friends, family, and those who inspired and encouraged me.

CHAPTER ONE

Francis Seto leaned his back on the hard wooden chair and shivered. It was four in the morning and although the summer weather of northern California was by no means cold, Francis' blood was chilled. Cold terror was like an invisible serpent that crept from his skin, through his bones, to his heart. He remembered the ghastly death scene of his two friends. Okay, they weren't friends, Francis admitted to himself; he didn't have friends. Dan and Jeff were acquaintances, workmates who he cared nothing about. Yet seeing their heads squashed like oranges, blood gushing from multiple slash wounds on the lifeless bodies, intestines poured out of the eviscerated stomachs like worms escaping from the ground, he felt like someone had pierced his heart with a cold steel blade. He tried to erase the images from his mind, but almost choked on his own saliva, and fought desperately the urge to vomit.

"Coffee?" the detective asked him.

He nodded.

"Black, okay?"

"Whatever." He never drank black, but now he didn't care.

Francis did not have a chance to take a good look at the detective until now. Sanders of the Mammoth Police Station was a short man in his early forties dressed in a tidy brown suit. His short blond curls and mischievous grin was that of a child, yet the lines on his face betrayed his years.

With an appreciative nod, Francis accepted the cup of coffee in both hands watching the detective seat himself comfortably behind the desk. Detective Sanders was staring at him with a penetrating gaze of dark green.

Francis sighed. It was going to be a long night. Instead of bringing the coffee to his lips, he wrapped his fingers around the cup as if it was the most precious item in the world. The heat from the cup warming his cold hands, it gave him the illusion of fighting away the terrorizing chill. He felt his shivers diminish.

"Still cold?" the detective asked. It was more like a grunt than a statement of concern.

Francis shook his head. That was a lie. There was no warmth in the world right now that can make his shivers go away. He thought about the unrecognizable, inhumanly mutilated bodies in the blood-covered room. He didn't like thinking about the slaughterhouse images, but compared to the other things he had seen this night, they were a soothing comfort. What really chilled his blood was not the ghastly death of his two friends. But the two phantoms that had appeared before him earlier: an apparition from the past that had haunted years of his memories, and a bogeyman that came alive from his worst nightmares.

Detective Sanders gently settled a tape recorder on the table. "This is just routine," he explained before Francis could utter a question.

The detective then read him his rights. Francis had heard it many times on TV. He never thought that he would actually have someone read it out to him. Clearly he was a suspect. The chair was uncomfortable, it was designed to be just that – he'd read it somewhere, probably in a crime novel. He couldn't lean back. All he could do was to lean forward, and leaning forward meant closing the distance, and a suspect would feel more pressured to tell the truth. Being innocent, he had no reason to lie and to feel afraid. Still, he wished he could have exchanged chairs with the detective while he was getting coffee.

"Let's begin by stating our full name." The detective pressed the button on the recorder. "I'm Benjamin M. Sanders, Mammoth Police Homicide."

"Francis Shun Seto."

"First, tell me what happened," the detective said calmly.

Yeah, so what the hell happened? Francis asked himself.

*   *   *   *

Francis was an ordinary guy who graduated from college and had an ordinary job working as a software developer for Bel And Biological Engineering Laboratories. He neither drank, smoked, nor misbehaved, and certainly had never set foot anywhere remotely close to the vicinity of a police station. What had happened was the stuff of nightmares.

The fire that broke out in the B.A.B.E.L research facility led him to the two-day stay in Mammoth, California. Andy, his superior, had suggested taking the short vacation. Francis agreed but was not enthusiastic about the vacation. He didn't know his coworkers well, and he had no intention of getting to know them better.

It was the third time he had been to Mammoth, a well-known ski resort area. He was there once three years ago in the summer with a couple friends and it had not been a pleasant memory. There were the occasional activities of fishing, hiking, and mountain biking, but nothing as exciting as skiing in the winter. Francis disliked outdoor activities because they were a waste of his time. Although he tried to keep in shape by visiting the gym every day for a half-hour workout, the daily routine was not exactly fun; he saw them as a necessity for health. For entertainment he would go to his computer games and science-fiction novels.

Francis offered to drive the five-hour trip from Los Angeles to Mammoth. Although his Honda Accord was not the perfect car for a trip, it was spacious and sufficient. One reason he wanted to drive was to avoid having to think about topics for conversation. All he had to do was to concentrate on the road. Meticulous by nature he wanted to be in control of his own car, and his own life.

Andy's cabin was at the bottom of a hill on a quiet, serene street under the shadow of a large oak tree. The simplistic wooden frame house belied the luxurious interior which was decorated with ornaments like of a royal manor. What caught Francis' eyes were not the delicate satin cushions, ornate tapestries, and silk canopied beds, but a stone pillar that stood proudly in the center of the living room facing the fireplace supporting the high wooden beams of the ceiling. Seemingly out of place with the wooden surroundings, the stone pillar was adorned with carvings of naked women with angelic wings. Each of them had their arms spread upwards, lips parted in sensual ecstasy, as if they were waiting with eager anticipation for something to descend from heaven. The scene was neither blissful nor comforting. A feeling of cold menace pricked at him and he felt the hair stand up on his arms.

They spent the rest of the day on the lake rowing and fishing. Francis got to know the others better; rather he felt more comfortable jesting and talking about mundane things with them. He told none of them anything personal. Most of the time they talked about sports, which did not interest Francis, maybe except for racquetball which he played quite frequently during his college years. So he talked about racquetball, he talked about school, and he talked about last time he was in Mammoth, skipping the details which he did not want to bring up. It was a waste of time. He was different. And they could never be his good friends. And he did not want them to be. He didn't need any friends.

The next day was spent idly while they mountain-biked and played poker in the cabin. Dan and Jeff seemed to enjoy the stress-relieving environment. Francis told himself that he could care less because he never took his work too seriously. Though he was on a paid vacation, he'd rather spend his time doing his own chores. There was never enough time to finish all the movies, computer games, and books he wanted to go through.

CHAPTER TWO

Francis lifted the cup and sipped at the coffee. It tasted like bitter Chinese medicine. Nevertheless it was warm and it felt comforting as the liquid washed down his throat. He wasn't so cold now.

Detective Sander's gaze never left his face.

He glared into the cop's eyes and shivered once more. He remembered staring into the eyes of the evil clown that stood next to his bed. It was like staring into the eyes of a predator poised to devour him any second.

"Where's Andy?" He was the only other survivor of the night's atrocity.

"In the other room," the detective muttered.

"Getting interrogated?"

"If you want to put it that way."

"We didn't do it."

"I didn't say that you did."

Francis suddenly remembered Sam, an old roommate from high school. He knew what Sam would have said, "I didn't think you had enough balls to do it, little worm." Francis' fists clenched tightly when Sam's face surfaced in his brain. Then he relaxed a little, calming himself. He took another sip from the cup, and there was a long eerie silence.

"Are you ready to answer questions?"

It wasn't really a question. He wondered when the detective's patience would run out. Not determined to test the man's limits, Francis answered with a shrug.

"What happened?" the detective repeated.

"I woke up in the middle of the night— "

"What did you hear?"

"Nothing." It was not exactly a lie.

"You just woke up for no reason."

If that was meant to be a reproachful question, it did not sound like one.

"I wanted to go to the bathroom," Francis said, hoping his face did not betray the truth.

*   *   *   *

He retired early that night, exhausted from the strenuous hiking and biking exercises, but more tired from the incessant, mindless poker games that they played. He fell asleep in the large canopied bed, staring at the silvery crescent moon that dangled outside the window.

A cold breeze woke him up in the middle of the night. Not remembering the windows being opened before, Francis did not mind it now, as the cold air was refreshing. He watched as the white curtains danced like the hem of a nightgown under the soft glow of the moon. Abruptly, an uncanny feeling of being watched shattered that placid moment of peace and silence. He turned away from the window and saw a figure on a chair leaning against the back wall of the room.

Silhouetted against the dim moonlight, the figure was as still and as silent as a statue. Glowering at the figure, Francis clutched the blankets around him, his heart thudding at an uncontrollable pace. The figure had an irregular shape for a head, with what seemed to be a horn protruding from the top. Francis did not let the interloper out of his eyesight. He didn't dare to blink. He was afraid that if he looked away for even a second, the creature would be upon him.

Even though he couldn't discern its features clearly, its glowing red eyes were like infrared beams scanning for his weakness. Their deadlock gaze lasted for what seemed like hours. Neither of them moved. Francis did not really believe in demons and ghosts, but he had read enough horror stories to admit the possibility of their existence. He didn't believe in God either, even though his mother was a devout Christian. Being baptized at birth and educated in a Catholic school, he at least knew how to pray, but never did voluntarily. He always thought that even if God were real, why would He have the time to listen to his prayers? Well, He better listen now. Francis locked his fingers into a devout clasp and muttered his prayer to God, asking Him to get rid of the nefarious entity that was before him. He closed his eyes, hoping that when he opened them, the vile entity would disappear like a figment of his imagination.

When he opened his eyes, the figure was no longer on the chair. It stood at the foot of his bed. It was a clown. The pointed pinnacle on its head was not a horn, but a hat shadowing an inhuman face devoid of emotion. Its eyes glowed red like flickering candle flames. Its lips were slightly parted; sharp teeth gleamed under the moonlight. Its gaze was that of a predator, one that sought pleasure crushing its prey before devouring it. Shivers went through his spine like waves of undulating spasms. He screamed, but no sound came. He felt a warm wetness spread from his crotch down his thigh.

He crawled back, desperately trying to escape, but like a puppet suspended in midair by a string, he had not moved an inch. His body was stone cold, unresponsive to his demand, frozen like a marble statue. The inhuman clown's arm pointed upward, sharp claws flashed and glistened in the crepuscule. When did it raise its arm? Francis never saw the movement even though his gaze never left the inhuman, pilfering monstrosity. The thing was going to strike him, and death was imminent. No, it was a dream, he told himself. It was a vivid dream, but a dream nevertheless. He closed his eyes and told himself that when he opened them again everything would be all right.

Half anticipating painful death, half expecting himself to wake up from the abhorring nightmare, he waited. A trail of cold sweat ran down his face and a fine wind blew in.

Thump!

Thump!

Loud as clanking drums, those were but sounds of his own heartbeats.

He opened his eyes. The curtains danced in the night breeze. There was no more evil clown. It was a dream after all. Quickly, he tumbled down the side of the bed, leapt toward the nightstand like an acrobat, and reached for the lamp switch as if it was a savior that stood between the line of life and death. The light blasted out and bathed the room in a dim orange. It was not until then that he had the luxury of letting a reassuring breath of air escape his throat.

His imagination must have been getting better, since he managed to scare himself almost to death. Pants drenched with urine, Francis promised himself that nobody would ever learn the truth of this day. Giving a small smile to reassure himself that the nightmare had passed, he quickly changed into a new pair of pants.

With his heart still beating at an incredible speed, and his hands still stone cold and shaking, he was afraid. What if it wasn't a dream? What if this cabin was haunted and an evil malevolence was going to subdue him? The verisimilitude of it was frightening. He believed in souls, karma, and reciprocation. He believed that he had never done anything wrong in life. Serial killers were not frightened of ghosts. What did he do to deserve this? No, it must have been a nightmare.

It had been a long time since he was afraid of the dark, but he was now. Easing the door open, he surveyed the hallway carefully. Whether it was a dream or not, he told himself that light was the nemesis of darkness. During countless stories and scenarios in his mind he had marked himself as a hero of the light defeating darkness. As long as he stayed in the light, he was safe. Light warded him against the unknown, light protected him. He considered the option of staying in bed until dawn with the lights on, but he wanted to go to the bathroom. He desperately needed a shower. If not for sanitary purposes, he needed to wake himself from his nightmare. Squinting towards the opposite wall of the hallway, he flipped the light switch and surveyed his surroundings as if he was a member of the SWAT team taking on terrorists all by himself.

Andy's door was closed. No sound came from below.

Studying himself in the mirror, he concluded that he looked like shit. He didn't look at his own reflection often. Though he was not bad looking, he didn't consider himself handsome. But now he looked like he'd been through hell more than twice. Turning on the tap water, he gave his face a refreshing cold splash. He stared at the running water for a while, and at the corner of his eyes he saw movement.

Fear welled up from the very core of his being. There was no conscious determination of danger, only an instinctive terror and an irrational alarm. He considered whether to look up onto the mirror, mirrors were portals between worlds, so some books had said. The world of reflections sometimes revealed to us more than the real world did. He looked up and saw her. He gasped.

Michelle.

A serene face as pale as ice, long black hair cascaded down her shoulders in natural waves. He stared into her emotionless, round, hazel eyes and shuddered. She was as beautiful as he had remembered her. But she was dead. Her lips were purplish gray, the color of meat that was left too long in the fridge. They parted slightly, but not in a sensual way. His terror was different from before. It was not the fright, apprehension, and panic of the hunted. It was a frigid, dreadful trepidation that was no less terrifying.

He spun around, hoping that she would not be there. But she was as real as the ground he stood on. She was not completely solid, but not transparent either, what was behind her could vaguely been seen through her softly glowing skin. She was translucent, like a computer-generated specter from a big-budget movie.

She wore the same dress she had on that night. White as snow, the vertical alignments of buttons that went all the way up to her collar fully adorned her womanhood. Her nipples were vaguely outlined on the gossamer fabric of the dress. She looked almost identical to how he remembered her. Except that she was devoid of life. And there was nothing erotic about this encounter, just pure spine chilling terror.

Slowly, she turned towards the doorway. Half gliding, half walking, she moved out of the bathroom with inhuman grace. Francis felt compelled, drawn to the specter. He followed her into the hallway and down the stairs into the darkness.

The soft glow of her skin became a beacon in the darkness. After the flight of stairs he found himself facing the stone pillar in the center of the cabin. The angelic carvings seemed alive, eyeing him with desire. Their legs spread as wide as their wings, waiting for him to gratify them. The sudden erotic hunger that he felt was eerie and chilling.

The apparition flowed past the pillar, turned a corner and disappeared down another flight of stairs. She was leading him to Dan and Jeff's room – the cellar.

He hurried down the stairs, taking two to three steps at a time, not wanting to lose sight of his ashen-faced guide. It was ironic that her ghastly glow seemed to have been protecting him from the darkness that wanted to devour him, but he wasn't sure that his cadaverous guide would do anything less at the end.

Reaching the bottom of the stairs with a thump, Francis noticed that she was nowhere to be seen. He smelled a horrendous stench, the stench of a slaughterhouse. As he held his arm to his nose, gagging, his other hand reached out blindly for the light switch. His hand came across something sticky. Ignoring it, he found the light switch.

The light blasted the room in a blinding blaze. He gasped at the scene before him, not believing his eyes. His olfactory senses confirmed the truth of what he saw. Falling down on his knees, he let the churned contents of his dinner poured out from his throat.

CHAPTER THREE

"Let me get this straight," the detective said as he raised an eyebrow. "After you have gone to the bathroom, instead of returning to your room, you went downstairs to the cellar to check on your friends— "

They are not my friends, Francis corrected him silently.

"—because you had a hunch. After you saw the scene you returned upstairs to wake Andy up and called 911. Is that right?"

Francis nodded. He did not tell the detective about the mysterious clown, or the ghost from his past. Nobody would believe him. And he didn't need anyone to believe him. He knew that none of what he had seen was his imagination. His two coworkers were gruesomely killed. It must have been the work of the evil clown. But why did the ghost of Michelle come to him? Or was she the one who killed Dan and Jeff? No, it couldn't be. Whatever the hell had happened, he was going to get to the bottom of it, and he was going to do it on his own.

"You heard no screams?"

"I told you, I heard none." He knew the detective didn't believe him, but it wasn't a lie. He simply left the supernatural out of it.

Detective Sanders frowned with disbelief, as he expected. "The room showed signs of struggle…"

"I am not a light sleeper," Francis interrupted. "And I have no reason to lie to you."

"I'm not saying that you did," the detective replied calmly. "It's simply my job to get to the truth."

There was silence and they stared at each other.

Sander asked, "Do you know the victims well?"

Francis shook his head. "They are merely acquaintances. I don't know anything personal about them."

"How long have you worked at…"

"B.A.B.E.L.," Francis reminded him, "Bel and Biological Engineering Laboratories."

"You worked in the same department for half and year and you don't know each other well?"

"I'm not a talkative fellow."

"As I can see." Detective Sanders closed his eyes for a short moment and let out a deep sigh. "Andy Roach, what do you know of him?"

"He's my manager, the person who hired me. I know him a little better than anybody else in the company—" but not by much. "I wouldn't call him a friend, he's just my boss."

"You seem to really keep to yourself."
"Is that a question?"

"Merely an observation. Did you have a normal childhood?"

"What's normal?" Francis didn't like where this interrogation was leading. He did nothing to deserve this.

"Were you abused?"

"Physically? No."

"Then how about mentally?"

"That's none of your business. I don't see the relevance of this. You know I didn't do it—"

"I don't know that," the detective cut him off abruptly. "Even if you didn't, you might know something that may serve as a clue to the case—"

Before Francis could utter a word, the detective silenced him with his raised palm. "You might not know that you know something. But anything insignificant you know might lead to something that helps. You do want to help us catch the killer, right?"

He could care less. He knew who the killer was. Well maybe not exactly, but he certainly knew a lot more than the police ever could. He nodded anyway. "Then stop asking about me. I have nothing to do with it."

"If you didn't do it, then you shouldn't be afraid of answering my questions," the detective reprimanded him with a scowl. That was the limit of his patience. "Do you have friends?"

"That depends on the definition of friends."

"This is not a game, Francis." The detective's gaze became a penetrating glower.

"I just thought we should resolve our issues with definitions," he said as he drew an intake of breath. He was tired of answering questions. He wanted to be left alone and he wanted to go home. "If you call people you say hi to when you pass by or people you occasionally eat lunch with 'friends', then yes, I have a few. Not many, but a few. But if you call people who you confide in with your personal problems, who you trust with your life 'friends', then I have none. And I'm not sorry about it. I'm not an open person. I enjoy being alone. And I want to be left alone now."

Detective Sanders leaned back in his chair and sighed. However his head nodded with approval. "That's much better, you'll be out of here soon enough. So what do you do at…"

"B.A.B.E.L." Francis reminded him again. "I'm a computer engineer. I do programming on the database and web interface."

"Do you like your work?"

"I don't mind doing it," he didn't see the relevance of the question; however he answered the question cooperatively. He was tired and he wanted to go to sleep. He didn't know where, and he didn't even know that if he could ever fall asleep again. But he needed to get away from here.

"What do Dan and Jeff do?"

"Pretty much the same thing. We all got hired around the same time."

"Do you know of anyone that might dislike them?"

Enough to pull out their guts and decapitate them? He shook his head and shrugged. "Not that I know of."

"What does Andy do at work?"

How the hell should he know? "He trains us and tells us what to do. He's a senior engineer and a manager."

"How did you get involved with B.A.B.E.L.?"

*   *   *   *

It was another day of interviews. Francis was in his best suit, actually the only suit he had. He had worn it in high school graduation. He felt uncomfortable in a suit, even though there were considerably a number of other seniors that dressed in business attire. He watched an Asian girl in a beautiful business suit walked by. If her skirts were any shorter, her bottoms would spill out. He watched her hips swayed as she trailed up the stairs in her high-heels. Why did girls look so nice when they dressed for work? Why did guys have to be so encumbered? Maybe it was only him that felt that way. He told himself that if he was the girl's interviewer, he'd be impressed, and it was by no means her intellect or credentials. The job was hers. He sighed with resignation. It was not a fair world.

He told himself that he better get a job offer soon. He did not want to graduate jobless. Once you've graduated, if you are jobless, then you are nothing but another career-less college-graduated bum. The world already had an excess of them. He didn't tell his parents that he wasn't going to medical school until earlier during his annual visits to Hong Kong. His father, being a dentist, questioned how one could make a living if he were not a professional. How little his father knew, and he called himself a professional. Francis told them he would find a job and not to worry about him. He knew they wouldn't. They just didn't want to find an excuse to be ashamed of him. They didn't care about what he liked; they just wanted him to make them be proud in front of other people. They wanted to say 'My son is a doctor' to their friends.

Fuck that. He wasn't going to be a doctor; he couldn't take another four years of school. With his grades, he couldn't even make medical school. Most of all, he did not want to stand around twenty hours a day healing the sick. Initially he wanted to be a doctor because he thought it was a respected profession and it would earn him a living, but that was the wrong way to approach a career. He liked computers. And the field was blooming with new technologies and demands everyday. So he decided to find a job in the field of information technology.

It wasn't easy for him, lacking good grades, extensive work experience, a degree in computer science, or social skills. Charm and charisma was not his forte, and one could argue that they were more important than credentials, especially in a job interview. He couldn't agree more. Stopping in front of the door to the career center, he reminded himself to smile at all times and pretend to be a people's person. Perception was reality.

Signing his name on the logbook in the front desk, he seated himself on one of the couches in the waiting lobby. He glanced at his watch, twenty minutes to his interview. That was perfect timing. He looked around and saw nervous students everywhere anxiously anticipating the call of their names, victims, waiting to be tortured with humiliation. Unable to fight back when they were humiliated, they were at their interviewer's mercy. Wanting the job, needing a career, their interviewer was that path to success, if only they could endure the torture. Each of the anxiety stricken students stared at each other with mortal hatred. In the career center everyone was each other's deadly rivals. Each day only one or two out of ten contestants would emerge victors. The rest of them were but the casualties of war, the bottom of the pyramid, losers of the society.

A shadow towered over him. He looked up, awakened from his reverie. A beautiful woman stood before him. She was dark-skinned, probably of Latin descent, with a lush mane of curly dark hair, wearing a black business suit with a low cut white blouse. She had a tag that said 'B.A.B.E.L.' on her jacket. Was she his interviewer? He didn't know if he should praise or curse his own luck. His throat was dry.

"Francis?"

He nodded and took her extended hand. He reminded himself to apply enough force to his handshake to assure of his confidence but not too much to indicate respect and humility. Such a superficial world, he told himself. Even a handshake was full of lies and deceit. He wished that he was in his imaginative world and that brandishing a sword was the solution to all problems. He put up his smile.

She sat down beside him, tugging at her skirt, making sure that not too much of her thighs showed. "I'm Sophie," she said with a warm smile. "I'm here to talk to you about the company and make you comfortable before your interview."

She had such good-looking lips. Francis discarded that thought and listened intently to what she said. "I'm with the Human Resources Department and I've been working for the company for about two years. Babel conducts research in different pharmaceutical and genetic fields. We sell a variety of products and always look for new ways to improve health. I guess I don't really need to go too much in depths into the history of the company or our products, if you've already been to our web site?"

Francis nodded. Going through a company's web site was often the first step for preparing for an interview. There was a Chinese saying, "Fully understanding your opponent in battle, you would always emerge as the victor." Originated in Europe, Babel went public in the States in 1997 after its breakthrough debut of the permanent cure for Cystic Fibrosis through genetic manipulation.

Learned from one of his biochemistry classes, Cystic Fibrosis was basically a disease in which a person's respiratory system fails to clean the lungs of dust and bacteria because DNA mutation in the cell membrane causes a failed chloride channel in the respiratory airways. A person with Cystic Fibrosis had serious chest infections, and only repairing the DNA sequence was truly beneficial to the patient. Genetic engineering enabled doctors to temporarily replace lung cells and cure Cystic Fibrosis; however, a patient had to undergo constant treatment because lung cells were replaced in the process of regeneration within the human body. The scientists at Babel had a high understanding of the human genome, and they were able to engineer a process to target the germ cells that lie deep to the epithelial lung cells, replacing the DNA sequence permanently. The permanent cure for Cystic Fibrosis was a breakthrough in medical history, and thus Babel became well known in the States. Babel also had a variety of dietary and health products like fat-burners and even a brand of human pheromone cologne that claimed to subconsciously attract the opposite sex. Francis didn't believe in those products, but nevertheless they sold well after the famous medical breakthrough.

The rest of his first round interview felt like a conversation, and Francis found that he liked the informal approach. It relaxed him. They hadn't discussed the job specifically, but mostly talked about him, his life, interests, and goals. While he tried to stay to the truth of most things, he also made himself sound more of an active, friendly person than he truly was. Occasionally she shifted her legs, crossing them in another position. Despite the almost embarrassing flash of thigh, Francis tried his best to fix his gaze on her eyes, which were no less distracting.

One of the things she said about the working environment that really captivated him was the recreation facility: an indoor pool, indoor racquetball courts, workout room, billiard tables, table tennis, even an underground arcade.

"There's a bar at the top of the recreation facility," she explained with pride. "It's opened to everybody, but employees get half-price discount on drinks. Babel is a big place, and we are encouraged to meet people and have a good time. I like going to the bar for a drink at night when I have to work late, sometimes I even go back there when I'm not working. It is as good a place as any. Maybe I'll see you there if you decide to work for us." She shot a quick glance at her watch. "Well, it's almost time for your interview. I had a very nice time talking to you." She shook his hand again and led him into the hall of doors beside the front desk.

The Torture Chambers, Francis thought. He wasn't at all frightened, perhaps just a bit anxious. After all the woman did do a good job of helping him relax, as opposed to other companies where you just sit down in front of two hard-faced interviewers and go through a series of humiliating interrogations. He had been through some computer company interviews where you had to take a test, or answer tricky impromptu IQ questions only geniuses could answer in that amount of time given. Or some interviewers asked moral situation multiple-choice questions which sounded so vague that you could not possibly know which answer was the one they wanted. And usually the answer you chose did nothing to reflect your own moral code or personality. Sometimes Francis wondered if the tests were designed to test your intelligence or ability to face different problems, but to give you mental pain and see for how long you can endure the torture.

That was the first time he met Andy Roach. Well over six feet, blond hair that was cut military short, his finely chiseled features were not daunting, but friendly, especially his beaming smile. As opposed to Sophie's attire, he was in a simple polo shirt. After a firm handshake and the customary greeting, he spent fifteen minutes talking about himself, what he did in the company, and the job functions of the position Francis applied for, occasionally giving Francis a chance to ask questions.

Andy had his undergraduate studies in Stanford, double majoring in Molecular Biology and Computer Science. He worked for a start-up software company and then spent three years at Babel.

Francis guessed that Andy was five years older than him. There were a few questions about school and work experiences, nothing specific or technical. They talked about interests and other things. Surprisingly, Andy played racquetball and video games, and even read a couple famous science fiction novels. Francis felt that they were quite similar. Perhaps he would be where Andy was in five years, a senior engineer. The interview was no more formal than the last one, taking about forty-five minutes but felt more like twenty. Nothing like torture, in fact Francis enjoyed it albeit feeling morally wrong to actually enjoy an interview.

"I think you're a pretty good fit with our company. You'll get a call within this week."

Those were Andy's last words before Francis was ushered out of the chamber.

It sounded good, Francis told himself. But you can never be sure. He was quite sure that Andy liked him, but he also knew that someone with better credentials could always emerge. He had done his best, now he was going to leave everything else to fate.

Sophie was in the front speaking to another victim. She looked up as he walked past, smiled and waved at him.

The next few days he was almost praying for the phone to ring. He was in his last rounds of interviews, the last chance he was going to get a job before graduation. Three days later he got the phone call from Sophie saying that he got the job. He was surprised that there were no second or third round interviews. Instead, he was invited to spend a day of orientation at the Newport Beach center. After seeing the working environment, he could decide whether to accept the offer.

The Babel research facility at Newport Beach was impressive. Five marble-colored high-rises surrounded a medieval-styled fountain. In the center of the fountain, a stone statue of a woman poured water from a vase. One hand was raised, as if she was a Greek goddess bestowing blessings on all those who surrounded and worshipped her. Each building had a pointed roof and was of a slightly different height than the others. Bathed in the golden gleam of sunlight, they looked like a cluster of crystals. The facility and the fountain made an odd contrasting pair, the fountain seemed snatched from ancient history, placing it right in the center of the technological advances of the future.

Two of the buildings were dedicated to research, one pharmaceutical, and the other genetics. The other three were Human Resources and Management, Accounting and Sales, and finally Computing Technology. But what caught Francis' attention was the three-story building across the fountain, the Recreation Center. That was the place that sealed the offer. The place had everyone in the orientation tour in awe. It had a vast underground arcade with games that came with big-screen monitors, a workout room with electronic monitoring equipment, extensive lockers and shower, seven Racquetball courts lined in parallel cells against a row of trench-mills and bikes. Everything looked like they had just been freshly out of a sports equipment store. A cafeteria with a variety of booths overlooked the pool area through glass walls. The bar was on the third level. Dark and decorated like a medieval tavern with wooden beams that lined the ceiling, it was large even for a restaurant, with small oak chairs and round tables scattered throughout the place. A large projection TV was in one corner. The far-side wall was situated with scattered billiard tables and a small disco dance platform. Francis was not a nightlife person who frequented bars and clubs, but the place certainly looked appealing to even an introvert like him.

The next thing he knew he was working there in the fall after his graduation.

CHAPTER FOUR

"Alright," Detective Sanders had his hands clasped, his chin resting idly on them.

Sanders' gaze was no less intense than before while Francis recounted his involvement with Babel. He left out as much details as possible, eager to only satisfy the man's curiosity.

"So why this vacation in the middle of the week?"

"Because of the fire."

Earlier that week, a fire broke out in the genetic research lab. It happened in the middle of the night. The fire did not seem to have been serious, as the next morning when he went to work, he saw no traces of damage and incineration except the occasional wandering firefighters and zealous journalists. The genetic research labs were closed down that day.

Andy told him that it was an accident caused by spilling of chemicals. Some said it was the works of AGTC, the Anti-Genetic Terrorist Coalition. That was what the people in Babel called the group of Christian zealots who protested against genetic research. They claimed that humans, as creation of God, had no right to meddle with God's creations. To do so was blasphemy, and thus evil. There were rumors that these people caused the various accidents that occurred throughout the States. There was no evidence linking the terrorist activities to the Christian group, to authorities they were only church communities holding protest events and forums. Their goal was to gain supporters so that the government one day would pass a law to forbid 'meddling with God's creations'. AGTC existed as an underground rumor, an urban legend.

Francis could not understand why people saw harm in genetic research. After all, people were born with genetic defects. Was it wrong to correct them through advanced science? God, if He existed, gave humans a brain to think and benefit society, and to do anything less was against what humans stood for. It was unbelievable how a twisted belief in theology can lead to thinking of something as good and noble as healing the sick, to be something wrong, evil, and even satanic.

However, there was one irony in calling the demented believers AGTC. Adenine, Guanine, Thiamin, Cytosine were the four nucleotides of DNA, the basic building blocks of all living things. The million combinations of our genetic information were made up of nothing else but these four basic chemicals, which defined who we were and how we functioned. And perhaps, the AGTC were the ones who would stand in the way of human attaining the first step to godhood, the power to not only manipulate life, but create it. The day when humans manipulated and created life with ease was the day when humans saw God as their peer. Perhaps they were afraid to live on without the guidance of a higher power.

Francis could never understand why, but his mother was like that. She attended fellowships and church gatherings, devoted what little time she had outside her work to God. When he was a child, for a time he hated God, because God took away what little time his mother had for him, He took away his mother's love. But when he grew up, he saw how silly he was to blame someone that he didn't even believe in. Mother was who she was, a devoted follower of God, who had no time to love him. He respected her belief because it was part of her, as his belief was part of him. He believed in his own power of imagination – it took him away from pain, it bestowed him with happiness that he could not find in the real world, it enveloped him in a world of love which did not exist in reality.

*　　*　　*　　*

"Faber, you've done it." A beautiful girl wrapped her hands around him and kissed him fully on his lips. "You've done it. You've defeated Lucifer, last of the ten sages."

Returning the sword to the scabbard strapped across his back, he lifted Rena up with his big arms as he strode across the blood and lifeless entrails of his defeated opponent.

He reached the computer terminal, and the red button. When he pressed it, everything would return to normal. He had thwarted the evil plans of the ten sages. The destroyed planet would then absorb the reverse entropy forces and spring back into existence. The universe would once again be in peace. And he was going to carry her back to his home and live happily ever after (that usually meant just a few days), until the next trouble came up.

*   *   *   *

"What's so funny?" The detective's coarse tone shattered his reverie.

Faber Bardsong, a master swordsman with no equal, a mercenary for hire who had never failed a mission, a bard who charmed hearts with his songs, a natural charismatic leader who led troops into battle, a savior of kingdoms and worlds. He was Francis' alternate persona in an imaginary dimension where technology and sorcery collided, and fate of the human race rested on one man's shoulder. Francis was living through one of the imaginary moments when Faber had triumphed once again over evil. He was grinning. No more dreaming, he told himself.

"As I said." For a moment he searched his brain frantically for where he left off before his thoughts wandered. "I was involved in modifying the intranet at the research facility, the one that burned down. Well, our project plan had gone to waste after the fire. So Andy decided that we should take a short vacation before things heat up again. He suggested coming to his uncle's cabin here in Mammoth. That's how we ended up here."

"Except that you didn't really want to come." It was another shrewd observation from the detective that accomplished nothing else except an attempt to intimidate him.

"Why do you say that?" if you want to play, I'll play. He went along with the detective's game of words.

"Well, it seems to me that interaction between people is not exactly your forte. So I thought you wouldn't have enjoyed a trip with your coworkers. Yet you came anyway because Andy was your manager and you didn't want to thwart his wishes and to appear as out-of-place with your coworkers. So you agreed to come."

"And tell me something I don't already know."

"Well, I don't see the reason to be belligerent about this." The detective cocked an eyebrow and added, "Did you notice how your friends were killed?"

Francis wanted to remind the man that they weren't his friends, but he decided that it would accomplish nothing. "Yes," he answered with a nod. "Gutted, blood everywhere, multiple slash wounds. The heads were—" he searched in his head for the right vocabulary to describe a smash watermelon but he decided to settle for the less precise. "—unrecognizable."

"So you took your time to examine them," the detective said in an accusing tone, which Francis disliked. He knew the man was trying to cast him into a trap.

"I did not have the stomach to examine them. One quick look was enough for me to recognize what had been done. I told you I have nothing to do with it. If I did it, at least I would have the wits to stage a break-in."

As far as he remembered, they were no signs of broken windows or doors indicating illegal entry to the cabin. But he was not surprised at that, because he knew what killed his coworkers. And he was probably going to be next on the list.

"Most peculiar, isn't it?" The Detective smiled, and Francis did not understand why, possibly because he had gotten his answers and seemed satisfied with them. "Well, looks like we're done here."

Francis took a quick glance at his watch. It was 4:23 a.m.

"You can go now." There was a loud click as the detective hit stop on the recorder.

Where? Francis thought, certainly not back to the place of death.

"Well, maybe not." Sanders gave out a tired sigh after shooting a glance at the clock on his desk. "It is quite late, and you have nowhere to go. There's still the matter of your belongings in the cabin. Tell you what. You can stay here at the station. Sleep on one of the couches outside or something, I'll be back in the morning. Then I'll take you back for your things and you can be on your way. Do whatever you wish afterwards, stay a few days and enjoy the fine weather here, or go back to LA, just stay out of trouble."

"And one more thing." The detective reached into the front pocket of his jacket and pulled out a business card. "Here's my card. If you think of anything that'll help us with the case, don't hesitate to call."

Francis took it and shoved it into the back pocket of his jeans. Andy was already outside, slumped on the couch like a big bear, still wearing shorts and a wrinkled T-shirt, his pajamas. His half-closed eyes jerked open when Francis took the seat next to him. For a moment they said nothing as they watched the detective give instructions to a brunette female officer behind a desk and stride out the door down the steps into the night.

"I'm sorry, Francis, about Dan and Jeff," Andy spoke in a barely audible voice. "I felt as if I have dragged you all into this. I hope God forgives me."

The mention of God reminded Francis that Andy was a Christian. If God even have time to care, if God even exists. "It's not your fault."

Andy laid a hand on his shoulder. "God will watch over them in heaven."

Francis said nothing.

"Are you alright?"

"I'm tired." He rested his head on one of the cushions and closed his eyes.

*   *   *   *

Francis was nine that year, when he still lived in Hong Kong. His father came back from a short vacation in Europe. Mother didn't go with him because her work didn't allow her to take vacations.

"Look at what Daddy brought you?" Father took out a doll. It was a clown. "I brought you this from Denmark."

Its skin was white, lips were colorless. It stared back at him, smiling a horrid smile. Under the copper-red hair, its clownish countenance did not belong to the kind of clown one saw in a circus but the kind that one would run into on a Halloween night that carried chainsaws.

"Here, hold it." Father held the monster out to him.

Francis shrugged.

"Alright then, it'll just sit here." Father settled the doll on top of his desk. It slumped down limp and lifeless. Then his father left him alone.

The clown was glaring at him, it was smiling. You don't want me, do you? But too bad you can't get rid of me. At night I will choke you to death.

Night after night, he was afraid, deadly horrified. It watched him sleep; it watched everything that he did. It was waiting, waiting for a chance to kill him. He wanted to be rid of it, but he couldn't. Mother would be very mad. Mother would not love him anymore. He didn't want that.

One night, in the dark, he stared at the dark shape of the clown that was on his desk. He saw the menacing shape move. Slowly it stood up. Lithely it jumped down from the desk to the carpet. Then it danced, a dance of death.

He screamed.

A burst of light shattered the darkness around him. Mother opened the door and turned on the light. "What's wrong, dear?"

"The clown," he said pointing at the floor. It wasn't there anymore.

"It's sitting on your desk."

"It was moving, it was dancing."

Mother smiled, it was a reassuring smile. But it failed to calm him. "You must have been dreaming. Now be a good boy and go to sleep, you still have school tomorrow." She kissed him on the forehead, nudging him back to sleep.

When the light was turned off, the darkness became a monster that did not hesitate to devour him. The clown was in the middle of the room, dancing. It was now translucent, glowing like an angel. Only that it wasn't one, it was a demon.

He didn't scream anymore. Watching the ritual of evil in silence, he knew that his mother would not believe him. He had to defend himself. He was brave, and he would not succumb to evil. Determined to guard himself, he did not sleep the whole night. However the clown did not touch him. When dawning light seeped in, the translucent entity of evil no longer existed in the room. The white devil-faced clown sat quietly atop his desk, studying him, laughing at his helplessness. Tonight, tonight I will kill you.

That morning he thrust the window open, clutched the doll by its throat, and flung it out with all his strength. He watched it arch across the sky.

From the fourteenth floor, it was a long way down. He smiled to himself because he had triumphed over evil.

The clown never appeared again, and somehow he had blocked out that memory. But now he remembered. And the embodiment of evil was no longer twelve inches tall. It was as big as a real man, and it was going to kill him.

*   *   *   *

Francis jerked awake in a pool of cold sweat. Rays of sunlight seethed in from the gaps of the blinds. Andy was already up, speaking with Detective Sanders. He stretched and was not surprised that his bone ached, probably more from last night's morbid ordeal than the uncomfortable position on the couch.

Washing his face in cold water, he took a look at himself at the mirror. Half expecting that something would appear behind him, he was glad that nothing did. He looked no better than he looked last night, a ghost. He needed a shower but knew he would not have the luxury of one until he was home.

Neither of them said much on the return to the cabin. The place was deserted except the yellow crime scene tape Francis had often seen on TV. He wondered if the bodies had been removed, but he was almost sure that the forensics team had already done all they could with the place.

Taking a quick look at the pillar and the angelic figures carved on it. He wondered what part they played in the evil that had taken place. For a moment he was transfixed by the sight before him, the angels' bare chests heaving, their depraved legs spread as wide as their inhuman wings, their tongues swirled. They spoke to him, urging him to perform immoral copulation with them. He shrugged and turned away, cursing at his own imagination.

It took them only a short while to gather their things. The detective bid them farewell, assuring them that he would let them know if any suspects were apprehended. They scurried into the Honda, finally glad to be away from the cursed place.

"What a vacation," Andy said with a deep sigh. "You look tired, Francis. Do you want me to drive?"

He shook his head. "I'm fine." He preferred not having to rely on another's driving.

"You're the kind that worries about car insurance and stuff like that, huh?"

"No, it's not that at all." Andy would never understand. And he did not intend to make him understand. He knew people who were overprotective of their own automobile, but he was not that kind of person. "I'm not tired."

The trip back down to LA would take approximately five hours. On a clear Friday morning with minimal traffic on the interstate freeway, it was a refreshing run on the road. Francis stared at the vegetation that flew by like bullets and thought about Michelle and the clown. Why had they come? Why did they kill? Why not him? Why not Andy? Why appear to him? What did they have to do with each other? What did they have to do with him? What did they want? A million questions crowded his brain.

"Who do you think killed them?" Andy's voice broke the silence.

"Who knows? Seems like a lot of serial killers are out on the streets these days." That was true; the crime rate of the Los Angeles area increased dramatically during the year. Either the police were less competent these days, or people found more varieties of illegal ways to entertain themselves.

"I couldn't really sleep last night," Andy commented. "When I can't sleep, I pray. I prayed for the spirit of Dan and Jeff, I prayed for our safety."

"I hope He listens." Francis had known Andy for eight months. It was the first time he mentioned the contents about his prayers or anything about

God or Christianity. He did not know a lot of personal things about his manager. But they had enough common interests to be more than acquaintances. They had played fighting games in the arcade together and challenged each other a few times in the racquetball court. Although he didn't have as much confidence in other things, Francis considered himself an adequate racquetball and an excellent arcade player. But Andy was better. He usually beat him two out of three times in both. Sometimes at lunch time or in between ball games, they would talk a little about their hobbies aside from their jobs. Yet Francis always kept in mind that Andy was his manager. Although he was less tense around the man now and felt more comfortable having fun with the guy, there was still a barrier between them, in addition to the barrier he had between everyone, keeping them from being friends.

"Francis," Andy said as he turned towards him, his ocean blue-eyed gaze, wide and intense. "Do you believe in God?"

Francis kept his eyes on the road, occasionally glancing at the rear-view mirror. He shrugged. "I'm still waiting to."

For a while, Andy didn't say anything, seeming to take time to analyze and ponder the meaning of his simple answer. "That's the first I've heard. But it's a good answer. So you want to believe, but there's just not enough evidence for you to have faith in God?"

"It's easy to believe, but it is hard to have faith," Francis answered. "We all like to have a higher power watch over us, provide us with explanation for things that we can't understand, for us to rely on."

"Francis, you really surprise me. I didn't know you're so philosophical."

"More like sentimental. And don't talk me into believing God."

"I won't. God will show you the way when He decides to. It all works out differently for us. I was going to ask you to go to a fellowship with me tonight. We don't make you do anything. It's just a gathering for people to talk with each other, trying to understand each other and themselves better. I thought you might benefit from it, especially after what happened yesterday."

Francis pretended to think about it for a moment, but he knew he was going to say no. "I think I'll pass."

"Sure, if you want to go next time, just tell me."

Francis remembered the fire and he wondered if Andy believed in genetic research. But he didn't ask, letting the calm silence once again encompassed them.

Andy's apartment was in Santa Ana, a small city next to Newport Beach, a lot closer than Brea, where Francis lived. Like him, Andy apparently lived by himself. Francis stopped the car in front of the town houses at the end of a cul-de-sac. In one of the better areas of Santa Ana, the street had a serene quality of an American suburban street. Andy gave him his number before getting out, telling him to call in case he needed anything.

It took Francis about twenty-five minutes to Brea, another town in the suburbs at the edge of Los Angeles and Orange County. On the second floor of a small apartment complex, his one room apartment was quite messy, as he had not cleaned the place in weeks. Though not tidy, he considered himself to be a hygienic person. He cleaned dishes and took out trash regularly. Since he did not cook and often ate takeouts, he managed to keep his place grease and roach-free. CD cases were spread all over the living room floor. He had to jump over them to get to his room. He switched the computer on, connected to the Internet, and checked his E-mail. There was none. He didn't receive mail often, except the occasional e-business ads and newsgroup messages, but out of habit he checked it often.

Taking a quick shower, he plunged headlong on his bed, falling within seconds. When he woke up, it was night and he had the lamp on, casting off the darkness that surrounded him. He was never really afraid of the dark before, but now he was. He did not want to find out what kind of surprises lurked in the gloom.

It was a quarter past eight on a Friday night. He suddenly had the urge to visit the local bookstore just around the block.

The Gibson's was what one called a haunted bookstore. The archaic place sat at the junction of two quiet streets; hardly anyone visited the place. Francis, however, was a regular at the store for a few reasons. Most people shopped online. Enormous virtual bookstores not only provided lists of anything one could possibly want in any sorted order one liked, also incessant reviews, recommendations, interviews with authors, and numerous services that one could never dream to obtain in a real book store. Not to mention low prices, instant shipping, convenient one-click buying methods really distracted customers from shopping in the real world. He enjoyed surfing on Amazon.com, looking at their products and reviews, but he still bought his books at the local bookstore. He liked to hold and flip through a novel before he bought it. It gave him an excuse to not stay home, and he could give Mark an occasional visit.

Mark, a young Japanese American, was small and slender. He was around five feet five, a bit shorter than Francis. During the brief conversations they've had since Francis moved to the neighborhood a few months ago, he learned that Mark was around his age, a graduate from UCI with an English degree, who was basically taking care of his parents' bookstore.

Mark had once told him that he was aspiring to be a writer. Francis had thought about it himself. Writing down his imaginations would be something quite enjoyable. But he knew that his parents would not have approved of a writer's career. They had a hard time accepting him as a computer engineer.

The young man was an avid reader and often recommended books to Francis. Sometimes they discussed thoughts provoked by a book. Francis never talked too much about his own personal life. Nevertheless he took a liking to Mark.

"Well, Francis. Nice to see you again, I haven't seen you for almost two weeks." Mark looked up from behind the counter and greeted him with a grin.

Francis glanced around. The Gibson's had the usual quaint noble look of a nineteenth century British bookstore, nicely paneled with wood, the books stacked neatly on black wooden bookshelves under a high-beamed slanted ceiling.

"Work was busy."

"The new Stephen King novel just arrived this morning," Mark yelled with exuberated glee.

Francis could almost picture him jumping up and down like a child. "Yeah, I know. Amazon.com had it a couple days ago. But I don't think I'm in the mood for another horror novel."

"Not you too!" Mark frowned with disappointment. "Falling under the spell of the Internet, losing all the fun of old-aged window shopping."

"Nah, I haven't really bought a book online. I just look at the reviews. The bashing between Jordon and Goodkind fans was something to read about."

"Which group do you belong to?"

"Neither, they both have their merits."

"Sometime we got to have a long talk about that. But not tonight, I'm sorry to say but I'm closing soon."

"Oh?" Francis was quite surprised because Mark was usually there until midnight, even on weekends. It was practically his second home.

"I am going out to dinner."

"A date?"

"With my sister."

"You have a sister?"

The bell rang, indicating the door being opened. "Speak of the devil."

Wearing a plain V-neck, long sleeve T-shirt and blue jeans, she was small and slender, perhaps no taller than five foot one. She had a short, boyish haircut and big round eyes. Her high cheekbones and pointed chin framed her pale face pleasantly. She gave him a warm, friendly half-smile adorned by a small dimple on her left cheek.

"This is Jessie, Francis," Mark introduced them.

He took her small hand, shaking it. Her grip was strong and confident, like a man's handshake.

"She's a cop," Mark whispered in his ear.

She shook hands like one, but she certainly didn't look like one.

"What was that, Markie?" she said softly, glowering playfully at her brother.

"Sorry, Francis. I guess we're closed now," Mark said. "Hey, why don't you join us for dinner? Unless you already have plans."

Francis was surprised that Mark invited him. He didn't know either of them well. "I'm not really hungry, just going to grab a taco or something. Thanks for the offer, though. I'd better be going. Nice meeting you."

He gave both of them a smile and quickly strode out of the bookstore.

The streets of the old town section of Brea were almost empty, bare branches clicked together in front of windows of old shops and homes. Despite the approaching hot summer weather, the air had an arthritic chill to it. A cold chill of portent swept over him as he walked back towards his car. Treading along the quiet street, he tried to avoid the overhung shadows cast by trees; the howls of dogs sent a shiver down his spine. Unknown things lurked in the dark, and he was afraid. *Why am I being so paranoid? I can't go on with life like this.* At that point, he considered that he should have taken Andy's advice to go to the fellowship; maybe he would have felt better. Maybe he just needed to go back home and forget himself with another novel. No, not this time. There were answers he needed, and he wanted to find them. His head pounded. He needed a drink.

He knew just the place to go. In just twenty minutes he was in Newport Beach, pulling into the parking structure of Babel.

A bar, the Raven was on the top floor of the recreation center. Just as the name suggested, the inside had a medieval cast to it. He remembered looking at the place almost a year ago during orientation. The place fascinated him, yet he never did find the excuse to come up here, until tonight. Everything was as he remembered, the dark atmosphere, the small wooden tables and chairs, the beamed ceiling; the place was like a conjuration out of a fantasy novel.

There were only a few people inside. A few executives huddled in front of the large projector in one corner intently watching sports highlights. Three ragged looking man gathered around the billiard tables, couples sat in dark corners huddled against each other. He settled in front of the bar and ordered a cocktail. After gulping it down, he ordered another.

At a table beside the bar counter, there was someone he recognized. Sophie's provocative skirt challenged every man's eyes. She was transfixed in a conversation with a burly man who sat close to her. Under the table, one of the his hands was up her skirt, brushing her inner thighs. She seemed to be enjoying it.

Francis sighed and glanced away. Other than the bartender who was busy behind the counter, he was the only one without company. He let his mind wander, fancying himself in a medieval tavern. He became the famous Faber Bardsong. With his long delicate fingers on the string of his lute, he told a tale of a legendary struggle between gods. Voluptuous barmaids brushed by, giving him kisses, and travelers settled around him, applauding his marvelous performance.

The scene dissolved around him and he remembered the first time he met Michelle – the ski trip during spring break in his sophomore year organized by the Science Fiction Club. It was the same accursed place, Mammoth, and he had met her in a bar. He wanted to get away from the group at night, as he didn't want to engage in their petty board games and idiotic group activities.

*　　*　　*　　*

Her face was that of an angel. Big dark eyes and small pouted lips; her long wavy hair poured from her shoulder down her waist in a beautiful cascade. She wore a white dress that almost brushed the floor. It was buttoned up the front to her collar but its sheer fabric only accented the wantonness of her womanhood. The outline of her nipples stood out like inviting pinnacles of pleasure, leaving his throat dry and his heart thudding as she walked by.

It was impolite but he found himself staring at her the whole night.

Finally, she approached and with a smile said, "If you stare at me any longer, I'd have to ask you to buy me a drink."

When he agreed to do so, she sat down beside him. He was tongue tied in the beginning, but he gradually felt more comfortable talking with the strikingly beautiful woman before him. In their conversation; she told him that she was studying Accounting in UC Berkeley and that she came to Mammoth with a couple of sorority sisters on a ski trip. He asked her why she was in a bar by herself and she replied that she enjoyed solitude once in a while.

Francis didn't remember how but he ended up letting her drive him back to her place, a cabin at the outside of the mountain. They continued their conversation after settling on the couch. He realized that he had never talked so much in his life, especially with a stranger and one so intimidating. Not remembering what they talked about next, perhaps about school, family, or even favorite movies, he recalled her telling him that he had beautiful eyes. Strangely he felt comfortable around her.

Then she leaned close to him, staring at him with her big dark eyes. Her hair smelled like roses.

His heart raced.

"Did you know that I could hear your heartbeats?"

"Is it that obvious?"

"I think it's nice." She gave him a little smile and leaned even closer until she was breathing on his neck. "I was wondering when you'd ever get around to kissing me. Then I decided not to wait."

Her lips brushed his, sending an electrifying thrill down his spine. It was at first sweet and utterly innocent, soft kisses of friendship and affection. Then her tongue parted his lips, probing his inner mouth.

Her hands guided his to her breasts. When he touched them, she let out soft murmurs of need. He kissed her neck. When his hands found the buttons of her dress, she gently pushed them away.

"What's wrong?" He frowned, worried.

She smiled slyly. "I am going to teach you a lesson today. You're going to learn to stop being a gentleman, especially when a girl is yearning to go to bed with you. Girls have dignities. And you are going to melt down that defense of being a lady. Here, kiss my hand."

He learned down and kissed her hand.

"Hold my other hand with yours."

He did as he was told, then needed no more instructions. He kissed her bare throat and unbuttoned her dress. Slipping his hand inside the fabric, he cupped her breast which fit perfectly in his hand. Her nipple stood rigid when the inside of his palm brushed it.

Lingering kisses trailed to her toes and back to her lips, silencing her moans. Her fingers slid from their intertwining entanglement of a lover's clasp and eased apart the metal teeth of his zipper.

She gave him a leering smile, got down on her knees and kissed his penis. She ran her fingers down the full length, while her tongue frolicked with his seat of pleasure. When she had him within the depths of her throat, he gasped, pulling at her hair.

He must have been dreaming, he told himself. Things like this did not happen to him, not him. This was one dream that he never wanted to wake up from.

The moment that she had him in a straddle, he felt his expending climax. Waves of electrifying spasms reverberated throughout his body. He remembered the first time he masturbated. It was almost like that, except this was a hundred times more galvanizing.

"I'm sorry." He didn't know why his first instinct was to apologize to her, but he knew that he had come too soon.

She only gave him a smile. "Your second lesson of the day. You don't apologize to women when you're making love to them. In bed, a woman likes to be dominated. Now you'll kiss me, fondle me, fuck me, make me feel like I'm in heaven, and stop apologizing to me."

"Yes, ma'am."

Lost in the passion with this woman he had just met he didn't know how many hours they made love after that, as time meant nothing to him.

*   *   *   *

Red faced, he noticed the yearning bulge of his erection under his jeans and glanced around. Pushing the thoughts of his first and only sexual encounter out of his mind, his gaze settled on the large projector on the far corner.

It was the ten o'clock news with a story of the murder of a high school girl in a Los Angeles park. The media had called this mysterious serial killer the Tormentor. He left each victim with a cut-off left nipple. Francis shivered as the gruesome scene of murder visited his head. What is the world coming to?

He left the bills on the counter and headed home.

On his way home, she appeared again.

Looking up at the rearview mirror, he saw her ghastly face. The apparition rode quietly in the back seat of his car.

The hair on his arm almost had a life of its own, each strand standing on its edge. He kept himself from gasping and screaming aloud this time. Through the mirror, he stared into her dead eyes.

Dread didn't keep him from keeping a watchful eye on the road as well. It was a car accident she had died in. Even though he was driving, it was not entirely his fault. He believed in retribution and reciprocation, and he had done nothing to harm her. For a short time he had loved her and thought fondly about the memory of the night. He didn't deserve to be haunted by her.

Gripping the wheel, he spun the car around, pulling onto the shoulder and halted next to an embankment. He turned around and faced the unwanted phantasm hitchhiker at the backseat.

"Just what the hell do you want?" he demanded.

CHAPTER FIVE

Jessie Ishimina stretched her arms and yawned. It was five on a Friday morning. The day was barely dawning and Echo Park was deserted except for the occasional joggers and the police vehicles surrounding the crime scene. She was in a very foul mood. It was the third time this week. She knew that when her cell phone under the pillow chirped, she was up for another gruesome sight. She stormed out of her car towards the crowd.

Terry Leo, her partner, stood calmly looking down at the body while the forensics personnel scurried around the scene. As always, he was dressed in a tidy Armani suit, with his dark brown hair combed neatly back. Almost six feet five inches tall, he looked like a GQ model with too much gel. He had the body of an American Gladiator, without an ounce of fat on his body. Women in the force adored him, and they were jealous of her. She liked Terry as a partner, not because he was good-looking, but because he was a smart and competent cop and she could trust him to guard her back when she needed it.

"What took you so long?" he asked as she approached.

"I was having a nice dream, so I decided to go on for ten more minutes or so."

When she stood next to him, they were like opposite ends of the world. He was tall, and she was only five foot one. Others considered him strikingly handsome, she considered herself plain. He always wore a suit, and she always wore jeans. She hated to be encumbered by fancy clothes when she might have to chase criminals. Though that rarely happened, she thought she'd look odd in business attire. Despite their differences in appearance, they worked well together.

"Was I in it?"

"No, I wasn't dreaming about fucking you, if that's what you're asking. That's the last thing I would ever want to dream about."

They joked about sex often. He always enjoyed claiming that all women in the world wanted to sleep with him. She was not surprised if that was true, but she didn't belong to the 'all women in the world' group.

She glanced down at the naked body that sprawled flat on the grassy ground. Involuntarily her hand flew to her mouth. Three years on the force and she was used to the blood and gore, but the world never seemed to run out of shocks. It looked worse every time. She did not have the urge of vomit anymore, but it was still very uncomfortable seeing a gruesome death scene. Bile threatened to rise in her throat.

Not able to make out the face of the dead woman, Jessie noted that her blue flesh had already started to decompose. The left nipple was cut off, with no sign of blood. The lower half of the body was still fresh. Under the flashes of camera light, blood seemed to be visible under the flesh of her thighs. It was the work of the Tormentor. Victim in her late teens or early twenties, raped and left nipple severed, upper body decomposing in an unusually high rate. The last two victims were also found in the vicinity of the Silverlake community after midnight. One was discovered in an alley behind a lesbian bar, and one was in a grocery store parking lot.

"Just how does he do that?" Terry was referring to the Tormentor's work. "It is just not possible." The police had named him the Tormentor. The press overheard it, and now everyone knew of the name. It was fitting.

The last two bodies had been in the same condition. The upper body so badly decomposed that the flesh were falling off from the bones, and the lower half appearing only dead for a couple hours, as if they were different bodies killed at different times and just patched together for display. But they all knew that it wasn't true. The last two bodies had completely decomposed down in less than two days. There were no insect infestations and chemicals used, at least as far as the coroner was able to tell.

Jessie watched uniformed cops fending off the press. For the police, the journalists always managed to get to the wrong place and the wrong time. No doubt someone inside had tipped them off. She had done so herself, when the truth needed to be told, but never so soon. The condition of the victims had to remain hidden from the press or the world would be thrown into a pandemonium. The FBI agents who had just arrived closely monitored the moving of the body. The Bureau had become involved in the case as a joint operation after the last victim was discovered. This time she surmised that they would have an advance team of scientists working with the body, trying to decipher the secret of the Tormentor.

So far the police had no suspects and no clues about the killer's identity. Since all three victims were found in Silverlake, Jessie surmised that the killer did so to taunt the police – a message that the police were not competent enough to catch him. He could be from anywhere in the Los Angeles area. But in order to get his message across, he would dump fresh blood in the same area.

"Let's get some breakfast," Terry suggested after the white van left with the body.

She nodded, knowing that another hard day of work was in store. Might as well start the day with a satisfied stomach.

They went to the Denny's a few blocks away.

Jessie ordered an omelet with white toast and Terry had scrambled eggs and sausages.

"You have a profile on the guy yet?" Terry asked.

"Just haven't written it down yet." She had studied Criminal Psychology at Stanford and had been taught to understand the criminal mind. Each killer she had gone after was captured after she had done quite an amount of crawling in the criminal's mind. And she did it better than anyone else in homicide.

"Let's hear it then." His dark eyes sparkled with excitement.

"I thought you'd never ask," she said, straightened her back and began. "The Tormentor is a male in at least his twenties, intelligent, confident, educated, perhaps works a dull, but respectable job. He lives with his family, in a middle-class area. He doesn't have a criminal record, just a normal looking guy with a grudge against beautiful women."

"You got to watch out then."

She glowered at him.

He made a face. "And how do you know all that?"

"First of all, the killing does not take place where we find the bodies. That means the killer has probably been killing them at home and then dumping them at night. The last two victims were both high school seniors who did not usually stay out late at school nights. They were abducted in the afternoon. As the Coroner's report suggests, though badly decomposed, the bodies indicated that they were killed after midnight. If the killer lived by himself, he would probably have killed them not long after he abducted them. It seems that he still lives with his family and possibly hides his victims in the garage or a cellar and acts only after midnight. Since both victims were still seen in school after five-thirty and missing afterwards, I assume that the killer has a regular job and he's not free until after five.

"He's highly intelligent. Condoms were used in sexual intercourse. No traces of foreign pubic hair on the victim. Either he's very careful or he shaves regularly. Victims all died from strangulation and no fingerprints were left. The victim's IDs were left deliberately. He seems to be confident in taunting the police that we cannot find him even though he keeps dumping the bodies at the same place. The last two victims were both beautiful, so I assume the same with this one. He abducts them for the hate, and not really for the sex. In his past he must have been hurt by beautiful women, especially ones around their late teens. There's an intense hate with the way he treats those bodies. The way he cuts off the nipple, the way he leaves them decomposing – a hideous display to the public, as if he's trying to tell us these beautiful features were just a facade and they're really ugly inside. Satisfied?"

"You never cease to amaze me," Terry said as he clapped his hands in mocking applaud, "but how do you explain how he manages to make the bodies that way?"

"Beats the hell out of me," she sighed. "And that's the Coroner's job, isn't it? Who knows, if you asked my brother, he would say it's alien abduction." "Fuck that crap." Terry gulped down his glass of orange juice and frowned in disgust. "There has to be an explanation for everything. Well, the last two victims lived thirty miles apart. We have no idea where this guy lives."

"We'll just have to wait for him to show up."

"You think he will?"

"You wanna bet?"

"You know, why don't you just become a profiler?"

"I like to get on the real trail, rather than advising asses like you from behind a desk. I want to hunt them down myself."

"Give you the thrills huh?"

She didn't answer him and gave him a distant look. It wasn't really about thrills. It just felt like the right thing to do.

"One more question."

"Shoot."

"Why the left nipple?"

She shrugged. "Signature."

"Do you think a jar of nipples would be sitting in his room?" Black humor was one thing that she learned spending considerable time at the force. Cops had to sometimes laugh at the violence around them. It keeps them from going insane.

"You're fuck'n gross."

"But what I don't get is which one is the left nipple?"

"Which one is your left hand?"

Then they both laughed.

The rest of the day was routine duty, for a homicide detective. The victim's name was Sandra Wiggins, an eighteen-year old high school senior from Arcadia, an upper-middle class area east of downtown Los Angeles. The identification was left close to the body – one nice thing that the Tormentor did. Usually unidentified victims needed dental records matching to confirm the ID, especially when their fingers were too withered away for prints. But for victims who did not take good care of their own teeth, it was a hassle for the police, and it usually took an unpleasant amount of time.

Mrs. Wiggins broke into a desolate cry at the news of her late daughter – her only child. Jessie stood mute in a corner watching the woman break down while Terry consolidated her. He was good at soothing women, so she let him do his job. With her fists clenched, she studied the various photos that scattered over the house. Sandra was a beautiful girl with a loving family. It was the third time this week that they had to visit the victim's household to gather information and to break the tragic news to loved ones. She was infuriated.

The Tormentor was taunting them. He wanted them to watch people suffer from the loss of their loved ones, he wanted them to hate him, he wanted them to hate him so much that they'll make mistakes the next time they saw him, and she was playing right into his hands. No, she told herself, she needed to be calm, and she was going to get that inhuman bastard no matter what.

Since they knew that the Tormentor was choosing random victims, they did not go into details of Sandra's personal life. From what Mrs. Wiggins said after she regained her composure, Sandra had good grades in school, was in the tennis team, had a lot of good friends, accepted to Columbia University studying journalism, was a loving kid with a bright future. And the Tormentor took all that away. Living only a mile and a half from school, she walked to school daily and Jessie figured that she was abducted on the way back.

"When I get my hands on that son-of-a-bitch, I'm going to skin him alive," Terry commented after they left the stricken mother.

"If he doesn't reduce you down to bones first."

"He can really do that, can't he?"

A sudden coldness swept up her spine. She remembered looking at the last victim's body in the mortuary two days ago. The bones were so white and clean as if the flesh had been washed off the body. What if the killer touched one of them? Could he have accomplished that by touch? Or did he make the victims consume some kind of chemicals? Whatever it was, the Coroner wasn't able to find anything, except the marks of strangulation that still remained on the worn flesh.

"I hope not." She sounded so unsure of herself that she suddenly felt very vulnerable and afraid.

The mood for pleasant chitchat was gone. In the car, they both realized how tired, physically from lack of sleep and emotionally from seeing the aftermath of loss of a human life, they were. Jessie studied the map on her lap, and suddenly she realized a pattern.

"Terry, Silverlake is the center of all three places of abduction."

"Which means?"

"That, for sure he'll be going back to Silverlake to dump the fourth body."

"Well, I thought you had that figured out already."

"It never hurts to be sure."

Terry only grunted and continued looking ahead at the road, hands tight on the wheel.

"Hey, haven't we been doing the same thing everyday?" She stretched her arms, feeling her ached shoulders.

"Well there's the day before yesterday, and then there's Monday. Every other day."

"Every other day?" She was almost shocked to hear the phrase.

"Yeah, so what?"

"That's it! He's murdering someone every other night. Which means tomorrow night he'll be in Silverlake. And I'm going to be there to take him down."

"You mean we," he added, "are you sure?"

She didn't have to answer him. They both knew that it was the absolute truth. A serial killer had to follow a pattern, once it was established. It was like the code of a killer, his mark, his creation of art. And he had to sign under his work to proclaim it as his, and he had to do it a certain way. To do otherwise would be betraying his own code of honor, unmaking his own creation, undoing his own identity. The logic of it was absurd, but she knew that it was how serial killers acted. And she was going to use that to her advantage, to apprehend him, to make him pay for what he had done.

"What are you doing tonight then?" Terry said as he pulled the car onto the freeway back in the direction of downtown.

"I need rest."

"Are you interested in dinner?"

"What?" She was startled. They had been partners for about a year and a half now and they had not really done anything together other than work. "Are you asking me out?"

"Yeah, why not?"

"You don't have a date with one of your bimbo girlfriends on a Friday night? That's news."

"That's why I'm trying to get one right now."

"Am I a backup or something?" She made a face at him. "Sorry, man. Got a date with my brother tonight."

"Bimbo girlfriends, huh?" he gave a disgusted grunt.

"They are how they look." She remembered meeting two of his friends one time at a bar after work. They all had the similar look, tall, blonde, buxom and brainless – not because they were blondes with D-cups, but because they still talked like Valley high school girls. "But I'm not going to comment on your sexual preference now."

"I used to like them because they're eager. But I know they only like me because of my body."

She let out a giggle.

"What's so funny?" he said, frowning.

"Like you for you body, like you for your mind, like you for your money. What's the difference?"

"You sound like someone who doesn't believe in love."

"On the contrary, I do believe in it. I just think most of the people in the world don't know what true love is."

"Then what is true love?"

"How the heck should I know? I'll tell you when it comes to me, but I really doubt it." She was in a serious relationship once, when she was in college.

*   *   *   *

She had met Joe in a party during her freshman year. He was a senior Art student at Stanford. They had dated after that and fell instantly in love with each other. He was dark and handsome, a sensitive and artistic man, and was very talented at paintings and sculptures. Yet he had a depraved lifestyle of debauchery – not a day went by without alcohol and drugs. The first time really being on her own, without having to take care of her brother, without having guardians, she was drawn to the lifestyle. Everything to her was new, not to mention he was superb in bed. So she had moved out of the dorms and into his apartment. That few months she was there she had lived her life without purpose – she rarely went to class and hardly saw daylight. But she was happy because she had thought herself in love.

That day she came back she had heard a woman's giggles in the bathroom. Joe often had classmates over. Women in class adored him because of his talents and his fun-loving personality. Sometimes Jessie felt jealous but she never doubted that he would be unfaithful to her. But when she heard the dissonance of his voice and another high-pitched voice from the bathroom she couldn't resist the urge to investigate.

Pushing the door ajar she saw him, naked, leaning comfortably on top of the toilet seat, admiringly focused at the woman kneeled before him – a red head with short hair, her face burrowed between his thighs. He brushed at her wet hair fondly as she performed, her lips moving eagerly along his shaft.

For a long moment she was stunned. Then she screamed. The woman grabbed her clothes and dashed out the door.

"I can't believe you did this to me. How long has this been going on?"

"It… it just came up."

"What do you mean it just came up?"

"I wanted my cock sucked. And she was eager to do it. You know you won't do it, for whatever reason you were never willing to tell me. I still love you and all. But I need this. You don't know how great it feels to watch a woman go up and down on you. It feels like you're the king of the world."

That's what love came down to, blowjobs. And he gave his reasons as if he was the righteous and she had somehow wronged him. He disgusted her. With so many tears in her eyes that she could hardly see, she yelled, "Get out of here."

"What do you mean get out of here? It's my fucking house. You get out of here." And she did and never came back to that place again.

*   *   *   *

"Don't be a cynic, Jessie. It always comes."

She smiled at him.

"You know, you have the most beautiful smile I have ever seen."

She laughed. "Terry, if you're trying to talk me into sleeping with you, you're doing a very poor job at it. And you know how the Department feels about this kind of shit."

"No, really, I mean it. And fuck the Department."

"Whatever."

As Terry pulled the car into the underground parking lot of the downtown headquarters, Jessie felt a rush of relief that she was going to get off work soon and see her brother. She had not seen Mark for almost three weeks now. She enjoyed her job very much, but lately everything seemed to have piled on her like a rock over her shoulder. Recently the crime rate in the Los Angeles area had skyrocketed, and the police had nobody but society to thank for.

After going back up to the office and typing her report, she was eager to be off. It was almost nine when she reached The Gibson's. She had almost grown up at the place. Actually, she and Mark didn't live with their foster parents until she was twelve. But all the fond memories of her childhood came from the bookstore, where she and Mark played games each day after school and were loved by two people whom they now called parents. All the bad things that happened before she was twelve were jumbled in her mind, blocked off, and nicely being secluded in an area of her brain that she never accessed.

Fewer and fewer customers came to the store as she was growing up. People went to the big chain stores like Barnes and Nobles, where they had everything in stock. And now more people shopped on the Internet for low prices and convenience. She had asked her parents to sell the store, because they weren't really making any profit. But Mark insisted on taking care of it. He had loved books ever since he was small, and being surrounded by volumes of books helped him aspire towards being a writer. In a way, she was still glad that the store was around, because it was where she drenched herself in childhood nostalgia. Sometimes she wished that she were back at those days, when the world consisted of only four walls, Mark, and her loving parents. The world was peaceful then. Now the world she knew was a horrid, senseless den of murderers.

As she pushed the door open, Mark was talking to someone. She already knew who it was; Mark had talked about him, the only dedicated customer. When Mark introduced them, Francis shook her hand with a smile. Dressed in a simple crew-neck shirt, he was lean but not tall, for the average Asian. His hair was parted neatly in the middle with the long strands combed to the side, his eyes were copper like the color of a new penny, and his face still had a little trace of baby fat on it. She didn't think him handsome, but when he smiled, he had a certain quality of warm boyish charm that she found attractive.

Mark murmured something in his ear.

She only heard 'cop'.

Giving her brother a stare, she asked, "What was that, Markie?"

"Sorry, Francis. I guess we're closed now," Mark told the man. "Hey why don't you join us for dinner? Unless you already have plans."

Now her stare turned into a glower. But Mark only shrugged.

"I'm not really hungry," Francis said. "Just going to grab a taco or something. Thanks for the offer though. I'd better be going. Nice meeting you."

He smiled at her again before stalking out into the street.

"Mark!"

"What?" He stared at her innocently.

"Why did you ask him to join us?"

"I thought you'd like him, he's really nice."

She arched an eyebrow at his brother and gave a long sigh. "If you're trying to play matchmaker, you have to do better than that. He looks like a freshman, for god-sake."

"He just looks younger than he is."

"And I didn't even mean college. How many times do I have to tell you? I don't need a man in my life."

"It's time to settle down, Jess. You're almost twenty-nine now."

"Not quite yet, and please don't remind me how old I am, and now let's get out of here."

They went to a favorite small Italian restaurant nearby. The food was excellent, the price was fair, and the environment had a distinct feel of a landmark place in Italy.

"Remember not to tell Mom and Dad that you saw me today," she reminded him after they were seated. She often visited her parents, but not in the past few weeks. Even though she wanted to, she had not the time and leisure to sit down with them just to chat. Both of them loved talking and they enjoyed hearing her daily adventures. But she didn't want to go home just to tell them she was too exhausted even to chat; it would worry them too much. At first they had disapproved of her being a cop. But in time they understood that it was what she wanted and enjoyed, so they accepted it. Jessie knew that it would make her foster parents very happy if one day she told them that she was done. But she knew she wasn't going to quit, at least not anytime soon. It was her mission, and she was far from completing it.

"I got it, my lips are sealed," Mark said, smiling. "So how's catching the killer business going?"

"Other than that I'm determined to take him down tomorrow, not much is going on." She had already told him about the investigation on the Tormentor briefly on the phone and her brother was fascinated. Though the nature of Tormentor's crime was supposed to be a secret, she trusted her brother and kept nothing from him.

"Do you have any hypothesis on how the Tormentor can be able to do what he does?" Jessie asked her brother. Though he was an English major, Mark minored in Folklore and Mythology and he loved everything that was considered "weird".

"Scientific?"

"I'd like it as scientifically sound as possible."

"I don't think you like alien abduction theory too much then?"

She confirmed with a nod and watched the waiter bring over the steaming hot dishes. She was famished.

"Well, how about that this guy is an escaped lab dog with special powers trying to take vengeance on mankind?" Mark's eyes gleamed with excitement.

"Nah, he can't be a lab dog, or a lunatic. He's an intelligent being committing structured crimes who enjoys playing with the police. He rapes his victims, not for domination or sexual needs, but a signature of challenge to us, and a message to the public about his hatred or jealousy of smart beautiful women. He looks common enough that even if he walks in here this minute, we wouldn't think twice—"

By coincidence, the restaurant door opened behind them. They both turned and looked with apprehension. A lovely couple walked in.

"Paranoid, aren't we?" Mark said with a half smile. "Well, maybe he's just some guy who stumbled across some kind of chemicals which disintegrates organic substances. So he decided to take on a role of a serial killer, since he thinks himself invincible with his new power."

"That's possible." She thought about it a moment, maybe she should pay more attention to investigating chemical or biotech companies. But she had no evidence and wouldn't know where to start. For all she knew, it could be some secret government project and she'd never get to the bottom of the truth. She had read and watched enough thrillers and X-file episodes to dismiss it as impossibility. But if the FBI knew something and was trying to cover it, they would have surely taken over the case. They were dealing with the unknown here, and anything was possible.

"You're going to confront the killer tomorrow, aren't you?" Mark said softly, as if he had sensed her thoughts.

"I sure hope so."

"Be careful."

She nodded.

CHAPTER SIX

Jessie's apartment complex was nicely nestled in the shade of a giant oak tree in the quiet suburban area of Pasadena, a close enough commute to downtown. Furniture was scarce in her unadorned apartment. A sofa, a bed, a coffee table, that was all. She had neither a TV nor a dining table. She rarely cooked. Maybe never, if one did not consider pouring boiling water into a cup of instant noodle cooking. Once in a while she went back to her parents' to have a decent homemade meal, but she hadn't done that in weeks. Her apartment was spacious, and seemed even more commodious with the lack of furniture and the high slanted ceiling. One could use the living room as a dancing stage without bumping into too many obstacles. She had her bed in the living room instead of the one bedroom in the apartment because she liked the idea of the abundance of space. It made her feel fresh and unrestrained. The more space, the less restrained, and the more free and comfortable she was.

Flurry jumped onto her lap as she seated herself on the bed and greeted her with a muffled purr. A beautiful Turkish Van with white fur and big brown eyes, he made soft purring sounds as Jessie scratched his soft fur. She loved listening to his purring as it calmed her. Most of the time she thought of her pet as a dog, a woman's best friend, because he lacked the whimsical nature of cats. While other cats would have come and gone as they wished, Flurry always stayed by her side when Jessie was home, giving out his soft friendly meow, asking to be petted, asking to be loved. And he often snuggled against her when she slept. While most cats despised water, Flurry loved having his fur soaked, and Jessie loved drenching the snowy fur ball until he was fully saturated.

After taking a long bath with Flurry, she got ready for bed and soon fell into a deep and peaceful slumber.

The next day she arrived at the office at ten, a little later than usual. The weariness was finally getting to her. Even though she had well over eight hours of sleep, her bones ached as if she had just been through a war, only which it hadn't even started. She made her reports to Lieutenant Blair, an obese bald man in his forties. She was sure that he was once strong, fit, and ready for the street, but now rows of fat jingled under his strained white shirt as he paced the floor. As far as she knew, most fat men were nice. Not to say that the lieutenant was not, he just irritated her. His flamethrower tongue turned on people at the oddest times, and often when an audience was present at times when grandiose was least expected. She had to watch what she said in front of him, as his earth-scorching retaliation for a breach of etiquette that none other could perceive, often resulted in a dauntingly embarrassing experience, one that she did not fancy living through. And the fact that he seemed to enjoy provoking her made her dislike standing in the same room with him even more.

She had once shot a killer in the forehead fifty feet away while he was holding a hostage at gunpoint. Her marksmanship was excellent, and she was proud of it. But Lieutenant Blair made fun of her in front of the whole force, "She could shoot as good as any man, if only hers was as big as a real man's."

Most laughed but she didn't think that was funny. Now she knew that Lieutenant Blair did not really mean what he said, but when she first joined the force she had a hard time understanding him. Despite his flamboyant, irritating attitude, he was a man of resources and talents. In between his blatant remarks, he often valued her opinions and listened to the hypothesis she made about suspects. And he often knew the right strategy, deployment, and commands in order to ensure justice being properly carried out. He was not simply a bureaucrat who climbed the ladder with only brownnosing and good test scores. He knew homicide and she respected him for that.

Despite the fact that Terry often had to restrain her from firing away in madness at the lieutenant, she had grown to like the man. She still preferred not to be within ten feet of him but she respected him nevertheless. The lieutenant's belligerent tongue was nothing other than a show of genuine affection. She didn't prefer that kind of behavior, but it was certainly better than getting hugged within the proud jangle of his belly.

In the unit shift change meeting, the lieutenant wasn't too affectionate. His mood was dark and tensed, as was everyone's. They were eager to catch the Tormentor, but they were afraid, afraid of the unknown, afraid of what he could and would do. Lieutenant Blair listened intently to Jessie's analysis and her conjecture about his appearance tonight. He did not reproach at her as he often did, but only solemnly nodded. She was dismissed to more paperwork at the office.

In an hour another meeting was held where the captain discussed the plan and deployment with the group and how they should handle the Tormentor if apprehended. They were to wound him, or kill him if necessarily. After all he was dangerous.

Jessie noticed a few unfamiliar faces during the meeting – the bureau. They offered no advice about the matters at hand, but attended as silent spectators. What was their plan? Actually she was quite surprised that the lieutenant did not doubt her conjecture. If she was wrong, it would be a total waste of resources, manpower, and time. But deep inside her heart, she knew that she was right.

*   *   *   *

At midnight they were cruising the streets of Silverlake. Other than the occasional silhouetted figures that lingered outside bars, the streets were calm and quiet. Silverlake had a large community of homosexuals, and there were more popular streets where gay and lesbian bars clustered together, alongside the occasion strip joints occupied by drug dealers, gangsters and hookers. Both Terry and Jessie hadn't patrolled the streets for a long time; it wasn't a usual part of their job. They specialized in looking for clues, investigating them, and hunting down the truth. Harassing suspects and breaking news to loved ones were the bonus.

Time crept by. Coffee mug in hand, Jessie watched the road wearily, half anticipating an emergency radio message any moment. It came after two hours of aimless patrol. On Orange Street, in front of Mahogany Bar, the victim was spotted.

Adrenaline pumped through her veins as Terry swung the car around. They both knew where the bar was, having passed by that place not more than five minutes ago.

A police vehicle was parked sideways in front of the massive wooden doors. The car was empty, siren lights still flashing. They rolled the car to a stop right behind the black and white. The street was quiet and empty, except a naked body sprawled face-up on the sidewalk and a young girl, with her face buried in her hands, shriveled a few paces from the body.

Jessie stepped out of the car, reached for the revolver holstered at her back, and closed the car door with her free hand. She switched the safety off her .38 Smith & Wesson and for a split second, pointed it at the girl who was huddled on the pavement. A mane of long, disheveled sandy hair covered her head where her hands did not. Jessie couldn't make out her face but she didn't seem to be a threat. Then she glared at the body on the ground. Hollow, cadaverous eyes seemed to glare straight back at her. She shivered and bit her lower lip.

The body's skin was as white as chalk powder, left nipple severed, no blood, still fresh and whole. It was no doubt the Tormentor's work, just that the decomposition had not, as yet, taken its toll.

Terry pulled the bar door opened. Jessie followed, both hands gripping the gun so tight that she was afraid that she would crush it apart. No sounds came within the bar. Something was definitely wrong.

A scream came from behind. Jessie spun around, startled. The girl whom earlier huddled like a helpless child was now wailing in terror, staring at her with dark mad eyes. The girl's eyes were transfixed at a point beyond her. Jessie figured she couldn't see her.

"Stay there and don't move," Jessie told the girl. Gripping her gun, she kicked the door opened and dashed into the bar. And what she saw inside immobilized her with terror. Bodies scattered across the place, only that they weren't bodies with flesh and blood. They were skeletons.

Where is Terry? She called his name as loud as she could manage. She knew doing so exposed her position to potential danger. But she also knew that she would have been dead anyway if the Tormentor was lurking in the dark waiting for her. Where the fuck is Terry?

Then she heard movement. Looking in that direction; she saw Terry kneeling on the floor. Leaning on a wooden-paneled wall, he wailed in pain like a child with his fingers cut off but wasn't allowed to scream aloud.

He looked up and stared at her with imploring eyes.

"Terry, what's wrong?"

Then she saw that his shirt was pulled open. His chest oozed and bubbled like the surface of a swamp. She stared with her mouth agape. He got him. The Tormentor got him. Terry was dying.

He murmured something, but she couldn't hear him. She leaned closer.

"Kill me, now. Please," he said it in a voice barely audible.

Tears welled up in her eyes as she held his hand. "No, you're not leaving me, Terry Leo. Damn it, don't you dare leave me!"

He pulled her even closer. "Please, Jessie," he whispered. His breath lingered at her ear like a painful sting of a needle. "And don't go after the Tormentor…"

She saw his flesh blackened, his face gone ashen and distorted in pain. She pointed the revolver at his temple, turned her face away. She cried. She summoned the strength to do what she must do. And at last she pulled the trigger, and felt his hand slip away from hers.

CHAPTER SEVEN

Francis groped for the faucet and waited for cold water. Eyes still closed, he splashed it over his cheek and brow.

He looked up at the mirror. Only his own haunted eyes stared back.

There was no one behind him. He had expected someone, or something, to be standing in the shadows, but no one this time.

Strolling back to his car in the empty rest area, he was determined to move on.

It was four o'clock in the morning, and he was on Interstate Five. There was still one hundred and eighty miles to San Francisco, and he could make that in a bit more than two hours. On impulse and desperation, he had decided to go to Berkeley. He was tired of Michelle's ghost haunting him. She was in the back of his car during the first hour of his trip – at first her dead, cadaverous eyes made his hair stand on its edge. But he was soon used to her visits. She did nothing to harm him, and she did not state what she wanted from him. She was simply there. And he had to know why. Retribution and reciprocation. What had he done to earn the visits of this desperate ghost? She must want something from him. He needed to find out what. So he decided to drive up to the campus of UC Berkeley to find out more about her. It was Saturday morning, and he hoped that the administration office would still be opened.

He looked up at the rearview mirror as he set the cruise control on his car at eighty. The back seat was empty, and he felt relieved. Michelle's apparition did not frighten him as much as it did before, but it was still disconcerting to find her translucent form watching him when he glanced at the traffic behind him. It almost discouraged him from looking into the mirror.

The road was almost devoid of cars. An occasional impatient vehicle passed by with the speed of lightning. Some drivers drove a hundred miles an hour. Francis knew that it was dangerous, and he wasn't in a hurry. He thought about how he was going to find information about her, after all he didn't even know her last name. He needed to find that out first. The accident, there had to be records at Mammoth. The cops would know. He shoved one hand into the pocket of his jeans. He still had the detective's card. When he looked up, he saw her face in the mirror again and jumped, almost losing control of the wheel.

When he regained composure, he studied her and began to realize that while she was translucent, her skin and her clothes had a substance that emanated a faint glow. It was as if she was constantly shifting in between dimensions. For a moment, the faint light that enveloped her made her look like an angel. She was still beautiful, dead and pale, but beautiful nevertheless.

The accident, he remembered it well.

*   *   *   *

He was sore from their lovemaking. He never thought himself capable of such strength and endurance. And he never imagined a woman so eager for him. It was as if he was living through one of his dreams. And he never wanted to wake up from it.

They lay limp in each other's arms. When the morning came, there were sounds and movements from outside the room. Michelle told him to ignore them. She said that her friends knew better than to barge into their room.

For the next couple hours they just lay in bed and talked. Francis told her a lot about himself, his family, and his past. He had never felt so good. Ever since high school and his trouble with his roommate, he had not opened up to a person. He was afraid to.

It had not occurred to him that she did not tell him much about herself, but she listened to him, holding his hands in reassurance. When he was done, she kissed him, urging him to make love to her again.

On the way to lunch, they almost had a headlong collision with a truck. Apparently drunk or simply incapacitated by other means, the truck driver did not notice his vehicle straying onto the opposite lane until the last minute, and pulled frantically at the steering wheel.

Avoiding the collision, Francis performed a ninety-degree turn. The car spun, dust twirled around them. The next moment the truncating vehicle was off the edge of the slope of the canyon. It wasn't a steep slope; yet the car flipped like a dying fish in a bucket while it plunged down the rocky incline.

The accident resulted in a few days of hospitalization for Francis. Luckily it wasn't anything serious, only a slight concussion. But he learned that Michelle was thrown out of the window and died instantly, result of not having a seat belt on. His remorse was heartfelt and canyon deep.

Maybe to Michelle he was just another guy, a one-night stand, but he had intended to ask her to be with him. No chance of that anymore. He had tried opening himself up, and it failed. He knew that she didn't die because of that, but it was true that opening himself up never did him any good. Then he was back to his realm of reverie, worlds of imagination, places where he controlled the flow of events.

*   *   *   *

At seven o'clock in the morning Francis parked his car outside the administration office of UC Berkeley. He decided to take a nap for two hours before looking for information.

Being dead tired, Francis was not kept awake by the beaming sunlight. When he opened his eyes it was already ten-thirty, a little later than he had planned. No nightmares visited him this time and he was glad. He didn't used to have nightmares, but he wouldn't be surprised if they visited him constantly now. Perhaps it was possible that his conscious world was already so much of a nightmare, so he was left alone in the unconscious realm.

He called Detective Sanders at a pay phone. He was more than eager to help him look up Michelle's last name in the database. It seemed that the detective had not been working in the resort area two years ago and was unfamiliar with the incident. Francis was stormed with questions before he got his answer. But he managed to just tell the detective that his inquiry was personal and had nothing to do with the murder two days ago. He assured the zealous officer that he would call again if he learned anything new. The detective probably didn't believe much of what he said, but he got his answer nevertheless. Michelle Siu-Ling Cheng was her whole name.

The administrative assistant in the office bought his fabricated story of being a friend from elementary school and having lost contact with her over the years. He pretended to not know about her death and tried his best to put up a shocked and stricken face. He wasn't much of an actor, but it seemed to have sufficed to cause the lady to lower her guard. As a matter of fact he was surprised that his plan actually worked.

"I'm sorry but I can't give you information regarding phone numbers to her family and such. I'm sure you wouldn't want it anyway, I can tell you that her family lived in New York."

New York? His heart sank. He was hoping that he could talk to her family. He remembered that she mentioned she had an older sister, one that was close to her. He was sure that he could find out more about her from her sister. "Are you sure you can't give me her family's number?" he asked the middle-age lady in a half-pleading tone.

She shook her head sincerely. "It's against the rules. I don't want to get into trouble. I'm sure you are a nice person. No offense intended, but the school can get into a lot of trouble if a family is plagued by anonymous phone calls. It would get me fired."

"I understand." He searched his mind, trying to think of something else that he could ask.

"Ah, this I can tell you," the woman's eyes sparkled suddenly when she looked up from the computer screen behind the counter. "Her last local address is a sorority house, Sigma-Pi. It's not too far from here. I'll give you the direction. Maybe you can find someone you can talk to."

She was a sorority girl, he remembered now that she mentioned it. But she had told him nothing else. Yet he had practically told her everything about his life. It only took him about a half-hour or so. Knowing next to nothing about her, he wondered what her dreams and goals were if she had not died. The woman gave him a piece of campus map, circling a building right off a street. Sigma-Pi, how cliché can a name of a sorority get?

The sorority house of Sigma-Pi was a beautiful mahogany and white building standing amidst towering trees and neighboring less adorned school apartments. Fraternities and sororities were places that governed people's happiness – their sex life. People would pay everything to get in, and being harsh did not come close to describing the initiation process. The rushing process was demeaning and torturing. Yet people went through it without complaints. He had heard wild stories like eating dog food, running naked on the street, and other despicable acts. However, those who got in were gods in their peers' eyes. He had never been within twenty feet of a sorority house in his life, and he never regretted it. He despised people who would literally cut off their own manhood to join an organization such as this and spit on others who valued their own integrity.

He strode up the stone steps to the porch and knocked on the wooden door. After five minutes, a girl opened the door. She was black, very attractive, with long wavy hair and light brown skin. Her green blouse was made of a sheer fabric like a nightgown and it did nothing to hide her voluptuous curves.

"Can I help you?" She had one fist planted on her hips and the other hand supported her on the frame of the door while she leaned leisurely on it. Her eyes darted up and down as if appraising merchandise.

"I…" the sight of her made a lump in his throat. Are all girls in the sorority so sexually appealing? "I was an acquaintance of Michelle. She used to live here?"

Her expression darkened for a moment, as if hit by painful memory, then she nodded. "Yes, she did. You a boyfriend?"

He ran his fingers through his hair absently. "Not really. I guess, just a friend."

"What do you want then?"

"I wanted to know more about her? Did you know her well?"

"I was her roommate," she said as one of her dark eyebrows arched up. "You said you were her friend. Then what else do you want to know about her that you don't already know? And why?"

"I guess I didn't really know her that well."

"You slept with her, didn't you?"

That took him aback and he instantly felt embarrassed. He even thought about turning away. But he knew that he must get his answers. He nodded.

"So why do you want to know her now?"

"We were in an accident."

"Mammoth?"

"Yes."

"And?"

He didn't know how to answer her, except the truth. He knew that she would not believe him, but that was his only choice. "I recently saw her again."

She gazed at him with her dark eyes for a long moment. "In your dreams?"

"No."

"Alright, come in."

CHAPTER EIGHT

They went through a living room in total disarray and mayhem. Francis was not surprised. The place looked like it'd been rampaged after the drunken Friday night parties. As she ushered him to a round, wooden dining table that would fit no more than three persons, she introduced herself as Sarah.

"So tell me." She settled herself comfortable across him, with one leg propping up on the arm of the wooden chair – a display of toned beautiful thighs.

She sits like a whore, Francis thought. But it only made her more delectable to the human eye.

"You believe me?"

"Yes," she said as she licked her upper lip. "Your soul told me you were not lying."

"Excuse me?" What the hell is she saying?

"Eyes are windows to the soul."

Great, now he was talking to a freak. A half-dressed sorority girl who looked like a model on Cosmopolitan telling him that she had just looked into his soul through his eyes. Life couldn't be more uncanny.

He told her, leaving out the details about the murders and the evil clown. She might believe him seeing Michelle's ghost, but he wasn't ready to take her to the next level. Then he told her briefly about how he and Michelle met prior to the accident.

"And you want to know why she haunts you."

He nodded.

"Well, I don't think I can be of much help. I knew her for two years, and quite well. She was active in school, a good student, but she also loved partying, like all sorority girls. She drank, smoked, and slept around as much as any of us did. She never had a steady boyfriend. Guys came and went."

Francis half-expected as much. After all, it wasn't like an angel descended from heaven that day and suddenly decided to love him.

"She was friendly, nice, and we all loved her dearly. Unlike the rest of us, she had good grades. She was smart, and she enjoyed life, every bit of it. She never had a problem with anyone and we were all stricken with grief when she passed away."

He listened solemnly. While she stopped, he did not know what to say.

"I don't think that really helped you, did it?"

He shook his head. "It helped, but just not the way I expected. I expected to be able to uncover something that I can do for her. Where's her grave?"

She let out a muffled giggle. "You think you're going to bring her flowers and everything will be okay? This is not a fairy tale. You know what? Maybe I can help you. I am a Psychology major. Let me ask you this, are you afraid when she visits you?"

"I was startled the first time. But no, I wasn't afraid. It just felt..." he searched for the right word to describe it. "Disconcerting."

"Did she seem like she wanted something?"

He thought about when he saw her in the cabin and then in the car, she was merely there. "No, I don't think so."

"Has it ever occurred to you that if she wanted something, she would have hinted it already? She's certainly not there for vengeance, as you told me you have done nothing to harm her before. And she's not trying to make you afraid of her. Maybe she's there to warn you about something?"

"Is that possible? Like a guardian angel?"

"Yes, precisely, like a guardian angel."

It made sense, and she was a lot smarter than she looked. He had thought her a bimbo, actually he had thought all sorority girls were brainless party girls. He was wrong. Michelle was an intelligent person, and so was this Sarah. He told himself that maybe he should not generalize people as much anymore. Then he thought about how Michelle showed him the murdered bodies. She was trying to convey a message, to warn him about danger. She was his guardian angel? But he hardly knew her. Maybe her spirit decided to watch over him after her death? A million possibilities popped up in Francis' head.

"I think a tarot reading will help you."

"A what?"

"A tarot card reading, you do know what it is right?"

Of course he knew what it was. It was the Gypsy's way of reading into someone's future with cards. He was just surprised that she knew how to do it.

"Normally it'd cost you, but I'll do it for free this time, just for you."

"You charge people?"

"Of course, I have expenses to pay too. And I'm very good," she licked her lip sensuously. "It's worth the money. Just hold on, big boy, Let me get my cards."

Francis swallowed. The way she boldly flaunted her sexuality made him feel very uneasy.

When she came back, she had a deck of cards with her. The cards had intricate designs, framed by gold, each as blue as the ocean. Gently she laid the deck on the table. Then she took her seat right next to him, cross-legged

Japanese style. She smelled like a blooming bouquet, and the closeness of her half-clothed body made him swallow and avert his eyes.

"I will explain the meaning of each card as I conduct the reading, I do this as a habit and it helps me concentrate. They do not signify the final meaning of your problem. I want no interruption and no questions. I will also use both the major and minor arcana cards."

Francis nodded, indicating his understanding. He didn't know much about tarot, but he knew that the cards were divided into major arcana and minor arcana. Minor arcana cards were similar to western playing cards, with four suits: wands, cups, swords, and pentacles, fourteen cards each, with the addition of princesses to kings, queens and princes. The major arcana had twenty-one unique cards. Most people read with the major arcana only because remembering the meanings of each minor card was difficult.

"I would be using the ancient Celtic method to conduct the reading. You are the Querent, the person with the question. You will ask your question and shuffle the cards. You will brush off all thoughts from your mind and focus only on your question. Otherwise my reading will not be accurate. Can you do this?"

"Yes," Francis muttered. "But what will my question be?"

"In one concise phrase, ask for the knowledge you want to receive." She glared at him with impatience.

Francis felt a cold shiver. He almost felt like living in one of his fantasies, where his future lay in a deck of tarots. The idea was absurd. Why was he here? He wanted to know why Michelle haunted him?

"I want to know the purpose of this entity Michelle and what she's trying to warn me of." That was his question.

"Focus, and shuffle," she commanded him.

He focused. He thought about Michelle, her ghastly apparition face, eyes that stared back at him from the voids of depth. And he slowly shuffled the cards. When he was done, he looked at Sarah, awaiting her instructions.

"Cut the cards to your left, and then hand them to me. Do not lose your focus."

She gently scooped up the deck, embracing it in her hands, before she closed her eyes. For a moment there was only silence as she was lost in solemn concentration.

Slowly, she flipped the first card off the deck.

Francis's heart was pounding. It was only a stupid fortune reading, he told himself. Why am I so excited over it? A certain compelling strangeness about the whole event made him want to go through with it. He reminded himself to focus on his question.

One card was placed horizontally in the center of the table. The card showed a woman in a plain white dress, kneeling piously in the moonless night with her hands clasped in solemn prayer. Stars of the night sparkled vividly. The drawing was elaborately beautiful, a combination of fantasy and reality, of a dreamlike quality. Francis had a feeling of being woven into a beautiful dream, or maybe it was a nightmare.

"The High Priestess," she said softly, breaking the silence. "The first card represents that which surrounds the Querrent, that is you. The unconscious, hidden knowledge, wisdom, and understanding."

She flipped the second card.

What does this all mean? He wanted to interrupt her, but he knew better. He had to wait for her to finish.

The second card was placed vertically right on top of the first, forming a crucifix. This card was in reverse. From what Francis could make of the upside-down picture, a hooded figure in a black robe held a wooden staff, and in his other hand fire sparkled from his palm.

"The Magician, is the second card that represents your opposing forces. He is the cunning trickster, deceit, manipulation, the power of destruction."

The third card was placed above the cross. It was obvious what the third card represented.

"The moon, your distant past: secrecy, instinct, psychic powers, dreams, and the irrational."

The fourth card was placed to the right of the cross, a picture of a couple lost in the pleasure of a fervent embrace of copulation. The vividness of the scene made him flush. With an attractive woman sitting so close to him, his mind almost wandered to places he shouldn't be. The question! He reminded himself to stay focus.

"The fourth card is the recent past, the lovers. Soul, choices, sexuality, relationship, love, beauty, attraction, perfection, harmony, unanimity, confidence, trust, and temptation."

That sure was a lot of meaning from a card which depicted a love-making couple, Francis thought as the fifth card was placed to the bottom of the first two. A court jester with a bright-colored hat juggled three balls while he smirked. There was no bane in the card but somewhere deep in Francis' consciousness, he had made a mental association with the clown. Suddenly the room had become dark and cold, he shivered.

"What lies far ahead," Sarah, now seeming like a mysterious witch woman, said with an unconcerned tone. "The Fool. A quest, journey, chaos, folly, delirium."

The sixth card completed a bigger crucifix, devouring the small one, making it vanish into the background of the depicted dreamlike scenes. A hooded figure with skeletal face held a long menacing scythe. Where its eyes should have been, there were only cadaverous voids that held nothing. Francis swallowed. He felt chilled to the bone.

Sarah's face darkened, her brows tightened. "Your near future, Death. Destruction, mortality, rebirth, reincarnation, failure, transformation, profound changes, renewal."

The seventh card was placed somewhere further to the lower right corner of the large crucifix. The card was reversed, on it stood a muscular figure holding an axe, a helpless man impaled under him, imploring help. It was the scene of an execution.

"Judgment represents your fear, loneliness, restraint, and sadness."

The next card was placed above the last. A lady in a dark dress floated in midair. She was not merely under the night, but standing amidst cosmos, and universes. Behind her stars and planets twirled in their paths as if they were alive. Bright light sparkled in her hands as if she was infused with a mysterious magic power, enabling her to navigate as she glided across worlds.

"The Star, the eighth card represents outside influence." The slight smile that touched her changed the dark mood from before. Francis didn't need to be a genius to know that this card represented goodness. "Hope, aspiration, healing, beauty, satisfaction, bright prospects, insight, preparation for new horizons, inspiration and reaching one's goal through hard work."

The ninth card was placed above the eighth, forming an incomplete vertical line next to the cross. It was a regular card of the minor arcana, the deuce of cup.

"Your hope of the future. The deuce of cup represents platonic love, friendship, harmony."

The last card completed the sword beside the crucifix. A tower stood majestically among slanting rays of sunlight.

"The final outcome: the Tower," she gave out a soft sigh. "It can mean a lot of things. The Tower represents catastrophe, the unexpected, divine intervention, punishment, deception, a reversal or change, a broken marriage or friendship, tearing down existing dogmas and structures, destruction of false beliefs, doctrines, and laws both secular and religious."

When she was done, she settled back into her chair comfortably and stretched her arms.

"So, what does this all mean?" Francis was impatient.

"Give me a moment." With her eyes closed and head lowered, the pause was as long as eternity. When she parted her lips, her gaze was as intense as a ball of fire. "The High Priestess is a representation of Michelle."

Francis looked at the card again and noticed the card was covered by another, but he remembered the serenity as the girl kneeled, praying in the middle of the night. Michelle also wore a long white dress, the coincidence was unsettling, he didn't believe in coincidences. This woman's glimpse into his future might hold more merits than she claimed.

"She is the hidden knowledge and wisdom within you. She's trying to help you fight against your foe, the magician, the power of manipulation and destruction. Your distant past holds a mysterious secret, something irrational, something powerful, yet dreamlike and out of the ordinary. Events are shaped by your recent past – your moment of trust and sexuality, the moment you were one with Michelle. What lies far ahead is a journey through chaos. But what lies close is something perilous – it can be death, or a profound change within you, a renewal, or a transformation. Your inner fear, fear of loneliness that restrain you from happiness, that fear affects your journey."

I'm not afraid to be alone, I am alone, I've always been alone. I always will be. But…

"But you shall receive aid through this journey. Someone, or something, guides and show you to the light. You will receive hope and inspiration to reach new horizons. What you want for the future, someone you can love and share, a soul mate."

Now he understood what platonic love meant. Was that what he wanted? Was it possible to have someone understand him enough to share everything with him? No, this was ludicrous. Soul mates were for people who lived through a fairy tale. He wasn't a realistic person, but love? He didn't have to dream about love, he just wanted to be left alone.

"At the end you will face the unexpected. It can be catastrophe, divine punishment, something so profound that changes your life forever. For worse or for better, I do not know."

"What am I supposed to learn from this?" Francis asked when she finished.

She shrugged. "It is the first time of my readings that only one minor arcana card appeared. After all, there are fifty-six of them."

"So?"

"That means that the reading had been significant, and very important to you. It might be too much information for you, but in time you will understand. Do you know the origin of the tarots?"

Francis shook his head.

"The origin of tarots is highly debatable. Some say it came from Egypt, that tarot was a form of communication. Some say it came from the Renaissance, or the dark ages, or even Atlantis. It is closely related to Jewish Kabbalah."

"This is all very interesting," Francis interrupted. "But what does it have to do with me?"

"Just listen," she scowled. "You need guidance on your journey."

"What journey?"

"The tarot showed that you shall embark on a perilous journey. And you need guidance."

This woman is insane, Francis thought. "Are you the star that's going to guide me?"

"Don't mock me, and no. I am only trying to help you, if you don't want to listen, you can leave now."

"I'm sorry, I'll listen." What could it hurt? He had come so far and found no answer to his problem. She was enthusiastic in trying to help. The least he could do was to show his appreciation and listen.

"Are you a Christian?"

"No."

"Do you believe in God?"

What's with people and theology? He thought about giving his usual answer, but then he decided against it because he didn't want to explain himself. He shook his head.

"I came across Kabbalah five years ago when I began to study the tarots. To some, it is a form of religion. To me, more like enlightenment. It is the doctrine that explains the entire universe being interconnected as one unified whole on a deeper level of reality. It is a scientific formula that explains why humans exist. Kabbalah means to receive. And at the very essence of all things, we exist to receive the spiritual light that is around us. Before the universe began, there was infinite energy, expanding as far as forever. The light is the cause of everything, the essence of infinite fulfillment. The light created the vessel, the effect, and it infinitely receives all that the light shares. The vessel is also known as Adam, and its nature is to receive. However the more it receives, the more it wants to be like its creator, to give and share, but it cannot. And the moment the vessel shuts off its receiving mechanism, it will learn to have the nature of its creator, to give, and it will become one with the creator.

"Man's nature is to be reactive. One does something because of the pleasure it gives him and because of the praise he'll receive or the benefits that is bestowed upon him. The devil is the enemy. Satan will direct you through receiving the light. He who controls time has the power to turn you away from self-fulfillment. He'll grant you pleasure and block you from seeing pain with the passage of time. He ignites our reactive impulses and robs us of energy. He motivates you to do the wrong thing and keeps you from seeing the truth. He's the counter intelligence of light.

"Time is the distance between cause and effect, the space between actions and consequences. The past exists at the same place with the present, but only marred by the passage of time. We must learn to see the past as clearly as the present, and as clearly as we predict the future. All men can become one with god, when they learn to share and give. When an obstacle occurs, one must realize that reaction is the real enemy. Shut down the reactive system and let the light in, express the proactive nature and never lay blame on other people or external events. Everything happens for a reason, and follows by a chain reaction of other events.

"There's a saying in Kabbalah: Any negative trait you spot in others is a reflection of your own. Only by fixing yourself, can you change others. We must take responsibility for the rotten stuff that happens in our life. We admit that we are the cause. Being the cause is one of the main attributes of the Light. When we behave like the Light, we become the Light. When we've accepted total responsibility, we have become God."

"Is that why," Francis said. "That you are telling me this? That you want to reach enlightenment."

"I don't expect you to understand everything I said, even I don't. I want you to understand what it is to be human, and why we do what we do sometimes. I read your future and lecture you about religious fulfillment, not because I want to hear your praises and gratitude. You probably think I'm a crazy woman."

He was going to protest, but she silenced him with her finger. After all he did think she was insane, and now he felt ashamed.

"I don't even do it because I want to reach enlightenment, because that, in itself, provided the paradox of reaction. I do it, because you need it. Otherwise, I might have just taken you to my bed and fucked your brains out for hours."

It was a joke, but he felt himself flushed crimson.

"I might yet decide to do that, it is very tempting. But you needed to hear what I had to say, because Michelle understood about Kabbalah more than I. She taught me a lot of things I knew. And if you remember the day that you met her—"

How can he ever forget?

"—She saw the loneliness in your eyes. Beautiful eyes they are, but they emanated a sorrow of solitude and desolation. She needed you so she could give you love and trust, and you needed her because you needed to receive. She was the light and you were the vessel."

"This is all very far-fetched, but I think I understand now, Thank you." What had he understood? Maybe he understood more about Michelle. Maybe she did love him. She listened to him, she gave him confidence, and she gave him love and friendship. But she sure did not come back for the sake of haunting him. She came to protect him, to warn him against a danger that lurked in the unknown.

Sarah nodded and a warm smile touched her lips.

After Francis bid her farewell, he walked along the street thinking about a great many things. The High Priestess, the Fool, the Magician, the Star, and the Tower. What did they each represent? What was he in the middle of? And why, why him?

CHAPTER NINE

The only thing she remembered about the previous night was that she cried most of it away. She hadn't cried in years. The most recent time was after her boyfriend Joe had cheated on her. And last night, she cried until her eyes were so swollen, as if stung by a bee.

The next day Jessie dragged herself to the office. Everyone stared at her staggering like a zombie. She did not need to look into the mirror to know that her ashen face was a hundred times more anemic and decrepit than theirs.

Everyone offered consolation to her. Losing a partner in the force was almost as bad as losing one in marriage. A partner was not only someone you work closely with, but a friend, comrade, sometimes guardian. And Terry was everything, and more. His constant bantering and jokes made her feel that work was fun; he gave her the courage to dismiss all the deaths that appeared in front of her; he made her work meaningful. She did not pay much attention to what people were saying to her in the office. She thought about Terry and what he said before he died. He told her not to go after the Tormentor. Like hell she wouldn't.

It was Sunday, but she had tons of paperwork to do. The abundance of forms that she had to fill out because of her partner's unfortunate demise was almost more overwhelming than the death itself. Fortunately, OIS did not give her a hard time even she had pulled the trigger on her own partner. The Officer Involved Shooting Team's involvement is standard procedure whenever a weapon is discharged by an officer.

She thought about the witness she came across yesterday. Her name was Mary Norton, a white female, twenty-seven of age. That was all she remembered, that was all she cared to remember.

She was going to talk to the witness again today, she was quite sure of that. They were going to bring Norton to the sketch-artist to attempt constructing the killer's portrait. Nobody was going to die tonight. She had one day. Yesterday night she was in the middle of a gruesome slaughterhouse where twelve died: two police officers, eight unfortunate victims in the bar, Terry, and the intended victim left outside naked and rotting on the street. No more, she told herself. She couldn't take it anymore. She was going to put a stop to the killing, even if it meant her demise.

Just what kind of power did the Tormentor wield within him? And how did he kill all those people in one stroke without causing a panic? And why? What did he want? Too many questions she couldn't answer. And her head was far from the state of clarity needed to be able to solve them.

"Jessie," Lieutenant Blair's voice was calm and serious, when she finally finished her papers in mid-afternoon. "You don't have to continue this case, if you don't want to. As a matter of fact, since the FBI is looking into it right now, if you wanted to take a vacation—"

"It's my case," she interrupted him.

"Look, you don't owe it to Terry."

"I owe it to myself."

"You don't have a partner anymore," Lieutenant Blair's gaze darkened, and for a moment he looked like a concerned father. "I can't get you a new one right away, everyone is occupied."

"I wouldn't want another."

"I don't want you going gung-ho and getting yourself killed."

"I'm going to make sure that I stay alive."

"You promise me, that you won't do anything rash."

"I promise."

"I'm assigning the witness to you. You still have to talk to the suits tomorrow, and you guys work things out yourself. The Bureau and the forensic artist are questioning her right now. You can talk to her afterwards. I want you to take care of her. She's the key factor of this case."

She was the key factor to winning the war. "Thank you, sir."

"You watch your back out there."

"Yes, sir."

She hadn't had the chance to take a good look at the witness the previous night. She had the chance now. Mary Norton had reddish brown hair that was cut too short, a thin face with a sharp jaw, and she wore thick black glasses that magnified her dark eyes, making her look quite ridiculous. She was average height, probably a few inches taller than Jessie, and was gaunt and scrawny, almost anorexic. Her skeletal arms were emaciated to a point of unhealthiness. She looked much older than her age. Her posture and the way she lowered her head when she talked made her look inferior to everyone else. She wasn't ugly, Jessie thought. But she probably was someone who did not think too highly of herself. Jessie told the woman who she was, that she was going to be in charge of her.

"You probably already answered a lot of questions before, but I would like to get acquainted with you and know more about you. So you probably have to say the same things to me again." Jessie actually skimmed through Mary's file before meeting with her so she probably knew the answers to most of the questions she asked. But Jessie needed to talk to her to get to know her, and perhaps befriend her so that she can help her catch the Tormentor.

The woman stared at her blankly for a moment. Her eyes seemed as if they were looking through the lens of a microscope. Then she nodded.

"Alright, well we can begin by you telling me what kind of job you have."

"I'm between jobs right now," she said, her voice soft, barely audible. "But I used to be doing accounting work."

"Where did you used to work?"

"B.A.B.E.L."

Jessie was familiar with the company. There was a recent fire that almost consumed one of the research centers. Orange County Police was looking into the incident. Some said it was sabotage, some said it was just a combination of power outage and the wrong chemicals at the wrong time and the wrong place. Nothing was found yet. A lot of riots with Christian fanatics that opposed genetic research happened concerning the company. They claimed that the fist of God struck down at the company. She thought the idea was rather ludicrous. When people were willing to believe something, they could believe anything. "So why did you quit?"

"Didn't like the people. They were snobs."

"I see, so are you looking for another job right now?"

She shook her head, eyes lowered. "Kinda taking a vacation for now."

"What do you usually like to do?"

"Not much. I stay home, watch TV, read magazines, and I spend a lot of time online also, talking to people on the net."

"Do you have a boyfriend?"

"No, like I said, I'm at home usually."

"You live alone?"

"No, with my mother."

"Your father?"

"Passed away when I was small."

"I'm sorry."

She only answered by a shrug.

"Do you frequent bars?" Jessie knew that she wasn't the kind.

"Oh, no. You probably wonder why I was in front of one so late at night. Well I'm nocturnal. I spend a lot of late hours online. I was out of drinks that night, so I walked down to the nearby liquor store. The Mahogany Bar was on the way."

"Do you drive?"

She nodded.

"But you chose to walk there instead, three in the morning."

"My mother sleeps right above the garage. I would have wakened her if I started the car. I didn't mind the walk. It was only a few blocks away. I could have used the fresh air anyway."

"Alright," Jessie at first felt it quaint that the girl would walk to a liquor store to buy drinks so late at night. But she admitted that it was a valid explanation, she would have done the same in her shoes. "What did you see?"

"I saw him." 'Him' was pronounced slowly, with fear and trepidation. "He dragged the body there, right in front of the bar. Then he went inside. I was so afraid." She was trembling. "I have never seen a dead body before."

"Did he see you?"

"No, I don't think so. He was in front of me all along."

"Did you get a good look?"

"Not a very good one, but I think they already made a sketch of him downstairs just now from what I told them. I only got a look at his side. He's Hispanic, tall, well built, and probably quite young. That's all I know."

"Did he get there on foot?" None of the police officers saw a suspicious car that night. Nobody saw how the Tormentor left, it just did not add up.

"I don't know, I assumed so, because I did not see him come out of a car. His car might have parked somewhere else." If it was, it was really well hidden from the police. There was a back alley to the Mahogany Bar, but it was too narrow for a vehicle.

"What happened afterwards?"

"Actually, the killer dashed into the bar because of the sirens. Two cops got out of the car and followed him inside. Then I heard screams, a lot of people screaming." She shook more violently now as if she was standing before a blizzard. "It went on for a long time."

"How long?"

"I don't know, a few minutes."

"And what did you do?"

"I took a close look at the body on the floor," she said and paused for a moment, seeming to calm herself. "It was so ghastly. I wanted to get to a pay phone to call the police, but they were already there. I didn't really know what to do, while I listened to the screams. My legs buckled and I just cried. People inside weren't just screaming, they were wailing, as if they were being tortured and burned in hell. "

Jessie understood what she was talking about. She had seen what happened to Terry. Terry did not utter one sound of discomfort, because he had courage to face death. But she understood how others would feel, with their flesh withering away. It is almost like being eaten alive, perhaps worse, because you don't know what's eating you, and you don't know when you'll die. You can only hope that death will come swiftly.

"What happened in there?" Mary looked up and their eyes met. Her eyes were teary, and for the moment she looked no older than a little girl.

"They didn't tell you?"

She shook her head.

Jessie thought for a moment about what she should tell her. "He killed everyone in the bar, the two cops, and my partner." She probably knew all that already, what she wanted to know was the how. If only Jessie knew herself.

"I'm sorry," she lowered her head once more. "But how? There weren't any gunshots."

"What did the FBI tell you?"

"That the killer used some kind of chemicals to kill the people in there."

"That's probably it, then." Jessie didn't really know what else to say.

"You don't have to lie to me, I know how he killed those people." Her gaze turned dark and intense, and Jessie suddenly felt a chill in her heart.

"You know?"

"Well I don't exactly know how. But I know the weapon he wielded."

Jessie gripped Mary's hands in hers, an earnest yet desperate gesture. "Please, you've got to tell me."

"This will only be between us. You can't let those agents know. They won't believe me, they will try to lock me up and put me into a mental institute," Mary said.

"I won't tell anyone, I promise." She gave her a reassuring grip. Mary's hands were so frail.

"Remember when I screamed, when you arrived and was about to follow your partner into the bar."

She nodded.

"I saw the woman who died. She stared into my eyes."

"You mean the body on the ground."

"No, I sometimes see things that don't belong to this world. She stood there and stared."

Jessie swallowed. "You saw her spirit." Damn it, she didn't even believe in ghosts.

"Yes, and I saw more. I saw the shadow that followed closely behind the killer."

"The shadow?"

"Yes, I don't know how to describe it. It looked part human, and part reptile. I only knew that it was Death."

"This thing, other people can't see it."

"That's right, like ghosts. Other people can't see them. My mom can't see them. But I see them."

"You saw this thing kill?"

"No, I did not. But I know that it did, I could feel its evil. It killed for that man."

Jessie felt herself shivering slowly. She wasn't sure if she could believe Mary, but she did.

"You believe me?"

"I don't want to, but yes, I do. Why, why are you telling me this?"

"Because I see the sincerity in your eyes that you want to stop him. I want to help you. I feel responsible, for not stopping you and your partner from going in there. I didn't know what to do. I panicked. I lost control, I broke down."

"It's not your fault. We wouldn't have listened to you. You might have saved me. The moment of hesitation you gave me might have saved my life." She understood that if she had gone in with Terry, before the killer left, she would have died alongside her partner. And that might have been a blessing, compared to what she was going to face in the near future.

"No, you don't understand. You are next."

"Next? What do you mean?"

"You are going to be the next victim. I can see death's mark on you. The Tormentor has marked you." Then Mary broke away from her grip, took off her thick glasses, buried her face in her palms, and cried.

Jessie's heart raced like the wind. Tears welled up in her eyes. She fought the urge to not let her emotion govern her. She was afraid, even terrified. But she was also excited, with her blood boiling. The Tormentor had marked her. That would be convenient for her avenging her partner. The only problem she faced now was she had to figure out how to defeat something that was more than human.

CHAPTER TEN

They didn't really say much to each other in the car while she drove Mary back to her house, a nice small white stucco building that stood in shadows of other compact condos on a sloped hillside. It was, as she had said, only a few blocks away from the bar.

After she bid farewell to her witness, Jessie passed by and took a long look at the bar. Two yellow strips made an X that sealed the crime scene, the ominous place where she lost her partner. Pulling her car along the sidewalk, she went to the entrance, pulled up the tapes, opened the door and stepped into the bar. It was dark, with only streaks of sunlight illuminating the now empty building. Most of the things had been tagged and cleaned away by the forensics team. Even devoid of furniture, the bar gave her the feeling of a very tight place closing in around her. And the chalked outlines of death danced around her like demons in the night. She felt vertigo that she did not feel the previous night. Last night there were too much death for her to notice her own claustrophobia, now the low-set ceilings wanted to crush her alive.

Quickly, she staggered past the point where Terry last made his stand, kicked open a wooden door at the back and went into the alleyway. She had already checked the place and the surroundings enough times last night. But she just wanted to be here once more. She studied her surroundings.

Where did the killer go? Where did he hide? She stared out at the slopes behind the bar and at the back of buildings in the distance. She saw the back of Mary's white stucco building. The killer could have hidden anywhere during the night while the cops were not around the scene. But her hunch told her that he had a hiding place around, and from her earlier suspicion, that he probably lived in the neighborhood.

Jessie had learned often to trust her own hunches sometimes instead of hard evidence. One of the first things she learned in the academy was that it was a cop's instinct that made a good, natural cop. Yet Silverlake and the surrounding area was still a big place, and from her guess, the killer would not have had any previous crime records. That meant a match could not be done. She shrugged with resignation and went back to her car.

While she drove she thought about Terry and could almost felt his presence next to her in the passenger seat. She wished that she could hear a wise-ass joke that he used to crack. They never truly amused her, but now the silence only created a void that was eating up her heart. She felt the hurt not only in her chest, but in her stomach, as if unseen blades were churning her insides. She recalled the feeling when she lost her father. Is this the feeling when someone loses a loved one? Except, she didn't really love Terry, at least not in a romantic way, though she cared about him as a friend, a partner, and someone she could completely trust with her life. He was part of her life. Maybe she could have even loved him romantically. He had certainly made his advances towards her when he first became her partner, and never really stopped, eventually treating it like a joke. Maybe they were only partly jokes. She knew that he was interested in her, even more so as they spent more time together. She didn't know if she regretted never giving him a chance. He represented everything she liked and hated in a man. He was the kind of men she was attracted to, just like her ex-boyfriend, but she knew that men like that could only hurt her.

She still remembered their first day and his comment about her. "I like women with tits, you don't really have much of that. But I've had more than a great time staring at your ass." A small smile touched her lips. It was a vile comment. But God, she missed him.

Her cell phone rang. It was Mark, saying that he was bored in the bookstore and wondered what she was doing. She told him she was busy and not in the mood to talk. Mark sounded disappointed at her tone before he hung up. She needed and wanted to talk to Mark desperately, but it wasn't the time.

You are next. She remembered Mary's words. She wished that she could disregard the woman's words. But the more she wanted to throw them away from her brain, the more she thought about them and the more she believed in them. She was seriously afraid, of the Tormentor, and the winds of death that he brought upon the world.

Why me? Why am I next? But that was not important. The question was how? How could she defeat the Tormentor? How could she defeat what she could not see? How could she defeat someone that seemed immortal? Mark would have ideas about that, she was sure. But she did not want to worry him. There was nothing that he could do for her. She was going to get through it alone one way or the other.

*   *   *   *

Angel Lee, the chief coroner, often looked deadlier than the dead themselves. With face and eyes that were grayer than death, she could give anyone a heart attack if one did not see her approach. Jessie had visited her often enough that she knew the doctor quite well. It often perplexed her that the doctor could claim that she enjoyed her work so well even when none of the pleasure was reflected on her face.

"Came to see Terry?" the doctor looked up from behind her desk and greeted her with a dry smile that often gave her the chills.

Jessie nodded.

"Not a pretty sight, and don't say I didn't warn you." She led Jessie into the adjoining room, a place that was freezing cold.

The drawer-like coffin opened with an unpleasant squeak and Jessie found herself staring into the cadaverous void which had been Terry's eye sockets. His head was a skull, all flesh dissolved. He was completely unrecognizable, as if he was a skeletal mannequin used for instructional display, only that it wasn't as white as those fake plastic. Taints of yellowish brown was on his bones, as if streaks of flesh still clung on dearly and screaming for final release. The dark mass of hair had fallen around the crown like lifeless worms. The sight was ghastly. It wasn't the first time she had seen a pile of bones, it was the fate of the Tormentor's victims. Some melted their flesh away slowly, some faster, but at the end, they were nothing but a pile of old, worn-out bones, a mockery of nature's cruelty of disintegration. But this time, it was someone she knew personally. She shivered and wondered if that was too, her fate.

Slowly, she turned away and brought her hands to her eyes, wiping away the tears that began to well up in her eyes.

Angel closed the coffin. "Want to see the others?"

She shook her head. After a long moment of silence, she looked up at the doctor, who was now leaning idly beside a tall glass window flipping through a magazine. "What about the girl?" The last victim of the Tormentor did not carry any identification with her.

"She totally melted away this morning at nine. Now she's nothing but a pile of bones."

"Were you able to learn anything new?"

"I monitored the whole decomposition process, from five till nine."

"How?"

"I cut off a chunk of meat and put it under a microscope."

"And what did you find out?"

"Absolutely nothing, no special enzymes involve. The flesh is basically going through normal decomposition, but in a highly accelerated rate. As if time itself surrounding the flesh is running ten times as fast.

Jessie thought about it for a long moment. She wasn't a science expert, but she knew enough about basic science to know that decomposition required air. "What if you put it under a vacuum?"

"Yeah, and you thought I never thought of that?" The doctor made a grimacing smile that was none too comforting. "It does halt the decomposition process. I have a few chunks under a vacuum for further studies. But I don't think it'll help us very much. The accelerated rate was not caused by a chemical effect, rather an entropic effect."

"Entropic effect?"

"Time, the force of entropy. The subject exposed to the touch of the Tormentor is in a state of accelerated time. Time runs faster, thus the subject decomposes faster. All the bodies decompose at a different rate, some fast, and some very slow. It seems that whatever that controls this force also commands the magnitude of its effect."

"How is that possible?"

"I can't give you a rational answer, Jessie. It is almost like...." it took her a while to complete what she wanted to say. "Magic."

Jessie gave an uncomfortable shrug and she took a minute to think about the whole thing. Angel said nothing and waited for her response. She thought that something was not right, as if there were holes in a theory, even if it was a made up theory. "I might not know a lot about chemistry and physics, but how does that work when the person is still alive?" She remembered seeing Terry's oozing flesh turning black as if they were dying prematurely in front of her. He was terrified, he didn't cry. But she saw the tears saturating his eyes, and the grimace of utter terror that accompanied them. It wasn't something she would like to ever see in her life again.

"Yes, you got a point there. I'm not totally sure about this. It's just a guess, but an educated guess, nevertheless. I believe there're two stages to the decomposition. The first stage when the subject is still alive, the cells undergo apoptosis, which has nothing to do with accelerated time in the second stage."

"Apoptosis?" Jessie had heard of the term before, but she couldn't place it or remember what it meant.

"Programmed cell death," the doctor said. "All cells have a limited life span, and they die and are replaced in all living bodies all the time. It is a metabolic process signaled by the nuclei in the cell that cleaves DNA, basically a natural process programmed by our own body. My guess is when the subject is infused with this," she paused a moment, searching for the right word, "strange power, his body first goes through apoptosis, until all the cells in his body die. And then the power takes on another form, a time acceleration, that renders the organic part of the body to nothingness."

"Nothingness?" Jessie asked incredulously. Things had to become other things. Conversion of matter, even pre high school physics taught her that.

"Just a figure of speech, basically turning back into air, dust, water vapor, eaten by bacteria, unseen scavengers in the air, who knows. Basically recycled back to the environment. Or as people in the ancient time called it, returning the dead to the mother earth."

Jessie took a minute to try to absorb everything the doctor told her. It made sense on a theoretical level but to her, it didn't make much real sense. To hell with it! Though it was her job to understand how a killer killed. But this was just too much. "Rape on the last victim?"

"It's all in the report. I did it all this morning, because of the priority of this case. Now all the other cases are backed up at least ten days. But anyway, yes. The last victim was raped. Vaginal tears, perimortem hemorrhaging, all the usual goodies. No evidence found with the rape kit, except the usual condom lubricant in the vaginal samplings."

"Thanks, doc. I better get out of here, got work to do."

The doctor gestured for her to wait and departed into the room behind her. Jessie stood motionless for a while, feeling uneasy in a room full of death. She felt tense, as if any drawer on the cabinet of death would pop open right now and a rotting skeleton would choke her to death. When the doctor returned, she had a large pile of folders in her hands.

"All twelve of them, nice and neat," Angel said with a half smirk. "Save me some time sending them to your office."

Talk and act as if nothing terrible has happened, and you've got a shield against what happens around you daily, and you wouldn't get hurt – the first thing a cop must learn. Terry was good at making black humor, joking about death. It had often lightened her mood, depersonalized her from victims. Jessie was never good at shrugging off all the deaths around her off as if they were dust clung to her clothing. She especially couldn't shake it off now, because it was her partner who died. And she was going to be next.

"I thought it was going to take me a long time to finish the autopsy reports. It did take me a while, but not as long as I expected. Most of them just died of natural decomposition, well, maybe not that natural, but already skeletons when they arrived. It did save me a lot of time."

Jessie looked away from the doctor while she took the reports. She didn't want Angel to see the tears, which did not come from mourning, but terror. Somewhere in her heart she had admitted defeat to the Tormentor. She had lost the hope of believing that good would triumph, that justice would be carried out, and she had lost her ego. And without ego, a cop had lost the only advantage he had over the criminal. He could not hope to win.

She shook her head, held the documents tight around her chest and headed out towards the exit elevator. Evil was trying to dominate her. No, she wouldn't have it. The killer was probably getting off on seeing her scared right now. All serial killers killed because they enjoyed watching the victim squirm under terror. It was never something personal. They killed because it was like sex for them, and they knew they could get away with it. A lot of them did get away with it. Real life after all was not like television or a crime novel where the good guys always won at the end. Investigation for most cases was often on hold, and the good guys were just sitting there waiting for the killer's next move. It took fresh blood to solve the old. Sometimes detectives even hoped for fresh blood, an ultimate irony for the good guys. Each time a victim was discovered, Jessie asked herself how many more must be sacrificed before they catch the bastard. This time she was next. She was the fresh blood. And everything was going to end.

No, she shook her head. She wouldn't have it. She would not succumb to evil. She was going to fight to the end, even if it took the last bit of her strength.

CHAPTER ELEVEN

Jessie had more paperwork to do, and that meant filling up the witness reports, organizing the autopsy files into the right folders, filling up more forms and statements. Detective work wasn't always out on the streets having fun. One often had a chance to take a break from the abomination of society.

She didn't remember deciding to take a break, but she was so tired that she fell asleep on her desk.

In a world woven by the threads of dreams, she was running in a dark forest, frantically shoving dense branches and leaves out of her way. Something was chasing her, something extremely unpleasant. She ran like the fate of the world was hung on her shoulders.

She tripped, fell, and was pulled by one leg along the dirt like a sack of trash. A huge tongue flickered in front of her. Her vision clouded, the shadowed figure in front of her was nothing but a blur. The reptilian tongue brushed her face. Oozing saliva burned her flesh. She screamed.

Screaming herself back to reality, she jerked away from the desk, panted, stood up and tried to calm herself. It's just a dream. But it seemed so real. She never had a nightmare that felt so real, as if the experience just spawned from her and now lingered as a part of her memories. She had nightmares when she first joined homicide and witnessed mutilations. But those were just nightmares. This was the manifestation of her terror devouring her from within.

She glanced at the clock. Eleven thirty-five. She had been asleep for more than three hours. Her stomach roared, and she cursed.

Then her cell phone rang. She took a look at the indicator screen. It said 'Lieutenant'. Fuck!

"Yeah"

"Jessie, whereyouat?"

"In the office."

"My God, you're working way too hard. Anyway, we've got something you might want to look at. There's a fresh crime scene at Newport."

"Newport Beach? That's Orange County, not our territory. Is it connected to my case?"

"No." Then why the hell was he calling her for? As if she hadn't seen enough. "But this one you will want to check out."

"Why?"

The lieutenant paused for a while, and she could picture him frowning, trying to gather his thoughts to answer her. "Okay, there's a remote possibility that there might be a connection. But that's for you to decide."

"The suits are there?"

"Yeah, and that too."

"Alright, give me the address. I'll be there in forty minutes."

She wrote the address down on a notepad. She knew exactly where that was, B.A.B.E.L. Corps.

"Thanks, lieutenant."

"No problem."

*   *   *   *

She had thought she wasn't going to see any more blood that day. There was quite a crowd surrounding the scene at the first floor parking garage inside Babel – Orange County PD, agents in blue and black suits, the assistant chief and a few of his goons, but no civilians. As she approached she could smell the coppery stink of blood. Despite the vast structure of the building, a stench of death filled the place. Under the usual flashes of the forensic cameras, Jessie studied the scene before her.

Lying next to a blood-sprayed BMW M3 were two bodies. The dead woman was Asian, in her late twenties or early thirties. Her face was covered with blood, but apparently not her own, as Jessie saw no apparent wounds on her, only clear strangulation marks on her exposed throat. The nail marks were deep, but not deep enough to draw blood. The victim was possibly dropped face down to the pool of blood that drenched the place and had been turned over by the police. The assailant was a woman, or possibly a male with extremely long nails. The victim's skin was unnaturally pale, as if she was stored in a fridge for quite some time. Her eyes stared lifelessly upward.

Jessie clenched her fist. Throughout the years she had learned to look into the eyes of the victims. Mostly they did not give her any clues, but they did give her the determination to right the wrong that was done to them.

The other body made her gag. She felt the bile rising into her throat and she was glad that she didn't have any dinner in her stomach. The body was cut, from head to groin, in half, the pieces lying next to each other like a meat market display. The pile of viscera lay like worms among the blood and flesh. When one of the forensic officers turned one half of the body around, the half brain seeped out like syrup — wet and slippery. It slid down and landed on the pool of blood with a thud, sitting calmly on a sea of red. It reminded her of a sunny-side-up egg, only the colors had all gone awry. She turned her head, gazing away from the scene.

When she found enough courage to focus again on the brutally severed corpse, she saw that the man was Hispanic. His distorted countenance did not betray his age, possibly before his forties, and Jessie found no stomach to study the corpse further. As she started to turn away again, she noticed one of the officers putting a gun into a plastic bag – a .44 Rugar Automatic. It wasn't an uncommon gun. Most people had one like that in the house for self-defense.

She found her lieutenant standing like a mountain gazing out at the silhouette shapes of the Babel office building.

"So what do you think?" He had his arms folded, and his words almost sounded like a disgruntled grunt.

"Well, other than thank you for the vivid display of human slaughter. I don't really think much of it."

"What do you think happened?"

She ignored the question. "I don't see the connection, sir."

He landed a big hand on her shoulder and then pulled her a few paces away from the crowd. "The Bureau's way too eager," he spoke in a soft whisper. "It's almost as if they knew something was going to happen. They have the OCPD working with them and they got here right after the call was received. They're on to something. And Jess, they want to talk to you in the morning. I think they want to take over your case."

She scowled at Lieutenant Blair. "No fucking way. You won't let them, will you?"

"I won't. But they'll just go higher and higher until they get what they want. The higher they get to, the more authority and the less they care about what you feel. And I won't be able to do jack shit about it."

"I know, I know." She was furious.

Most cops hated FBI intervention. It cost them their dignity when their territory was invaded, and they felt incompetent. But this was not about her territory, it was personal. She was going to do everything to keep her case. She was going to confront the killer on her own terms. She needed to avenge Terry and everybody else the Tormentor had slaughtered. For a long moment she said nothing, trying to calm herself. "And you think this is somehow connected?"

"Maybe."

"The weird ugliness of it sure does strike a resemblance. You mentioned somebody called in?" but she saw no civilians in the compound.

"Anonymous call, some guy with a heavy Chinese accent."

"Could be the killer." Just last year she solved a case in which the Good Samaritan was actually the cold-blooded serial killer. He pretended trying to save the victim and was eager to help the police to catch the killer. He kept them in a tizzy for months. If she and Terry had not successfully laid a trap for him, they would never have caught him. Criminals had a lot of innovative ways of challenging the police. Not only did they thrive on the suffering of the victim, they enjoyed toying with the good guys.

"Well, you still haven't answered my question. What do you think happened here?"

She thought about it for a moment. "Looks like a car jack, or robbery, or attempted rape, could be all of the above. Possibly the Hispanic male had a partner, a woman, or a guy with very long nails, could be a transvestite. This person killed the woman, they got into an argument, and then he decided to eliminate the partner. Then he got away. He could have made the call or somebody else who didn't want any trouble." She took another moment to review what she just said. "That's not right, is it? Why cut the guy open like that, and what kind of weapon could make such a clean cut? It doesn't make sense. The woman's purse's still there, isn't it? And she doesn't look sexually assaulted. The car is still here. Probably too messy to drive away with, but wouldn't have been that way if he just shot his partner and left with what he wanted."

"Well, if it's that simple I wouldn't ask you to take a look at it."

"Thanks anyway. So that woman was from the bar over there on the other side?" She remembered the quite impressive recreation facility here. She was here with Mark a year ago.

"Yeah, they are probably rounding up the people over there and asking questions now."

"And it's got nothing to do with me, so I'm going home."

"Good night, Jess."

"You too. And thanks again for the nightmares."

When she walked back to her car, she was thinking about her case, or what's left of it. And she noticed that she had mindlessly walked past where she parked. When she turned back, she had a sudden feeling of being watched. It was cop instinct, as if someone had pricked the back of her neck to alert her of being under surveillance. Her eyes looked up from the concrete floor and surveyed her surroundings – there were only a few cars in the first floor of the parking lot. She noticed a metallic-colored Honda sitting in front of her. A figure was inside.

Driven by curiosity, she walked forward and stared into the open driver-side window. The figure turned around and stared back at her with round, copper eyes that had a quality of sorrow about them. She recognized him. Two days ago he still had the faint boyish charm about him. Today a mask of desolation occupied his countenance. He was startled to see her, but that moment of surprise flashed by quickly and he was back to looking bleak and devastated. Something traumatic had happened, she thought.

"Hey," she uttered.

"Hi," he muttered in return.

"Francis, right?"

He nodded and then ran his fingers through his hair, looking for a while lost.

"Jessie," she reminded him.

"Right, I remember. Detective, right?"

"You okay? You don't look so good."

"I'm fine." Then he looked away from her, staring straight ahead, out his windshield, at the nothingness out of the night.

When he turned back at her, she felt a sudden moment of fright. She could feel hair standing straight at the back of her neck. The air around her was wrong, as if an unseen force was right there studying her, ready to devour her. She shivered. Suddenly, she felt something cold touch the base of her neck, trailing up to the short tails of her hair. She spun around. There was nothing there.

Turning back to look at him, she caught an amused curiosity on his face, but he said nothing. She calmed herself, noticing that the unseen menace around her was gone and the pacing of her heart slowly subsided to its normal beat.

"What're you doing here?"

"I work here." He gazed at her, a moment of intensity mixed along with nervousness.

"It's Sunday night."

"I was having a drink."

"You waiting for someone?"

"No."

She wanted to ask again what he was doing here, but then he continued. "I had a little bit too much alcohol. So I'm just resting a bit until I can drive back home." He looked pale, in fact too pale to be anything near drunk.

"How long have you been sitting here?"

"I don't know, an hour? I fell sleep for a little while."

"Did you see or hear anything unusual?"

He shook his head. "Am I supposed to have seen something?"

"Just asking, someone died around the corner over there."

"Oh, I didn't see anything," he said calmly, not surprised. "Are you investigating?"

"No, just happened to pass by. Actually I'm just leaving. Do you need a lift or something? You don't look like you should be driving."

"I'll manage. I still have to get to work early tomorrow."

"Alright, I'll see you later then."

He only nodded and stared away at the wall.

He didn't ask her what happened around the corner, did he know? Could he have been the anonymous caller? But he didn't have an accent, and he wouldn't have stayed around. Maybe he was just the type of person that didn't get curious, and certainly didn't enjoy a conversation. What a strange man, Jessie thought. Solemnly, she walked back to her car. It had been a long day, and eagerly she waited for tomorrow. The true confrontation would begin on the next day. Not only did she have to fight for her case, she had to fight for her life.

CHAPTER TWELVE

Francis didn't pay much attention to the road when he drove back to LA from Berkeley. He thought about Michelle and the night they were together. Her ghost didn't appear in the backseat again. Though he was ready for her and knew that her apparition would no longer cause him fear. Maybe it was because of sunlight. But he knew that the sun would not stop her from showing herself. He guessed that for now he had completed the first of his tasks and she was satisfied and for the moment needed to haunt him no longer. He felt like living through one of his fantasies, that he was looking for clues to solve a mystery. Part of him didn't like what was happening around him, but part of him felt that he had a purpose, a spark in the dullness of his day-to-day life. He often dreamed of an adventure. And reluctantly, he was pulled into one now.

Dead tired, Francis could hardly keep his eyes open. He glared at the violet sunset sky of the smog-covered Los Angeles city as he glided downhill on the Interstate-5 and decided to take a detour to Westwood before going home. He wanted to have a walk around the UCLA campus as he hadn't been there for months. He pulled onto the 405 freeway and exited Westwood Boulevard. When he passed by the Federal Building, he saw a huge throng of people holding up crudely written signposts. That was a regular spot for protests. "God Forbids" was written in black on a piece of cardboard. "No Genetic Engineering" was written on another. His coworkers had named these people A.G.T.C., fanatics who rumored to have burned down the Babel labs. Francis shook his head, not understanding why people actually would give a damn about what scientists did for research.

He stopped by Starbucks Coffee to pick up a cup of iced cappuccino and then pulled into the parking lot of the university campus. It was now twilight and he trotted aimlessly along Bruin Walk, breathing in the refreshing cold air, watching students scurry about with their books and bags. He made a stop at the arcade in Ackerman Union, his usual hang out place between classes. The place had changed quite a bit. With new machines and different interior settings, it was still the good old place. Though the arcade in the recreation center of Babel was actually superior, he felt attached to the place because of the four years of memories. He didn't understand the nature of his sudden need of nostalgia but with the help of frosty caffeine in hand, he was now more alert. He was ready to continue his drive home.

*   *   *   *

He knew he was dreaming. From time to time he was conscious inside the reality of his dreams. He was back at the cabin in Mammoth. And he was standing before the ghastly massacre scene of his coworkers. The walls were red. All covered in blood, not a spot was missed. Blood dropped from the ceiling, forming a crimson puddle on the floor. The regular thuds of the syrup-like droplets sounded like heartbeats, his own heartbeats. That wasn't the way he really remembered it. How many times do I have to see this? He cursed.

He heard laughter behind him, before him, all around him. The evil figure of the clown walked out of the shadow. Its leather-booted feet stepped on one of the heads. And Francis watched the head pop like a watermelon smashing onto concrete.

The evil clown held him entranced with an ominous red gaze, and slowly it closed the distance between them. One step, eight feet. Another step, six feet. Another one, four feet.

"Fuck you," Francis said. "I've had enough of this crap. I want out of here now."

To his surprise, his demand worked.

He was back, back in the darkness of his own room.

Michelle's face was but a few inches away from his own. He had gazed into her eyes, and through her translucent face at the ceiling right behind her.

He jumped out of his own bed in trembling astonishment.

When he gathered enough courage to look at his bed sheets again, she was gone.

"Damn you!" he swore that if his heart were any weaker he would have died of a heart attack. He was no longer terrified of the marauding phantom, but to have her that close when he least expected it was an abhorring absurdity all by itself.

The light was flashing on his answering machine, the number two was displaced on the indicator. Who could it be? He rarely received phone calls. He pressed the play button.

"This is Detective Sanders. I just got the autopsy reports of your friends today."

They weren't my friends, Francis silently corrected.

"Nothing unusual, I'm just keeping you posted." There was a long pause. "Despite the fact that I do believe in your statement, you are still the prime suspect. Frankly we got nobody else right now. Hopefully something will turn up soon. Meanwhile, be careful up there. If you have any additional information that can assist in the investigation, please do not hesitate to call. I'll talk to you later."

The next message was from Andy. Francis recognized his voice right away.

"Just calling to see how you're doing. If you need to talk to anyone, give me a call. Otherwise, I'll see you on Monday. May God be with you."

Yeah, right. Francis hit the delete button and fell back into his bed.

*   *   *   *

He spent Sunday at home, doing what he usually did on Sundays – playing old video games, reading unfinished novels and eating Thai food takeout for lunch and leftovers for dinner. Often feeling that someone or something had him in close surveillance around the corner, he had trouble concentrating on what he was doing. He felt like he was living in a place filled with hidden cameras and wire taps, with no way of getting away from them.

Books, games, and stories that usually took him to wonderful surreal places of imagination no longer did their jobs. He felt trapped within reality, a reality where he didn't want to be in. The momentary pleasure of the sense of adventure and purpose he had yesterday had been gone, replaced by a dark bleakness tormenting his soul. He felt empty, haunted, and miserable.

At around 10 p.m., he felt like getting away from the house and drove to the recreation center at Babel, ordering a cocktail drink at the bar. There were even fewer people than last time.

He didn't know for how long he sat watching a basketball game on the projector holding an empty glass in his hand. When he went back to the parking lot, he felt detached from his mind.

Less than ten feet away from him, a Hispanic man held a woman at gunpoint, in front of a BMW. The man's dark eyes met his just when he looked up from the ground, and for a moment they held each other in a locked gaze.

Francis turned away, hoping the man would ignore him. What could he do? He's no hero. This was reality. He was not a knight in a shining armor. Reality was cruel, bad things happened, and people got away with it. Maybe the woman was going to be raped, maybe the car was going to be jacked, and maybe even someone would die. That was just one of the many cruel facets of life.

He quickened his pace, furthering the distance between them. But when he glanced back, he froze. He saw a third man who wasn't there a moment ago. This man was very tall, at least seven feet, towering over the gunman. He wore ragged clothing that was medieval in design and quality, a jerkin and a tunic; a sword hung over his shoulder. The blade was gigantic – it was as long as the man was tall and as wide as two outstretched palms. The man looked like a ruffian who had walked right out of the dark ages.

Something was very wrong. Francis studied the strange swordsman, and noticed that he had a translucent quality to his being. It was almost like staring into, and through, the apparition of Michelle.

Then he watched the swordsman's giant hands close around the gunman's shirt collar and lift him up away from the woman he was holding at point blank.

"What the fuck!" The gunman dropped his weapon and swung his legs frantically, like a lynch victim struggling for his life.

The swordsman dropped him before one hand went to his back for the hilt of the sword. Then the enormous blade came down with a two-handed thrust that was faster than the strike of lightning. There was a spray of blood and the body toppled on each side of the blade like a split apple.

Wide-eyed, Francis watched the woman through the mist of blood in the air. There was no fright on her oriental face, only a smirk on the corner of her mouth.

It was a good time to run for his life. But Francis did just the opposite. He walked closer.

Stopping before the pool of blood, he stood face to face with the woman. The giant stood at the side with his arms folded, sword back in the scabbard, oblivious to the blood before him.

"You can see him," the woman said. "Then you must not live."

Like the wind the blade came for him. He jumped back out of harm's way. At that moment he felt the change, another presence within him. He was a shell that held two souls. A force manifested itself, taking shape before him. The long white dress and beautiful mane of dark hair, Michelle's phantom stood before him, stood as part of him.

She took a graceful leap into the air. The gossamer fabric of her dress clung to her; the wind blew the strands of her wavy hair back. Sailing through the air like a crossbow arrow, she landed a powerful kick in the swordsman's face.

Francis felt the vivacious vigor of each of her movements, and the sheer force of her attack shook within him. He watched the swordsman stagger backward while the woman clutched at her face as if she was hurt by the blow. There was a flash of silvery metal, the blade coming in a swing. Michelle dropped low to the floor, spun her leg, clutch it around the giant's left foot, flipped herself around, and brought him to the ground.

Instantly, she launched her next attack. Leaping atop her fallen opponent, she forced her weight onto the figure below her, focused at the center of the chest. The swordsman's arm reflectively rose as air was forced from his lungs.

Shifting sideways, she wrapped her legs around the giant's hand like the blade of scissors – a Jujitsu arm-bar.

Francis had taken a quarter of joint-locking grappling martial arts during college, but he never anticipated it to pay off in such an inexplicable way. She knew what he knew, as if she was part of him.

Like pulling a lever, she pulled the thick arm down until it was between the swell of her breasts.

Francis heard a thunderous crack of joints, which was accompanied by a scream – the woman's scream, high-pitched like a banshee's wail.

Ignoring the momentarily incapacitated opponent below her, Michelle was upon the wailing woman. Her phantom hands closed around the woman's bare throat and nails bit into her flesh like sharp teeth.

Francis, at a distance, watched the woman's face contort in fear. At the same time he also watched through Michelle's eyes as the woman gasped for air and struggled in vain to cling to her life. He felt the life draining out of the woman and power coursing through him. The woman gave out a last spasm then fell limp and lifeless before him.

Shaking violently, not in terror, but in ecstasy, Francis felt an electrifying thrill running through him a hundred times more powerful than the first time his seed flowed inside the warmth of a woman.

Not knowing how long he was drenched in the sea of ecstasy, when he regained his senses, Michelle was no longer there. There was no more medieval swordsman, only blood, intestines, two parts of one human body, and a dead woman lying face down amidst the blood.

Feeling sick and dirty, he detested himself. Not because he had killed someone through self-defense, but that he had enjoyed the process more than he had enjoyed anything else in his life.

He turned and stumbled away but he lacked the strength to run, as if suddenly the weight of his body had increased ten fold. Tears welled up in his eyes. What have I done? What is happening to me? Am I going insane? Was all of that real? Did I really kill somebody?

Reluctantly, he looked back at the scene, trying to absorb what happened. He knew he had a vivid imagination. Was the imagination taking control of him now? Did he belong in an asylum? But it felt so real. That's what a mad man would have said. He looked at the bodies again. Was he still hallucinating? Or did he really kill someone? And why did he have that intense feeling of pleasure? What did it all mean?

Struggling with his headache, he didn't understand and he didn't want to understand. He wasn't sure if he could accept the truth. With barely enough strength to walk, he needed to get away, but felt responsible. Staggering to the pay phone right around the corner, he picked up the receiver and dialed 911.

"911 operator, state your emergency," said a clear, brisk, female voice.

"Bodies, people die." He tried his best to fake an impression of a person who could only speak broken English.

"Your location, sir?"

He hesitated a moment, thinking of the best way to say the address.

"Are you currently at the crime scene?" the operator asked again.

"Yes." Then he remembered the police could track his location through the pay phone. "Parking lot B, floor one."

"Your name, sir?"

"No, no name."

He hung up and staggered back to his car. Switched the ignition on, he found his hand lacking the strength to pull the gear from park to drive, not to mention he couldn't even grab hold of the steering wheel. He was ridiculously weak, like a person who just recovered from a fever moments ago.

Leaning back, Francis let the nausea swept over him.

He didn't know for how long he had been in his car, only half conscious. His mind raced like the wind along the thin line of sanity. Faintly, he had heard the roar of cars pulling into the parking lot and the rumbling of crowds. The noises were far away, yet they seemed so close. His perception of everything around him was changed, as if more doors now opened from his mind to his soul.

He sensed someone approaching his car. He didn't turn his head, but he saw nevertheless, as if he had developed a wider range of peripheral vision. He heard loud clicks of boots striking cement. And he watched her approach.

Jessie, he remembered. What was she doing here? Then he remembered she was a cop. But he didn't think she worked in Orange County.

"Hey"

He turned and this time watched her with his real eyes. The banks of her hair, tumbled down both sides of her face to her chin in disarray, as if she had just woken up. Her eyes reflected discontentment and weariness. He had often thought that women with high-cheek bones and short hair were unpleasant to look at; she wasn't very attractive, but she was far from being ugly. Nevertheless, he was in no mood to relish her looks.

"Hi," he responded quickly, as soon as he found his own mind beginning to wander. Not wanting to appear rude, he certainly did not want to look suspicious.

"Francis, right?"

He nodded. What did she want? He didn't need petty conversation. He wanted to be left alone right now.

"Jessie."

I know who you are. "Right, I remember. Detective, right?" He didn't know what else to say, he just wanted her to go away.

"You okay? You don't look so good."

"I'm fine." He looked away from her, staring straight ahead at the night through his windshield. What do you want, please go away. Maybe he was afraid that she'd discern his thoughts from his eyes. Suddenly he felt his perception alter. He felt himself watching her. He felt his hands closing around her throat. He turned back to her and saw the apparition of Michelle between them. He was watching Jessie through her eyes. And her hands were closing around the throat of the unaware detective. No! He commanded in this mind, and Michelle halted and slowly drifted away to the side, she watched him like an angel of death.

He was worried that the phantom would not listen, but she had. He wanted nobody else to die. He looked back into Jessie's eyes. They had widened with fright. Could she see what he saw? No. But he was not sure. Was Michelle only a figment of his imagination? But why had his perception changed? Was it the result of him being one step closer to insanity?

He commanded her again, and Michelle complied, circling to Jessie's back.

Her ghostly movement was so graceful that she appeared to have ridden the currents of his thoughts. She raised a finger and gently mussed the hair on the back of Jessie's head.

She spun around.

She felt it! It was real!

She stared blankly into Michelle's eyes. Jessie could not see her.

Francis had the peculiar sensation of watching the frightened detective from two places. He could see her back. And he could see her face. It was too much for him. And proving Michelle really being there only took him another step closer to losing his mind. It wasn't possible. She was a ghost, yet she wasn't. Because she was, in some way, part of him, as if she was part of his soul.

Jessie turned back to look at him, her pupils darted around, trying to hide her dread. Her nose winkled and she blinked profusely for a few seconds. He wasn't sure if he should feel even remotely amused, but at that moment he did.

"What're you doing here?"

He thought about what to say to her, and wondered what it would take to get her to leave him alone. "I work here."

"It's Sunday night."

"I was having a drink."

"You waiting for someone?"

"No," he had his own alibi worked out. "I had a little bit too much alcohol. So I'm just resting a bit until I can drive back home."

"How long have you been sitting here?"

"I don't know, an hour? I fell asleep for a little while."

"Did you see or hear anything unusual?"

He shook his head. "Am I supposed to have seen something?"

"Just asking; someone died around the corner over there."

"Oh, I didn't see anything." He tried his best to look surprised. "Are you investigating?"

"No, just happened to pass by. Actually I'm just leaving. Do you need a lift or something? You don't look like you should be driving."

"I'll manage. I still have to get to work early tomorrow."

"Alright, I'll see you later then."

He nodded.

Good riddance. He watched her go in the rear-view mirror. Francis wasn't sure that he wanted to be in that state of increased awareness anymore. It was all too weird for him to handle. As the footsteps subsided, Michelle stood alone gazing out at the darkness. He wasn't sure how it worked, but he called her back. And she drifted like currents of air, through the barriers of the steel car doors, into his body until she was one with him. The whole process felt so natural that it unnerved him.

He realized that the more he understood, the more he did not. Michelle was real. She was not merely a ghost. She was part of him, part of his soul, part of his mind. He did not know how much control he had over her, but he did command her actions. Not only could he see through her eyes, he seemed to be able to feel through her skin. What is she? How have I gotten this power? And why have I gained this power? Why had I felt so much enjoyment when she, no I, killed. And did I kill Dan and Jeff? He wasn't so sure that he had nothing to do with it now. He had killed and rejoiced in the blood bath. And he had wanted to kill again. Even now he hungered for that sensation of thrill. Oh my God! What have I become?

But then, he realized that everything could be just a dream – his vivid imagination coming alive, or he was going out of his mind. He wasn't sure which theory he preferred. He only knew that something was definitely wrong with him.

CHAPTER THIRTEEN

For the whole night he sat up on his bed and stared at the empty darkness that surrounded him. The bleak void was no longer a stranger to him. He watched and studied the darkness with an inhuman keenness, no longer afraid of the unknown that lurked in the shadows. What was around him was part of nature, and he let himself relax and be enveloped in nature. He was like an owl that sat comfortably on a branch, bathing in the sweet sweep of the night.

He savored the moment when he had sucked the life force out of that woman. He had rejoiced from her pain and anguish. He shivered in excitement when he had felt the force of life burned inside his body.

Then he told himself that everything was just a bad dream. Soon it would go away.

Dawn came and light swept in. He fell asleep.

The alarm clock sounded like an exploding bomb. It was nine in the morning. Francis guessed that he was asleep for about three hours. There weren't any more nightmares. His head thudded as if someone was constantly pounding on it. He considered calling in sick, but decided against it. Not wanting to stay home any longer, he convinced himself that his headache was only momentary, which it was.

The drive back to Newport Beach was short and the traffic was minimal. Not much of his attention was on the road. His mind raced with the thoughts of the incident yesterday. No longer clouded by the ecstasy he had felt, he still longed for that feeling. He suspected that it was like drugs, once you've experienced the high, you would always long for it. He concentrated, but the more effort he put into focusing on the problem, the more he started confusing himself. He understood that he had a vivid imagination, but he always knew the boundary between reality and fantasy, and treaded carefully in between.

What he experienced was beyond scientific explanation. Francis knew it had not been an insane encounter of his imagination because someone died and it was the truth. Michelle's phantom existence was as real as the existence of his own body, if not soul. He had control over her, he had felt it. She was part of his awareness. Normal people could not see this phantom of his. Jessie did not, but that woman last night did. She too had a phantom of her own. Who was she?

Perhaps he needed to pay a visit to a shrink. Maybe his imaginations had rendered him schizophrenic. A person afflicted with schizophrenia could not make a distinction between dream and reality. Was he a freak turning demonic or just sick in the head? He had no proof of either, he could just be dreaming.

Back in the office, his cubicle was on the fifth floor in a secluded corner near the aisle by the elevator. The location provided easy access in and out of the floor without his getting noticed. He enjoyed sneaking in and out without his coworkers talking to him. He didn't have to say the customary "Good morning, see you later, how was your weekend?" and other meaningless chatter. Usually, his work area was quiet, as Dan and Jeff who worked across him were not loud-mouths, but today it was as silent as a graveyard. It was a graveyard.

Francis turned on the monitor and logged on to the Babel IT network. The Windows 2000 interface came on and he noticed he had a couple new emails. There were a couple advertisements, one from Andy, and the last one was from anonymous@babel.com. Ignoring the one from Andy which most likely concerned the next task of his project, he went straight to the last mail and double-clicked on it.

Lilitu,

You must save her, tonight, 8:00 pm at the Gibson's. Beware the breath of the Tormentor. In saving her, you shall redeem and save yourself.

Your one and only friend.

Although he did not recognize the name Lilitu, he did know Gibson's, the bookstore he frequented. The message was odd, but the mail was for him. Someone wanted him to be there tonight for something. The Tormentor, he didn't recognize the name at first, but finally remembered that he heard it from TV. Tormentor was the name that the media gave the recent serial killer who was frequenting the Los Angeles area. Whoever sent out the mail wanted him to save someone in the bookstore from the Tormentor. He wondered who and why.

The mysterious sender of the mail had signed his own name as 'Your one and only friend'. Francis tried replying to the mail and only wrote "Who are you". He clicked the send button and half a minute later the mail bounced back with an invalid address. He had suspected as much. But if the sender wanted his address totally untraceable, why did he put @babel.com at the end of anonymous? It was a hint indicating that someone inside the company was watching him.

Francis shook his head, brushed aside all the questions in his head, and tried to concentrate on his work. Most of his programming was done on a web content management system called Vignette's Story Server. Like any other common web software system out there, it interacted with a large database, converted raw computer codes into HTML output for the Internet.

He couldn't really focus that well that morning but he managed to fix a few bugs in his codes and completed a couple of testing routines. When his mind began wandering, he thought that maybe he could trace the sender of that Email. He couldn't do it himself, but he knew someone who could.

Kyle Gideon, system administrator, was a tough looking man in his late thirties. He wore a pair of silver wire-framed glasses below his shiny balding head. Although only average-height, he had a strong build and the tough look of a man who had been in the military. In spite of the rough image of his appearance, he had good manners, a cordial smile, and exceptionally shrewd eyes. Francis always found him helpful when he ran into problems with his local system or network.

"Francis, I heard what happened. How are you holding up?"

That question was the exact reason he was trying to avoid running into people. It was a waste of time, and he didn't even know what to say. *Gosh, I hate dealing with people!*

Francis quickly threw him a question. "Is it possible to trace an anonymous email address by looking up the log on the server and retrace an IP address?"

"Yes," Kyle nodded. "But it depends on how well the sender tried to cover his tracks. He might have deliberately routed his mail through different servers throughout the world, and then it becomes impossible to be traced. Well, not impossible, but the effort and time that it requires may simply not be worth it. You need something traced?"

"Yes, it's not very important though, if you don't have time."

"I'll run an initial trace for you, but anything beyond that I can't promise. Give me the send time of the mail."

Francis did and watched the man go at it. He made a note to pay attention when Kyle logged onto the mainframe system. At that moment when the username and password was requested, he stared at the keyboard and the hand movements, and thought he saw each key being pressed clearly.

0638Fish1ng. He committed the password to memory. He never knew when he would need to use it. A little leverage always helped, especially in a dangerous situation. He switched his focus back to the flashing cursor on the monitor. Francis was not good at system administration but he had a general understanding of how things were done. He watched Kyle pull down the log and trace the sending computer's name and IP address. Kyle starred at the screen for a long moment and finally muttered, "It's routed internally."

Francis suspected as much. "Thanks for your help, Kyle." He darted out of the office avoiding more conversation.

So he had just proven that someone in the company was watching him. He felt vulnerable. That person was spying on him, plotting, and manipulating him. Suddenly he felt a raw chill crawling over his skin, he shivered.

CHAPTER FOURTEEN

It had been a long day. Jessie stretched her arms and yawned as she stepped out of her car in the apartment garage. She had attended the inquest – a formal inquiry and investigation of the consequences leading to her partner's death. She had shot her partner but under the unusual circumstances, they did not make it suspend her. The rest of the day she drove around the Glendale neighborhood conducting a house-to-house search for the Tormentor. She was sure that he was somewhere in the vicinity. But she couldn't find any clues, as she had suspected. She felt like an automaton doing blind police work without her partner. She was lost, desperately afraid, and there was nobody there to provide her any comfort, to lend her a shoulder to lean on, to joke around and make her forget. For a moment she leaned on the door, burrowed her head in her arms, and surrendered to the overwhelming surge of emotion.

Not until after a moment which seemed like an eternity, she regained her composure and staggered towards the elevator. She never did like riding inside elevators, they were claustrophobic. Even though she had forced herself to overcome her claustrophobia soon after she joined the police force as it was interfering with her work, she never did annihilate the feeling of discomfort in confined spaces. Instead she embraced it as part of her life. Many things were not comforting: blood, rape, murder, death, betrayal, the confinement of space seemed so insignificant.

A strong anxiety overwhelmed her as she reached her apartment's door. Something was wrong, definitely wrong. A cop's instinct could never be explained by rational reasoning. Jessie un-holstered her gun, her other hand reached for her keys. She turned the key in the lock and pushed the door slowly open. Light from the corridor swept in. With a firm grip on her weapon she pointed forward and studied every silhouette in her apartment. She noticed things were in disarray because they were casting the wrong shadows. An unlawful entry had been made. Someone had been and could still be there.

For a moment she stared into the shadows. Then she quickly flipped the light switch on and blasted the room with white light. She knew she had a momentary advantage over the intruder because he was going to be blinded by the sudden brightness. Noticing the mayhem, the scattered items, and broken jars, she pointed her gun at the most likely places where an assailant would hide. She knew her home well, and she knew where she would hide if she needed to surprise someone.

Scanning with her eyes, she swallowed, found nothing, and only listened to the thumping of her heart. She checked all the corners one more time to make sure, and finally she concluded that she was alone in her apartment.

Then something caught her eye. On the wall next to her cabinet were letters in red. They looked like dripping blood.

Gibson's   Death   8

The store. Whoever did this knew about the bookstore. Mark. She was supposed to be next. Damn, what did this have to do with Mark? She would never forgive herself if anything happened to her family. Jessie looked down from the red letters to the white feline skeleton below. It was Flurry, in the Tormentor's signature. She cursed, knuckles turning white from gripping her Smith &Wesson too hard, she felt like she was crushing the handle, if not the bones of her hand. A quick look at her watch told her she only had forty-two minutes until eight. That was not nearly enough time to get to Brea, even with sirens on.

Jessie never recalled moving so fast in her life. She loved her brother, and the bookstore. It was where she grew up, where she had her fond memories, where she was happy. She wasn't going to let the Tormentor destroy her childhood and her family.

She thought about calling for backup as her vehicle sailed down the freeway. Though she wasn't sure how to confront the Tormentor, she didn't want to drag others into her predicament. She thought about how Terry died. No matter how many cops guarded her back, the Tormentor could kill tens, if not hundreds, in one stroke. This was one battle she needed to fight on her own. She thought about calling Mark to tell him to close early and head home, but that could prove even more dangerous than it already was. The Tormentor could be lurking in the area waiting for the right time to strike. If she bent the rules, the Tormentor could simply followed Mark home to kill off his whole family. She would have a better chance to make a stand where she knew Mark would be.

Each minute on her watch ticked away slowly as the surroundings flied by. She was moving through the world like an arrow in suspended time, with a bomb whose timer was approaching zero.

7:59, she was there. She leaped out of the car. With the gun in her right hand, she rushed into the bookstore.

Mark looked baffled. "Sis, so nice of you to drop by. What's with the gun?"

Jessie gestured for his silence, pointed her gun at every corner of the bookstore to check for any possible intruder.

"There's nobody here, Jess. What's wrong?"

It was then the wooden door swung open and the ringing bell almost stopped her heart. Her weapon swung toward the door – there was nobody there. A cold breeze swept in. The door swung back to its original position. No one, no one was in there.

Jessie felt something, something that sent a terrible chill down her spine. Something made her bite hard at her lower lip until it stopped her from trembling and dropping her gun. Something was in the room, she couldn't see it, but she could feel the menacing coldness that embraced her like the devil's grip. For a long moment she just stood there letting death stroke her. She studied the unseen presence around her, trying to find a weakness so that she could confront it, only realizing that she was as helpless as an infant.

The wooden door flung open with a bang. A man stepped in. Francis. His gaze for a moment locked with hers before landing somewhere in between them, Francis turned pale.

Involuntarily, she followed the movement of his eyes and her aim shifted to his line of sight. Nothing, there was nothing there.

Suddenly Francis leapt towards her. Catching her in an embrace in mid air, he threw his weight atop her, crashing onto the wooden-tiled floor.

A sharp electrifying pain pierced through her back as the man knocked her to the ground. Her gun slid out of her reach. And he was on top of her, panting on her neck. Her brow furrowed in confusion.

"Shhhh…" he muttered into her ear.

In her peripheral vision, she saw the wooden counter shatter, then beginning to disintegrate like a stone wall being turned into grains of sand.

When Mark crawled from behind the debris, she let out a sigh of relief.

By that time, Francis had pulled himself up and was looking out the door, searching for something. In a moment, he came back to stand before her, extending his hand. "It's gone."

"What's gone?' Mark exclaimed behind them. "What happened?"

Francis gave no answer, but only stared into her eyes – a gaze that was neither cold nor warm, only penetrating, and carried with it a potent sorrow.

Jessie didn't know what he was doing here. But she was sure he was not here to harm her. His eyes had told her that much, if not his action. So she took his hand without a doubt and let him pull her up. She didn't have her gun with her anymore but she was not in a hurry to find it. Whatever was in there a moment ago, her gun would not have done her any good.

His hand was so warm that it comforted her. For a while she hoped that he wouldn't release his firm grip. But he did, when he heard Mark exclaiming in agitation about the disintegrated counter.

"Look, I can't explain this," Francis muttered softly. "I was just passing by."

Jessie reached for his shoulder, but the gentle nudge seemed to startle him, as he jerked back a few steps, protectively leaning against a bookshelf.

She wanted to walk forward, but she sensed that he felt uncomfortable and decided against it. One minute ago he stepped in like a hero, now he was like a child cowering in the corner. "You saw something. Tell me what you saw."

He shook his head. "You wouldn't understand."

"Try me."

Then her cell phone rang. She silently cursed. "Hello, Jessie here."

"Jessie," It was a female voice. She didn't recognize it right away. "It's me, Mary."

Mary's quick breath revealed distress

"What's wrong?"

"I'm so sorry, Jessie. He has me. He has me. He wanted me to call you. He says he wants you to be in Echo Park. I'm so afraid. Please, please, don't let him hurt me."

The shock almost stopped her heart. How could that happen? "No, I won't. Where are you right now?"

"In the car. I don't know..." then the connection was severed.

Jessie stormed outside and dashed back into her car, ignoring the scene in the Gibson's. The Tormentor had her one witness. She was in his game and he was playing her like a pawn. Tonight, another execution would be carried out.

She regretted not asking Francis more about the nature of her nemesis. But time was running out. Her family was safe at the moment. But with the Tormentor still alive and lurking about, the world was on top of a bomb ticking itself to explosion.

*   *   *   *

At 6:08 p.m., Francis finished his tasks for the day. He was surprised how efficient he had been. Normally, he would have had no incentive to work so fast because he never had a pressing deadline, and he was always nonchalant about his job. But today he went on writing new components, debugging codes, testing new functionality, one thing following the other in succession like a ripple effect. He surmised that a busy day made him forget about his disposition, his plight, and his urges.

He craved the sensation that had excelled any feelings he ever had, when he took that woman's life, the moment that hapless body writhed and died, and that moment power flew inside him, that moment he felt whole and complete, that moment he was no longer flawed, no longer inferior. It was like when he held Michelle in his arms three years ago, it seemed the world was in his hands and he had everything that he ever wanted. Happiness, excitement, pride, vanity, indulgence, longing, a cascade of emotion had surged through him, leaving him forever scathed and changed. Only it was so fleeting, one minute he was whole and the next he was empty. It was evil, yet so deadly attractive, and he was drawn to it. He questioned his own sanity, his humanity, even his identity. He was no longer sure who he was. Francis Seto was not someone who bathed and rejoiced in another's blood. He hoped he really was in a dream. But it felt more and more like twisted reality. Yet, work had made him temporarily forget about all his worries.

Seeking more distractions, Francis went to the video arcade inside the Babel recreational facility. He was in front of his favorite fighting game machine, King of Fighters 2000. When he played he had forgotten himself. He was no longer Francis; he was the character he chose.

After a few short rounds with the computer artificial intelligence, someone pulled up a chair beside him.

"Mind if I challenge?"

Francis already knew who it was before he spoke. Andy, just like him, was a regular in front of the machine. In fact, they were the only ones who really played and knew the game. When Francis first started working in Babel, he was very surprised that his manager actually played the same game he adored so much and was a good match with him, if not better. They had spent countless hours in the virtual arena. At first Francis felt uncomfortable having fun with his boss, but he had gotten used to it over the few months. He never did try to know Andy more than necessary, and he felt a gap between them. Not one that was denoted by rank, superiority, or age, but the impenetrable barrier he felt with anyone in the world. A thick bubble stood between them that was not likely to burst despite their similar interests.

After a quarter was inserted into a slot and Andy picked his favorite characters, the match started. A game with Andy was often mind-boggling and exciting. They matched each other quite evenly. Francis was better at using systematic attacks, combos that was most efficient in different scenarios and doing the most damage. Andy was a good strategist. Though he was not as good using the most efficient moves to attack, he often could catch him off-guard doing something unpredictable. Sometimes his mind games were so deadly that Francis often found himself trapped in a predicament. Offensive and defensive, a flurry of blows, and Andy won at the last second with only one more drop of energy. The game was close, it often was. They were both excellent players with considerable room for improvement; therefore the game was never dull. New strategies were always waiting to be discovered and tested against the opponent. Francis cursed at his loss and inserted another quarter, lost again.

"You're losing your touch," Andy said with a half-smile. "I must be working you too hard today. You want to go for a game of racquet ball instead and win back some dignity?"

Francis stole a glance at his watch. "Nah, not today, I got to get out of here."

"Great work today by the way. I'm beginning to think maybe I don't need to hire more guys to replace..." Andy didn't finish the sentence. Realizing his mistake, he continued with a casual smile, "Well, anyway, don't work too hard. Have a great evening."

Francis' heart was pounding during the drive to the Gibson's in Brea. He had no clue what to expect, and he certainly had no idea how to react. He felt like a pawn on a chessboard, or a puppet controlled by the threads of someone's grand scheme.He found a parking spot a block away from Gibson's and gently slid his vehicle into the space. 8:01 p.m. Whatever was going to happen must have already started. Hurrying towards the store, he saw a Lexus RX four-runner with flashing sirens double parked in front of the store. The driver-side door was still halfway opened.

A small, cloaked, hooded figure was staring at the bookstore window. Francis thought it strange that someone would wear a heavy cloak in summer, but he ignored the figure and went straight for the door. Pushing it open, he strode into the store to find a scaly lizard that stood on two feet like a man. It was something Francis expected to appear in his world of imagination, an abomination that walked out of a fairy tale, something that did not belong to the real world. He desperately wanted to wake up from his nightmare. He noticed two other people in the store, Jessie and Mark. Jessie was holding a gun in her hands, and her eyes stared into his for a brief moment. There he saw a reflection of his own fear.

She had her gun pointed at him; however he did not feel threatened by it. She couldn't see the lizard in the room, just like she couldn't see Michelle. The monster turned towards him, studied him with glowing red eyes, its tongue flicked, taunting. With disinterest, the scaly fiend turned back towards Jessie, its real prey.

When the scaly head jerked back in an attack stance, Francis focused and called for his own inner power. Michelle materialized before him. There was something different about her this time – in her hand there was a long thin blade. The moment he commanded her to strike, the lizard's jaw opened and an arrow of spit fired towards Jessie's heart.

Francis leaped and launched himself at the oblivious woman, knocking them both to the floor. As they hit, he felt the splintering explosion behind them as the arrow impacted upon the wooden counter.

Meanwhile, Michelle's sword bit into the scaly hide of the monster's right arm like a venomous snake. Quite embarrassed in his position, Francis muttered a sound into the detective's ear, advising her to be silent. It was the only thing he could do to calm her. If she couldn't see what was going on in the room, she must have been clueless and frightened. He shifted his focus back to the battle and watched the counterstrike as a scaly arm with shiny claws went for Michelle's throat. Francis swallowed, watching the blow missing by inches, as Michelle agilely leaped out of the way, pulling the sword out of his other arm with both her hands.

The giant lizard retreated a few steps, stopped its frenzied movement, and began to lose substance. Like fog, it was dissipating into thin air. Francis knew he didn't deliver a fatal blow. It must have hurt, but didn't hurt enough to annihilate a manifestation, or whatever it really was. The assailant must be calling it back, just like his calling Michelle, assuming they were the same kind of entity. Whoever his enemy was, was hurt, and was retreating. Then he remembered the cloaked figure outside. Getting up, he slid the door open, thought about looking outside. Then it occurred to him that it was safer to send Michelle outside to act as his eyes for a quick surveillance, that way he wouldn't run into an ambush. Nobody was outside, the sirens were still flashing, and only the hot summer wind blew.

Francis turned back to the store and for a moment studied the counter where he had carried out transactions so many times. It was now a pile of dust and splinters. He stared at Mark, and then Jessie. The expression of dread and blank terror never left their faces. He didn't know what to tell them. He hated dealing with people. The prospect of it was even more frightening than dealing with a hostile lizard from an unknown realm with spit that could disintegrate and claws that could shear human flesh with ease.

He wanted to run away. He had done his part. He didn't want to deal with them. On the floor, Jessie looked so fragile and helpless. Though he was tempted to escape, he walked over to her and extended his hand. She took it; it was so cold, and she was shivering. He felt her calm as his hand held hers. Her newly gained serenity in a way quieted the frustrating commotion within him. He still didn't want to deal with them, he didn't know them, he wasn't responsible for them, but he no longer felt the need to run away.

Hearing Mark's disgruntled voice break the silence, he released Jessie's petite hand.

"Look, I can't explain this," Francis muttered. What do you want me to say? What do you want me to do? "I just passed by."

There was a gentle nudge on his shoulder. It startled him. Jessie and Mark were now both looking at him quizzically. They wanted answers. He was trapped in a corner, with nowhere else to turn.

A cell phone rang. Saved by the bell! He didn't pay attention to the conversation, but Jessie soon scurried out of the bookstore as if her life depended on it. Mark called out after his oblivious sister, in vain. The sirens soon faded away with the wind.

"Francis, tell me, tell me what's going on?"

"I can't, I don't know how."

"Please," Mark's hands were on his shoulders, shaking him. "My sister is in danger, isn't she?"

Francis nodded.

"Tell me, please," Mark begged.

"You wouldn't understand."

"Then make me understand! Something was in here, wasn't it? Something was going to attack us and you interfered. It was the Tormentor, wasn't it?"

The Tormentor. That must have been what he just faced, the mysterious serial killer whom he heard from the news on TV. "I don't know," it's just a dream. No, it's not a dream. "I don't know, and I don't understand."

"It was going for Jess," Mark said observantly.

Francis was surprised how calm and shrewd Mark was, but he didn't answer him.

Mark pointed at the debris. "There's got to be an explanation for this. I have heard a lot of weird stories. Jess told me about how the flesh of the victims wither away within hours until they become skeletons."

"Just like the table." Francis bent down and studied what was left of the counter.

"And I know that you know what's going on. Tell me, please."

Francis stood back up, studying Mark's determined gaze. "Like I said, I don't fully understand it. What you call the Tormentor is someone human, flesh and blood, just like you and I, I think." He wasn't sure, but it was as good an educated guess as any. "What he controlled, a manifestation of power, something that ordinary people can't see, stood in this room and attacked you. I stopped him, and he called his power back and escaped."

"So the Tormentor's power is to disintegrate anything that he attacks?"

Francis stared and pointed at a golden metal knob that rested like a gem within the pile of rubble. "Maybe not anything, flesh and blood, wood, not metal." He thought about it for a moment. "Just carbon-based matter."

"That makes sense, I think. You have a similar power, don't you? What is your power?"

Francis thought about yesterday night, and he lied, "I'm not sure."

"So you are saying that the Tormentor is flesh and blood and can be killed. But my sister won't stand a chance because she's not going to be able to see this manifestation. Francis, you have to go save her."

He shook his head.

"Please help her, my friend." Mark gripped Francis' arm.

Friend, Francis silently repeated the word. It sounded foreign to him.

"She's everything to me. Please don't let her die."

When he saw the tears that running down Mark's cheeks, he felt his stomach churn. Though Jessie was no doubt a brave and competent detective, she was fragile and helpless against something she could not see and she needed his protection. And Mark, he was a good person. Francis didn't want to see him mourn for the rest of his life while he could have done something to prevent it. He had felt inhuman when he killed the night before. Now it was the chance to redeem himself.

CHAPTER FIFTEEN

Mark wanted to go with him to Echo Park, but that was a very bad idea. Not knowing if he would survive his second encounter with the killer, Francis knew he was better off alone. He wasn't proficient at the art of persuasion, and since convincing Mark wasn't very effective, so he resorted to force. He had Michelle pin the guy up to the wall. For a moment Francis was afraid that Michelle would crush Mark's fragile bones. He was glad that at least she was good at listening.

Francis figured that it was a good opportunity for him to test out the extent of Michelle's power, in what little time that he had. He sent a mental command to Michelle, making her stay in place holding Mark by his collar. Ignoring Mark's screams, he ran out of the store towards his car. About fifteen paces out of the store, he was suddenly thrown backwards. Breaking his fall with his elbow, he regained his balance and tried to move forward, only finding that a gravity-like force was holding him in place, preventing him from going any further. For a moment he felt like a magnet in a vortex of a powerful electromagnetic field.

He turned around and took a few steps back towards the store. He did that with ease. That was it. That was the range of Michelle's power. If Michelle and he were one and the same, that meant she could only be separated from him so far, fifteen paces, no maybe twenty. He commanded her to release Mark and he called her back to him. The feeling of Michelle joining with him was still staggeringly alien to him.

He returned to his car, and this time, no unknown force threw him back. Mark yelled from behind, running towards him. But he had started the ignition and was well on his way.

Traffic had cleared off a great deal as night approached. Though both the killer and the detective had at least a fifteen-minute head start, Francis suspected that he would catch up, provided that he didn't run into any accidents.

Who is the Tormentor? He at least learned that it was the person that stood before the store window. If that person wielded the same power, then he must be bound by the same restrictions. If Francis couldn't be more than twenty paces from Michelle, that meant whoever the Tormentor was, phantom and human would not be far apart from each other. If he could keep the lizard busy, Jessie would have her chance with the real killer. They had a chance to win, if only he could get there in time.

*   *   *   *

Jessie stepped out of her car, flashlight in one hand, and the revolver in the other. She held both close, and was ready to fire. The flashlight was giving away her position, but the park was so sparsely populated she was sure that the Tormentor knew exactly where she was anyway. The light was necessarily to find her target but more so to pierce the fearful darkness. She needed to be reminded that she was the light among darkness.

There were a few cars in the parking lot. People came here to jog at night and some came for a date so they could make out in front of the lake. There weren't a lot of places where you could see water in the San Gabriel Valley, so the small lake in the park was special. Though there were cars, she hardly saw anybody around her. And she had no way of knowing if the Tormentor had arrived with Mary already. She suspected as much, because she did not use her sirens to get here faster. She was playing the Tormentor's game now, and she wasn't ready to bend the rules, at least not until it was the right moment.

"Jessie!" a figure uphill called her. She recognized Mary's voice and started up the small slope. A car pulled up from behind her, but she didn't look. Her heart was pounding. *Where is the Tormentor?*

Mary was leaning against a large oak tree. Jessie flashed her light at Mary and saw her bleeding arm. Mary was in a light-colored tank top which was soaked with blood. Jessie studied the laceration on her arm – it was a deep cut, which seemed to have been caused by an object with a sharp blade.

"The Tormentor did this?" Jessie asked.

The girl nodded, her cheeks wet from recent tears. Jessie gave her a hug and let her cry silently on her shoulder. "You're okay now, where is he?" Her hands were full, but the girl needed comfort. So she managed to brush Mary's hair with her knuckles while holding the gun tight in her right hand.

"Jessie!" Someone was running towards them.

$$* \quad * \quad * \quad *$$

The Tormentor's scaly arm was raised, prepared for the strike. Francis wasn't going to reach her in time. He focused and called, hoping that it wasn't too far. Michelle floated across the grass like a water jet cutting across ocean waves. Bathed in the moonlight, her long white dress flowed behind her, like a bride of death – imposing, lethal, yet dissonantly beautiful.

In the enveloping darkness, he saw Jessie, oblivious to the danger behind her, holding someone in an embrace – A girl. *The girl.* The pieces began to come together.

He quickened his pace. *The closer I am to Michelle, the closer Michelle can get to the Tormentor.*

$$* \quad * \quad * \quad *$$

A shrill scream almost deafened her. Jessie pulled herself away from Mary as blood spurted like a small geyser from Mary's shoulder. The flashlight dropped to the ground, but her grip on the gun was still strong.

She saw a silhouetted figure running towards them. She pointed her Smith & Wesson towards the shadowed darkness, ready to pull the trigger. Then she hesitated, remembering a familiar voice calling her name just a moment ago.

"Jessie, don't shoot!" It was Francis, who barely had enough breath to convey his message. "She is the Tormentor!"

What? She spun around. Mary was gone.

*   *   *   *

The creature dodged the second slash at the head, spun, and landed an explosive blow on Michelle with its tail. The sudden attack threw Francis back a few paces. He clutched his teeth as he felt the sharp pain shock his body. If his surmise were correct, whatever damage Michelle received would reflect on his own body. The only consolation was that he knew the same rule applied to the Tormentor. His whole upper left arm was numb, but it didn't stop her from reaching Jessie, he was almost there.

The next attack came. The arrow-like acidic spit was launched, not at Michelle, not at him, but at the unaware detective. He watched the greenish liquid sail across the moonlit sky. He jumped towards her, knocking her out of the way, to only watch the gelatinous liquid sink onto his shoulder.

He felt himself fall on the grass, not feeling his arm anymore. It didn't really hurt, as he expected to. He lost his connection to Michelle. He was lost, and alone, in the darkness, an eternal darkness that was consuming him bit by bit.

"Francis! Don't let go, Francis!" He opened his eyes when he felt the teardrop hit his face. He never expected his life to end so soon. There was still so much more to accomplish in life. He lifted his right arm, and he wanted to hold her for a moment. But he didn't have enough strength. He felt content. At least the last thing he looked at in this world was beautiful.

He watched the lips of her small mouth parted, she was saying something. But he couldn't hear anymore. Death was spreading all over him like a contagious disease.

*   *   *   *

She couldn't stop the tears. She didn't cry often. Now the tears ran down her face as if they had a mind of their own. Before her, someone she hardly knew, had saved her twice. Now he was dying in her place. It should have been her. His eyes stared into hers. The courage, compassion, sorrow in his eyes were overwhelming. Yet he only smiled, and then closed his eyes.

"He can still be saved." A concerned voice came from the shadow of the giant tree a few paces in front of her. She saw a tall figure, vaguely silhouetted in the shadows, leaning leisurely against the large tree trunk.

"Who are you?"

"That is of no consequence," he said, pointing.

Jessie's eyes followed a limping figure moving down the slope towards the parking lot.

"If you can end the Tormentor's life in time. You can save him," he said making a deliberate gesture of looking at his wrist. "You have approximately ninety-five seconds."

"You are saying, once the Tormentor dies, the damage can be undone?"

The figure tapped his watch.

She didn't care who that man was, or what scheme he was plotting, she had to save Francis and end the world's greatest pestilence. She wiped the remaining tears off her face, gave the holster a firm tug, and ran into harm's way.

*   *   *   *

When Francis opened his eyes, he wanted to see angels. But what he saw was his worst fear carved in an inhuman face, the face of the clown. Evil, malicious red eyes glowered from a hideous countenance and the fright that emanated from malevolence situated a stronger hold on him than death itself. Immobilized and without hope, he was surrounded by death on one side, and something worse on the other.

The face came closer and closer until it was only an inch away from him. Its jaw opened, showing him the sharp, protruding teeth. Francis wanted to shut his eyes, but he couldn't. He didn't know if it was death or fear which held him in trance.

The moment he prayed for death, he felt strength returning to his body and he was able to move again. He stood up and griped his own shoulder, where the acidic arrow had penetrated. It was whole, with no sign of damage. He looked around. His nightmare was nowhere to be seen. What did the evil clown do to him? Could it be possible that the evil entity saved him? He shook his head, refusing to believe it.

Jessie, where was she?

In a distance, he heard gunshots.

*   *   *   *

Under a streetlight, she suddenly lost feeling in one ankle. Losing her balance, she fell. Jessie managed to fire off two shots from her gun, just before she hit on the ground.

Her target, too, toppled, not far from her.

It was over.

Then the figure before her struggled to rise.

It wasn't over.

Mary, covered in blood, staggered towards Jessie, until her face was illuminated under the same circle of light.

Jessie pulled the trigger, or she thought she did. But she only dropped her gun. In horror, she watched her hands turned charcoal black. She could no longer feel her hands.

Mary laughed.

Jessie could see the two bullet wounds on her now limp right arm. Blood gushed from her. "Why?"

"Why? Why? Why? Why?" Mary, her hair disheveled, covered in both wet and dried blood, looked like a hideous hag that visited children at night to steal their souls. In contempt, she spit out, "For my whole life, I had to put up with people like you, people who have everything. I'm sick of you, I'm sick of the world. Now, I am bestowed with power. I am better than the likes of you. It gives me much pleasure, to watch you writhe in pain, to beg for death. You call me the Tormentor, I find that appropriate."

Suddenly, Mary fell to her knees on the ground, both hands gripped her head; her face was distorted in pain. "Fuck, you promised, you promised to make the headaches go away. You promised to let me keep my power. You promised, you lying fuck!"

Jessie was befuddled by Mary's sudden outburst. But only until then she had time to realize how wrong she was. She had not even a glimpse of what the true Tormentor's identity was. And she had to pay for her mistake with her life. Francis too, paid his life for her mistake. And many more people would pay. She was a good detective. She was a hunter who was good at psychoanalyzing, tracking, catching her prey. She had stopped countless killers in the past. Her past success had made her overconfident. And the desire for vengeance clouded her judgment. She should have been more careful. Now she had become prey and it was too late.

Father would have scolded her for her mistakes. Yet he would still have been proud of her.

She closed her eyes. She could no longer feel her limbs. Pain burned within her body like a flame that was consuming her alive, yet she was so cold. For a long moment she struggled. She couldn't let herself succumb to the grip of death. But the more she struggled, the more she felt the remaining grains of life slipping away from her, and finally she gave in, letting the darkness embrace her.

CHAPTER SIXTEEN

He was too late. The circle of light illuminated the parking lot like a spotlight on an arena. Jessie was unconscious, if not dead. Her flesh was an inhuman charcoal black. The Tormentor, a girl with disheveled dark hair covered in blood, had both hands clutched onto her temples. She screamed, wailed, and cried in a voice straight from an asylum, disturbing and terrifying.

Francis and his phantom surveyed the vicinity with the utmost caution. When Michelle realized the lack of immediate danger, she stood like a statue waiting for his command. Having Michelle guard him, he felt safe enough to check Jessie's pulse. At first he was afraid to touch the charcoal flesh. Her skin looked like it could sear his flesh off, and it seemed so fragile as if it could fall apart any moment. He was surprised to find her skin extremely cold, as if it was freshly out of a freezer. Nevertheless, he was glad when he found a pulse.

She was still alive, but only barely.

Francis looked towards the wailing Tormentor. He saw the bullet and multiple slash wounds on her arms but he knew that they were not the cause of the Tormentor's pain. He did not feel sorry for the serial killer. He was determined to end her life, to save Jessie.

Seemed to have sensed his discontentment for the killer's existence, Michelle was already upon the mad woman without his direct mental command. Her phantom hands clasped the woman's throat.

The power of the life force surged through Francis, spiraling down his body, and flowing through his spine. Every vein felt the pleasure and excitement. He watched Michelle's phantasm lips slightly parting, as if sexually content. Through her eyes, he watched the contorted woman's face, the way she grasped, the way she screamed, the way she twisted and struggled. It was at once repulsive and unbearably erotic, a cocktail of sensation almost too much to bear.

*   *   *   *

He felt so weak that he could hardly move. Though he felt not as incapacitated as his last experience, he had trouble retaining strength just to stand up. Averting his eyes from the now pale and desiccated cadaver which was once known as the Tormentor, Francis went to check on the unconscious detective. Natural color returned to her skin, her breath was slow and regular. She was once again whole, unscathed. For a moment, he just watched the serenity on her face.

He needed to get out of Echo Park. Someone was dead, a cop unconscious. He wasn't ready to deal with the police. She showed no sign of consciousness but he needed to get her out of there nevertheless. Picking up her gun, he slipped it back into her holster. Then he lifted her up and dragged her back towards his car.

On the way back he drove slowly. He gripped the wheel firmly but felt displaced. The ecstasy he longed for was just as satisfying as it was the last time, but this time he was prepared for its potency and was less incapacitated by the shock.

It was almost ten when he carried her back into his apartment. Stepping over the junk on the floor, he went straight into the bedroom and settled her comfortably on his bed. There was a considerably amount of blood on her shirt, mostly not hers. He figured that it was probably better to let her dirty his sheets than to help her change. It was the first time a girl was in his apartment. Even though she was not invited, he did not want to feel like a pervert.

He watched her sleep. He had read about rapid eye movements but this was the first time he saw the flickering eyelids of REM sleep so close. Remembering he now had a guest in the house, he thought to make his place more presentable. After a quick shower, he spent the next hour cleaning up his living quarters.

"Can I have some hot tea?"

The voice startled him while he was stacking his last pile of CDs onto the cabinet.

"Oh, you're awake." He studied her for a moment and thought about her request. His only reaction was scratching his hair.

"Let me guess," she said, smiling. "You don't have tea."

"Right."

"How about warm water?"
"I'll heat it up right away."

She chuckled.

After giving her the glass of water, Francis led her to the couch then sat across from her and watched her gulp down the water. He felt quite awkward watching her, so he averted his eyes. He wanted to say something but he didn't know what to say.

"Thank you, by the way," she was the first to break the silence. "For saving me, and then saving me again. There are a lot of things I want to talk to you about, and it's going to take a while. First of all I really need to take a shower, if you don't mind. And I need a change of clothing. Have you seen my cell phone, by the way?"

Francis shook his head.

"Darn, I probably left it in the car. Oh well, that's for the best anyway. At least now I can have some peace and quiet. But I really need to call Mark to tell him that I'm okay."

"Oh, the phone is over there," Francis said pointing. "Apologize to Mark for me if you could."

"Oh?"

"I pinned him up on the wall."

She raised an eyebrow.

"I didn't do it exactly myself, it's a long story."

"One that probably has to wait after the shower." She picked up the phone.

Francis didn't really pay attention to the conversation. He went into his room to look for a clean T-shirt and towel. Pacing the room while his guest showered, he had a million questions in his mind.

When she stepped out of the bathroom, he couldn't help but give out a chuckle. He wasn't a big man, but his T-shirt had covered her like a tent. At the moment she looked ridiculous.

"Very funny," she said smirking and wrinkled her nose at him, then settled herself cross-legged on the couch.

Francis realized that he had not really had a long look at her. He had met her briefly the first time in the bookstore, then when he was almost incapacitated at the Babel parking lot, and finally tonight under hostile circumstances. He remembered when she cried, she was like an angel that watched over him before death almost claimed him. He had thought she looked boyish and plain the first time he met her, but he realized how wrong he was. Though her hair was not long, the few strands that dangled in front of her pale face made her look pleasantly attractive. Most angular-faced women looked crude and rebuking, yet her high cheekbones, together with her big round eyes and small lips, framed her face nicely in a feminine and soothing way. She had an air of toughness about her, but that all went away when she smiled. The small dimple on her left cheek shined with thwarted softness, making her look sweet and cordial.

"You don't talk much, do you? You just like to stare."

"Oh, sorry," he said averting his eyes, embarrassed.

"You are so shy, just like my brother," she said giggling. "Anyway, I thought you..." she paused for a moment, seeming to search for the right phrase. "Were gone. Someone was there, and he told me if I could end the Tormentor's life, then you'll be saved."

"Someone? Who?"

He understood now. The devil-faced clown was controlled by someone else, and that someone had killed in the cabin in Mammoth, warned him about the Tormentor and saved his life. He did not know the agenda of the mysterious clown, but he needed to find out who he was.

"I couldn't get a good look at him. It was dark, and my eyes were blurry." She averted her gaze, embarrassed about the tears she shed. "Anyhow, I went after Mary. And she got to me. But suddenly some kind of lethal headache seemed to have claimed her. She went on ranting about hating the world, hating people like me. And she was cursing at someone, for not fulfilling a promise or something and not making the headaches go away. Then I lost all my senses. I thought I was dead."

There was another long moment of silent before she continued. "I want to know, I want to know everything."

"I can't tell you." Francis lowered his eyes. He wanted to tell her everything so much, but he couldn't.

"Why?"

"Because I don't believe any of it. This is just a nightmare. And when I wake up, this is all going to be gone."

She did not respond to him, but stood up, walked over, and stood next to him.

He flinched and moved a few inches away until he hit the side of the couch and couldn't move anymore. She was too close. He felt like she had invaded his private territorial boundary. He felt uncomfortable.

"I'm not a figment of your imagination, Francis." Her dark eyes glimmered, and she seemed to be reading the depths of his soul. "I saw what happened. Or rather, I didn't see what happened. But I experienced everything you experienced. I don't know what you can see that I can't, that's what I'm trying to find out. But I am real, the Tormentor was real, and so is everything that happened around you."

He opened his mouth, wanted to say something, but nothing came out.

"And don't tell me that I am probably programmed to say this because I'm part of your dream. I've already had this conversation many times with my brother. You like reading, don't you?"

He nodded. He didn't need to ask her how she knew. The fact that he went to Gibson's regularly and she probably saw the stack of novels in his room after she woke up would have been a big clue.

"Avid readers are dreamers," she continued. "Because books can take them to places, worlds that they can't normally go. A character in a well-descript story can make you feel different emotions. A good book can make you forget about yourself and live through dreams like real life."

That was exactly why he enjoyed reading so much. There wasn't anything to feel good about in his real life. Therefore he loved the adventures books could take him on.

"But you do know when you are dreaming, and when you're not?" It wasn't really a question. "I can't say that I know you very well. But I know you're not a freak. You may not be normal, but that only means you're unique and extraordinary. And you know that fantasy and realism don't collide in your head. You are not dreaming."

"I'm not afraid of being a freak. I'm afraid of what I have done."

Francis thought about the woman in the Babel parking lot – the pain on her face when he drained the life out of her, the ecstasy he felt that consumed his every desire. He longed to kill again, and he did so. The wantonness of the redress was like a depraved addiction, one that he was ashamed of when it crossed his mind, but it was one that he couldn't stop thinking about. He stunk of evil. If real life had an adventure in store for him, he didn't want it to be this one. He didn't want to kill and pleasure from it as if it was sex. If everything was real, he would hate himself so much that he'd rather die. He was afraid, and for the first time he felt the pain of his loneliness like a knife through his soul. He had nobody – no family that understood him and no friends that would listen to him, he was like the sole survivor of a holocaust. He couldn't help but let the frustration, the aggravation, the trepidation, and the sudden surge of emotion inundate him. Tears flooded his eyes.

Like a mother, she caught him in an embrace, letting him burrow himself on her shoulder. He let go of himself and cried. She gently brushed his hair and patiently held him. Her embrace was so warm that it calmed his raging heart. His mother had held him when he was a kid, but it felt more like duty than love. Michelle had held him, but it was lust and sorrow that brought them together. This was something entirely different. He felt friendship and care. He felt some of his burden of fear and loneliness subsiding, not a whole lot, but enough to make desolation seemed further away.

"Tell me, tell me what happened. You will feel much better after you've let it go," she said in a soft, placating voice.

Her warm breath was more soothing than the breeze of the summer sea.

"I know you are afraid of the power you have acquired. You are afraid of what you have done. And you are probably afraid of what you have become.

But you saved my life. And I think I deserve to know who saved me. So tell me about you, tell me about what happened to you. And let me be the judge of you."

He noticed that she said "judge" with such emphasis, as if she was the singular authority that could deem him worthy.

Then they let go of each other. Jessie moved back a little bit to give him space. He felt a little embarrassed that he had sobbed like a child in a woman's arm, but he felt comforted, and he was ready to speak.

"This is off the record." It wasn't a question, more like a demand, or a requirement for information exchange. She was a cop after all, and he could not possibly risk her putting everything he said down on papers, even though it was far-fetched and unbelievable.

She nodded.

*   *   *   *

Jessie listened while he told the tale. He began by retelling the accounts of the Mammoth trip and what led to that company gathering. He was not eloquent, but she was impressed that he did manage to give her quite a cohesive and descriptive account of details, including how he felt about certain things at certain times. From time to time he left out some certain bits that she thought were important and she had to ask him to recount it. A few times he went off track to talk about college and how he got into Babel Corps, however he mostly stayed away from topics of childhood and personal life. She did not mind the distraction nevertheless. Though she wanted to understand the truth behind the Tormentor and Francis' power, what she really wanted to understand was him. He needed her friendship, and she needed his.

He told her about the trip to Berkeley as he tried to unravel Michelle's past. Jessie asked him about the previous encounters with the real-life Michelle and he showed a brief reluctance to answer and took a few moments to restructure his story.

Jessie learned about the gist of their brief meeting and her death. She surmised that Michelle was a big part of Francis' life, despite the fact that he only knew her for one day. He seemed to have treasured the memory. From the way he recounted his experience, she felt a strong reluctance of opening up and sharing his feelings. She felt the barrier that he had guarded himself with. Understanding and respecting his need for privacy, she did not pry further for details. She too had memories that she did not want to share with anyone.

He next recounted his experience in the Babel parking lot, when he first learned control of Michelle's ghost.

She wasn't sure if she completely understood it, but he had made her draw the conclusion that Michelle was some kind of psychic energy controlled by Francis' mind. The Tormentor and the dead woman in the parking lot had similar powers. This was something that she would need to run Mark across. She was sure he'd come up with some creative theories to the whole ordeal.

When Francis recounted the parking lot incident, he seemed agitated and ashamed at himself, even though it was self-defense.

He was close to breaking down. Jessie did her best to offer him reassurance and gear him away from the guilt, which was mostly centered at the pleasure he experienced while Michelle drained the life out of her victims. It was something sexual, something erotically addictive, and something so powerful that made him doubt reality entirely. She couldn't possibly know the full extent of horror he experienced, but she understood why he wanted to shut it away and think of it as a fantasy. When he killed and rejoiced in the blood, he saw himself as a demon. But he was not a demon. He was only a sweet innocent young man, a victim of society, or his own twisted fate. She wasn't sure how she'd deal with it if she were in his shoes. To physically enjoy an act that you so mentally despised was a contradiction that could easily tear someone apart. Yet, in some way he had mastered this fear while he convinced himself to tread between the thin line of fantasy and reality. If not for his bravery and compassion, she'd be dead, twice.

Their conversation continued. He told her about the mysterious email that brought him to her, his first engagement with the Tormentor, and then the confrontation at Echo Park. For a while they discussed about the Tormentor's power. She told him about the apoptosis and the reverse entropy theory the coroner had conjured up. Then he recounted his second encounter with his worst fear, the clown. And it turned out somehow the clown saved him. She suspected that both the clown and Michelle were similar, and it must be the work of the mysterious observer in the shadows. While the process of cell degrading had already started on Francis and she failed to end the torment, he would have died but the clown miraculously reversed the cycle of degradation. The how was not as important as the why. More importantly, Jessie thought that understanding what the clown symbolized in Francis' life was the key to unraveling the mystery.

Michelle was a memory dear to Francis, and the clown was his inner fear. Jessie wondered if it was a coincidence that they both reappeared in his life at the same time. She had heard about the paranormal experience Francis had with his father's gift during his childhood. That was one piece of the puzzle. She couldn't tell if it was real or a fantasy. Jessie thought that perhaps along the way the clown had represented the lack of love and understanding from those around him, something that had become inherently evil to him, and he was afraid of it, like he was afraid of being lonely. She wondered if the clown was the embodiment of that fear that he would end up alone forever. And it was possible that the clown was also part of Francis. She had read Steven Kings' Dark Half. The clown could be Francis' unconscious part, the evil half, the fear. She didn't like her analysis and she was not going to confront him with it. While Francis was making so much progress communicating with her, she was not going to provoke him with something that had no basis. She didn't believe there was an evil side to Francis. Looking into his beautiful brown eyes she already seen the torment and struggle he had gone through accepting that he killed those killers and enjoyed killing them. He didn't deserve to suffer anymore.

There was one thing that Jessie understood, from the mysterious email and the man who warned her. A mysterious architect is orchestrating their action behind the scene. It sounded like one of Mark's conspiracy theories. Someone out there knew about her, about the Tormentor, about Francis. And that mastermind was manipulating them like pawns. The battle with the Tormentor had ended. But another battle had just begun, one that was even more dangerous. Both she and Francis were drawn into it. But for now, they needed rest.

"It's all real, isn't it?" Francis said softly.

She nodded. Her fingertips brushed the top of his hand, she wanted to hold his hand and give him reassurance, but he shrugged away. "You are not a demon, Francis. You killed because you had to. You killed to save me. If the world is not thankful for you ending the Tormentor's life, I am forever grateful. So is Terry, my late partner, and all the other victims who had perished. This new power you have, you may not like it. You may want it to be a dream, but you have to accept it as reality. Despite however evil you think of it, use it to do good, use it to help society. And you have done just that, and you should be proud, and not ashamed of yourself. Maybe God gave you a little bit of advantage over the normal people, and maybe you're the one that's needed to give balance to the world. So accept your power as part of you, accept the new Michelle like the old Michelle, like the memory that had become part of you. And in accepting her, accept other people, and yourself, and live life as it should be lived."

For a moment he seemed dazed. She appeared a little bit surprised at her own speech. Then he nodded, and smiled.

She looked at her watch, it was 2:43 a.m. "I got to go."

"It's late, you can stay. I'll sleep on the couch."

"It's alright. I still need to take care of something at home before getting back to work tomorrow." She thought about the mess there, and she decided she didn't want to think about it.

"Alright, let me drive you back to the park then."

"I think I'll take a cab. You look too tired to be driving."

If he'd insisted that he wanted her to stay, she might consider staying. But he only said, "Good riddance then."

She grinned back at him. After she called the taxi, she went through the threshold of the front door.

"Thanks," he muttered.

"For what?" She knew what he was thanking her for, but she wanted to hear him say it.

He stared at her with his round copper eyes, reluctant to even mutter a word. She gazed back at him in anticipation.

"For…" he said slowly, softly, but with great effort, as if the words themselves were devices of torture. "Making the fear go away, making me stop doubting myself. And, building a bridge."

She gave him a dimpled smirk. Despite the fact that he didn't like saying more than necessary, she liked his choice of vocabulary. She understood him, a bridge between his world and the outside world. There are still people in the world who cared. She cared. She was his friend, or she would like to be his friend. But she didn't build the bridge. It was always there. She just showed him the way.

Jessie knew that he still didn't trust her, and he still didn't consider her as a friend. It would take her a lot more effort to have him offer his complete trust and friendship. She didn't know why he thought that he could trust nobody in the world and nobody cared about him. She wanted to know who Francis really was and what made him the way he was. But for now she had made him happy, and it was a good start. One day, he'll walk across that bridge and embrace the bright new world on the other side. She nodded.

"You haven't told me much about you yet."

She didn't know if she was ready to do so, as shadows hung in her past. "I can tell you over dinner, but only when you tell me more about you."

"Are you asking me out?" For a moment, he looked surprised. But his half grin betrayed bliss.

"Nope, not at all. But I'm giving you a chance to ask me out."

"Okay."

She raised an eyebrow at him. She was waiting.

He ran his hand absently across his hair. "Alright, would you like to—
"

"Seven, in front of Gibson's," she interrupted. She was going to miss the cab if she had to wait for him to finish his sentence.

There was a battle ahead of them and this new friendship that bonded them in a great many ways, making them feel not so alone anymore. But for now, they needed the rest.

It was then she realized that in many ways they were similar. He had consciously shielded himself from the rest of the world. She thought she was open, but she had unknowingly shielded herself from people, from love. She knew there had been chemistry between Terry and her, but she never gave him a chance. It's too late now. Terry is already dead. She told herself that it was time to move on and put everything behind her. No longer would she let the past consume and destroy her.

CHAPTER SEVENTEEN

Through the darkness he stared into her eyes through his own. And through her eyes he was staring back at himself. He no longer felt the need to illuminate his room, it was but a luxury. Darkness had become his companion.

"Michelle, I know you can hear me. You have a mind of your own, don't you?"

He watched her pale, ghostly face. For a moment her lips seemed to have slightly parted, but her expression did not change. Her face was serene, devoid of emotion. He was certain that the ghastly entity knew how to act on her own. She had first appeared to him in Mammoth and led him to the dead bodies. Then she protected him in the parking lot and strangled the Tormentor without his direction.

"You just want me to think that you're listening to my commands, but you don't have to, do you? So talk to me."

He almost thought she shook her head. But it was only his imagination.

"Shake your head," he told her.

And she did, like a mannequin swaying its head, eerily unnatural.

He willed her to stop. Just before he decided to banish her from the room, back to his body, he remembered the sword. And at that moment the thin blade materialized in her hand. Just like her, the blade was translucent, as it didn't really exist in the corporeal world.

"You took that from the woman in the parking lot, didn't you?" Francis thought that some sort of power had passed to Michelle when she strangled that screaming woman. He remembered the giant broadsword that the woman's phantom carried. Michelle's sword was not the same. It was a thin

Japanese blade, instead of something from the European dark ages. He had never seen a katana up close, but he knew what it looked like. "So what did you take this time?"

She only stared blankly at him. Through her eyes he could see how clueless he looked.

"Good night, Michelle." He knew that he was only talking to himself. He closed his eyes and commanded her to come back. Feeling her presence fill the void of his physical body, he felt whole again.

*   *   *   *

In his dream she came to him, just as he remembered her, lively and beautiful, with the long white dress and the perfectly combed black hair in natural waves.

He was in a bar, the only patron. And he watched her play the piano. He was aware that she was dead, but strangely undisturbed by it. Her long white fingers danced across the keyboard, and for a while he lost himself in the overlapping cascades of melody.

"Why do you come to me now? What do you want with me?" he said, so close to her that he could smell the flowery fragrance of her hair.

"I loved you." She smiled faintly. "And you loved me, Francis."

He shook his head, he wasn't sure about that.

"Yes, you did. That's why you remember me so clearly. That's why you treasure the memory so much."

"Is that why you became my guardian angel?"

"You are your own guardian angel, Francis."

"The Michelle that is inside me, that's not really you, is it?"

She leaned close and kissed him on the tip of his nose. "I am part of you." As she did so, she began to dissolve – pink lips fragmenting into fractal patterns of light and dark, dark eyes giving way to a glittering display of retinal sparks.

*   *   *   *

"The entire biotech sector on Nasdaq has recovered from its fifty-two week low as Babel corps announced today that the fire did not damage any important ongoing research. The facility had sustained no structural damage and will continue to be used as Babel's main research center. Two billion dollars worth of computer and medical research equipments had to be replaced but there was no loss of data, and projects were mostly only hampered for a two-week time period. Despite the loss, the first quarter financial report was forward-looking in nature. The company's venture into E-commerce was a success. Vice president of operation United States, Dale Lore, had indicated yesterday at the press conference that the profit from eBabel.com had grown from 1% of the company's profit to 3% from the last quarter. Mr. Lore said that he had intended to expand E-commerce to 10% of the company's revenue and have eBabel.com target different regions of the world instead of only the United States in the coming three years. Today, the company's share price raised from its 52 week low of 55.7 to 85 opened this morning—"

Like I care. Francis hit the button on the remote to change the channel. The eight o'clock morning new was on.

"A body was found this morning in Echo Park by two early joggers. The cause of death is unknown. The police suspected work of a serial killer who was involved in a murder last night in Orange County. The victim—"

The phone rang. He quickly muted the TV.

"Dad, what a surprise. What is it?" Francis asked him in Chinese. His father never called him, unless he needed something.

"Your mother wanted me to check on you."

"I'm fine."

"How's work?"

"That's fine too."

"How's the company doing?"

"What do you mean?"

"The stock price was at an all time low last week."

"Dad, I really don't care."

"You should. Don't you care about your options?"

"They don't vest until three years later. And really, I don't care."

"Well, you should. The harder you work, the better the company will do. And in a few years, you'll be a millionaire."

He didn't even want to argue with him. "I thought you didn't like me getting this job?"

"Well it's not as noble as being a doctor, but I'm sure you'll be making as much as a physician in a few years."

"Nice hearing from you again, Dad. I need to go to work now."

He hung up, feeling a little bit agitated. His father always was good at giving him that kind of feelings. What a great way to start the day.

When he got to the office he logged on to check his emails. Andy had sent one about him asking if he wanted to play racquetball this afternoon. The second piece of mail was from the same unknown source.

Lilitu,

You have done well, in passing your first test. And know that, this is but the beginning.

Your one and only friend.

The message made him look furtively behind his back, as if someone was watching him from a hidden corner. Whatever. He turned his focus back to the computer. He was irritated that someone presumed to know all the truth and watched from his safe hiding place, like God.

He opened the browser window which immediately displayed his default intranet homepage. He and the other guys had built the intranet from scratch and he was proud of the piece. Every working day the intranet front page displayed a different article that was about the company, which employees were encouraged to read. He read it. Sometimes the articles were interesting, sometimes they weren't. Francis knew that a whole team of people were hired just to manage and be creative about the contents in the company's site. He thought it was a bit excessive just for educational and recreational purposes for employees, but it was Babel's principal that each single employee should know what the company was doing and cared about it like family. That was why the recreational center and the bar were built. He wondered if that was why he took the offer to work there, despite the match of his background and interests, a generous salary, and desperation that he couldn't find any appropriate jobs.

The article today was about anti-addiction drugs that the company's research center was developing. The new drug was a superior, less-addictive alternative to methadone, the once-a-day narcotic that has been used for decades to block the craving for heroin's euphoric effects:

The combination pill Suboxone is made up of buprenorphine and naloxone. The drug buprenorphine blocks heroin's effect. After heroin is injected or snorted, it travels through the bloodstream to the brain and nerve cells in the body. The body changes heroin into morphine, which goes to the synaptic cleft, the space between nerve cells. There the drug competes with the body's neurotransmitters for spots on the nerve cell's opiate receptors. Once on the receptors, the morphine triggers a chemical response that produces a high. Buprenorphince competes with morphine in the synaptic cleft, preventing the drug from binding to the receptors and blocking its effect. Burprenorphine lasts longer than morphine, so if any morphine makes it to a receptor, the buprenorphine takes its place once the morphine wears off. The naloxone, on the other hand, remains inactive unless a recovering addict tries to abuse the drug by crushing it into a powder, adding a liquid and then injecting it. The activated naloxone starts an extraordinarily painful withdrawal. In effect, it punishes those who misuse their treatment. The combination pill was nearing the end of clinical testing and will go through FDA approval in the nearing months. Babel Corps expect to see its worldwide appearance in addiction treatment clinics in the beginning of the year 2002.

He clicked through the links to other news and suddenly thought of something. The Internet was the information highway. He could technically find anything that he needed to find. He clicked on the search engine button and entered "lilitu". Thirty-six matches came out. He couldn't help but wondered why he did not think of it the day before.

He clicked on one of the links and scanned down a list of definitions. The name Lilith came up as the English version of the original Hebrew Lilitu. He clicked on the first link and read the page.

The figure of Lilith, daughter of the goddess Mehitabel, is a very complex one. Her image differs from culture to culture, becoming more and more demoniac as time goes on and patriarchal values begin to gain dominance.

In ancient Samaria she was regarded as the "left hand" of the Great Goddess Inanna. She assisted her by bringing the men to the goddess' temples, to worship her by participating in "Tantric" rites with the temple-women. As a result of this role, Lilith became known as seducer of men and as harlot.

Among the Semitic speaking peoples of Mesopotamia, she was first a figure similar to Lil, a Sumerian goddess of destructive winds and storms. When Hebrew/Semitic morals became dominant in the Near East she was equated and merged with Lamashtu, a demonic female spirit (sometimes witch) known in Syria as a killer of children. Here she acquired her characterization as a winged demon of the night (Talmud), as dangerous vampire and succubus (Zohar), as mother of the incubi and as screeching night-owl (Bible).

Other legends show her to be the magically beautiful first woman to share paradise with Adam, a female "made by god" in a manner similar to how the "Lord" "made" the first male. Here, then, she is the original first woman, an independent and free virgin who would not submit to Adam's attempts at sexual domination. After leaving both the first male and the prison of paradise she was replaced by a less independent and less equal Eve, a woman not "made" from the Earth but from a rib of the man Adam. It is said that Lilith is but one of twenty names by which that first woman was known and each name is supposed to contain a "secret of sexual mysticism". These "secrets" most likely represent the erotic teachings and sexual techniques that were taught to initiates and worshippers in the temples of Inanna, Ishtar and Astarte ~ teachings and practices that threatened the new patriarchal leaders and their attempts to make woman into a dependent, monogamous servant of their households. "There is no doubt", says Ean Begg, "that the Queen of Sheeba in the cabbala, the Zohar and Arabic legends, is identical with the Near Eastern goddess Lilith, who is also associated with the concubine of Abraham, Hagar 'the Egyptian', whose son Ishmael, having been begotten on the Black stone of the Ka'bah, became the ancestor of the Arab peoples."(Begg p38)

In the Hebrew mysticism of the Qabbalah, Lilith is associated with the lunar position on the Qliphotic Tree, the so-called "World of Shells" that contains the "negative" and dark energies. Lilith also absorbed the local deities Abyzu and Ardat Lili.

Fascinating, Francis thought. He clicked the 'back' button on his browser and went on to other links. Some thought of Lilith as a goddess, some saw her as the queen of demons, some thought of her as a seductress who stole the seeds of men – the first succubus, a creature spawned from myth and legends. Others argued that she appeared in the bible as a serpent. Some folklore said she was Adam's first wife. He thought about Michelle. Seductress, demon, goddess, succubus, Michelle was Lilith. Michelle was the seductress, but in his mind she had been a goddess. When she fought, she was a demon. When she strangled, killed, and sucked the life out of the others, she was the succubus. That's why he was called Lilitu, as Michelle was part of him.

Feeling a presence nearing his vicinity, he knew someone was approaching. He was no longer surprised by his keen perception of his surroundings, as he was already used to Michelle's power – Lilith's power, his power. Quickly he added the index page to his bookmarks on his browser, so he could get back to it later and resume his research. Then out of habit he opened a work related application to pretend that he was busy doing something.

"Hey, Francis." His manager was in a white T-shirt and shorts, looking sporty. "Just wondering if you want to go for some racquetball today."

He thought about it for a moment. "Yeah, we can if we go early." He wouldn't pass up a chance to be out of his office, but he didn't want to be late for his date tonight.

"Three sounds good?"

Francis nodded.

"See you at the courts then." Andy turned around and left, without asking him how he progressed with his assignment.

*   *   *   *

Jessie couldn't believe how exhausted she was. After she had driven home she did not go to bed right away. Instead she spent the rest of the morning cleaning her apartment, which included her attempt in vain to wipe the blood off the wall and clean up Flurry's carcass. She wanted so much to give her cat a proper burial, but she only had time to leave him at the garbage dump. She had two hours left to sleep, and spent it tossing and turning and trying desperately to come up with a story to tell her lieutenant about the Tormentor's death while leaving out Francis' involvement.

Lieutenant Blair had looked doubtful when she told her story. But she knew he trusted her too much to doubt her words. She hated taking advantage of the relationship, but she had no other choice. She wouldn't even have tried lying to him if she hadn't left too many signatures at the scene in Echo Park – bullets and shell casings. She had told him about the confrontation at the park and that a mysterious third person intervened and killed Mary. Then she was off in a car chase after her savior but got into an accident which rendered her unconscious till morning. That accounted for her inability to call in to the office before the body of the Tormentor was discovered. The lieutenant was dubious of her story, but only reprimanded her for being reckless and not calling backup.

She then reported to the FBI, which she hated because of their arrogance. They saw themselves as better than the police and they were coming in to clean up the department's mess. But this time it was different. Jessie felt that the Bureau was hiding things from her, probably trying to cover the trail of their investigation. They did not seem shocked when she told her blatant lie. Their only concern was to steer her away from finding out the truth. They knew things that she didn't know. But she intended to find out. Her case on the Tormentor was officially closed, and the lieutenant did not put her on rotation, just telling her to finish up her paper work and take some time off. Like Hell she was going to stay in the office in front of the computer. There were too many loose ends to tie up.

So she had skipped lunch to come back to Silverlake. Stepping out of her car she stretched her arms and readied herself to confront whoever was at Mary's residence. If Mary did not lie entirely about her family, she still had a mother, one that the police still hadn't gotten around to notify. They were busy autopsying the body. Normally next-of-kin notification would have taken place first, but the Bureau always had a different way of doing things, plus it was the Tormentor this time, which made any wrong procedures right. For her she only needed the truth.

She gathered up her courage and walked up to the hillside white stucco house. She knocked and waited. After a long excruciating moment, the door was opened by a middle-aged lady who had curly blonde hair so light it almost seemed white.

Jessie put a smile on her face, showed her badge, and introduced herself.

"If you're looking for Mary, she's not here." As polite as the lady tried to sound, Jessie sensed a little bit of impatience and weariness in her words.

"I'm not really looking for Mary, but I'm here about Mary."

Her face darkened.

"I'm sorry, Mrs. Norton."

"Oh, just come in." The woman was not as shocked as Jessie expected her to be. She was ushered in and took a seat at the vanilla white couch in a small but cozy living room. "She's gone, isn't she?"

Jessie gave a solemn nod. She was never good at sentiments. She hated it. Terry had always done it for her. She wasn't sure if he liked it at all, but he knew she despised it and he took that responsibility every time without a word of complain. She sure missed him. Everything seemed to remind her of him lately. Silently, she told herself that she wasn't going to miss him anymore. Forward, look forward. Never look back.

"She broke the law, didn't she? And you guys took her out," she said slowly. The tone wasn't accusatory, but each word was like a sharp knife piercing Jessie's heart. She was glad that the monstrous killer no longer roamed the world. But inside that shell of an inhuman killer, she was just a girl, a daughter. And this woman loved her daughter.

"No." She wasn't sure what question she was replying to anymore. "I mean—"

"Yes, I know what you mean."

"What was Mary like?"

"She was a lovely child," the woman answered without hesitation. "Her father died young. I'm her stepmother but I loved her like my own daughter." Tears welled up in the woman's eyes. For a moment she looked away and did not say anything.

Jessie waited patiently. She was actually surprised how cooperative the woman was in telling her about Mary. The most important thing she needed to find out was the why but not the how. Little pieces of the puzzle, if she could put it together, maybe she would have a better understanding of the grand scheme of the truth.

"She was always studious and quiet, didn't have a lot of friends. Got perfect grades in school, but never seemed to find enjoyment in life." She let out a long sigh before continuing. "She was a good kid, but we weren't so close. Not the mother and daughter relationship I would like to have. We never really talked about personal things. But I know that she's not the kind of person that would kill…" She averted her eyes. A small stream of tears ran down her face, a face filled with pain and regret.

"So did you know about her activities?"

"No." She shook her head, wiping away her tears with the back of her hand. "But I suspected something was wrong. The drastic change in her personality terrified me."

"When was this?"

"A few months ago."

"After she quit her job?" Babel corps, the nexus in the vortex of chaos and trouble. Both Francis and Mary were employees of Babel, so was one of the victims in the parking lot. The death of Francis' coworkers in Mammoth, the recent fire, and other added-up details suggested something wrong and sinister was going on in that place, something she intended to find out.

The woman nodded.

"Did she say why?"

"She said she needed a break, that's all."

"So how did her attitude change?"

"She became belligerent and started to talk to me in a different tone. I thought she was drinking or taking drugs. And she was home less, which I thought was a good thing. Sometimes she didn't come home until dawn. I was concerned, but I was afraid to ask her. I was afraid of the tone she was going to use to talk to me."

"Do you know if she has any friends that I can talk to? Perhaps a boyfriend?"

"I don't know. She was very quiet before and never had any friends. But recently there were a few calls for her. Usually it was a man with a deep voice looking for her, but he never left a name or number."

No luck there, Jessie was hoping that she could find at least a friend that knew Mary somewhat so she could understand her a bit better. She could ask around in Babel Corps but she doubt if Mary would have made friends in the company. Someone in the company might have instigated the change in Mary, but she would hate to have to go into the lion's den to investigate, especially now that she was pretty much freelancing, she couldn't even look up phone records. She thought about Mary's last words, which she remembered clearly. "For my whole life, I had to put up with people like you, people who had everything. I'm sick of you, I'm sick of the world. Now, I am bestowed with power. I am better than the likes of you. It gives me much pleasure, to watch you writhe in pain, to beg for death."

"Oh, so rude of me," Mrs. Norton suddenly interrupted her thoughts. "I forgot to ask you if you wanted coffee."

"Yes, thanks." She needed one. "Black, please."

"It'll be a minute." The woman moved towards the adjoining kitchen.

People like you, people who had everything. The victims, all girls, pretty, popular, had good grades in school. Mary was jealous. She despised them. And someone bestowed her with power; someone tipped her over the edge. Someone instigated the hate inside her heart and made her a monster.

"So how did you know she broke the law?" Jessie asked, calling into the kitchen.

The response wasn't what she expected – a loud bang, gunshot, shattering of glass, and a thud. Shit. Revolver drawn, Jessie leaped up and carefully proceeded into the kitchen. Mrs. Norton was on the floor, gunshot wound in the chest. Jessie bent down, while keeping a watchful eye at her surroundings, and placed her fingertips to the woman's throat, searching for a pulse in her carotid artery. She was dead. The round was so perfectly placed that it must have pierced her heart. With circulation halted in an instant, she did not bleed much. Death was instant, peaceful. Jessie was glad that the poor woman did not suffer much, but she certainly did not deserve this ending.

There was nobody in sight. The patio door had a large crack with a bullet hole. The killer had made the shot from outside. With her free hand Jessie slid the glass door open and stepped outside. For a moment she became distracted by what she would only describe as a strange, yet beautiful, phenomenon. A graceful fall of small rocks tumbled down in front of her in an exotic rhythm. That moment she was unfocused and vulnerable. She realized her mistake and snapped herself back to alertness.

On the other side of the patio, the ground sloped steeply all the way to the bottom, there was the bar where Terry was killed. Nobody would have survived the fall and she saw no movement between the sparse Southern California vegetation. The only escape was up. She looked at the second story. It was inaccessible from where she stood. The patio didn't even have a roof. In a mile radius she was alone, only the fine wind blew. It was impossible. She stared down at the scattered pieces of rocks on the wooden tiles. Something didn't add up. The rocks did not belong there. She looked above again, letting the midday sun blast fully into her eyes. The killer escaped to the second level. She did not know how, but she was sure of it. There was no other way.

Darting back into the house, she went up the stairs, her gun leveled in front of her. Alert at all times, she was ready for anything that would come as a surprise. She went up to a hallway with two doors on opposite sides. They were both closed. She had to take a guess. If she picked the wrong one, the killer would be further out of her grasp. If she picked the right one she would chance an ambush.

She went to her right. Crouching low, she nudged the door open and found herself in an empty bedroom with neatly piled bookcases. She removed herself from the doorway and positioned herself in a more fortified position before surveying the room. Nobody was in sight. The adjoining bathroom door was ajar and she noticed the wide-opened medicine cabinet above the sink.

Bottles scattered in mayhem across the floor. Someone had rummaged through it.

When she heard the hurried footsteps down the stairs behind her, she cursed. She picked the wrong room, or did she pick the right one? She followed like a hunter, and did not even hesitate when she heard the gunshot from outside the house. A white Toyota Camry was backing out of the sidewalk. The bastard had popped her tire.

She ran out onto the middle of the street, planning to take a shot at the fleeing car but it was already too far out of range. The road was all the way downhill from her position so she concluded it was her unlucky day.

A loud horn blasted behind her. A middle-aged Hispanic driver with a full beard stuck his head out of the window of a blue mini truck, muttering obscenities at her for blocking his way. She spun around, pulled her badge out, and realized that she didn't really have to. The driver's face had turned ashen when he saw the gun.

"LAPD, need to borrow your vehicle." With a revolver two inches from his head, the driver turned out to be extra cooperative. She was in business in matter of seconds. Stomping on the gas pedal, she tore away and resumed her pursuit.

Turning a sharp corner right onto Glendale Blvd, she hung on to the steering wheel and clenched her teeth as she felt the truck almost topple to one side. She realized that if she was going to catch the assailant she could not possibly do it in the truck. The acceleration was inferior, and turning at full speed was too dangerous.

The ninety-mile-per-hour speed was the truck's limit, and the car in front was losing her. Barely making it through a yellow light, she cursed. Grasping her firearm in her left hand, she leaned out the window and aimed. Faster, come on, faster. She needed to get closer to get a clean shot. It was a red light ahead, and the white Toyota was trying to make a right turn. She was in luck. Her first shot popped the tire like an over-inflated balloon.

She stomped on the brake, fifty feet away from the red light. The Toyota had gyrated onto the sidewalk, hammering head-on into a fence. The driver's seat was empty. Fuck! Where the fuck is the driver? Thirty-feet, she was still going sixty-five miles per hour. The tires screeched like the scream of a dying squirrel.

The next thing she saw made her forget about how to make it through the red light. In front of her small rocks floated in the air like an asteroid field in a space movie. There a man stepped onto them as if they were some sort of celestial stairway. For a moment she locked eyes with him. Piercing blue eyes sent a chill down her spine. Twenty feet, she was at thirty miles per hour. The moment the light turned green, she approached the intersection. Just as the last batch of interweaving traffic slid by, she realized she was under the levitating staircase.

A thunderous clash on the rooftop told her that she had just added an un-welcomed passenger. She ducked to the passenger side of the truck, before hearing a distinct pop as a bullet penetrated the roof to bury itself in the seat just inches away from her head. With a rush of adrenaline, she pumped random bullets above her.

She had hoped for a dead body rolling to the side of the street. But while she hoped, she already heard the movement of her predator hovering above her. Therefore she didn't pay attention to where the car was going; her first priority was to get out of her predicament.

She slipped her gun into her back pocket and kicked the passenger door open. She watched the scenery fly by before her like a flashback recorded on tape in fast forward mode. Releasing a deep breath, she got ready to jump. To her dismay she found herself unable to make her move. Her left hand was stuck to the rail of the passenger doorframe, as if she was attached there by superglue. She struggled, but to no avail. Above her the predator was approaching. She first saw the man with his blond hair and wild blue eyes, then the gun, gleaming tauntingly bright in the sun. If she didn't do something about her plight, he was going to get a clean shot at her in a matter of moments. Staring towards the end of the truck, she aimed for the back tire.

The next series of moments was a cascading chain reaction, one thing happening right after another so forcefully that they seemed to happen all at once. The tire blew, and the truck's balance on the road was tipped. Jessie found herself one too many inches too close to the road and death as the now lopsided truck skidded. The vertigo was so overwhelming that she thought she was going to faint, but she told herself to hang on. Her villain lost his grip on the rooftop and fell back like a jettisoned piece of trash. At the same time, her hand jerked free, and she too, lost her balance plunging head-on onto the road.

Jessie covered her head with her arms and rowed onto the cement like a bowling ball. She clenched her teeth as sharp pain pierced her arm, glad that she was wearing a fairly thick long-sleeve shirt. It was now ruined, but better that than her arm.

Surprised at how quick she recovered from her fall, she watched the truck collide into a parked sedan before surveying her surroundings for her weapon, which landed a few paces away from her. Her other hand had already found her backup revolver – a small .25 Popper Beret hidden by her left boot, and tucked it safely away in the back pocket of her pants.

About fifteen paces from her, the killer was pulling himself up. Glancing around, she saw a fairly empty parking lot with ongoing traffic on the other side. There was nowhere to hide. With a firm grip on the Smith & Wesson, she gradually closed her distance, one small step at a time.

The villain – a small, scrawny white male with disheveled blond hair, turned and faced her with no gun in his hand.

"Freeze," she ordered. "Put your hands above your head."

The man ignored her and took one step forward. An obscene smile glowed from the corner of his mouth.

"I'm warning you, I will shoot."

He took another step and they were now ten paces apart.

She fired.

The silvery bullet stopped in midair about a foot before its target.

She fired and fired again.

Now three bullets hung in midair like stationary satellites that orbited around a planet.

Fuck. She had three bullets left in her clip.

The man continued his approach, nine paces, eight paces.

She was on her own against a foe with inhuman powers, with three more bullets and a backup revolver with another six which would probably do her no good. Her mind raced for a plan.

She fired her last three consecutive shots onto her target. The last one, aimed at the forehead, hovered only a few inches away from his skin. She made an empty click on her trigger, indicating to her opponent that she had no ammo left before dropping the gun onto the ground.

"How would you like to die?" the man asked, the obscene smirk never leaving his face.

Seven paces. The next moment was going to be a true test of her career marksmanship. Not to mention the remaining .25 didn't really offer a good aim, it was meant to be a concealed weapon used to fire at close range. She wasn't sure if she was up for it. And she was less sure about when it was the right time. Francis had told her that there was a limit to the range of his power. This man was still approaching, that meant he was still too far away to kill her. She needed to be as close as possible to make her shot, but she didn't know the threshold of both their limits. She had one chance and screwing it up would mean instant death.

"Who gave you your power?" she asked.

The man didn't answer. Six paces. It was still too far away for her to be certain.

Five. That was the right moment.

She reached for her backup weapon. Pulled, aimed, shot.

A stream of blood trailed down the man's forehead. The second bullet had punched the first one in, just not deep and fatal enough. She couldn't believe she made the shot at all, as the chances were slim. Double tapping with the .25 was harder than shooting an arrow and penetrating one that already bulls-eyed. It was not good enough. Four paces.

She fired again. Or not, she did not fire, she could not. The trigger was unwilling to budge. It was already too close. Too young to die, she told herself. Then she lunged and threw herself onto him. She hammered the bottom of her revolver handle onto a hovering bullet right before his forehead. Her blow impacted, threw both of them onto the ground. Watching the blood splash, she hammered and hammered in frenzy until the outer bullet was so deeply buried in the man's forehead it was like a part of his anatomy, and until she was too exhausted even to breathe.

She looked down, onto the pool of blood and the bolted bullet. The face of death looked back at her, and she gasped. Reaching into the man's shirt pocket, she found a white bottle of pills and slipped it into her pants. Then she collapsed in the pool of blood, unable to move. She was exhausted. Watching the clouds slowly moving across the horizon above her, she waited for the sirens.

CHAPTER EIGHTEEN

"I'm very disappointed, Ishimina. You are supposed to be on vacation." Lieutenant Blair scowled down at her. But there was a smile at the corner of his mouth as he extended his hand to pull her up. "You look like shit, by the way."

"Thank you." She let him pull her up. The firm grip was reassuring and soothing, assuaged her blues, and made her forget about the blood around her.

"What trouble have you gotten yourself into this time? And how did you do that?" The big man pointed at the bullet that half protruded from the dead man's forehead, making him looking like a unicorn of death.

"Long story."

"Well, you type up the report."

"Tomorrow." Stealing a quick glance at her watch: 2:30 p.m., she decided to make a trip to the Coroner before going home to take a long shower. Actually she had a bubble bath in mind. Then there was dinner with Francis afterward. She had time but she had to get going.

"After that, you are going to take a vacation."

She nodded, but the lieutenant's one single eyebrow went up in question. "A real one, Jessie. And no more cowgirl shit."

"Right, I could use one." She could, that was true. But she still had little pieces of puzzle to put together. She was not going to miss that for anything. Not to mention, whoever was behind all this had really pissed her off. She was going to get even with him, or them. Not only was that for Terry, Sandra, Mary, Mary's mother, herself, Francis, but everyone that had to endure an anguishing ordeal that they did not deserve.

One of the uniformed cops drove her back to her car and helped her replace her flat tire. On her way to the medical center in USC, she drove slowly. She had enough excitement for the day, if not for the rest of her life.

"Ishimine, surprise, surprise." The coroner looked up from her documents, her face as pale as the lab coat she wore and as expressionless as the death she inhaled. "All covered in blood, if it wasn't for your jolly movement, I would have thought you were coming in a body bag."

Jessie returned a smirk and stuck her tongue out. Long ago, she had learned not to take the coroner's dark insults and jokes too personally. "Always the cordial Angel."

"Let me guess, more bodies?"

"Not yet, but getting here."

"Want another personal moment with the dead? Not a good sight, don't say I didn't warn you."

"Need to ask a personal favor."

"As long as you're not asking to keep one of the bodies as souvenirs."

She showed her the bottle. "I need a chemical analysis."

"What am I, your SID lab?"

"I kinda need this off the record."

Angel scowled.

"I know you're a busy woman. Well, this is very important." Jessie knew she could get Angel to do this for her. She held all the cards in her hand. "I'll let you know everything that goes on in the investigation."

"Everything?"

"Everything." A person looking at dead bodies every day could use some strange phenomenon and conspiracy theory to spice her life up. "As a matter of fact, this bottle may contain the key to—"

"Let me guess, the apoptosis and the reverse entropy effect," she interrupted like an excited kid with a new toy.

"Maybe."

"You got a deal."

Jessie beamed. "Here's my cell phone number. Just give me a call when you got something." She wrote her number on one of the post-it notes on the desk. "Remember, this doesn't leave the room."

"Just you, me, and the dead all around us."

It was probably more because of the cold air in the room than the creepy comment Angel made, Jessie shivered. "Alright, time to hit the showers."

It took another half an hour to get back to her apartment in Pasadena. She was not enthusiastic about going back to her place mainly because Flurry was no longer there, and it was still a mess. Some unwelcome stranger had violated her space, her privacy, her world.

Feeling moody and blue, it was time for a bubble bath. Running hot water in the bathtub, Jessie threw her bloodstained clothes into the laundry basket and poured some Epsom salts into the tub. Then she sank into the warm liquid heaven and spent the next hour doing her own version of rebirthing. When she emerged from the womb, she was as unscathed as a newly born, with no trauma whatsoever. Well, not until she had to think about it.

Then it occurred to her that it would do her some good to spend a few days at home. She picked up the phone and dialed.

After a few rings, the other line was picked up. "Hello?"

"Hi, Mom."

"Jess? How are you? It's nice to hear your voice again. It's been a while. How's the case going?"

"I'm fine. Did Mark say anything about my case?" She hoped he didn't. She really did not need her mom worrying over her right now.

"No, he just said you got into some trouble, but he doesn't know the details."

"Well, I'm fine now. I'm kind of officially off the case for the moment and I'm going to take a few days of vacation."

"You can use some time off, Honey. You seemed to have been overworking yourself."

"I'm a workaholic, Mom. I was wondering if I could come home for a few days and catch up on some old times."

"Of course, Honey. You're always welcome at home, your dad will be very happy to see you. Are you coming over for dinner?"

"I got dinner plans, Mom. Maybe tomorrow. I got to do some packing now, I'll see you tonight."

"Okay, take care."

She wasn't an overly messy person but organization had never been her talent. Opening the closet, she snatched a few shirts, T-shirts, pants, and underwear, throwing them into her suitcase. She knew she probably had everything else she needed in her parent's house. If not, she could always go buy supplies from the supermarket just around the corner. Her leather-bound diary went into the suitcase too. Ever since high school she had the habit of writing diaries. She liked the idea of looking back, when she was old, at some of the happy things in the past. As for some unhappy things that occurred in the past, she was willing to forget. She did not write daily though, maybe once or twice a week. Sometimes the intervals were longer, maybe a month, sometimes even a year or two since she started working, depending on if there was something significant to write about. There were a lot to write about now, and she was going to do some of that tonight. Although none of them were considered happy, she thought it was something worth reminiscing at an old age, if she lived that long.

Then she put on an old pair of blue jeans which she hadn't worn for a while and a small white tank top which exposed her waist a little, just enough to be sexy and not enough to make her a tramp. She checked herself on the mirror. She still looked good. One good thing about her job was that it made sure she stayed in shape. She had friends from college that got flabby in just a few months of office work. She was not the kind of person who cared too much about vanity, but then she was a girl. Not to mention a single girl who had not dated anyone for years.

Jessie looked at her watch, 5:32 p.m. There was still plenty of time. She lay down on the couch to meditate and think about the case. Then it just occurred to her that she no longer had a case. In spite of that, it was her case until she understood the whole thing. She hated unsolved puzzles. She thought about what she was going to do tomorrow, the idea of a real vacation was very tempting. But she needed to find out who the man today with the strange power was, and hopefully she would find out what kind of pills that bottle held. She had no doubt all the clues would point towards Babel Corps.

The key to the mystery was Francis. She barely knew him, but she knew she could trust him. She was seldom wrong about people, though she was definitely wrong about Mary. Her mistake almost cost her life, but she vowed to never make that mistake again. There was something about Francis that spoke to her and told her that she could trust him. Aside from the fact that he so selflessly saved her from peril, the spark of innocence that gleamed in his eyes indicated a soul incapable of falsehood, a soul enveloped in an inner turmoil with what he believed as evil. It was a mystery that she felt drawn to him. And that mystery was shadowed by something gargantuan. She envisioned something evil sitting on top of a tower looking down at her, amused at how little she had accomplished, or how far she had advanced someone's diabolical plot. Babel Corps, the Tower of Babel, it had a familiar ring to it.

She called Mark at the bookstore.

"What's up, Jess?"

"What do you know about the Tower of Babel?"

"It's in the old Testament."

Yes, that's right. How did I forget about that? "The tower that people built in order to reach God and the heavens. It enraged God and He made the builders talk in different languages thus they can no longer communicate with each other, right?"

"Right, that's the gist of it."

"Where else does it appear?"

"In some Sumerian legends, but it's basically the same idea, nothing special. Why are you asking this all of a sudden?"

"Just trying to ponder the meaning of Babel."

"Babel Corps?"

"Yeah."

"You think it means something? I think it's just coincidence."

"You know how I feel about coincidences." There are no coincidences, as all things happen for a reason.

"Right, when are you going to tell me what happened the other day?"

"Later tonight, I'm staying at home for a few days. I'll be coming by the shop later, to meet Francis for dinner." She paused for a second before continuing. "And I don't want to hear anything from you."

"I wasn't going to say anything. Just glad to know that I still have a perfectly healthy sister."

"I'm far from being healthy. Anyway, catch you later."

CHAPTER NINETEEN

Francis walked into Gibson's. The pile of debris from the previous night had apparently been cleaned up. In place of the destroyed counter stood a foldable desk.

He greeted Mark, who seemed to be busy cataloging a stack of books. Jessie looked up from her magazine and smiled. She was in a tank top as white as snow, a little of her bellybutton was exposed, and her tummy was as flat as a washboard. Her hair was combed differently, from one side to another covering only one ear. She looked adorable.

"Hey," he muttered, trying to make his stare polite and unobvious.

"Hey you." She hopped over, acting jolly and energetic.

"You look like you're in a good mood today," he commented.

"Trying to be," she said smiling. "You'd never have guessed what happened today. I'll tell you on the way."

"Where are we going?"

"To this small Italian restaurant on the corner. You ever been there?"

He shook his head.

"My favorite restaurant. I'm craving for some Gnocchi right now."

"Noki?"

"Let me guess, you're never had that either. You've been so deprived."

He answered her with a smile.

Mi Piace was a small Italian restaurant that was just around the corner, a less than five-minute walk from the Gibson's, a place he often passed by but never paid attention to. It was not fancy, but quaint, charming, and comfortable.

He had never been to Europe but he'd imagined that Mi Piace was what a hometown restaurant on a side street in Italy looked like.

Even the waiter was Italian looking – tall, dark, with a thick accent. He ushered them to a table next to the window with a nice view.

Francis scanned the menu. "Where's this Noki thing?"

"It starts with a G, under pasta."

"Oh, I see it. I think I'll give that a try."

"Do you like potatoes and pasta?"

"I love potatoes."

"Then you're going to like it."

"So what happened today?" Francis asked after they ordered.

"I visited Mary's residence, talked to her mom for a while, very nice lady. I would have liked to talk to her a bit longer, but someone paid us an unexpected visit. He popped a bullet into Mary's mother."

"Holy…" He did not complete his phrase. His jaws went slack.

"Shit, right. That's what I said. You don't have to be polite in front of me, I'm a cop, remember. I spill out foul obscenities everyday, just to make the bad things I see a bit more okay."

"I'd like to ask you how you came about being a cop. But I think I'll let you finish your story first."

"Yes, I'll tell you that part later. Let me finish my little adventure first." An exquisite aroma flowed by as the waiter brought the dishes. "Or maybe not, stomach calls. Didn't get to eat lunch, I'm famished."

Gnocchi was a kind of pasta made with mashed potato and flour. It was soft and tender, but not too squashy like mashed potato, solid enough to be chewy and distinctly delectable. Francis really enjoyed it.

"You need to get out more often," she said with a half smile, still chewing her potato pasta.

"Why do you say that?"

"Because you look like you just ate unicorn meat. Anyway, talking about unicorn. Let me continue my story. So this guy popped a bullet into Mary's mother from outside the patio while she was making coffee for me in the kitchen. I ran to the patio, downward slope on the other side, it was almost like a cliff. The only thing I saw was rocks falling down like rain right in front of me."

"Falling rocks?" Francis asked, not really understanding.

"Well, you're not going to believe this, this guy used the rocks to climb upstairs."

"How?"

"Well, I don't find this out until later, that he can levitate things around him. He built a stairway of floating pebbles and climbed up."

If not for his near-death confrontation with the Tormentor yesterday, he would have had a hard time believing her.

"I'm getting ahead of myself here," she went on and told him about the car chase, how she blew her quarry's tire, but the assassin built a bridge of levitating rocks and climbed onto her truck. That her hand was stuck on the door and how she got out by shooting the back tire of the truck and almost killed herself. And in the last standoff she fired multiple bullets at her target to only have them float futilely around him. Then she went into the details of how she lured him close enough for a double tap, and ended up just physically hammering the bullets into his forehead with the butt of her gun.

Francis could imagine how frightened she must have been, fighting a foe with inhuman powers. He was that scared the night before, even though he had his own powers. She had nothing but her gun, her wits, and courage.

Her cell phone hummed a tune. "Sorry, usually I don't take calls over dinner but this is important."

"Hi, Angel." For the next minute or so she just listened. Her expression darkened. It must be bad news. "Thanks anyway, I'll talk to you tomorrow."

"Damn it," she scowled. "It can't be." She looked away, lost in a reverie of deep thoughts.

Francis wondered if sometimes he would look like that when he stopped paying attention.

"Sorry." She looked disappointed. "Bad news. The bottle of pills I uncovered from the assassin; I had the contents analyzed by a friend. She said it was just aspirins. What's your take on all this?"

"Let me think about it for a moment," he said, taking a couple minutes to analyze the situation. "Someone sent an assassin to take out Mary's mom. She knew something important. Then the assassin also uncovered a key piece of evidence from the medicine cabinet, which is only a bottle of aspirins. Doesn't make much sense, does it?"

It was more an observation than question, and he didn't expect an answer. But her sudden silence was a bit daunting. He knew it was not true but he felt as if he had upset her. He searched his mind for something else to say.

"What did you think the pills were?" he asked. "Perhaps some kind of power-inducing substance?"

"That's what I was thinking."

"Perhaps the pill could disguise itself as aspirins."

"Not very likely, then why would someone be sent to retrieve it?"

"Right." He suddenly felt quite stupid.

"Unless he did not know that it was only aspirins, and was only following an order to remove the evidence. In that case, Mary did not know that they were only aspirins."

Her analytical reasoning amazed him. And something clicked in his mind. "That's what killed Mary."

"What do you mean?"

"Before I…" He tried to find a more appropriate word to say over dinner other than killed, but couldn't. "You know."

She gave a sympathetic nod.

"She had some sort of terrible headache and while she struggled, she kept on saying 'They promised'. If she was referring to the pills, maybe she was relying on them to sustain her power. But if they only gave her aspirins, maybe they wanted her removed. And the person who was ordered to clean out the evidence did not know those were just regular pills."

"And it would be prudent for that person not to know." Jessie followed his thread of thoughts. "If they could not survive without the pills, whoever made them had absolute power over the people they gave them to. They can't possibly let anyone know that they are passing out fake pills to remove people."

That made a lot of sense to Francis, but who is passing out the pills? And no, the major question is…

"Are you on any pills?"

He shook his head. "Not that I know of."

For a moment, they did not speak but only stared at each other, thinking, pondering, and calculating all facets of possibilities.

"Francis, are you sure?" Jessie broke the silence. "Think about it. This is important. Has anyone done any clinical test on you, put any foreign objects in your body, given you any pills?"

"You think Babel Corporation did this?"

"What do you think, Francis?"

"They're the prime suspect, I agree with that."

"You work there; Mary worked there; the parking lot victim, your co-worker's death, pills, research, everything points to one place."

She made a lot of sense, but he worked there. He did not like the idea of being an unwilling lab rat. He thought about his few months of work, he was only in the IT department. He had not even been to the research building. Nobody made him take any drugs he did not want to take. They did not even make him go to any clinic for a drug test. He had not had a needle poked into him since he was a child.

"No," he answered her firmly. "I can agree that you suspect Babel Corps for being the villain. But they did not do anything to me, I'm sure of that."

"Then how do you explain your power?"

How the hell should I know? "I can't."

She averted her eyes and let a few long moments of silence slide by. They were long torturing moments.

"I'm sorry." Her gaze fell back on him. Her dark watery eyes for a moment held him entranced. "This is supposed to be pleasant dinner, now see what I did. It's just that I hate unsolved mysteries, it's one of my many vices."

"It's alright." Her one glowing dimple on her left cheek did make everything cheerful and bright. He wanted to complement how lovely her smile was, but he was too embarrassed to do so. "It's been pleasant so far."

"Let's get the check," she said. "My treat." Before he could protest, she continued. "For thanking you about yesterday. Next one is yours. I want something big and expensive."

Next one?

"Kidding."

Is she kidding about next time or is she kidding about something big and expensive? Never mind. "Thanks."

"Hey why don't we go get something to drink?" she suggested. "You know of a place we could go?"

"I do, but I'm not sure you wanna go there." The only place he knew.

"Try me."

"There's a really nice bar in Babel recreation center."

"Oh, I know about it. You guys are a bunch of spoiled brats!" "You don't know the half of it."

"You don't think they'll put funny research stuff in my drink, do you?" She contorted her face which looked ridiculous.

"Nah."

"Alright, then I'm in for another adventure."

*   *   *   *

When the passenger door of the Honda Accord swung itself open, her heart leaped. She looked across the car to Francis, who looked away and smiled guiltily.

"Tell me you didn't do that."

"Guilty as charged." He was trying to hide his smirk, but wasn't having much success.

Apparently her astonishment was somehow amusing. She didn't find it very funny though, especially she could now deduce an unseen thing was standing in front of her, Francis called her Michelle, but she neither saw, felt, nor understood what it was.

"Please don't do that again. It doesn't take that much effort to walk over here and open the door for me, right?"

"You want to shake hands with her?"

Or with it, whatever the hell it really was. Today, and yesterday, she was almost killed by one of these things. Absolutely not. "No."

"Come on, aren't you curious?"

To know what it feels like to be touched by a ghost? The idea was making her flesh crawl. "Not really, no."

"You know that's really just part of me, unless I'm still dreaming."

"I know," but is that the truth? What is the truth? "It's a little unsettling, I don't think I'm ready for that today. You know, I'm glad you've come to terms with your imagination so well already. It's a big step from yesterday."

"Just learning to get along as I go along."

Questions danced through her mind. Was he really sure about reality? Had he accepted what he had done as truth? Or was he just considering himself living in a fantasy? Actually she was hoping that the last few days were a fantasy, it was too terrible and unreal. Pain, fright, tears, and anxiety, merged and entangled inside her like long forgotten parts of her old self.

They were both silent as he drove. That moment of quietness and solitude was soothing. It made her remember times she was in Terry's car. He talked often, but sometimes he was quiet. He knew when to be quiet, and it was comfortable. A good partner was not always necessarily someone you constantly talked to, but someone that you could be next to and be silent for hours and still felt comfortable.

"You are a pretty gentle driver, aren't you?" He was only driving around sixty-five miles on the freeway, which was unusual for someone his age.

"I try my best, especially when there's an officer next to me."

"Oh, I don't do traffic tickets."

He didn't say anything on the remaining short journey to Babel Corps.

Jessie stared blankly out the window. The five highest buildings in the coastal commercial town of Newport Beach surrounding a beautiful fountain that glowed in rainbow colors made up the compound of the "Gateway of the Gods." While a stunning sight in daylight, it was dark and ominous under the cloudy night. The nexus of evil power was glowing, smiling tauntingly at her, and luring her into the den of evil. She shivered and shook her head; what was she thinking? Though all the circumstantial evidence led to this place, it didn't mean that it was the source of evil. Nevertheless, as they approached the place, it only brought her anxiety and unease.

Francis did not park the car too far away from the scene from the previous night. She guessed it was his usual spot and also the closest distance to the recreational center. It was after ten at night but there were still quite a number of people in the compound. Some walked back after a hard day of work back to their cars, and a few were strolling into the recreational building in shorts, tank-tops, and work-out towels.

The Raven, on the top floor of the recreation center, was a bar with a British Pub feel to it, with atmosphere that rivaled the top lounges she had visited in San Francisco. The place was spacious, large enough to accommodate an upscale dinner party. There were quite a few patrons there, some concentrated near the big-screen TV on the far side, some laughed at the pool table, and some just stared intently at each others in an intimate conversation, occasionally sipping at their beverage. The place was relaxing and somewhat romantic. It was a privilege to be working at the famed Babel Corps.

They picked a small table in a quiet corner. A dark-haired waitress in a short skirt came to serve them right away. She ordered a Bailey's On The Rocks and Francis ordered a Screwdriver.

"Is that your favorite drink?" Jessie asked after the waitress strolled off. Even she couldn't resist looking at the swaying hips. She didn't find it a turn-on, but she liked to observe how other women used their bodies to get attention.

"No, not really," Francis said smiled; he shook his head and for a moment looked slightly embarrassed. "Just the only drink I know."

"You should give Bailey's a try, it tastes kinda like coffee."

"You a coffee drinker?"

"I love coffee. Bad habit since college, couldn't stay awake in class until I have had a nice cup of hot coffee."

"And donuts too?"

"Well, my partner, no, ex-partner," why does Terry always come into mind? "Liked donuts, just like every other cop. But they're just a big clump of sugar and grease. You know, cops like donuts because it's open 24 hours. But I rather go to Denny's."

The waitress came back, placing their drinks on the table. She then turned to Francis and smiled at him, deliberately ignoring Jessie.

What a flirt, Jessie thought.

She let Francis try her drink first and he nodded with approval, saying that it tasted a lot like iced cappuccino.

"So do you get a lot of late night shifts?" he asked when the waitress finally moved out of her sight.

"Not a lot, but sometimes there'll be a few nights during an investigation when we're trailing a suspect closely. In the Firecracker's case, we had gone four days straight without sleeping following our target. That's when the coffee kicks in, and the late night donuts for him and Jack-in-the-box for me time."

"Firecracker?"

"That was about a year ago. The killer was a Vietnamese American who used fireworks to kill his victims. He was a sneaky bastard, and twice he almost got us blown up."

"So what happened at the end?" A light sparkled in Francis' eyes. For a minute he was like a little kid trying to get his mother to tell him a bedtime story.

"I shot him in the head." She lowered her eyes. Killing had never made her feel good, even when it was fully justified. Sometimes she felt that it was as bad as not being able to catch the bad guy. "There was no other choice, he was holding Terry hostage. He had already killed seven victims, including two officers, and he told us he would make the best fireworks with both of us. With Terry's head under the barrel of his gun, we were at a standoff in the parking lot. Out of sheer luck, a cat tripped over one of his traps and got blown to pieces, instead of me. That sneaky bastard had the whole place trapped with thin wires. He didn't anticipate the cat and was befuddled for that split second, and I took the chance."

For a moment, she thought his out-stretched hand was going to reach for hers. Her heart suddenly shuddered briefly. He only reached for his drink. Must be the alcohol, she told herself. She was a wild girl the first year in college. In her past she was drunk every night and she did everything: smoking, weed, and all sorts of debauchery. The first time leaving home she wanted to experience life. She straightened out after two quarters of bad grades, a broken relationship, and loss of confidence in men. She went back to schoolwork and thinking about her career goals. She hadn't touched a sip of alcohol ever since. She needed it tonight though, because she felt like she had walked through hell twice in a row.

"It isn't easy, is it?" His large, gawking brownish eyes were suddenly magically mesmerizing. She found herself light-headed and lost.

"No, it never is. No matter how justified it is."

He was going to say something, but then he changed his mind and looked away.

She knew what he was going to say, recalling what they talked about yesterday. He had enjoyed the moment of his kill, but that was not his fault. It was what the power was doing to him. He was afraid to become evil. And that in itself was goodness, she thought. Though she didn't say anything, she knew that he understood.

The waitress came back and asked them what they wanted. They both ordered Bailey's this time.

"So why did you want to be a detective?"

"Oh, that. It's a long story." And many parts she did not want to go into. "But to make it short, my father was a cop. He died when I was fourteen."

"I'm sorry."

"He was killed by someone he put in jail, a victim of vengeance."

"Escaped criminal?"

"No, that's the irony of it. The killer actually studied law after he got into jail. He appealed due to improper ways of obtaining evidence and the lack of it. He built a case and was released after two years. Killed my father three days later."

"Was he ever caught again?"

Jessie shook his head. It always hurt when she was reminded that her father's killer, and the person who hurt her, was free in the world and did not have to pay for his crime. "Things quieted down, and he just got away." Then she shifted her eyes away from his gaze and blankly studied the blinking images on the projector all the way on the other side of the room. They didn't mean anything to her, just a way to distract her so she didn't have to focus on the sad, disturbing images that were popping up in her mind. Every time she thought about what happened, her heart and stomach felt like they were going to burst and she was petrified with an unquenchable pain.

"Are you all right? I'm sorry that I made you upset."

She took a deep breath and gulped down the rest of her drink. She told herself to focus on other things: Mark, the store, her new loving family, and she was instantly better. "I'm okay. Don't worry about it. It's not your fault. I haven't thought about the past for a very long time. I've put it all behind me. I didn't become a cop to follow my father's footsteps, or to bring justice to him. I just wanted to understand. Why they do what they do, and to stop them from doing more, so there aren't more people in the world getting hurt. And of course, justice, doing good, solving puzzles, even sometimes the thrill of hunting down the bad guys, those come with the job and they bring satisfaction, but sometimes I just wish that there were no jobs out there for us to do. And that means no one is getting hurt."

The waitress came by and she ordered another drink. This time she didn't find the attire as offensive. "Anyway, the first thing I learned about being a cop was that most of them really did get away. Serial killers are the hardest kind to catch because they have no motives, they do it for sport and some even do it to challenge us. They leave us little signatures, evidence, clues to taunt us, to see how many victims have to die before we figure out what's going on. Sometimes we even hope for fresh blood, that's what we call new victims. When a killer stops, we cannot do our job either. It's a big moral dilemma for us. Do we want him to kill more? Or do we want him to stop? Though it is out of our control, we always wonder how many more people have to die. And not until we get the son-of-a-bitch we won't be able to get a good night sleep."

The waitress came with her drink and for a long moment Jessie was dazed by her own outburst. She swallowed her frustration and again looked to the far corner of the bar for comfort. Many times she questioned if she liked her job and thought about quitting. But she didn't know what else she could do, each time she caught the villain she was infused with satisfaction. It was her duty to stop them, maybe in some way it was redemption for her father's untimely death, and maybe it redeemed herself from her abuse. Her job was to understand them, to find out why they kill, but the more she thought she understood them, the more she found out she didn't. There was one more thing she realized after meeting Francis. Perhaps there was an appealing nature to evil itself. Because each time when she put her mind inside the criminal's and embraced that very darkness that was the core of their souls, she felt a fascinating gratification – something that was almost similar to the way Francis experienced when he took lives. It made neither of them evil. It was just a brief moment of joy and satisfaction that kept them going.

"So why do you think a serial killer kills?"

Jessie suddenly felt exposed, as if his gaze had penetrated her thoughts and he had read everything in her mind.

She took a deep breath before answering, as if her life depended on what she was going to say. She told herself that she always overreacted a bit when this subject was touched on, but only because her whole life she was trying to figure it out, and through that process had shaped the path of her life. "When I was in school, I studied Criminal Psychology. Textbooks said that people become violent because of traumatic experience. Abuse, and unbalanced childhood, some wanted to exercise revenge. But it's all bullshit."

There was a curious gleam in his brown eyes that asked her "why" when he looked up, a little bit shocked at her use of language.

"A lifetime of abuse doesn't make a person evil. A person can be abused all his life and still not be able to hurt a tiny life. Being wronged just means that you have first hand knowledge of what it feels like, and you know what you shouldn't inflict on another person."

When his lips parted, she was afraid that he'd ask her "How do you know about that?" or "Can you personally testify to that?" It was not something she wanted to discuss. But he did not.

"So you think people can be born evil?"

She nodded. "Everyone has an evil side in themselves. I call it darkness. Some are dominated by it. The right kind of love and education could steer a person away from that path, abuse and torture can enhance someone's evil side. But it is not necessarily true that an insane killer did not grow up in a loving family, or an abused child has the excuse to grow up to be a messed-up person. It's all inside his or her brain, heart, and soul. All of us have darkness inside our soul. And the only thing that matters is whether we contain that darkness, or let the darkness consume us."

"So what happened to you and Mark after your father died?"

She was glad that he changed the subject. It was starting to make her blood boil and she'd probably end up embarrassing herself, if she hadn't already by raising her voice and saying bullshit. But she was a cop. They were expected to be rude, even on a date. At least she hadn't said the f word yet.

"Our mother left a long time before that. So after the incident we were placed in a foster home. They moved us around a few times to people who wanted to adopt us. I was a big trouble maker then." She smiled faintly as she thought about the things she had done before. "For the family we didn't like, I caused so much trouble that the family couldn't stand us and had to send us back. Finally we moved in with the Gibsons. They loved us and both of us really liked them. They treated us just like as if we were their own. And we lived with them ever since. They are our real parents now. I have not forgotten my real father, but he's now just a faint memory in a long forgotten past." He was still important to her, he was the person who steered her towards her path, not only when he was alive, but more so after his death. Yet now his existence only belonged to nostalgia and flashback she tried not to bring back to her mind. She so wished that he was still alive, and wondered what she'd be like if things were different.

She realized that her thoughts had wandered and Francis had watched her reverie and said nothing. After the third drink she had a slight headache from the buzz, but she felt relaxed. She looked back into Francis's eyes, and wondered why she liked looking at them so much. The copper color looked out of place, almost fake, as if he was wearing contacts, but she knew he wasn't vain enough to do so. It wasn't unattractive though.

"Francis, I really like your eyes."

He blushed and turned his face completely away.

She only gave out a small giggle. "Really, did one of your parents have brown eyes?"

He shrugged. "I don't know. I have never seen my biological father. My mother said he's French."

"That explains it." She couldn't tell that he was of mixed heritage. Sure his eyes were not typically slender and his features were not completely oriental. Nowadays it was hard to tell if someone had mixed or straight blood.

"No, it doesn't really explain it," he said with a sly smile. "I took genetics in college and according to the textbook, genes with light colored pupils are recessive to the genes with dark colored pupils. In other words, dark eyes are dominant so a mix can only have dark eyes."

"It makes sense, I think."

"Anyway, I'm just a mutant, or plain weird."

She laughed. She did that for a long time, because she had not laughed in a while. "You said your last name is Seto? Is that Chinese?""

He nodded. "That's from my father, the guy my mom married after she had me."

"I thought all Chinese last names are single syllable."

"Most of them are." He scratched his chin. "Mine actually comes from an official title originated from the Zhou dynasty, its one of the exceptions among mostly single syllable surnames among the Han Chinese. There are other barbarian tribes integrated into the Chinese civilization with multiple-syllable family names. Some changed their names and some didn't. I must be boring you."

She shook her head. "History is fascinating. So you know Chinese history pretty well?"

"Yes, I was in Hong Kong until I was fourteen. School was quite intense there. I basically knew both Western and Chinese history back and forth from the beginning of time."

"I haven't been to anywhere in Asia. I have only seen it in the movies. Perhaps I should go sometimes. How do you like Hong Kong?"

"A lot of people, crowded. I think I like the States better."

"Because you don't like people?" She was being blunt, maybe a little too blunt. It's the alcohol.

He smiled, shrugged, averted his eyes and didn't say anything for a while. "Not until now."

She didn't know what else to say and only nodded in acknowledgement. She thought it was a sweet thing for him to say.

"Tell me about your childhood, your parents, and what it was like growing up." She wanted to know why he didn't like people.

He swallowed and looked away for a long moment, before beginning.

*   *   *   *

Francis Seto came to the world in the year 1977. Born and raised in Hong Kong until he was fourteen, he had never met his biological father. His mother Eileen was a journalist for one of the few English television channels in Hong Kong and she conceived him before marrying Elias Seto, a dentist. Francis had often questioned if his parents loved him. And what was love?

His mother was a busy woman. She came home late at night; often by then he was asleep. She would come into his room quietly, and kiss him on the cheek. She woke him up every night, but he pretended to be asleep. He liked the kisses from his mother, they made him feel loved, or the illusion of it. Francis saw more of his mother on TV during his childhood by watching the news and talk shows where she appeared every night.

His mother was a beautiful woman, and Francis thought that it was why Father loved her. Father watched her shows every night, and Francis watched with him. Getting tired of watching his mother on TV as he grew a little older, he would rather have her spend more time with him in real life. Nevertheless he watched, because his father did. Maybe it was a way to tell his father that he loved Mother, so that he would love him as he loved Mother. Maybe it was a way to tell himself that he loved Mother, because if he loved her, she would surely love him back.

"Why does she do that?" Francis remembered asking his father. He remembered his mother often blew the long strand of hair out of her face when it fell. Then she would take a moment to stop what she was saying, and proudly brush her long wavy cascade of lush black hair backwards. That happened so often that it sometimes seemed more deliberate than coincidence. Mother still did that. Father had only answered him with a grunt when he was six and he had let it go at that. He never had much conversation with Father. He understood as he grew older. Mother brushed her hair on TV because it was pretty, and people liked watching things that were delightful to their eyes, despite the mostly dreary and superficial content in Mother's talk shows.

He questioned himself if his father loved him, as often as he questioned about his mother. And he would answer himself with a melancholic no. His father treated him well, as well as any father who could have treated his own son. Yet it was out of respect, not out of love. His father respected him because he was the son of the woman he loved, but nothing more. Father didn't talk much and sometimes Francis wondered if he truly was not his father's son. Because he was a lot like him – quiet, most of the time keeping to himself. Francis liked his father because he provided for the family, bought anything he wanted, never scolded or hit him for any bad deeds. Maybe a father like that was what a lot of children dreamed of having, but for Francis it didn't feel quite right. It didn't feel like having a father, it felt like living in a stranger's home.

The day after he tossed the clown Father got for him from Denmark out the window, he had endured a beating, by Mother. It was the first and only time she had ever beaten him. He had thought that Father would at least scold him for what he did, but he did not even ask why. Francis knew why, he bought him something just to show Mother that he cared about her son. After that was accomplished, he did not care about his rebellion. Mother at least loved him enough to be disappointed at his actions. He didn't enjoy being flogged, but in the following years he sometimes yearned for it. Despite being painful, it was evidence that someone cared.

Francis often tried to learn who his real biological father was, but his mother only told him was that he was a Frenchman she met in China during a vacation. Mother said that he saved her from almost getting killed by a drunk driver. They fell in love shortly after that and later on he returned to France.

Mother never gave Francis any details. She never had time to, except maybe on TV. His name was Jean-Pierre. She didn't even know his last name. Francis wondered how many Jean-Pierres there would be in France. It was more common than a David in the States, or a Fiona in England.

Not many people knew that Francis was not fully Chinese. His French decent was not something to be ashamed of, but Francis told no one about his heritage. He often kept to himself, and he told no one that Elias was not his real father. Francis did not look Caucasian. Perhaps his eyes were a bit rounder than most stereotypically viewed slender-eyed Orientals and his hair a bit browner and softer, but his ancestry never came into question. There were Chinese who looked more Caucasian than him, and he saw himself as a full Chinese because he grew up enveloped in the culture.

To Francis, his childhood was like a collection of colorful fairy tales. He was quiet in school and he didn't have many friends. Yet he was never bored because he had a vivid imagination, and he depended on that imagination to get through his childhood days. He loved watching cartoons, and then he liked video games and computers, then science fiction and fantasy novels. All of them served one single purpose, to take him on a wild, fun trip across the realm of imagination. In that land he could be anything that he wanted: a master swordsman who slew dragons and rescued damsels in distress, or a powerful sorcerer who turned the tides of battles which decided the fate of worlds. In his imaginative worlds he was a hero, someone important. In the real world he was just one of the many zillions of people, he was nobody. He was happy living through endless adventures in the chimera realm of fantasy. He found true friendship and love there, something that did not exist in the real world.

His parents soon noticed that he spent much time in his own room with his own toys rather than playing with other kids. His mother asked him to go out more often. He only nodded. He knew that his mother did not have the time to notice his social activities. His father did and probably informed his mother. Yet as his grades at school were still more than satisfactory they didn't really care. When he was fourteen, his parents suggested sending him to boarding school in the States. They had asked him if he wanted to go, but he knew that he probably didn't have much choice so he nodded. He knew that they wanted to detach him from his toys so he could have an ordinary social life. They did it out of love for him. That's what he told himself. But sometimes during the long, lonely night on the top level of the bunk bed in the Boston boarding school, he wondered otherwise. They were tired of having him around, even though most of the time he was just in his own room. They were ashamed of his being so abnormal, the child with no friends who always kept to himself, sitting in front of the computer or in bed reading a book giggling to himself. They wanted to strip him of his only possessions, and they had gotten rid of him. But he still had his imaginations, his worlds. They could never take that away. With that, he didn't need love or friendship. He did not resent his parents for putting him in a boarding school. Even though in there he had no freedom to do what he liked. He had to study with the others, play sports with the others, eat with the others, and make friends with the others.

He rarely spoke, not because his English was not fluent, but because that was how he was. His mother had appointed a British tutor for him when he was small teaching him proper speech. From all the variety of books he had read his English was better than most foreign students. All he had to do was to change the British accent and he almost spoke like an American, when he wanted to.

There had been two people in his twenty-four years that he had trusted. The first one was his roommate in boarding school during eleventh grade. A big, burly Korean guy named Sam roomed with him for that year. Sam was popular and talkative, and he often initiated discussions of different topics before they went to sleep. Francis ignored him in the beginning, but later their confidences went from homework, class to family, philosophy, hobbies and even girls. They became best friends, and Francis relied less on his fantasy world to make him forget about his real-life problems. He told Sam everything, and Sam told him everything. Well, everything that Sam wanted him to hear.

As the end of his junior year approached, Francis had gotten to know a girl. Her name was Rosa and she was from Spain. Her dark blonde hair was like honey that poured around her creamy, white shoulders, and her green eyes were like sparkling emeralds from the treasure chest in his imaginative world. They were often in study groups together. Whenever she brushed close, Francis felt his heart thump uncontrollably as if it wanted to jump out of his confining body. He was so in love with her that he never knew what to say when she smiled and gazed at him with her big green eyes. He wished that she were a distressed damsel in his heroic world of fantasy. But the real world was a sad place, he never knew what to do or say.

"You like Rosa?" Sam asked one night.

Francis knew it was a mistake, but he couldn't help letting his secret out.

"Well, she's got big tits," Sam commented. In his eyes he only saw breasts.

Francis didn't mind that, but he'd like to think that there were more qualities to girls than just their boobs.

Sam was popular with girls because he was tall, big, talkative, and handsome. Francis himself was small, and being quiet did not help. He didn't know how to talk to the opposite sex; in fact he didn't know how to talk to anybody, except Sam, who told him that he was going to help him by tutoring him on how to approach her.

Eventually Francis became more outgoing and had gotten to know Rosa better, often asking her to study with him alone as an excuse to spend more time together. Francis appreciated Sam's advice, and he kept his roommate updated on his progress with Rosa every night. Francis and Rosa became good friends. He was happy, and this time he was happy in the real world.

One day, all that bliss came to an end. Francis came back from the library to find the wooden door to his dormitory room closed, a thin trail of orange light seeping from the crack below and a soft moaning noise of a girl came from inside. He knew what Sam was doing because it was between their agreement that when one of them wanted to bring a girl back to the room, the other had to give them privacy. Unfortunately, Francis never had the chance to take advantage of that privilege, however Sam often did. He claimed to have slept with girls from the school ranging from freshmen to seniors, and Francis believed him.

It was two in the morning and apparently Sam was still busy 'doing' it. Even though the library was closed, Francis decided that he could probably stay in the lounge and read until Sam was done. Right before he walked away, he heard a familiar voice.

"What about Francis?"

Francis recognized that voice.

"What about him?" That was an impatient grunt from Sam.

Francis carefully pressed his ear to the door.

"What if he comes in and sees us?"

That was Rosa. Francis swallowed hard, his heart beating so fast that he could hear it for the whistling leaves which seemed to be laughing at him outside the hallway window. It couldn't be Rosa, Francis told himself. He must have been mistaken. Sam knew that he liked Rosa, and Sam was his best friend. She must have been someone else who sounded like Rosa.

"That little worm, he doesn't have enough balls to walk into the room, not when I'm fucking. He knows I'll kill him."

Francis swallowed again, and heard the exploding noise of the clump of saliva settling down his dry throat. Fist clenched, his knuckles turned white.

"Don't be so mean, he's kinda cute, in a weird sort of way." She giggled and moaned again.

"He doesn't have enough dick to satisfy a horny cunt like you."

She moaned louder this time.

Francis' chest was heaving and his clenched fist was shaking. No, that cannot be Rosa. Rosa is a sweet innocent girl. And Sam, he's just saying all that to impress the girl. He doesn't mean it. He calmed himself. His hand went to the doorknob and turned. The wooden massive door slowly squeaked and swung open.

Head thrown back, Rosa was straddled on top of the man below her. Her face was contorted in ecstasy. Sam's one hand cupped her breasts, the other around her hips, guiding her to and fro atop him. His eyes were not closed, he watched her intently with a leering expression, as if admiring a trophy. A dim light in the corner of the room flickered with the rhythmic movements of the couple. Shadows danced on the far wall of the room, oak branches thumped, leaves whistled, and crickets sang. It was an orchestra playing a harmonic song of disdainful laughter. You are a loser, Francis.

He hated Sam, he hated Rosa, he hated the world, and he hated life. He ran and he cried. He never stopped crying until dawn came. When he couldn't cry anymore, his eyes were so sore that they burnt and stung him like fire. He never talked to Sam or Rosa again. That day he retreated back to his world of imagination, the world in which he had total control, the world where friends did not betray him. And he was happy again.

*   *   *   *

Jessie was speechless after his recounting of his childhood. She could feel the sorrow he felt. Though it was by far not a horrible childhood, it was lonely. And she did not think her mere words could comfort him.

After a long period of silence, she decided to change the subject. "How did you get into doing computer programming?"

"I guess I've always liked computers. I find it a lot more comfortable dealing with a computer than socializing with others."

You're not doing so bad right now, she thought.

"I didn't study computer science though," he continued. "My parents wanted me to become a doctor, and I went along with it. Perhaps I didn't dislike the idea at the time so I gave it a try. I was good at chemistry in high school. I ended up studying Biochemistry at UCLA. As the years passed by, I became more disinterested in the medical field, and working in labs and doing hospital volunteer work numbed me even further. Of course my grades would scarcely be sufficient for me to get into medical school anyway. I decided that I should do something I liked, or rather something that I've been doing for a long time already. So I took some programming classes in school to brush up my skills and found a part-time job doing Internet related work. Well, then it got me into Babel."

"So how do you like the work?"

"It's mildly challenging and I don't mind doing it. But to tell you the truth, I lack the passion for my job. Like the passion you have for yours. I can see the fire burning in your eyes when you're talking about hunting down the killers. I don't have that for my work, everyday I go to work and time just passes by. "

It was true. She had a fire burning in her when she crept into that dark mind of a criminal and trying to solve the most intricate of puzzles. But she wasn't so sure anymore. She was a bit fed up with the horror she had to deal with. "You feel like you're not destined to be a computer programmer?"

"If there's such a thing as destiny, yes."

"I believe it."

"Me too."

"Perhaps in the future you'll run across something you feel passionate about."

"I hope so."

"Say, does Babel keep all their research projects on computer?"

"Yes, in a database somewhere."

"Would you have access to that?"

"Nope, I have access to the web interface that deals with the database. But I don't have the passwords to directly extract data."

"Have you ever done any hacking?" The talk about computers reminded her of someone she knew and suddenly she had an idea.

Francis shook his head. "That had never been my thing."

"Assuming if someone were to hack into Babel to look for something, would you know where to begin?"

He thought about it a while and nodded. "As long as you have the passwords, you can get to what you want from the intranet. What are you suggesting?"

"You want to know what kind of secret projects they are running, right?" She suddenly realized that she was still within the company compound and she nervously spun around to see if anyone would overhear her. Nobody was around.

He nodded with a sly smile, seemingly amused at her nervousness.

"You making fun of me, Francis?"

"Would I do that?"

"I didn't think so. Anyway, what I'm saying is that I know someone who's pretty good at hacking. He helped me on a case once. If I were to get him to help, unofficially, do you think it'd work?"

His brows narrowed. He was scrutinizing and judging her integrity. Then he smiled. "I think that'll shed some light on our situation."

"Alright, I'll give you a call tomorrow morning, at home, right before you go to work. I'm going to hunt down my friend tonight. Those hackers are more nocturnal than vampires. I'm sure he's going to have some questions to ask you before he can do the actual hacking. You can get into the office anytime, right? Even after midnight?"

"Yes, I can go to work anytime I want." He sighed. "This is going to be dangerous."

She didn't reply right away. If Babel was the villain who would send out an assassin with supernatural power just to wipe out evidence that did not prove to be evidence, who knew what they would do to protect the heart of their computer system, the vortex of true power. "It's going to be fun," she assured him. So much for my vacation.

It was already two o'clock in the morning when they decided to head back. He drove her back to the bookstore.

Before she took off, Jessie decided to lean over and give him a soft, friendly kiss on the cheek. She startled him, as he answered her with a confused look. She gave him a smile and told him that she had a great time. And she had to reassure him twice until he believed her.

She really did have a good time. Because he was a good listener, she felt comfortable talking to Francis. They had the possibility of becoming good friends. Though she made mistakes judging killers, she was never wrong about friends.

Exhausted as she drove to her parents' house, she found everyone already asleep. Her room was bit compact but cozy, with a fresh clean aroma to it. Mother had probably done some extra cleaning for her right after she called today. Jessie hopped onto the bed and stared blankly at the ceiling for a few long minutes just to bathe in the pleasant reminiscence of nostalgia.

The happiest years of her childhood were spent in that room. The bed she had not only slept in, but studied, read, and written her diaries in. She slipped her hand into her suitcase and took out the leather bound diary. Mother had gotten her into the habit of diary writing in this very room. She never wrote anything before she was fourteen years old. Some things were burned into her memory and others she wanted to forget, none pleasant enough to be worth a revisit, even if it was a brief sojourn or even a quick flashback slideshow, afraid that pain would devour her from the inside. It did once, and she only thought about looking forward and never thinking about the past, but living here changed her. She learned how to savor the good memories, which often made her feel that life was worth living, once again.

She opened the diary and flipped to a new page. Nothing had been written for months. The last time she wrote something, it was after she solved the Firecracker case. She was thankful, if not to God, to fate, destiny, and most of all, the cat, for letting her live, just by sheer luck and chance. Biting the tip of her pen, she thought about where to start. Finally deciding that she'd start by recounting bits and pieces of the Tormentor case, she wrote about Mary, Terry's death, and meeting Francis. This week she lost a true friend, but gained a new one. She ended the page with "And life goes on".

Right before she was going to crash and not wake up for at least twelve hours, she remembered that she had to make a phone call. She flipped her cell phone open and scrolled through her contact list. Under the entry "Hacker" was the phone number of Robert Hernandez, or the underground operation center as he called it. They had met over a year ago on a case involving a murder ring on the net, and he had helped her on various cases since.

She knew that Bob was the only person who could unofficially help Francis and her uncover the secret behind Babel Corps. She pressed the dial button and waited patiently for the other side to answer.

CHAPTER TWENTY

Despite the alcohol, Francis still fought with his pillow before truly being submerged into the dream world. Although Jessie had convinced him that he was not schizophrenic, he still questioned his sanity and the reality of the world around him. As much as he was worried about his own perceptional integrity, he was more disturbed at how much he longed for the sensation. He was either insane, or evil. There was no other choice. Neither was easy to accept. There wasn't any alternative to his problems, except to uncover the truth. He had to find out the true nature and purpose of his power, knowing the truth was more likely to condemn than to free him, but that was not his choice to make, but the path he must walk.

Though for the first time in his life, he had someone to talk to, someone to listen to. There was somebody in the world who cared about who he was, and what problems he had. He no longer felt like the Lone Ranger strolling across a vast, lonely world. Someone else listened to him. Of course he was not sure if Jessie really wanted to be his friend. Nobody ever did. He still remembered the night when Sam and Rosa broke his trust and convinced him that he was forever alone in the world.

He wasn't entirely sure if Jessie was offering her friendship. There were many motives that he could think of. Thanking him for saving her life, or even feeling sorry for how lonely he was, or even using him to solve the mystery behind everything. He was the key, the only connection, to uncover the mystery behind Babel. She knew that, and that's why she was keeping contact with him, to satisfy her curiosity, to exercise vengeance on those who wronged her. No. He shook his head. He did not want to think that of Jessie. She had a genuine sweetness about her. He liked her, and he'd liked to care about her. Don't care too much, or you'll get hurt, a voice in his head hissed with admonition.

He dreamed about high school again. He dreamed about Rosa's dark blonde hair and beautiful green eyes. He dreamed about confiding in Sam his deepest secrets. Then he dreamed about the moment of betrayal and his junior year that shattered like a crystal ball dropped onto marble floor. Bits and pieces of memory did nothing except to taunt and haunt him like a bogeyman inside an old closet.

When the alarm clock went off, he swung his arm and silenced it; however the phone woke him up shortly after.

"It's me, Jessie."

It took him a while to gather his senses and he realized yesterday had seemed like one of the episodes of his dream world. He was having a hangover, from an attempt at friendship. He grunted in acknowledgement, wondering what she wanted.

"Hey, I talked to my friend, Bob. And he's agreed to hack into the Babel mainframe. There are a couple questions he told me to ask you. You probably need to write this down. Are you ready?"

Francis hopped out of bed, staggered to his desk and grabbed a pen and piece of paper, feeling like he was still dreaming. She told him a series of things for him to find out, like file location, network firewall, database, web server, IP addresses, mainframe system, his level of access and possibility of gaining higher access, a whole bunch of technical terms that she probably did not understand. He knew some of the answers, but some he needed to find out, and some he didn't even have an idea how to look for. He knew he would be kept busy for the rest of his workday. That was at least a good thing, because it would take his mind off Lilitu, friendship, and the thin line between what's real and what's not.

"Can I call you back at home at around six o'clock?" Jessie asked.

"Better make it seven." He knew that it was probably going to take him quite some time to find out all the information and that using the work phone was out of the question.

"Alright, I'll talk to you later then."

Francis was both relieved and disappointed at the strictly business conversation with no mundane exchange. She was treating him like a witness from her case. Friendship was a luxury. He didn't need friendship.

The rest of the day at work he spent looking up information. He was not a system administrator, so half of the things he was supposed to find out were hard to get to. But it helped that he had acquired the login password to the mainframe system the other day with his keener senses, so he could familiarize himself with the setup and file directory structures of the system.

He had expected another anonymous Email from his secret friend and he was a bit disappointed that it did not come. Though the messages often shed more enigma than answers to his situation, it was part of the excitement.

He spent hours trying to pinpoint which area he needed to breach to find the right information. At last he found it in the Research and Development section of the Babel intranet content management application. Though he thought he knew the intranet inside and out, there were apparently a lot of areas he never knew existed and he didn't have access to. Under the section Science and then Projects he found the first security blockade. A message prompted him that he did not have the right authorization to enter that part of the site. The information he needed resided somewhere inside the application, he was sure about that. His heart pumped as he felt that he was a step closer to finding out the truth about everything. He felt adrenaline surge through him.

The day went by quietly and he got most of the information he needed. Though he didn't get any real work done he was sure that he had already made it up the day before. That was the benefit of working in a big corporation environment, without constant supervision and micromanagement.

He was back at his apartment at half past six and eagerly waited for Jessie's phone call. When the phone rang, he picked it up instantly.

"Francis, Bob's on the other line here."

"Hi, Francis. Please read out the info you found out." Bob's voice was deep and asserting, somewhat like a politician's. Francis couldn't help but wonder what kind of man he was.

He started with the first line on the notepad. Occasionally Bob asked him for clarification, but for the most time he just listened.

"Okay, good job, Francis. Let me see if I got this right," Bob said. "The data we need resides in an Oracle Database, and we've got no access to the database. The only other way to access it is through the web front end, and that's the Vignette Story Server Version 5 Web Application Server sitting on the Netscape Enterprise Server 3.6 which can interact directly with the database. That you have access."

"Only limited access to certain areas."

"Yes, I understand, but I believe I can change that. I'm not very familiar with the Vignette application product, but I'm familiar with others. I'm sure I can figure it out in a short amount of time. Now I believe that the firewall you have is quite high security. It'll take me quite some time to break through it if I were to work from home. How's the security at your office? Can you go in anytime?"

"Yes, I can go in anytime."

"If I were to go in with you—"

"Bob, are you sure this is a good idea?" Not having said anything for a while, Jessie's tone was cautious.

"It'll save a lot of time," Bob reassured, "and a lot more risk-free. If I were to break in from the outside, I could be traced. I need at least two days of preparation to make sure I can cover myself with planned decoys, and I'm not sure if I want to do that for free. A giant corporation like Babel really knows what they're doing with the firewall. However, if I were to go in from inside, I won't be causing any security breaches at all."

"What do you think, Francis?" Jessie asked.

"He's right. It'll be better if we bring him in." He was sure it was not very risky. There was virtually nobody around the office at night. And most importantly he wanted to see how a real hacker worked.

"I need two hours to research the technology a little bit. Then I'll be ready to go."

"Alright," Jessie sighed with resignation. "Francis, I'll pick you up at nine thirty. Then we'll swing by Irvine to pick up Bob."

"Just give me a ring and I'll come down in a jiffy," Bob said in a rush before he hung up.

"How's your day?"

That question left him staggering for a moment. It took him a while to switch from the hacking wavelength to the chitchatting mode. "Oh good. Busy day. What about you?"

"Relaxing, I slept, ate, slept. I feel like a pig now. Anyway, are you excited?"

"A bit. But I don't think it's going to be that easy. We're going to run into trouble."

"It wouldn't be fun if we don't, right?"

He answered her with a grunt. He was not sure if he was having fun, or constantly looping through a series of horrible, unending nightmares.

"Anyway, you probably want to take a nap now, I'll call you when I get to your place."

Francis was thinking the same thing. He was dead tired, must have been the lack of sleep from the previous night.

When he lay on the bed he was hoping to be reinvigorated with a short sleep but all he did was stare at a static point at the ceiling. He used to daydream about exhilarating journeys in his worlds, but now he was drenched with excitement and anticipation. He wondered what answers he would get this day and what kind of danger he would run into. Then his thoughts wandered back to the sensuality and pleasure of the kill. He tried to shift his thoughts away, but he had no easier time of doing that than falling asleep. Like a drug, the sensation of his kill beckoned him, seducing him with that promise of savoring pleasure. The more he tried to stop himself from thinking about it, the more focused his mind became on it. And the more he thought about it, the more he loathed himself.

Francis had never been proud of himself. He did not understand people, he did not have friends, he did not feel loved, and most of the time he did not exist in his own world. But he never hated himself. Self-loathing was despicable. He did not need empathy, he did not need hope, he did not need love, and he did not need happiness. But he needed his self-value. He needed to sustain his morals and to believe in the principles of what was right. Without them he was nothing. All his life he had not needed acceptance from other people, not his parents, not anyone he knew, but he accepted himself as who he was. Now he was starting to doubt the very essence of himself. He was treading toward a path of destruction.

Why is this happening to me? This isn't real. No, this is. Why am I trying to escape? Am I as much a coward as an immoral self-loathing bastard? I've always been a coward. I've never tried to face the problems in the real world. I escape and let them resolve themselves. It has always worked. Why isn't it working now? Why can't the world just leave me be? Why am I thinking about this now? Why don't I wait for the answers? What if I don't get answers?

His mind was a maelstrom of incoherent thoughts. They were so potent that, for a while, he felt as if his soul had been corroded away by those ideas. He then asked himself why he felt so frustrated. After all he had saved a person's life, and in doing so he had gained a friend. But he knew that deep down in his heart that was not reason enough for excusing himself from the atrocity. He had done something good, something he should be proud of; but the extent of that pleasure in comparison to the carnage was infinitesimal.

When the phone rang, he realized how much time flew by. Jessie's voice brought him back from maze of deep meandering thoughts. He got ready quickly and rushed downstairs, in anticipation of getting some of the answers to his questions.

"Excited?" she asked.

For a while, he just watched her dimpled smile. She had such a soothing smile that he wondered if he were to look at Jessie more often he would not have so many questions in his head. He might not even want to daydream.

"What? Something on my face?"

"Just looking at your dimple."

"That's a genetic defect."

"Defects can be good."

"Just like your eyes?"

He looked away, closed the door of the car and buckled the seatbelt. "I am just a bit nervous."

"Yeah, me too."

He looked at her again; she looked back. Then her smile turned into giggles and soft laughter. "Nah, there's nothing to be nervous about. I figured I survived a gunfight with someone who can stop bullets in midair, nothing can be worse."

"I guess." But you never know.

Irvine was another thirty minutes away. He did not pay attention to the road at all. Occasionally he chatted with Jessie, but most of the time he was still lost in deep thoughts.

Bob was not what he expected him to look like at all. From the deep voice, he had expected Bob to be tall, an imposing presence. But he was dark and short, even shorter than Francis, almost scrawny. Bob's eyes darted around like he was a thief preparing for a crime. With his wrinkled T-shirt and shorts, he looked like he came straight out of bed.

After Jessie introduced them to each other, she asked impatiently, "Got a plan, Bob?"

"No worries, Jessie. I've gotten it all figured out. This is going to be a lot easier than I thought. It's certainly not like hacking into FBI headquarters."

Francis shot a quick questioning glance to Jessie, but she only shrugged.

"Okay, here's the plan," Bob continued with his deep, commanding voice. "You told me you have access to the mainframe. You'll get me in there and I'll alter your username privilege to Story Server. Now you will log on with the same ID and you should be able to get into the project you couldn't get into before. You would have access to view the code of all the templates. Though you still would not have access to edit and use any of the templates, you can now duplicate the whole folder and dump it into your development area. With some changes to the path names, you should be able to view the whole area with the same database calls."

Francis shut his eyes and ran the whole process through his head one more time. "Yes, it seems that would work." He was amazed that in two hours, the guy had become more knowledgeable about a system than he was.

"Of course it'll work," Bob grunted with pride.

"Sounds cheesy to me," Jessie commented as she pulled her four-runner onto the ramp to exit the freeway.

"Cheesy, what do you mean cheesy?" Bob complained with a disgusted look which he could see in the rear view mirror.

Then she laughed.

"You have no idea what we're talking about, do you?"

"I didn't understand a single word you guys said."

Then they all laughed. The tall buildings of the Babel complex came intio view. The moment had come. Francis no longer felt nervous. The sound plan, or Jessie's melodious laughter, probably the combination of both, had managed to lift a heavy weight off his heart and cleared some of the smog off his brain. He no longer wanted to doubt his own self-value. He only wanted answers.

CHAPTER TWENTY-ONE

Jessie was never privileged to work in a high tech company environment. She had worked in an office, but offices of government agencies were different. They usually were composed of individual desks instead of secluded cubicles connected together. Francis' cubicle was in a serene corner quite close to the elevator. With a smile, he had commented that he liked the location because he could get in and out of the office without detection. She wasn't sure if he really enjoyed his shyness and loneliness as much as he claimed to be. He had enjoyed talking to her, or maybe she was just giving herself too much credit.

While the two computer geeks settled themselves before the machines, she strolled around the premises exploring the intricate cubical maze, making sure that they were alone and the work would not likely be interrupted.

She circled the cubicles, visualizing what it would be like working there. She thought she would not like it. Although it was not overly crowded to evoke her claustrophobia, it was monotonous and dull. She preferred to be out in the field breathing danger, excitement, and adventure as regularly as possible. But lately she was inhaling a little too much of that, maybe in the future she would decide working from an office.

When she finished scouting, she found the two so focused on their work that they did not even notice that she was there. She pulled up a chair from the adjoining cubicle and sat behind them.

"Are you in?" Bob muttered.

"Yes."

"Alright, duplicate and move the files." Bob's deep, serious voice gave him a divine, commanding presence. In the virtual world, he was a god, omnipotent and powerful. There was nowhere in the universe that was called the Internet he could not reach.

Francis was not doing as much typing and he seemed to be accomplishing most of his task by clicking and dragging. Jessie was not totally computer illiterate. She could turn on a computer, dial online, check her email, and operate most of the word processors and spreadsheet applications that were utilized in an office-environment. But she knew next to nothing of how a computer really worked, how to program logics, or even how to troubleshoot any minor problems that occasionally happened with computers. If anything out of the ordinary happened while she was on one, her only solution was to scream for help.

"Are you done switching the path names yet?" Bob asked impatiently.

"Not yet, it takes time, man. There's quite a bunch of them."

"Well, hurry up, dude."

"What's the rush?"

"Well, I don't want to sit here all day and wait for your ass."

"If you were helping instead of just sitting there and bitch, it'll go a lot faster."

"I'm a hacker, not a freaking developer."

"Semantics."

"No, I actually know shit, and don't get paid for it."

The boys are just getting along fine, aren't they? Jessie smiled to herself. Common hobby breaks the ice.

It took about an excruciatingly long half hour before Francis was done. For a while she heard only the rhythm of her heartbeat, a symphony of both excitement and anxiety. Secrets were about to be revealed. It was easy, almost too easy. They encountered no obstacles – it was never a good sign.

"Alright, use your browser and type in '/Sandbox/Francis/test1'," Francis instructed.

Jessie focused her attention on the computer monitor in front of Bob. A few seconds after Bob typed in the correct path a white page surfaced, a single underlined word 'TEST' showed up like a flag in a field of snow. Jessie understood that in a browser, underlined word usually meant a link to somewhere else. Bob placed the cursor atop the word and clicked.

Another page surfaced. This time it was more colorful, a blue logo on top said Babel Labs. Immediately below that was a heading "Area 2140869". Under that were three underlined phrases with one below another, they were links.

Project Pillar

Project Lilitu

Project Cydonia

"Here goes, let's see if Francis' programming worked out or not." Bob placed the cursor over "Project Pillar" and clicked. For a while nothing happened.

"What's taking so long?" Jessie asked impatiently.

"This happens when a lot of data is being pulled from the database." Francis pointed to the bottom of the Internet browser, where a progress bar indicated something was being loaded. "It takes time to complete the request and render the page, it's still going. There."

A page of text filled the screen.

"Put a disc in." Bob issued another command. "We'll save the text to a disc and you can view it at home."

Francis quickly opened the top drawer of his desk and took out a small box. He took a diskette out and insert into the desktop unit.

Bob manipulated the cursor above the file tab, and then went down to the save command. When the capturing was done, Bob hit the back button and returned to the menu page with the three links. He proceeded to the next link, "Project Lilitu."

Right after it was clicked, Jessie saw a flash and the screen suddenly blacked out. And she saw something else, something danced across the screen for a split second. It was a small creature of some sort, but she could not describe what it looked like. It looked like one of the wacky screen savers.

"Did you guys see that?"

"See what?" they said in unison.

Right at that moment there was a bright spark of light on the bottom of the desk, right behind the desktop computer unit. The sudden burst shut down the computers and the screens were now blank.

"Fuck," Bob exclaimed. "We triggered some kind of alarm, the disk?"

"I got it." Francis held it tightly in his hands while he examined the desktop. "How is this possible? How can both computers be short circuited at the same time?"

"I think we should get out of here," Jessie suggested.

Bob stared blankly at her. He was dazed, lost in a reverie. Francis, on the other hand, displayed extreme reluctance.

Francis gripped her wrist firmly, the touch sent a sudden electric shock up her nerves and it made her shiver. She stared into his pupils and felt the sorrow emanate from them, with power so great that she seemed to have been folded into a forlorn space where she was desperate and alone.

"Lilitu, that's Michelle. We've come so close."

She put her other hand on his to reassure him. "I know. But we got something. And let's get away with that knowledge we got. If we are greedy, we might lose it all."

"You're right." Embarrassed about his contact with her, he flinched and turned his face away. "Let's get out of here."

Francis led them to the elevator just around the corner. Jessie's heart was thudding vehemently, knowing that whatever Babel was going to send against them was going to be extremely nasty. And she did not care to face another assassin with inhuman power, even though she now had Francis with her. But she knew that Francis did not care to engage any enemies. Every time his power was unleashed, he seemed to feel very depressed and questioned his own sanity and value. She didn't want to see that happen again.

In the elevator, Jessie watched the digital floor number decrease. She never could feel comfortable in an elevator. The claustrophobia, the danger of being in a transportation device out of your control, the anticipation of never reaching destination, the vulnerability. She was reaching for her gun.

"What are you doing?" Francis asked.

"Just getting prepared."

It's not going to do you any good. Jessie thought he was going to say that, but he kept his mouth shut. Her gun saved her on the previous day, it was the only good luck charm she had. But she decided against un-holstering it, she did not need to alarm Bob. And she certainly did not need the security guard from the lobby to be suspicious. Her anxiety was clouding her judgment.

Bob was peculiarly quiet. It wasn't like him. He didn't know the extent of trouble they could be in. So he had no incentive to be alarmed or frightened. Maybe he was just shocked that even a hacking expert like him could not foresee the triggering of an alarm system.

There was a rush of relief when the elevator door opened. The security guard eyed them suspiciously as they hurried out of the building but said nothing. They were silent all the way to the parking lot.

The moment they were in the car, Jessie let out long breath of air. Nobody followed them, no one attacked them. They were safe. She noticed this time Bob had taken the shotgun position and Francis sat in the back passenger seat.

Just as she was going to start the ignition, Bob leaned over to the back. "Francis, can I see the disc?"

"Oh, sure." He tossed him a black diskette.

The instant Bob got the disc, he ripped it in half.

"What are you doing?" Jessie stared at him.

The answer for her was an insane laugh of a madman, a laugh of a villain's triumph, a laugh that belonged in an asylum. Jessie had no idea what was going on; she reached for her weapon.

By the time she had her revolver aimed at Bob, a cold wind stroked her face, despite the lack of circulation in the enclosed compartment.

The lunatic laughter became a tormenting scream, as Bob was thrown backwards, choked by an unseen force. He grasped at his own throat, gasping and struggling as if he was drowned in the deep end of the ocean.

Jessie felt a drop of sweat ran from her forehead. She held her revolver tightly, unrelentingly, but that was all she could do. "Francis, what are you doing? You are not going to kill him, are you?"

"No, don't worry." His voice was not as reassuring as it should be. Jessie bit her lip and watched Bob cease his struggle and fall limp on the passenger seat.

"It's gone," Francis said and pointed outside, upwards towards the ceiling of the parking structure.

"What's gone? Where?"

"This thing that occupied Bob's body. You can't see it. It's one of those."

"Where did it go?"

"You see the electronic wires on the ceiling?"

Jessie rolled down the window and stuck her head outside. She saw the wires that lined the ceiling, providing the neon lights with electricity. "How?"

"Let's get going. I'll explain, I think... I mean I'll try to explain."

She turned the ignition on, slid the car out of the parking space, and proceeded towards the exit. She had thought something else was going to come at them, but they were out of the Babel compound safely. "Is he okay?"

"Just fainted. I only choked the wind, not the life, out of him." Then from the back seat, he leaned forward so close to her face that he was almost breathing at her ear.

His warm breath and the closeness had the sudden effect of placating her. She did not feel totally calm, but she was a lot less edgy than a minute ago.

"I feel that I'm gaining control over Michelle."

Talking about the thing as if it was a real person had always made her feel uncomfortable. To her Michelle was like a phantom of death, the other side of the coin known as Francis, the unknown. The unknown was always unpredictably dangerous.

"If I can help it, I am going to try not to kill anyone anymore."

She did not know what to say to offer him comfort. She simply nodded, and doubted if he even saw her from behind.

"Something that's similar to Michelle and the creature that the Tormentor controlled took over Bob's body," he continued. "I chased it out. It escaped and dissolved into the wires on the ceiling. I think the creature is electricity based."

"Electricity based? How is that possible? I thought your power is some kind of energy, something that would be similar to a ghost."

"Yeah, but that thing has more to it. In a way it is the same as the others, some kind of energy form. It's slightly translucent the way I see it, but it also carried charges of electricity with it. I think it can bend itself totally into a form of pure electrical energy. I think it attacked us through the computers and overloaded them and it escaped into the wires."

"But how did it take over Bob?"

"I don't know."

"What did it look like?"

He thought about it for a while. "Small. Have you seen the movie Gremlins?"

"Yep." It was one of her all time favorites as a kid.

"You know when that little creature turns evil?"

"Yes, when it snacks after midnight."

"Right, that's what it looks like, except it seems to be cloaked in electricity."

That's what she had seen in the monitor, and she thought she was hallucinating. "I think I saw it on the screen right before the computers shut down."

He stared at her as if he was seeing a ghost.

"Anyway, where are we going right now?"

"Back to Bob's place. So how do you feel about losing our precious hard earned data?"

"Well… I would really have to lose it to know what it feels like." The initial painful tone turned mordantly sardonic.

"What?"

"I still got it. I gave him a blank disk."

"Thank God."

"And God has nothing to do with it. Thanks to my fast reflex and quick thinking."

"And incessant gloating." She watched him return a smile in the rear view mirror. She was glad that he no longer looked depressed. Earlier today he seemed lost and apathetic. Now he looked alive again with a purpose. Just like her, he wanted to know what was on the disk, even though it was only a third of the information they sought. The disk could be just enough to shed a beaconing light on their predicament.

Lost in thought, Jessie was driving instinctively, and they were already within blocks of the destination. Bob stirred as she approached the apartment complex.

"What happened?" the man grunted.

"You fainted," Jessie told him, trying to decide what to say.

"I don't faint."

"First time for everything."

"Not in the middle of hacking."

"We triggered some kind of alarm," Francis interjected. "Something short circuited the computer and must have shocked you."

"That's not possible." Bob glowered at both of them, defiance in his eyes. "Even if there were some kind of alarm in the server side, it should not affect anything on the client side. The most they can do is wipe out the database and track our IP address. And I don't remember getting shocked."

"Believe it or not, that's what happened. Anyway, thanks a lot. Bob, I owe you one."

"You owe me two. And no, I don't mess up and I don't trigger alarms."

"You didn't mess up." Please don't pry anymore. "You did great. I owe you a big one."

"Two big ones."

"Yes, two big ones."

"How are you going to repay me?"

"You'll think of something."

He scoffed at her and grunted again. "So you guys got the stuff you need?"

While she was thinking about how to answer him, Francis cut in. "Yes, we got it. Thank you."

Bob was going to say something. When Jessie gave him a hard stare, he turned away and opened the passenger door. "Alright, I'm not going to ask what it is. See ya."

Francis hopped onto the passenger side after Bob was gone, his eyes dancing with excitement. "Let's go back to my place and check the disk out."

"I can hardly wait."

On the journey back they were both quiet. Francis was eager to take a peek at the data they stole and was so hyper that he was fidgeting in the seat like a schoolboy who waiting to get out of class.

Jessie was afraid that anything they could steal from the Babel database could be junk data. But now that someone bothered to protect it with security measures, she could conclude that it must have been something really important. Even though they only had a third of the information, it could be just enough to show them the way.

"You still think you're schizophrenic?" she asked him halfway back to Brea.

He thought about it for a moment while he stared blankly at the oncoming traffic. "I reckon if this is a dream, I might as well make the best out of it."

"Yeah, that's the way to live life. One thing the other cops told me when I joined the force was to enjoy life as much as I could, because life is too short and it could be over before you know it."

"So did you?"

"It's hard to say if I really enjoyed life when I became a detective. I enjoyed work so much that one could say I had no life at all. I ate thinking about homicide and went to sleep thinking about homicide. It gave me a lot of spiritual fulfillments though. Sometimes I treat it as some kind of redemption for the college days. Back then I enjoyed myself a little too much, having done every crazy thing you can think of – drinking every night, smoking pot, being wild and out of control."

His eyebrows went up. "Really? You don't look it."

"Looks can be deceiving. Actually, no, I did look it… if you met me back then when I was a freshmen, I'll probably scare you. But I got tired of that empty lifestyle." And Joe cheated on her, making her feel like everyone in her circle of friends where just a bunch of creeps and lowlife, herself included. "Not to mention my grades were tumbling and I almost got kicked out of school. I just snapped and decided to get myself together. It wasn't easy. Sometimes I wished that I never strayed. But now that I think about it, I wouldn't be me right now if I weren't me back then. We all learn from our mistakes. That makes us who we are."

"There's a saying that one must comprehend the past in order to embrace the future."

"Who said that? Anyway, right, that's what I meant. What was I talking about originally?" She had digressed so much that she forgot what they were really talking about.

"About enjoying life." Francis reminded her.

"Right. So what about you?"

"What about me?"
She gave him a hard stare, and he smiled.

"Me? I think I have never tried to enjoy life. I think of life as dull and mundane and people in this world just don't like me."

I like you, she thought. Is that so hard to accept so you have to think that you are just imagining all this?

"So I turn to other things, like books, games, my own imaginations. In other worlds I have control and I forget about this one. I hardly live in this world at all. But spending time with you I feel like this world has its merits too, and not to mention it has been exciting and I've been enjoying it. Part of me says that the real world is not supposed to be exciting, so that part started to doubt the reality of this world. This whole thing could be a dream. And of course taking responsibility for killing people frightened me, even if I did it to protect myself and to save you. It doesn't make it any easier. And part of me enjoyed it so much that I felt myself becoming this hideous monster. If this was a dream, I could go back to my dull and mundane life without ever having killed anyone, without ever having witnessed any atrocities, without ever having some freaky super power that brings disaster."

Without ever knowing me.

"But this is not a dream, is it?"

Jessie couldn't really answer that one, not for sure anyway. Sometimes, she had started to doubt reality.

"For good or bad, I'm in this already. I might as well accept what I am, what I have become, and make the most out of it," added Francis.

"You know, it's not a bad thing to have dreams and to live in an alternate world, if that's what keeps you alive and happy, as long as you don't lose track of the real one. Nobody is asking you to live in this world a hundred percent, but that fifty, or thirty, percent of the time you are here, you might as well make the best of it, make it as good as any of your dreams are. Sure, the real world is unpredictable and it is beyond your control, there are people who may not like you, events that you may not want to happen, because in here you don't play God. You are a pawn of a greater design. But it does not mean that you have to be unhappy here, it's all up to you to make the best out of life. Life is like a roller-coaster ride, with its ups and downs. But without the downs, you will never cherish the moments when you find true happiness. Your ability to be able to escape does not make you weird. It can be your strength also. Emotionally, you are less vulnerable and stronger than people who are always trapped in reality. You should be glad for the way you are."

"I've never looked at it that way before."

"It's not too late to start. There are moments when I feel really sad and lost, and I don't want to deal with the world, that's when I try to hang on to my good memories. For me, they are like your dream worlds. They help me diverge my attention and temporarily escape my problems. Everyone in the world escapes, just because you do doesn't make you a coward or a loser. Without an escape, you could be spiritually crushed. But just know that your problems are here, your world is still here, you still live in it, and you can't escape forever. And you have to face them when you are ready."

It took him a long moment to digest all that. "I never thought someone could understand me."

"You never gave anyone a chance."

"Thank you, Jessie."

"Oh, what for?" She never liked to give people an easy time, especially guys.

"For listening and understanding. It sure feels good to spill out all the things in my mind."

When Francis's apartment came into view, the conversation ceased naturally. Jessie found a street parking space and quickly slid the car in. If there was one other thing she could be proud of herself other than her marksmanship, it was her parking skill. She could complete the narrowest of parallel parking spaces with just one stroke.

When Francis opened the apartment door and switched the light on, they saw a piece of paper on the floor slipped in from the crack of the door. Francis picked it up and then his expression darkened instantly.

He handed the piece of paper to her:

Lilitu,

Do not use any electronic devices with an interfacing monitor screen or you will be under attack. Do not view the information. Meet me at 11:30 am at Mecca. Follow the direction: Take 10 East, exit Mecca north. Travel 3 miles north until you reach a big advertisement board on your right. Exit your car there, walk northeast up the small knoll. There I will reveal myself to you, until then, be cautious.

Your one and only friend

She studied the piece of paper, trying to find a clue about it. At first she thought it was a computer printed message, but when she ran her fingers across the letters, she could feel indentations. It was done by a typewriter – one of the old style ones that really struck each letter onto the piece of paper by force.

"Damn it, we're so close to knowing the truth," he exclaimed.

"Is this whoever friend of yours to be trusted?" She knew all they had to do was to turn a computer on and load the disk in.

"I don't know, I have gotten two messages from him with the same signatures. It seemed that he was trying to give me hints and help me. It seemed logical that we should not use a computer at this moment because that's how Bob got attacked. The same thing can happen to one of us."

Right, it made sense. What was I thinking?

"Where's Mecca?" asked Francis.

"I know where it is. It's a bit east of Palm Springs." She remembered seeing it last time on the way to Las Vegas. There was a shopping outlet in Palm Springs, and Mecca was about ten exits past that. Mark had the habit of reading out road signs, when he was not tired. Sometimes it was amusing and sometimes profusely annoying. The name Mecca had stuck into her mind and she recalled instantly where it was. "It's pretty much in the middle of nowhere. The direction is sort of vague but I think we should be able to get there without any problems."

He gave her a long disapproving look.

"What?"

"You're not going."

"I am too."

"It's too dangerous."

"I can take care of myself. And I'm coming. The message does not specify that you have to be alone. No more negotiations."

"Damn, you're a persistent one, aren't you?"

"Yes, one of my many vices."

"Just how many more do you have?"

"I don't keep count."

They both laughed. There was nothing funny about it, they could not view the information they took and felt like being watched, and they were probably in more danger then they could ever comprehend. The comic relief relaxed them.

"Want something to drink?" He sat up and broke the silence.

"I'm fine. So what's the plan tomorrow?"

"I need to get back to work first. Since both of my computers are fried, I will act surprised and talk to Andy, my manager, and get him to look into the problem and have them fixed. I should be able to take off right after. I'll be excused anyway since I can't get much done without my desktops. This way nobody would be suspicious. Then I can drive us to wherever that place is."

"If you don't mind, I'll drive."

"Why?"

"It's a personal problem."

"You don't like my driving huh?"

"Yes, you drive like a girl. But it's not that, I have issues with the compactness of the interior spacing of your car."

"It's not a very small car. And you sat in there last time anyway."

Not by choice. It was our first time out and I didn't want to be like a sissy. "I'm a bit claustrophobic, I told you right?"

He nodded.

"Well, it's not serious, it's not like your car would make me faint or something, but I just prefer more space. And I love driving anyway." She often sat in Terry's car though, because he had a Landrover, and it was huge. There it was again; she was thinking about Terry, and how much she missed him.

"Okay."

"Pick you up in front of your office building at ten?"

"Deal."

"You're not going to look at the stuff inside the disc without me, are you?"

He smiled, shook his head, and his brown eyes gleamed with a regained sorrow. She wondered if it was because he was seeing her go, or it was because he had the information in his hand and could not look at it, or maybe he still preferred to be in a dream but in fact was not. The thin line of truth and mystery was devouring him inside out.

She might have taken a step forward in understanding him. But part of him was still an enigma. And a fraction of that enigma could be contained in that disk. They had it in their hands, but looking at it now could forever destroy them. That was the irony of life.

She bid Francis good night and headed back. She was emotionally drained, thinking too much and could not stop. Talking to Francis made her think about what she had been doing all theses years, things she had lost and thing she had gained. When her head pounded with an aching pain, she knew she needed some rest.

CHAPTER TWENTY-TWO

Francis ran along the dark, ominous corridor. His heart pounded, his leg was sore. Footsteps stalked him. Not knowing what he was running away from and where he was running to, Francis just continued forward, being pursued by his own fear. A shrill cry, a high-pitched wail from a female halted him. After seeing a sliver of light he turned a corner, and found himself in a room.

It was a lavish, opulent room with a crackling fireplace, cushioned divans, gold chandeliers, and adorned brick walls. Then he saw it and his heart almost stopped.

It, his fear, his nemesis, the clown dressed in ridiculous silk clothing, a face painted white and eyes that gleamed an evil red. It held Jessie's bare neck with one clawed hand. One sharp claw trailed back and forth, stroking her exposed throat, leaving a thin trail of red.

Jessie stared blankly at him with an expression of horror. Francis could sense her trembling from a distance. Her mouth parted, perchance she wanted to scream or plea for his help, but no sound came out. He wanted to save her, but his feet felt like they had been encased in stone.

Sensing his helplessness, the clown pulled Jessie's head towards its face. Then the evil being began kissing her, a deep, long kiss of death. A tear ran down her cheek.

He struggled and couldn't shake himself free.

He closed his eyes, could not watch the terror. And he struggled again, but to no avail.

Time passed.

When he could move again he opened his eyes and found himself in the dark, drenched in cold sweat on his own bed. Another nightmare. He cursed.

Gathering his senses, he reached under the pillow and felt the floppy disc. For a while he held on to it for assurance. He wondered if it was the disk that was causing his nightmare, or if it was the anxiety of wanting to see the information. Or was it the terror of anticipating the aftermath of knowing the truth? Why was he so afraid? Was the truth going to destroy him? Or was he going to destroy himself before the truth?

He did not fall back into a slumber for the rest of the night and finally he watched the sunlight stream in through the half-closed blinds. When bright light enveloped the room, he got up and took a cold shower.

He left his apartment at eight-thirty and went into the office half-dazed.

Discreetly, he checked both of his desktops and confirmed that they were in the same state as last night, short-circuited and nonfunctional. Then he went to Andy's desk and informed him of his problem.

"Alright, I'll call IT and get your computers fixed," Andy said, his eyebrows rose, not quizzically but seemingly amused. "You don't look so good, Francis."

"Didn't get much sleep last night."

"Why don't you take the day off? Get some sleep and let's do some racquetball tomorrow morning."

Perfect, Francis thought. "In the morning?"

"Well," he scratched at his short blonde hair. "I got some personal stuff to do in the afternoon and I thought we both could use some refreshing exercise in the morning. And there's not much going on at work anyway, all the projects seemed to have been stalled after the fire and the accident, and the hiring is not going any better. You seemed to have made a lot of progress in the last few days. I need to catch up with you. I'm not complaining though," He let out a small smile that was supposed to be reassuring. "Work can focus your mind and make you forget other things. Well, so can an intense game of racquetball. Anyway, why don't I meet you at the courts around ten-thirty tomorrow?"

Francis nodded. He was not in the mood for racquetball. But he complied anyway, eager to get out of his manager's presence, in case that he would change his mind again about him having to work the afternoon.

There was still almost an hour left before his rendezvous with Jessie on their secret mission. He was not in the mood for arcade games but he went to the recreation center anyway, trying to forget his psychological problems. Sitting in front of his favorite machine was not the same anymore. He played mindlessly, and was losing to the computer opponent even at the easy levels. After each loss he fed in quarters like an automaton. Time drifted forward in a painfully slow manner, like an hourglass that refused to let go of its sand. When it was time, he waited at the circle in front of the main building.

She was as prompt as always, arriving one minute and a half early.

"Hey it's me again." She offered a beaming smile when he opened the passenger door. Her one dimple glowed with a heartwarming softness that seemed to put his mind at ease.

Is she really happy to see me? Or is that just her customary greeting face?

He managed to smile back, but no words came out of his mouth.

"Not in a very talkative mood today, huh?"

"Oh, it's not that. Just been thinking."

"But you do that all the time."

"Oh, I guess so. You're in a good mood today?"

"Yeah, you could say that. Put the bad memories behind me. Staying with the family makes one happy."

Francis wished he could say the same thing.

"And I'm quite excited about today. It's our first adventure together."

"More like second."

"The last one doesn't count. We weren't really cooperating and I was mostly unconscious."

They laughed. Thinking about it, that day was very dangerous for both of them, they could have both died. But he could laugh about it in hindsight now.

"It's like I'm your new partner now." That almost sounded awkward coming out of his mouth.

For a long moment she said nothing, he had thought that he had said something wrong.

"Yes, you are." She grabbed the coffee mug sitting idly between their seats. "To our new partnership."

"Oh, I don't have a cup."

"Come on, give me a virtual one."

He knocked her mug with his fist.

"You better watch my back and not die on me."

She seemed to have said it half-jokingly but when he thought about it, he realized that whoever was waiting for them could be out to kill them. It was dangerous. One or both of them could lose their lives at any moment. Prepared to give anything to know the truth, even his life, Francis wanted to know his power, to know himself, to know his place in this world. Even though the phantom of his power had seemed to bring him misfortunes and pain, it also brought him a friend and a purpose. He still believed that his power was a curse, and somehow it turned him into an evil killing machine, and he would do anything to get rid of it. But on the other side of the equation, he felt alive with a purpose, whatever that purpose was. Not just a reject of society, he was here for a reason, his power was here for a reason, for good or evil. He felt important, important enough to be an assassination target.

As for Jessie, Francis wondered why she was doing this. Was it to satisfy her curiosity, to have vengeance against the power behind the killer of her partner, to see justice done to the villainous source that forged the Tormentor and murdered innocents, to repay a debt of his saving her, or just to help him because he was her friend? Why don't I just ask her? No, I don't know how to ask. Does it really matter? No, I guess not.

He looked outside the window at the sky, dark and gloomy, with an occasionally streak of sunlight breaking through the darkness like a spear. Like his mood the sky was confusing. It didn't know if it was going to let it all go and rain, or let the sunlight pierce through so it would become a bright and sunny day.

"Having one of those deep thought moments?"

"Oh, you could say that." He shook his head, a bit embarrassed for not saying anything for a long while. "Just thinking about the whole thing."

"So you have an idea who we are meeting?"

"Don't have a clue. Could be someone out to kill us."

"Aren't you the sentimental one? I thought you said yesterday it's someone who's been helping you."

"Or manipulating me."

"To what end?"

"I don't know. You know, one of those conspiracy theory movies, everyone is the enemy."

"At least you don't think you're a schizo anymore, thank God." She was somewhat amused.

"Are you prepared for any contingency?"

"I have my gun so I just point and shoot. And then there's plan B."

"And that is?"

"I just cower behind your back and squirm like a little girl."

His almost jumped when he heard that.

"You looked like you just saw a ghost."

"I did see one."

"Well, if you don't think you're up for the job."

"Who says I'm not up for it?"

And then she giggled. "It's every little girl's dream to have a guardian with superhuman powers."

Is it every little boy's dream to be a superhero? And I'm not your guardian. Comrade, maybe. I can barely help myself, not to mention protecting anybody else.

The conversation about their potential plight ended there. They were making good time east bound on the Highway 10 as traffic was almost minimal. As they get further inland, civilization became sparse and the desert root of Southern California began to show. Scenes of rocks, sands, the road, with the Joshua trees and cactus and the occasional malls and houses which looked so much like anywhere else in the United States flew past their windows.

After they passed the Palm Springs outlet shopping center, Jessie told him they were almost there.

Seeing the sign "Mecca" Francis felt the race of his heartbeat and the rush of adrenaline. The mystery was about to unfold, at least one part of many. And he was going to be one step closer to the truth.

"Three miles north, right?" Jessie asked as she pulled the car off ramp.

He didn't even have to reconfirm with the note in his pocket, having read it too many times the night before. Not that it helped him in anyway on his situation, but it did serve as something for him to focus on.

Slowly they drove northbound on a narrow street. There were no oncoming cars, no vegetation, and no buildings. Surrounding them was only the wind, the sand, and the desolation.

"Where does this road lead?" he wondered.

"Beats me, some people like to live in the middle of nowhere."

As the road curved right, they saw a billboard which stood high, alone, and out-of-place in the surroundings which the hands of civilization had not touched. The advertisement was for an online community for women with newborn babies. A place for them to get advice, meet people in the same boat, and share experiences with them.

"No wonder all the dot coms are going down the drain," Francis commented. "Imagine the chance of someone seeing the commercial."

"Hey, we saw it." She pulled the car to a full stop onto the side of the road. "But I guess unless we plan to have a baby, there's not much help in it. We're ten minutes early by the way."

Francis ignored her joke, knowing that she was just trying to lighten his mood. He stepped out of the car to have a look around.

At first he saw nothing under the gray sky except miles and miles of endless sand. He scanned his surroundings and finally something caught his attention. About a good thirty to forty paces away, there was a small knoll and on top of it a figure waving at him.

"Do you see that?" he asked her as she stepped up behind him.

"See what?"

He pointed.

"No."

"Aren't you supposed to be the one with good eyes?"

"What gave you that idea?"

"You did say you were a legendary marksman."

"I did not say legendary. And you're the one who's probably got some enhancements to your vision."

"Why do you say that?"

"Remember, you said that you saw the password to the mainframe?"

"That was due to speed, not distance. And this is really not that far away."

"Why don't we both be civil, stop arguing, and just walk closer to the damn thing?"

"Why didn't I think of that?"

She rolled her eyes upward and let him lead her towards the figure.

As he walked closer, Francis could see that it was a little girl in a purple dress. She was small, blonde with her hair tied up in a knot. Francis surmised that she was no older than nine.

"Please tell me you see her now," he muttered.

"See who?"

"This is not funny."

"I'm not trying to be."

"Damn it." He felt the goose bumps on his skin and the lump in his throat. He was afraid and anxious, not the same kind of fear as when he met the evil clown but it was fright, nevertheless. Fear of the unknown. "Just stay behind me."

"It's one of those?" It was more an observation than a question.

"Aha."

He took the next steps with utter determination and courage, trying to grasp the power within himself, to be ready to unleash it at any moment. There was never a sensation of confirmation that he was in charge of his power, but he felt Michelle's presence within him. That sensation was soothing, and reassuring. What he first saw as unreal and a curse was now so attached and so integrated inside him that he now could find some comfort in a dangerous situation.

Just like Michelle, the little girl was slightly translucent. She did not stop waving. There was nothing menacing about her. But there was something eerily unnatural to her posture, her motion, and especially her smile. The figure could be bait to a trap, or salvation to their predicament. There was only one way to find out, to go forward.

He walked up the sand dune with Jessie clinging close to him, almost breathing on his neck. He had never seen her so nervous and on edge, he guessed that after having a few close encounters with the supernatural, she knew that even her skills could not put her in control of the situation. After all she could not defend herself against what she could not see. He was there to protect her, if only he could protect himself.

When he was only a few paces away from the little girl, he stared into her emerald eyes, into the dark clouds that were behind her. She wasn't exactly a living creature, but he could swear that he saw a glimpse of intelligence in her eyes. It was similar to the evil he saw in the clown's eyes, remorse in Michelle's, and the hate in the Tormentor's.

"I've been waiting for you," the voice said, surprising him. The phantom was talking. And her voice was sweet and melodic. However it did not quite fit with the image of a child, it was the tone of an adult.

"Jessie, did you hear that?"

"Yes, and it's creepy." Her grip on his arm tightened.

"Who are you?" Francis demanded.

The moment he was anticipating her answer, a beeping noise came from behind him. It was Jessie's cell phone.

When he turned around, she had already flipped the lid open. She was reading the screen instead of answering it, indicating that it might have been a text message. Her expression darkened.

"What's wrong?" As soon as he said that, he saw a flutter of movement at the corner of his eye. The little girl flung her hand out, knocking Jessie's cell phone to the ground. She then stepped on it with her purple shoes and shattered the phone into bits and pieces.

He was not sure what was happening, but he readied Michelle nevertheless to defend them. But the little girl already disappeared into the thin air. Left with them was only the remnants of a cell phone, shattered. He thought Jessie was going to scream, but there was only a blank look on her face.

"Hey, are you alright?"

For a minute she did not answer him. Then he gripped her shoulders and shook her, and awareness finally stirred in her eyes.

"What, what happened?"

"Your phone rang, and the little girl knocked your phone down and stepped on it, and now that's what left of it."

"Oh I see."

Oh I see? That's all you have to say? Something is wrong here, very very wrong. And where's the little girl? "Let's get out of here," he suggested. He knew that it probably was not the right thing to do, but it was the only thing he could think of at the moment.

She did not say anything on the way back, and the continued blank look on her face was a bit disturbing. Liveliness was always part of Jessie's character. To see her like this was like seeing her devoid of her soul.

As they got to the car, she turned the ignition but it only gave a cranking noise. Francis took a look at the indicators on the dashboard and saw that the battery was dead. Realization came to him.

Michelle reached for Jessie, while Jessie reached for the holster at her hips.

Don't hurt her. The thought was more a plea than a command. And he was hoping that it would work as both.

Michelle's phantom hands closed around Jessie's throat, and immediately the possessed detective dropped her gun.

Francis clenched his teeth, channeling his thoughts in his psychosomatic control over his power. What control he had over it, he pushed mentally, exerting the limit, breaking the boundary. She was his friend, and he would not have her killed. He felt how fragile her neck was, he had felt the rhythm of her breath, the song of her heartbeat. He felt the blood pumping through her arteries, her life surging through her veins, her life which at this moment was his, his alone.

When Michelle released her she was unconscious, but still alive.

A hiss of relief went through his teeth.

A creature that was made out of pure electricity flowed out of her body. No taller than eight inches, it stood on top of Jessie's limp body and grinned at him as if it had triumphed over a battle that had not even been fought.

Kicking the door open, Francis jumped back and rolled onto the ground. He did not know what that creature of electricity was capable of, but he was sure that he did not want to fight inside an enclosed space with Jessie in it.

The creature also jumped down from the car. Its body sparkled like lightning. Slowly it was advancing upon him.

Katana in hand, Michelle charged her enemy like a valorous knight. He wasn't sure if he commanded her, maybe his subconscious did, or maybe she was simply acting on her own accord. No matter, because he was already drawn into the fray.

The blade made a wide arc in the air and passed through the foe with ease of a knife cutting paper. The creature did not even attempt to dodge. It was almost too easy. However, where phantom blade met supernatural lightning, only a bright sparkle answered. There was no sudden death, no fatality, and no victory. He could not hurt his foe. The sword had hurt the Tormentor, why does it not damage this creature? Perhaps because it is electricity? But he thought the entities were like ghosts. If Michelle was a ghost, and so was the Tormentor and this creature, he wondered how this entity was different, invulnerable to physical attack.

Now it's not the time for a science lecture, not to mention it's on a subject that makes no sense. He needed to focus on the battle, but that moment of hesitation had already cost him. Michelle could not get out of range when the electric energy discharged.

Francis felt the electricity surge through him. His limbs became numb and out of control. Unable to support his own weight, he crashed onto the ground, kneeling as if he was a devoted worshipper of a deity who suddenly appeared before him. Imagining that his body would hurt, Francis' mind was too busy to notice. The enemy approached, slowly and cautiously. It was calculating for its next step as it was not sure if he could still defend himself. Once he lost control of his limbs, he had also lost control of Michelle's. She also kneeled on the sandy ground like a hapless, stricken soul. She was the one who took the hit, and he was the one to suffer the consequences. The foe's target was now him, not Michelle, because he had proved to be more vulnerable. However, his enemy's host was nowhere to be found. He was at a definite disadvantage, but he was also beginning to understand the bizarre twisted rules of the game a little bit better.

Death was but three paces away, he was not afraid. Because he felt like he had already been there before, it was not a time to panic, but a time to plan and plot. He noticed that the gleaming creature did not shine so brightly anymore. If he guessed correctly, the creature fed off electricity in order to survive. Apparently it followed them inside the battery of the car. It took a little bit too much and the car did not start up. Now when it had discharged energy to assault him, it had been cautious to not deplete its source, so it only immobilized him. He was sure if the creature was fully charged, it could kill him in an instant. It also had a secondary power, to reside in someone's body and exert certain control over that person, like it did with Jessie and Bob. The entity could not control him because he carried no gadgets. Jessie used the cell phone, and Bob used the computer. Not the simple act of using it, but rather, staring at the screen rendered someone vulnerable to the creature's control. That was why the note specifically told them to not use any electronic devices. That was why they were out here in the middle of nowhere – where there were no electric wires hanging from light poles, no oncoming traffic, where the creature of lightning had no place to hide, trapped, and was vulnerable.

He looked into the two empty voids that were the creature's eyes, and wondered how it was going to kill him. No doubt the creature could rip his throat out with ease, now that he was unprotected. He struggled again, but he could not feel his body. The only thing that was clear was his mind, the one thing that could not save him.

A sound of unexpected whistle distracted his assailant so it turned away to watch the little girl in the purple dress who had seated herself comfortably on top of Jessie's Lexus. Her feet were dangling and she was like a jubilant child sitting on a swing. Francis did not know how long she had been there, but the most important question was: was she there to save him?

A dark green jeep pulled over on the opposite side of the road. A man walked out with something large in one of his hands. There was something familiar about the figure, but Francis could not make out right away who it was. Crouching low, the man seemed to gather his strength for a brief moment and then flung the object in his hand upward. As it traveled in an arc across the sky, Francis saw that it was a container of clear liquid.

The little girl leaped up after the spinning container, intercepting it in midair with utmost precision and style that belonged to a circus acrobat. Right above the creature of electricity, only a few paces from Francis, the impact in the sky sent silver gleaming sparkles pouring down like fireworks explosion. Francis could have sworn that there was a strange order to the downpour. Instead of a chaotic explosive impact and water splashing everywhere, the water fell in a streak-like order as if it was rain from the sky. Not one drop hit his face. They were all targeted towards his assailant. He watched the already dimming creature diminished even more as droplets of clear liquid impacted its hide of inhuman energy. It dropped to the ground, struggling and trying to crawl out of the way. It managed to drag itself a few paces away from Francis, towards the mysterious figure by the green jeep.

It did not go very far until it finally gave up. A thin layer of ice covered its now lifeless body.

As the man slowly walked towards him, Francis was able to command his own body again. Wearing a plain white long sleeve shirt with khakis and shining black boots, the man was bald and had dark eyes that gleamed intelligently behind his glasses – Kyle Gideon, the network administrator at Babel Corps.

A hand extended to him, Francis took it and let himself be pulled up, his muscles ached painfully, but he was whole. "It's you." He was sure that it sounded desperately stupid when he said it, but he did not know what else to say.

"Yes, it is I." They watched the little girl in the awkward purple dress walk over to the icy corpse. Then she stepped on it with merciless contempt on her small face, effortlessly grinding it down into small crystal shards. "I wouldn't care to see the real body of this person."

"Whatever happens to the…" Francis was desperately searching for a word to describe the phantasm power. But he took so long he decided to skip the word altogether, "also happens to the person who controls it?"

"Yes, and you will learn about it."

"That little girl,"

"Her name is Cao."

"She has a name?"

"They all do. She likes to be called that." The little girl sauntered over and gave Kyle's lower limb an affectionate hug. Kyle mussed her shiny blonde hair and she giggled in response.

"But she's not real."

"Oh, please don't upset her. She's as real as the sand you're standing on."

Francis shook his head and looked over to the black Lexus.

"Don't worry about her, she's okay."

"Just who are you?" And who am I? What world am I in?

Kyle reached a hand into his shirt pocket and pulled out a business card, handing it to him.

"FBI?" Francis stared at the card, astonished.

"That's who I really am. And I'm working undercover investigating Babel Corps."

"How many of you are there?"

"Just me."

"Why are you telling me this?"

"Because we have a common enemy. And I need your help."

"To do what?"

"That's to be determined. But first you must go home and look at the information you got yesterday. You must understand the situation you are in."

"You have seen everything in the database?"

"Just a part of it."

"Why didn't you just give it to me? Why this game?"

"Because you have to earn my trust. I don't know who you are. I just know that they have an agenda with you. There are certain things that they want you to accomplish, and then they want to eliminate you. And besides, we had to get rid of the sentinel guarding the database, and we had accomplished that."

"Project Lilitu." He remembered what he saw yesterday, the information he was so close to getting and yet couldn't.

"You are Project Lilitu." The stress in his voice sent a shiver down Francis' spine.

Is he but a simple experiment of a corporation? "I didn't get everything from the database."

"Just study what you have, and then contact me. My cell phone number is on the card. We'll talk again when you are ready. Let's jumpstart your car"

For a while Francis just stood that numb and confused, not knowing what to believe. He went to check on Jessie as Kyle pulled his jeep head to head with the Lexus and connected the cables. She was warm, breathing regularly, and sleeping like a baby.

For the first few tries the engine only grunted impatiently but it wasn't long when it sighed with resignation and shook joyously with success.

"You might want to replace the battery when you get back," Kyle warned when he removed the cables and closed both the hoods.

"Thanks, and I have one more question."

"Shoot."

"Are you the only one fighting against Babel?"

Kyle took a long moment, as if he was pondering the consequences to answering his question. "In a sense, yes. I am the only one working with the government and I have not recruited anyone from the inside. However there's someone else who is also an enemy of Babel. He knows of me, but we do not work together. Not yet, anyway."

"Why?"

"Because I don't agree with his methodologies and let's just leave it at that. We have the same goal and for now we are just approaching it differently on our own. In time you'll know of this person. We'll talk again, take care and trust no one."

Then he was gone.

CHAPTER TWENTY-THREE

She was holding a dim candle, surrounded by the unknown of darkness. Taking a step forward, she tried to examine her surroundings with a calm mind. Beyond the faint protective circle of the illumination, she saw that she was in what seemed to be a long hallway of dolls. Some looked like clumps of asparagus, some looked like scarecrows, and some looked so evil as if they were spawned from hell itself. She was surrounded by dolls, dolls that ranged from the Victorian era until the modern days. There were piles of them, stacked on top of each other.

Hearing a sobbing noise, she took a few courageous steps forward and found someone kneeling on the floor with her head lowered. She recognized that it was Mary, her thick glasses blocking her face.

"The Tormentor is coming, help me." Her pleading voice was barely audible.

But you are the Tormentor!

From darkness a scaly arm with sharp claws came and snatched Mary from behind right by her neck, like holding a dangling wine bottle. The next second she was gone, devoured by the darkness around her.

The dolls wailed.

*   *   *   *

Jessie opened her eyes. She looked around and noticed she was in the passenger seat of her car. Francis was in the driver seat, focused on the road ahead of him. From the side view, his face was a mixture of bewilderment and intense concentration, as if he was meditating his way out of a labyrinth of utter confusion, completely oblivious to his surroundings.

"When are you going to stop staring at me?"

Maybe he wasn't completely oblivious, Jessie corrected herself.

"Oh, you noticed?"

"Aha, I told you my senses are sort of, in a way, enhanced."

"What about your olfactory senses?"

"Why? You haven't been taking showers?"

"Not since I took one at your apartment."

"Then thank God my nose doesn't work any better than it did before. I just see better, that's all. Anyway, are you okay?"

"Yes, felt like I had a good night sleep." With a nightmare. Then she reached over and pinched his face.

"Ouch! What did you do that for?"

"Who says you can drive my car?"

"You didn't object when I picked up the keys."

"Alright," she said with a long, exaggerated sigh. "For you I'll make an exception. Drive on."

"Yes, ma'am," he said right away like a diligent little boy.

"Are you going to fill me in for what's happened, or am I going to have to pry it out of you?"

"You don't remember what happened?"

"The last thing I remembered was—" when the cell phone rang. She reached down her pocket trying to locate her cell phone. Then she noticed her empty holster, and the gun on the floor. The next moment she was terrified of what she tried to do. "I didn't —"

"Yes you did, and don't worry about it." He took a long moment to gather his thoughts, before telling her a condensed version of what transpired between her lapses. After her cell phone rang and the little girl destroyed it, she looked distant and seemingly possessed. Then she tried to assault him in the car but he subdued her with his powers. Then that creature of lightning came out of her and almost killed him. But Kyle, an undercover agent, saved him.

"Do you know this guy?"

"We work in the same department, so I've met him a couple times."

"Do you think he can be trusted?"

"I don't know what to think. He's been monitoring me, helping me, and he saved me and tried to enlist for my help. But it could all be a scheme, a trap for something bigger."

"Let me see his card."

Francis handed it to her. She studied it for a while and thought it looked legitimate. But business cards are only printed, and even badges could be faked. She knew a way to find out if the guy was legit or not, it was standard police procedure. "Could you get to the rightmost lane and slow down?"

"What for?"

"I want to get to the next call box."

"And?"

"Just to satisfy my curiosity."

He did so without any addition inquires or arguments and soon she saw one of the yellow call boxes for roadside emergency on the side of the freeway. As he pulled over, she fished out a calling card which she had not used for a long time and a list of numbers from her wallet. Silently she cursed at the inconvenience of no longer having her mobile phone.

She called the FBI headquarters at Quantico. As the operator answered, she identified herself as a LAPD officer. She then asked if there was indeed a Kyle Gideon in the Bureau. The operator told her to wait for a while as he checked on her credentials and searched the directory. After the operator confirmed his existence, she asked what operation Kyle was assigned to. As she had surmised, the operator said the information was confidential. She hung up, her curiosity satisfied.

"Kyle checks out okay," she commented when she climbed back to the car.

"Let me guess, you called FBI headquarters." Francis observed, not looking surprised at all.

"Right." She adjusted her seat, suddenly feeling uncomfortable, or maybe just strange because she had never sat at the passenger side. "It doesn't mean anything though. If it is true that some kind of biological experiments give you freaks super powers, the government is going to do anything to get this power, if it's not already involved. Who knows whose side the FBI is on? It wouldn't be hard to–"

When dark shadows seemed to have cast over his face, she realized she said something wrong. "Look, I didn't mean that." Why did she say freaks? It was just the first word that came to her mind.

He stared at the ongoing traffic that flew by them, looking distant. "Don't worry about it. I don't get hurt from other people's words. I'm used to it."

"Francis, I'm not other people. I am your friend. I said something wrong and you should be angry."

He turned to look at her, and his brown eyes gleamed with a distant, remorseful sorrow. Then he put his hand on her shoulder and gave it a slight squeeze of reassurance that almost bordered on affection. "Don't worry about it. You're not other people. But I'm not angry, I know that you don't think I'm a freak, and that's all that matters."

She nodded.

"You aren't afraid of my powers, are you?"

The question took her aback, and she had to take a moment to think about it. He's not a killer. I can trust him. "Are you kidding? If one day you do something that I don't like, I won't hesitate to kick your ass."

He smiled. She smiled back at him, and soon the smiles turned into laughter that they shared on the way home.

*   *   *   *

In eager anticipation, Jessie watched Francis turn his desktop computer on and insert the floppy disc into the groaning machine. After Windows operating system booted up, he clicked on an icon on the desktop and opened up a small black window. As he was typing, he explained that he was moving the files from the floppy disc to the internal hard drive of the computer so that the files could be accessed more easily and a backup would coexist in his own computer, in case something happened to the disc.

Jessie was not quite a computer illiterate. And that was not the way she knew how to move files. "Why do you move them like that?"

"It's easier to type in the command prompt than to drag and drop," he explained. "For computer nerds, anyway. Manipulating stuff in the windows environment is essentially the same thing as typing in a line in the command prompt, it's just a higher-level presentation of the same procedure. Done."

Then he opened another window which belonged to a text editor, not the generic note pad that she often used that came with the operating system, but something else possibly that Francis was more accustomed to. Next he opened the file and flooded the white area with texts. To Jessie's surprise, the texts were clustered together instead of being displayed nicely as she usually saw on the computer screen. And in between words there were occasionally tags of a computer coding language that she knew nothing about.

"This is a source code of a web page," he explained further, sensing her curious uncertainness. "What we call an HTML page, it's interpreted by a web browser. Let me—"

"Look, you don't really have to explain everything to me. I know you've been waiting to find out about the truth—"

"And it could wait a few more minutes. You are part of this too, and I'd like you to know exactly everything that's going on. Unless you don't want to know."

"Of course I do. You know curiosity and I are best friends."

"I thought so. Anyway, I'm going to use a browser to view the page instead of a text editor, that'll be more viewable."

"Okay, since you're getting so good at explaining things, I'll let you get a little bit more practice. Could you explain to me what we did yesterday? I haven't got a clue."

"And I thought you were smart."

She smiled at him.

His eyes focused, at a spot behind her. One of his hands disheveled his hair and then absently combed it back to place, as he gathered his thoughts.

"Okay," he said as he cleared his throat like a person who was readying a big public speech. "Think of the whole thing as having three levels. The outer level is the web, what you see on the Internet, what you see on screen, it is the display of the information. The lower level is the database, where the information subsides. The middle layer is the one we hacked into, the one that connects the top and bottom. It is the layer programmers manipulate, writing code that extracts the data they want and feed it to the display layer in the fashion that they see fit."

"So the information we stole was actually on the internet?"

"No, it was on an intranet, sort of an internal net that's not accessible by the world. You can only see it inside Babel Corps. Even so it was password protected. That's why the fastest way to get the information we wanted was through the middle layer, since both the top and bottom layer was protected by heavy security. When we changed the programming, we sort of turned off all the security to the top layer without having to worry about the bottom layer since it was already connected."

Even in laymen's terms, the whole idea still sounded complicated, but she was starting to grasp the idea of how something worked in the internet. "So do all web sites have three layers?"

"No, there're two kinds of websites. There's static and dynamic. A dynamic website contains three layers like I mentioned, and it's constantly changing, which is governed by the bottom layer, the database. A static website only has the top most layer, the display, and it doesn't change unless someone changes the HTML code, which was what you saw in the text editor."

"So not all pages in the Internet are dynamic?"

He shook his head.

"So what makes someone wanting a static or dynamic web page?"

"It depends on what someone wants to do online. Let's say you wanted to put a homepage up, and it just wanted to introduce yourself and say hello to your friends. You can do that in five minutes, and it'll make sense for you to do it static. It's low cost and easy to maintain, while setting up a dynamic environment is costly. Some companies spend millions building and maintaining a system like that. However, there are things that you can conveniently do on a dynamic system with a snap of finger if it's properly setup, as opposed to tons of hours of work if you only had a static system."

Jessie arched her eyebrows.

"Let's say you want to build a news network like CNN.com, if you were to build it statically, you would have to write thousands of pages and every time a news article changes you have to change thousands of pages that connect to that news article. If you were to build it dynamically, you would set up the database to contain the news. While you put in the appropriate logic to filter out information on the middle layer, you can control what you want to present on the display layer."

"So what happens when you want to change a news article?"

"Provided the system is setup efficiently, the programmers don't have to do anything. What happens is they would have written an internal application, one that resides on an intranet, for editors to interact with the database."

"That's the lowest layer."

"Yes, correct, where all the news articles resides. The writers type in the news article via a web interface that's similar to a text editor, so they can submit it to the database. Then perhaps editors can look at it, review it, and submit it further down the line if there was a workflow system built it. When it's ready, it would be tagged as ready in the database. Depending on the current date and time, the middle layer of the system would pick up that article to display on the Internet. There could be a thousand pages linking to this particular article, but nobody would have to change anything except the person that wrote the article."

"Which cannot be conveniently done in a static environment."

He nodded with a slight smile. "You catch on quickly, maybe you can make a good engineer yet. Anyway, that's the gist of it. Of course there's a lot more to web development than what I just said, but I'm not going to bore you with any more details."

"No, it's really interesting. Thanks for explaining. Now I know much more than I knew before. And I sort of know what you do for a living now." She surmised that the Internet side to Babel Corps worked in a similar fashion. Before when he told her that he was an engineer at Babel, she thought he was catering to lab equipments or research computers. Even when he said that he worked on the Internet, she still assumed that is was something biotech research related. She never did know that there was such a complicated process behind a web site, even for a company that only had a very small role on the internet.

"Well, I never thought I could explain the basic concepts behind my job in ten minutes."

"That's a good thing, right?" She was a little perplexed by his comment.

"Of course. Let's just say I never thought I was going to explain things in detail. I was never good at explaining to people what I do. I tell others that I'm a computer engineer. It usually stops there." And his face seemed to say that he never really cared if anyone understood what he did, or if anyone cared to understand.

"Give yourself some credit. You're very good at explaining things. Maybe someday you can be a teacher."

"Nah," he shook his head, half smiling. "Anyway, let's get to the real juice."

*　　*　　*　　*

Project Pillars

Overview:

The purpose of Project Pillars is to study the latent abilities of the human brain. Studies had found that the undeveloped area of the hippocampus carries the potential to develop abilities that exceed the normal human mind. A fused drug of P.I.L.L.A.R. (Pro-Ile-Leu-Leu-Ala-Arg) and modified Herpes viral vector, while inserted into blood, can cross the blood brain barrier and directly modify human brain cells in the hippocampus (refer to section 2). The modification process is almost instant as soon as the drug reaches the destination. Two effects have been seen so far for a person who has taken drug: the brain accepts the changes and he develops latent abilities; or the neural activities in his brain has increased a hundred fold to the point of the neurons become cancerous, causing instant brain death. While further studies have been conducted to determine why certain human brains could not accept the changes in their hippocampus, no data with conclusive results has been collected. Though research scientists of the project have developed a theory as to why certain human beings accept the changes and some don't. It is entirely plausible that certain sequences of genetic codes dictate that possibility of change, and it is similar to that some people are tongue-rollers, and some simply are not. However, current limitations of technology makes it quite improbable for scientist to confirm this scientific speculation, much less target the correct genetic sequence.

For a person who is genetically compatible with the P.I.L.L.A.R. drug, the neuron activities will slightly and gradually increase in the hippocampus. This change is not harmful right away, however, the increase neural activities over an extended period of time, can prove malignant to the human brain. An oral dose of an alternate form of the drug, called P.I.L.L.A.R.E.R. (Pro-Ile-Leu-Leu-Ala-Arg-Glu-Arg), has been devised to lower the neural activities to a less harmful level. However, the drug's effect is not permanent, it must be applied periodically. There's no fixed amount of time one must take the drug, the time needed seem to differ on each individuals. The average time is two weeks. Symptom of severe headaches is a clear sign indicating that the dosage is needed.

A person who has been injected with P.I.L.L.A.R., and survives the process is termed a host, or a gifted one. Although it is a genetic selection, scientists of the project believe that only those with a quality of inner strength can survive and accept the power bestowed upon them. A gifted one's mind is able to cast some sort of psychic projection onto this plane of existence, what we termed as a Pillar. A Pillar is a projection that exists between planes, or dimensions. It is believed that a Pillar exists both in the living world and a spiritual world; however, it is only a speculation. Further studies of planes, dimensions, and Pillars are ongoing on a daily basis, but the concepts are not for us to grasp within the near future. The types of Pillars that exist seem to be countless, and not one Pillar is the same as another. Similar to an individuality of a human being, not one person is identical to another. Throughout studies of the limited subjects we have, we have devised a system that separates Pillars into categories, and we have also fully analyzed the limitations and attributes of a Pillar and how it coexists with its host in our planar existence (refer to section 3). However what we have found so far is but a grain of sand in a vast desert. Thus, further studies are being conducted in learning the truth about Pillars. We believe that the power of Pillars has been with the human mind since the beginning of known civilization. It has been hidden deliberately by our genetic makeup, and only to awake when the survival of the human species depend on it. Thus it is vital that we fully understand this power within us, this next step of human evolution may save us all from our eventual doom in the future.

*   *   *   *

"Fuck me!" Francis exclaimed and smashed his fist onto his desk.

And that was the first time Jessie heard him use foul language. Cops said it all the time, she said it all the time, and it never meant anything. But she knew when he said it, it meant an awful lot. Putting her hand on his shoulder, she grasped it and tried to give him reassurance. He was shaking, with a mixture of fury, frustration, and most of all, fear.

Not knowing what she could say to calm him, Jessie's eyes could only linger on the computer screen among the lines of text. It took her quite some time to digest what she read meant to her, and most of all, to him. And she scanned the paragraphs again and again, trying to find faults with it, trying to prove that it was nothing but a joke. But deep inside, she knew it was real. That was the truth behind everything.

She was afraid to look him in the eyes. When she did, the anger had subsided. Hiding behind the brown eyes, Jessie saw a child lost in the corner of a dark closet, afraid of the dark, afraid of being alone, like she was so long ago.

Jessie embraced him, like a mother embracing a lost child, and letting him rest his head on her shoulder. He was shaking, not as violently as before, but with no less dread in the uncontrollable quivering. He burrowed himself on her shoulder, and silently cried.

"They injected me with that shit," he muttered, his voice was barely audible.

"You don't know that, Francis." She didn't know what else to say. She only brushed his hair, and ran her hand along his back.

"They must have. And if I don't get that drug, I'm going to die."

"You're not going to die." Babel, the Pillar Project. Just how many people are being experimented on this drug? How far does this thing go? And her friend, is he going to die? What if Babel gives him an antidote? Does it mean he'll be forever under Babel's control? A shiver feather-tickled the back of her neck, trailed down her back and spread into her arms. She too, found herself trembling. Her heart ached.

They were both silent for a moment that felt like eternity. They clung to each other, finding hope in each other's arms.

"When?" Jessie found herself unable to organize a coherent sentence.

"When what?" Francis pulled away from her arms, wiping away tears and avoiding her gaze all together.

"When did you get injected?"

"I don't know."

"When did you first see Michelle?"

"The night in Mammoth, when…" he paused, staring at the computer screen with the now blinking screensaver, as if it gave him inspiration. "That bastard."

"Who?"

"Andy. Only the four of us were on that trip. Only two of us survived. He must have injected everyone with that drug."

"And the others didn't make it." She was starting to understand the big picture.

"That's why he smashed their…" the words were stuck on his lips.

"So that no evidence of brain tumors can be found in an autopsy," she concluded for him.

He nodded in reluctant agreement and turned his focus back to the computer screen. Moving the mouse, the screen flashed back to its original state. "Let's get this over with."

The next section of the document covered the science behind the P.I.L.L.A.R. drug. Francis read it slowly, scrolling down in a gradual pace. When he was finally done, he stopped at the page just above section three.

She had to admit that she could not understand much of it.

"Monstrous, but brilliant," he commented.

"What does it say?"

"I'm not entirely certain myself, I would assume even a doctor in biochemistry would have a hard time grasping the ideas presented here. Give me a moment to think about it." He stared at one of the charts on the screen, eyebrows arching; then he continued, "The P.I.L.L.A.R. drug, a mixture of a protein, DNA sequence, and a virus that is designed to cross the blood brain barrier and target hippocampus of the brain."

"What is the blood brain barrier?"

"It's sort of a gateway between blood vessels and brain cells determining what substances that it would let passing through, think of it as an extensive filter system. The brain is very fastidious when it comes to blood supply. I think glucose and a virus can pass through, that's why they fused the targeted mutagen with a viral vector. Okay, when the virus carries the protein and DNA into the right place, it sort of rewrites part of the genetic sequences of brain cells. It's basically gene therapy done on the brain. Nobody has ever done this before."

"Then this is a breakthrough in medical science?"

"Oh, it's more than a breakthrough. It was a breakthrough when Babel cured Cystic Fibrosis permanently by gene therapy. This is a miracle. Editing brain cells is a million times harder than changing permanent lung cells. A brain is responsible for so much, like regulation of hormones, coordinating movements, interpreting senses, memory, just one tiny miscalculation can turn a person into a turnip or simply redefines his humanity. This is crazy. We're talking about science fiction coming to life.

"Sorry, I'm digressing. Anyway, what I was going to say is only less than thirty percent of a human brain is normally utilized. By modifying the hippocampus, one is able to exercise his brain in a more efficient manner, so to say. One of the side effects of this process is the gradual increase in neuron activities, if the person belongs to the group that doesn't die right away. This becomes malignant and is fatal after a period of time without further treatment."

"Is this similar to cancer?"

"Yes, it's just an uncontrollable growth of cells. That's when the second form of the drug comes into play. It works as an inhibitor."

Before she could open her mouth to ask him how an inhibitor worked, he continued. "Your body is regulated by biological systems that involve inhibitors. I wished I paid more attention in class when I was in school. I can't give you a definite example right now. But the basic idea is that your body makes a lot of biochemical substances for different functions, but an excess of those substances can be harmful. Your body needs to know when to stop making something and take a rest. Some substances work as inhibitors, and your body keeps track of how much an inhibitor's made or received. When it reaches a certain level, your body will stop that process until that inhibitor is depleted. Sometimes an inhibitor is just a byproduct of another regulatory system, that's how the intertwining biochemical systems regulate each other. The neurons in your brain have a similar process, made by neurotransmitters, and they too can be inhibited by a substance called cyclins, which regulate the cell cycle of mitosis. Since the whole process is not natural, the body doesn't know how to regulate the increasing neural activities. The drug stimulates the body to complete its regulatory functions."

When he stopped, she took a couple minutes to absorb what he told her. And as complicated as it sounded to a person like her who barely scratched the surfaces of life sciences in college, she understood it, in a mundane sort of way. "Thank you, Francis."

He raised one of his eyebrows, showing genuine incomprehension.

"For taking time to explain."

"Oh, no problem. I think I did it as much for my sake as yours. It was a little bit too much for me to take on all at once, saying it out loud in a skeletal sort of way actually helps me make sure that I understand it also."

"Okay, if you say so."

"Let's get on with the rest of it."

"Wait," she said, suddenly realizing something. "This is awfully convenient for them, isn't it?"

"What are you talking about?"

"People who undergoes this experiment, even not by choice, if they do make it out alive, they will be forever subjected to Babel's mercy. Because they need the ..." She could not find the strength to say the rest of the words, she knew that it hurt so much that it was like a knife stabbing into his heart.

He looked away, saying nothing.

*   *   *   *

Section 3 – Pillar Systems:

The following section breaks down the study of the planar psychic projections into different topics. And it is based on the research done on limited number of subjects, so the data is not an absolute presentation of the universal truth. Any Pillar exceptions can occur anywhere, anytime.

Types of Pillars:

Pillars can be separated into three different categories:

Type A: The gifted having total control over his Pillar. In this type the Pillar does not have any inherent instinctive or intellectual abilities of its own accord. It cannot act on its own without commands from the gifted.

Type B: The gifted having partial control over his Pillar. The degree of partial control can vary from case to case. A person can have only little control over his Pillar, or having almost as much as control as one that belongs to type A. This type of Pillar shows a considerable level of intelligence, being inversely proportional to the level of control its host has. The less intelligent ones know how to guard themselves in self-defense, or how to complete a task on their own, with little supervision. The more intelligent ones can even be whimsical in nature, and will do things in their likings, even object to command against their nature or habits.

Type C: The gifted having no control over his Pillar. The only control he has is perhaps activating or deactivating the projection, although this too, isn't absolute. In rare cases, Pillar of this type has even proven to be parasitic, draining the life energies and killing off the host without the host being able to turn it off. This type of Pillar, although rare, is very dangerous. Though not all is parasitic in nature and entirely uncontrollable, some show extreme intelligence, as much as a normal human being, if not more. It can even communicate with its host. If it takes a liking to its host, it'll do his biding and protect him with all costs, after all, a Pillar and its host exists as one physical entity.

Note: The type of a Pillar will affect the visual range of its host. A gifted belonging to group A can see whatever his Pillar sees, no matter how far the Pillar is away from him. However a type C gifted one will have no visual connections with his Pillar and will not be able to keep track of his own Pillar if it's out of his own visual range. A type B falls somewhere in between.

*   *   *   *

When Jessie looked up at him, she couldn't read any emotions in him. The anger, terror and confusion seemed to have temporary subsided, perhaps the intensity of those emotions was somewhat diluted by the awe of scientific breakthrough, and a thirst for understanding. His countenance was that of a blank canvas, one that conveyed no emotions. She wondered what he was thinking.

"I'm a type B."

"Huh?"

"I have a lot of control over Michelle, almost as much as I want to, without being too cumbersome. But she also knows how to act out on her own on certain occasions."

He was calling Michelle a she, and not it. She wondered if he still thought of her as the person he met long ago or simply a projection of his brain, as this document suggested. What was she really? Was she a spirit, a guardian angel, a masquerade in disguise of a psychic projection from a scientific experiment? Or was she truly nothing else but part of Francis, a facade of a shadow deeply rooted in his memory?

*   *   *   *

Laws of Pillars:

Law of Action and Reaction: A Pillar is a representation of its physical host in between planes. They cannot survive without each other (with the exception of some parasitic Pillars). What happens to the host happens to the Pillar, and vice versa. A gifted with an injured right arm will also have a Pillar that has an unusable right arm (with the exception of non-humanoid Pillars). A Pillar knocked ten feet backwards would have the same effect on its host, and vice versa, no matter how far away a Pillar is away from its hosts.

Law of Physics: A Pillar has to obey the physical properties of this plane of existence while it is away from its host. That means it will stand on the ground and cannot move through walls, it breathes air. Unless the Pillar is of an elemental nature, or has some inherent abilities that enable it to defy the real world law of physics, it has to behave as any normal beings must behave. A Pillar can only be activated in the vicinity of the host; however, deactivation can happen anywhere, a Pillar can be called back immediately with no regards of distance. However the law of physics must apply, in the way that there must exist a path between a Pillar and its host for deactivation to successfully occur. That means if a Pillar is trapped in a room with four solid walls, deactivation cannot occur.

Law of Detection and Interactivity: As Pillars are beings that exist between planes, objects belonging to this world cannot harm a Pillar. A bullet and a car cannot harm a Pillar, but a Pillar can inflict damage to objects of this world, including its host. Thus a person without a Pillar can never guard itself against a Pillar. A non-gifted cannot see a Pillar, unless that Pillar had manifested itself considerable power so that it could be even seen by a non-gifted. This exception is rare and applies to Pillars of a gigantic size and considerable physical power, or if its inherent nature allow itself to interact with non-gifted in a way based on sight.

Law of Boundary: A Pillar cannot exceed its inherent maximum possible range, which applies to the greatest distance between a Pillar and its host (refer to attributes of Pillars for details). This distance is always a straight line discounting objects that block its paths. This limitation does not apply to projectile weapons or wide area effects. This law can be utilized in survival and combat situations to a considerable advantage. For example, a Pillar holding onto the edge of a cliff can ensure that its host will not fall and hit the ground, provided that the maximum possible range is not greater than the distance of the vertical fall. And the strength of the Pillar can support the force exerted by the free fall plus the exertion. The law applies when the maximum range is reached, and the force is usually proportional to the weight of the host.

Law of Effects and Abilities: Each Pillar has its own different ability that has a different set of rules regulating it. That rule can never be broken unless the Pillar has exceeded its own limitation and grown into a different state. A Pillar must continue its own existence in order for its abilities to take effect, unless it is a permanent effect. That means temporary effects will be wiped away when a Pillar or a host ceases to exist.

Law of Conservation of Energy: A Pillar uses energy of its hosts, which is ATP, the very same form of energy that the biological systems of a human body uses. Utilization of Pillars cannot be continued incessantly, energy must be replenished. The level of energy usage varies depends on size, physical power, and level of activity of the Pillar in a particular session.

Attributes of Pillars:

The different attributes of a Pillar can be separated into the following categories: The same attributes belonging to a normal human being falls in the middle. That means that in each category, there exists Pillars with greater power than a human being or less powerful than a normal human. This does not apply to range because it is only an abstract value measuring distance.

Strength: the physical power of a Pillar, the force it applies, the damage it exerts on another, and the endurance of damage it could receive. From studies it is concluded that strength of a Pillar is inversely proportional to range, but not necessarily inversely proportional to speed.

Range: the maximum distance (in a straight line) between a Pillar and its host. It seems to be true that Pillars with extreme ranges have very weak physical power, and Pillars with destructive strength have short ranges. Although no exceptions have been seen, those that fall in between the spectrum don't seem to adhere to any patterns.

Speed: how fast a Pillar can act and react. The fastest of Pillars can move close to the speed of sound, seemingly to defy the laws of nature. However, the slowest can move slower than a human being.

Growth: the potential of a Pillar to become more powerful, this includes improving its other attributes, learning or improving its inherent abilities, or completely evolving to a totally different state. Some Pillars exist as beings in their early learning stages, and some simply lack the ability to grow. The concept is similar to a human child, or an adult. A less powerful Pillar is more likely to grow faster, but it's not to say that an already powerful Pillar cannot grow, or a relatively weaker Pillar is not already at its final stages of growth.

*   *   *   *

The end of the document certainly gave an impression of an unfinished job, but that was all they had for now, already a lot to absorb right away. Jessie did not know if she understood everything, but she more or less had an idea of what Pillars were and what they were capable of doing. If she had read this document before, she might not have been courageous or insane enough to chase down one of them, going head to head without any help. When she was investigating the Tormentor, everything was a mystery. What they stole from Babel answered a lot of questions they had, but it also introduced a hundred more concerns, like a virus spreading in a nightmare. What is Babel trying to accomplish? Just who is under Babel's control? Is Babel funded by the government? How many gifted are there already in the world? How are they going to fight against such an overwhelming power? Or are they? What is Francis going to do? Is he going to die? Or rather, is Babel going to force him to do something he'd rather choose death?

She didn't know what to say, how to comfort him. While she was lost in thought, Francis brought two glasses of ice water from the kitchen, handing her one.

"What are you going to do now?" The ice-cold water settled in her stomach like a foreign substance. Though refreshing, it was also chilling and unsettling.

"I don't know," he sighed. "Andy, he must be a host, he'll know how I can get the drug to save myself. I promised to play racquetball with him in the morning. I'll see what happens then."

"What are you going to do? You're not going to confront him, are you?"

"That sounds like a plan."

"That's too dangerous. You don't know what kind of power he has."

"I'm going to take that chance, who knows how long I have left." His tone was unnaturally calm, for a person whose fate was out of his grasp, and the clock was ticking away every moment.

"Then I'm coming tomorrow."

He almost protested, but stopped. "There's no use arguing with you, is there?"

"You know me best." She tried her best to smile and didn't really know if it actually looked like one.

"Ten-thirty, at the courts. It's just at the bottom of the building we went to last time, the one with the bar. You'll probably have to go on your own, since I need to work in the afternoon, if they fixed my computers."

"No problem." She took a look at her watch, it was already three. "We totally forgot about lunch, you want to get something?"

He hesitated, and looked troubled. "Actually I'm not really hungry."

"Not in the mood, huh?"

"I guess not."

"I'm sorry, Francis. If there's anything I can do—"

"Actually, it'd be great if I could be alone for a while."

He doesn't want me there. He is kicking me out. Why does he just want to be alone? Whatever problem he has now, isn't it better to talk it out with someone? "Okay, I'll see you tomorrow then. Anyway, this is my phone number at home, if there's anything, don't hesitate to call." She wrote it down on a piece of paper.

He nodded and then ushered her to the front door, as silent as a broken radio.

He needed to sort out things on his own, without her distraction. Maybe she was the one who didn't want to be alone. Ever since Terry left, it felt like she had missed a big part of her life. Though he was only a partner on the job, he became someone she confided in, her one true friend. And when it came to romance, she had successfully constructed a wall around herself.

Walking to her car, she wondered why she thought about Terry and her non-existent love life every time she saw Francis. Francis was still a big mystery to her. Sometimes she felt like she knew everything about him, and other times, she knew next to nothing. At times he was childishly charming, and then he was so annoyingly unfocused as if he was living in another world. She did think that her presence and her friendship made him take great leaps from his social reclusion. Every day he was becoming a little bit more pleasant to be around. And she felt that she was a big factor in helping him become a better person. That accomplishment gave her joy and fulfillment.

She did like him though, maybe not the kind of like she'd have hoped for, meeting a guy. He was not someone that she could admire and rely on; more like meeting her own little brother all over again, someone who needed a strong hand to pull him up from the childhood fantasy that still lingered. Yet she liked him nevertheless, maybe it was the childishness in him that made the foundation of friendship between them so strong. Outside the tough detective exterior, she was a child at heart, and afraid of more things than an average adolescent. Especially now that a dark cloud loomed over the world, yet she felt less threatened than she felt alone.

CHAPTER TWENTY-FOUR

The rest of the day she spent at Gibson's, always the place of nostalgia and comfort, with Mark as company. She detested being alone now more than ever, yet she did not want to tell Mark what she had recently learned. Normally, she'd tell Mark everything. She knew that Mark would not doubt her, because he was her brother, who trusted her. Yet it was because he would believe her that she would keep her lips sealed. She could not even begin to guess the danger that knowledge would bring, and she could never drag the only family she had into peril. She had already done that once, and she was lucky that nobody got hurt.

Mark tried to pry it out of her. She simply brushed away the subject with small talk. He was much safer not knowing the truth behind Babel.

Picking up a new thriller that just arrived at the store, she sat down and tried to immerse herself in a story. But after reading a few pages, she found that she could not concentrate, so she decided to take a walk.

There wasn't much to do in the suburbs, only the occasional gift and antique shops, restaurants, and cafes that scattered along the antiquated street of the town center. Borders was around the corner, but she was hesitant to go in there, even to buy coffee, because she would feel like she was betraying the family business.

A brief yet heavy downpour soaked her wet before she could find shelter. Reluctantly she returned to her car and decided to head home for a warm shower.

She spent the rest of the day cleaning up her room, throwing away things she no longer needed and held no sentimental value. Deciding to sort through old photos and albums, she realized that she rarely took any pictures ever since she joined the force. She could not find one picture with Terry in it. Ten years from now, she was not even going to remember what he looked like, if she lived that long.

Her mother came in and sat down, asking her how she had been doing. Jessie was close with her foster parents, especially her mother, but it felt like an eternity since they had a proper conversation. Homicide occupied all her life, sometimes even her dreams. She told her mother about her partner's death in detail, but subjugated to intensive censoring, resulting in a version that excluded the supernatural.

An uninterrupted dreamless night fully rejuvenated her for the morning. Putting on a workout outfit she had found in the depths of her closet left from her college days, she headed for the one place she should avoid, yet kept revisiting, drawn to it like moths to a flame.

She was fifteen minutes early, but Francis was already waiting for her in the lobby. In a white T-shirt, shorts and the plainest white tennis shoes, he sat cross-legged on the couch, lost in thought like a Buddhist monk in meditation. She had to put herself directly in front of his line of sight to get his attention.

"Oh, hay." It was a perfunctory grunt, but she told herself that he was overjoyed to see her. After all, who wouldn't? She was in her cute little outfit from the college days, and she almost felt young, almost.

"How are you feeling?"

"White and fluffy."

She raised her eyebrow.

"Like a lab rat."

She laughed.

"It wasn't really meant to be funny, I'm okay, I guess. No broken bones, not yet. Not lost in a schizophrenic world. Just feel like I'm violated."

"I'm sorry, Francis." She knew how it felt to be violated, she knew.

"It's not your fault, really. Anyway, you need a card to get in, but I can sign you in as guest. Andy's not here yet, he's always late. We could play for a while before he gets here."

"I don't know how to play racquetball. I didn't come here to play."

"Then why are you in that outfit?"

"Dress for the occasion."

He gave her a long look.

"Alright, I'll play." She sighed. "But you'll have to teach me."

"Deal. It's really not that hard, you can play tennis, right?"

She nodded. She used to be on the high school tennis team, but that was high school. After that the only time when she moved her aching bones was when she was chasing down fleeing suspects or witnesses who wanted to avoid trouble. Thankfully stress often kept her in shape. "What about Andy? What are you going to do when he comes here?"

"Don't worry about it. I'll think of something."

He seemed confident about the whole thing so she had to let it go.

Francis had his own racquet and he went ahead to check one out for her at the counter. The fitness center was lavishly built with neon lights and glass panels that separated individual workout areas. Abundant treadmills and bike machines that looked like they had never been touched surrounded one side of the racquetball courts. The back walls of the courts were glass, letting the audience from the cardiovascular machines view the action inside as they exercised. This is the place owned by people who do experimentations on people, without their permission, she reminded herself.

Both the courts and the workout area were almost empty. Jessie figured that since the facility was only opened to employees, the majority would frequent the hours after work. Francis picked a court that was closer to the entrance, went in, and indicated for her to come along.

She dropped the small bag with her wallet and both her guns just aside the glass door, making sure that she had them in sight, entered the room, and closed the door.

The racquetball court was like an interrogation room, except emptier and bigger, and the see-through side of the room was not shielded by a mirror. She looked up. The ceiling was high enough to make her feel at ease. Considering the pristine silence, the room was probably sound proof. She looked at the glass door behind her and wondered if the thick glass was bullet proof also.

Francis briefly explained the rules of the game, his voice causing a faint echo in the hollow room. As far as she understood, the area between the two lines on the floor in the middle of the room was for the serve. For a legitimate serve, the player had to stand between the lines, and the ball had to hit the front wall once and the ground area behind the second line once, all the other walls, including the ceiling, which to her was indeed a strange concept, could be utilized as many times as possible, or not at all. A legitimate return was to hit the ball anytime after bouncing back from the front wall, and just like tennis, the ball could only touch the ground once.

He gave a few pointers to her stroke and she decided she was just going to play the game like tennis. The ball was blue, sized somewhere in between a tangerine and an orange. He threw it up and started a slow serve as she was ready.

Watching the ball slowly sailing towards her, she hit it with all her might in an overhead stroke. He returned it with ease, but harder. She hit it back, and he returned it, this time, slightly off-angle, bouncing once on the side wall, and then to the back. She gave chase but couldn't get to the ball in time.

"You're not too bad at all," he said in an encouraging tone.

"What are you talking about? I just ran around the room in a circle like a mad chicken."

"Nice way you put it," he said smiling. "That's normal for someone who just started. It's like a pinball machine or pool table. The ball bounces, and you have to anticipate where it's going to land. And remember, every time the ball touches a wall its speed and angle changes, almost like doing a physics problem while playing."

"Gosh, I hate math."

"It's really not that bad, it'll come naturally. Just remember, the moment right after you hit the ball, don't stand there like a statue. Go back to the center of the court, and be ready for the return."

It took her a few times to understand why. Sometimes she returned the ball and stayed at one side, and became trapped as her opponent returned the ball to the other side. Just like tennis, she needed to be always mobile enough to get from one side of the court to the other.

They did not start a serious game, just rallying, hitting back and forth, so Francis did not explain to her the official rules. Francis taught her more tricks as she was getting accustomed to the trajectory of the ball, and improved her performance. He told her hitting the side wall of the court to the front wall corner on the other side could make a deadly drop in the front. To make a high drop at the back, one should hit the ball high up in the air and rebound to the back of the court from the ceiling.

The game was simple, yet complex, and required one to be agile and alert. It was a strenuous exercise of both the mind and body, yet it was fun. After a short while she was exhausted, having to pause to catch her breath.

A man was waiting outside, stretching as he observed them. He wore a tank top and basketball shorts. He was tall, well built with powerful arms.

Jessie retrieved her bag and opened the glass door to step outside.

"I'm Andy," he greeted her with a smile. Square-jawed, broad shoulders with short blonde hair and penetrating blue eyes, he was unexpectedly handsome.

"Jessie." She shook his hand.

"Francis tearing you apart in there?"

"It's my first time, and it shows, doesn't it?"

"No, not at all." It was probably just a polite lie. "You picked it up pretty quickly."

"It's your turn now. I'm exhausted." She also thought that his voice sounded familiar, but she couldn't place it.

He nodded, still smiling. And Jessie watched him stride into the court. When she had heard of Francis' manager, she had expected a person that looked more like the stereotype information technology professional, fat and nerdy, like Bob the hacker. Though Francis by no means looked like a geek, he just looked like a lost college kid still trying to find his classroom, or his place in the vast world. But Andy, although only in a tank top, looked like someone politically influential and charismatic, perhaps someone with a high rank in the army, someone who could penetrate her soul just with a glimpse of his blue gaze. She wondered if he was a gifted.

After exchanging a few words she could not hear outside the court, Francis and Andy started rallying back and forth, practicing and warming up. The atmosphere totally changed while the game started. Both players crouched low, their attention focused, their faces determined. Francis' serve was powerful and the ball often streaked low in a straight line towards the back right corner of the room. Andy liked to serve the ball high up in the air, no less powerful. It seemed he was taking an advantage of his height to keep the ball a tad bit higher in the beginning. Both of them were equally skilled, having no trouble returning serves and hitting the ball to the oddest places in the court. Andy was the trickster, often exchanging his offensive tactics dropping the ball to the front and back, and alternating between sides. Despite Francis' physical disadvantage, he was determined to save even the most impossible returns to put himself back into an counterattacking position. Andy was a lot taller, and leaning low he could usually get from one corner to the other with less of a big leap than Francis. However, Francis was lithe and fast, with seemingly unlimited energy sprinting back and forth, and he was good at returning Andy's powerful strokes to spots he could not reach. A few times he even succeeded in returning the ball flat on the ground, which Francis had explained earlier as a death blow in racquetball, sort of a hit that targeted the ball right at the angle where the front wall intersected the floor, resulting in the ball rolling back like a bowling ball, impossible to be countered.

It was a good match. And Jessie enjoyed watching the rivalry between them. She had never seen a professional racquetball tournament, but she would guess that what she saw was not too far off. And of course she didn't mind watching the sweating, glistening hard bodies. For a while she forgot about the mission they were here to accomplish.

Until after a few games, when Andy avoided a drop he could have saved, dropping his racquet, and leaping out of the way. The two of them faced each other with scornful anger in their eyes. Francis was thrown backwards, pinned to the wall by an unseen force. For a moment he seemed transfixed, crucified on the wall, his face a rictus of agony. Then he slowly slumped to the floor.

Jessie reached for her gun, opened the glass door, and rushed in. Pointed the gun at Andy, she was shaking, and was not even sure if she could aim straight. She sincerely prayed that it would not come down to firing it.

Andy turned to her, and she noticed there was a deep cut on his arm. The flesh around the laceration was turning charcoal and spreading out like an outbreak of Black Death. There was an odd familiarity to it, almost like déjà vu.

"Don't move, or I'll shoot."

CHAPTER TWENTY-FIVE

Francis had spent the previous night thinking. He no longer doubted his own sanity because he knew he could have never dreamed up such complex scientific experiments for the sake of negating reality. In fact, he was trying to escape it by telling himself that he was still in a dream.

All he asked for was to be someone normal, to live a quiet, mundane, normal life. He never had any ambition to be rich and successful, and he certainly did not have some kind of life long quest to win the Nobel Prize. He just wanted to live his life and being able to face himself. Perhaps he did not want to disappoint his mother, even though it had been a long time since he had felt her love. Maybe he wanted to be happy.

He was now cursed with this parasitic power called Pillar. It had haunted him and made him do things that he was not proud of. He felt ashamed to kill, and more so for rejoicing in the blood bath. Every time he thought about his power, he vividly remembered the joy of drenching himself in the essence of stolen life, and he yearned for every moment of it. Like a powerful drug it seduced him. And as he longed for it, he hated himself, and he hated Babel for changing him.

For some time he wanted to give up. He was going to die if he did not get the drug to keep his head from exploding. It'd been a week since he had discovered Michelle; maybe he still had another week, or less. But he'd rather die than submit to the will of Babel. He would not become part of the evil corporation and doing their sinister deeds just to cling to that thin thread of life.

His life was taken from him, and he was as good as dead.

His thoughts drifted, and he tried to revisit his imaginary adventures. Except that he could no longer focus. What would Faber Bardsong have done if he were in his place? The hero would rid himself of that curse and hunt down the ones who had bestowed it upon him.

But that was an imaginary figure he had created, a representation of what he would never be in real life. He was not powerful, charismatic, eloquent, brave, and did not have comrades who were willing to die for him. He was just a lonely guy trying to live a normal life.

He was not going to fight against a world dominating power all by himself.

But he was not alone. Jessie was there for him, and there were other people like Kyle, who was also struggling against the grasp of Babel. He had nothing to lose trying to find the truth, and no matter how slight the chances were, maybe he would find a way to cleanse himself of the curse.

No matter how bad Francis felt about himself during the past week, he had done things that he never imagined doing. He had fought, saved someone's life, made friends, and he had taken himself one step closer to the truth. He was never going to be someone like the idol of his childhood, but he did not have to hide behind his shame. He had already become something more.

That thought became a spark that ignited a fire inside him. That fire of hope extinguished the sadness, confusion, and the shame inside his heart. These few days, he admitted to himself, he was happier having someone to talk to. Just when he started to have a glimpse of what a true friendship was like, he found out he was not going to live. And in the racquetball court he played like he had never played before, as if he was playing for his life, his hope for the future. He won the first round and Andy the second one. After the two games he was exhausted, and he had almost totally forgotten what he had come to the courts to do, to confront the man who might yet be the one responsible for what he had become.

In the middle of the third game, when Andy was reaching for a drop in the corner, Francis decided to surprise him. He commanded Michelle to block Andy's path, knowing that a normal person would run through her.

As expected, Andy dodged to the side to avoid the impact, turned, and regarded Francis with his blue gaze.

For that moment, time seemed to be suspended. Francis felt a chill in his heart as Andy's scornful gaze penetrated his defense. The ball dropped and rolled. Francis saw movement in the left corner of his eye, a figure that moved so fast it was a blur. It was the clown, wearing the face of a devil. Foregoing his own safety, he commanded Michelle to attack Andy.

Michelle slashed out with her katana with an unmatched fury, and at the same time the clown was upon him. He clearly saw punches landed on him like bullets from a semi-automatic machine gun. Each one of them broke something on his body. And as he was thrown backwards onto the wall, he felt himself shatter like a fragile glass doll.

If not for his enhanced perception, his eyes would not even be able to follow the shadow that trailed behind each of the clown's punches. And to his horror, he had felt that Andy was holding back. If he had not, each punch would have gone through him as easy as a knife shearing paper.

He slumped in so much pain he no longer felt his limbs. Michelle had only been able to make a small cut on Andy's arm before she too collapsed in the corner of the court, a lifeless mannequin. Something was spreading on Andy's arm, a devouring darkness.

Jessie had come in with her drawn gun. He wanted to tell her to get away. He struggled to find his voice, but could not. Pain was the only thing he perceived, the only thing he tasted, the only thing he smelled.

The next moment was one of miracles. The pain subsided, and he felt himself becoming whole again, his broken bones mended themselves. He looked up, the color of flesh was returning to Andy's blackened arm.

"Put down the gun, detective," Andy said calmly.

"I'm okay," Francis found the strength to stand up. "Do as he said."

Backing away from Andy, Jessie went to help him stand, checking his body for injury while still keeping a suspicious eye on Andy.

"You're the one who injected me with the drug," Francis accused. He was sure now.

"That was my mission, but no, I did not."

"What do you mean?"

"In Mammoth, after I had injected the others, I went to your room." His eyes were downcast. "You defended yourself with your Pillar. Or I should rather say, your Pillar defended you, in your subconscious. You've had it all along."

"You lie!"

"That's the truth, you don't need P.I.L.L.A.R.E.R. to keep yourself alive."

What is he saying? That he has his Pillar all along.

"I've had my Pillar since childhood," Andy admitted.

"What?"

"Yes, yet we are all drawn to this place."

At first, Francis did not understand Andy's statement. Then he understood that he meant although they got their powers from separate sources, they still ended up meeting here in Babel by coincidence – which led him to thinking about his dead coworkers. "But you killed them."

"I did what I had to do," Andy sighed. "Babel's order for me was to inject P.I.L.L.A.R. into the three of you. I had hopes that all of you would have made it, but they did not, and I was forced to end their lives. Believe me, I was relieved when I did not have to deal with you."

"If you don't need the drug to stay alive, why are you following their orders?"

"To convince them of my loyalty. It is necessarily..." he paused for a moment, with pain in his eyes. "For a greater good. Just like Kyle, I presume that you've known about him by now, I'm fighting against Babel. Not one night do I not pray to God for forgiveness, for murdering innocents. You must think me a murderer, but I had to prove my loyalty to Babel, so that everything that others and I have worked for, would not be in vain. In time you will understand."

"What have you done to me?" Francis' strength had fully returned, his pain gone, like chalk markings erased from a blackboard. He felt as alive as ever.

"I restored you, that is my power."

"It was you, that night, at Echo Park."

He nodded, solemnly. "Babel gave you a mission, even though you didn't know it. You were supposed to eliminate the Tormentor, who had gotten out of control. Kyle knew about it and suggested that I gave you a hand when you needed it. So I followed you and restored you when you were under the Tormentor's power. Just like I worked on myself right now, I could easily reverse the cell death process, returning the cells to their normal state."

Francis stared at him, not knowing what to say. He was a murderer, and a savior. Francis hated and distrusted Andy more than ever, but part of him also wanted to thank him for saving his life. The conflicting emotions were ripping him apart.

"I hope you will see that as a token of my friendship, and an apology for deceiving you, as well as the atrocity that I've committed. I ask neither for your gratitude, nor your acceptance of my apology. Only try to understand why I had committed such sins. There's a meeting tonight at the church, please come. Come and you will understand." He turned to Jessie. "And please come tonight not as a detective, but as Francis' friend. There are things that I will reveal the world cannot know."

Jessie nodded.

"The Revelation Church of Christ, 113 Belville Avenue, Brea. Eight o'clock." Then Andy strode out of the court as if nothing had happened.

CHAPTER TWENTY-SIX

Everything happened so suddenly. One moment he was going to die, the next moment he was told that he had his power all along. Perhaps the experimentation had started long before he was working for Babel. Francis did not know what to believe anymore.

"How are you feeling?" Jessie asked. They were sitting outside the court after the ordeal, staring at the now empty battlefield.

"Confused. It feels like I have lost control of my life, or actually I've never had it."

"That's not true."

"Saving you, fighting the Tormentor, it's some kind of orchestrated scheme."

"I don't believe it. You saved me because you wanted to. Not because someone programmed you to do it. I would have died if you didn't show up. And actually the Tormentor would have too. They gave Mary aspirin instead of the real drug to ensure of her death in case you did not survive."

"That's why Mary looked like her head was hurting, before I…" he could not finish the sentence. "But it feels like everything was a setup. Even getting this job and coming here to work. Especially that."

She put her hand on his, squeezing it. Her hand was cold, nevertheless it gave him a friendly reassurance. "Don't give up, Francis. Your life is in your own hands, and you know it."

Now that he did not have to rely on a drug to survive, he could freely uncover the truth about Babel, about himself. Pieces of a puzzle were coming together: the Clown, Michelle, Pillars, and Babel. However he thought that those pieces only added up to a tiny part of a much bigger puzzle.

"And are you up for church tonight?" Jessie asked. "Is Andy a Christian?"

"Yes, supposedly quite a devout one." Devout enough to kill for something he believes. Faith was forever a mystery to him. "He's asked me to go to church before, but I never agreed…" He never liked church, because it took his mother away from him. "I don't really want to go, I don't trust him. But I guess we have to, just to give it a chance. See which side he's really on, what he's doing behind Babel's back."

"What are you going to do now?"

"I was thinking of going back to check if they replaced my computers, then… I don't know. Not really in the mood for work."

"Want to go shopping?"

"I'm not much of a shopper. But I guess it beats work."

"Not very enthusiastic, huh?"

"What do you want me to do? Beg you to take me shopping?"

"My, my, aren't we edgy today!" She wrinkled her nose disapprovingly and said, "After a shower though."

"Oh, definitely."

*   *   *   *

They went to South Coast Plaza, one of the largest shopping malls in California. Although conveniently close, Francis could not recall the last time he had been there. Shopping was not one of his preferred past times. He often went into specific stores, bought the things he needed and exited the shopping area like a criminal on the run.

However, he did not have as bad a time as he had expected this time. They spent hours stopping in each section of the mall, looking at small gadgets, trying on clothing, and taking ice cream and coffee breaks. Although he did not buy anything, he had an enjoyable time.

Jessie bought quite a handful, mostly clothing. Although she was not the dressy type of a girl, she was a girl after all. Girls went into a mall and they shopped, that was the universal way of life, or so Francis thought.

Arriving at the church a little before eight, they followed a few people into what seemed to be a large room on the side of the church. Francis guessed that was where they held the fellowship meetings. He had felt a little uneasy stepping into a church, as he had felt such hate for it as a child. His mother had spent her spare time in a holy place which caused him to be jealous. When he was a grownup, he had always wanted to believe in God, but never really embraced faith.

Seats were arranged as in a large classroom or a small lecture hall. Francis and Jessie sat towards the back. The fellowship session seemed like a racial melting pot, except that the age group seemed to be limited to late teens and young adults. As the place became congested, a middle-aged Hispanic man introduced himself as Father Raul, welcoming them to the fellowship. It seemed that the Father only meant to welcome them and did not stay under the spot light for any period of time. Andy, dressed in a formal shirt of dark blue and a black tie, took over as the Father sat down in the front row. Francis had never seen his manager wearing formal attire, as he often dressed casual at work. In Francis' eyes, Andy looked out of place.

"I see that there are some new faces among us," he said, his voice slightly amplified by a microphone clipped on his collar. His blue eyes scanned the room, memorizing faces. "Welcome to our weekly meeting." He then went to read a passage from the New Testament about Jesus and his disciples, part of a story that Francis vaguely recollected from his childhood scripture classes in Catholic school. The words drifted by his ears like Greek.

"Do you know why we are here today?" Andy raised his voice slightly, catching their attention. "Why? Why are we here today?" His voice became thunderously demanding.

"To fight." People around them answered in unison.

"To fight what?"

"Evil!" They shouted like a lynch mob.

"Evil, yes, evil in disguise of science. Genetic scientists, corporations, working against God's will. Trying to change the essence of what makes us humans, trying to change the destiny that God has planned for us. We are God's children, that has always been our place, in earth or in heaven. It is not our destiny to play God, to create and alter life, much less to alter our own very biology. We have sinned, we have contaminated God's work, we have committed blasphemous acts, we have desecrated our own existence, and we have angered God."

"But it is not our fault!" someone in the front row exclaimed with anger.

"Yes, I know." Andy lowered his voice, sounding almost regrettable. "But we as humans must answer our sins together as an entire species. God no longer will punish us by floods and diseases. It is up to us, to steer our own path; however, the consequences can be far more disastrous. So far God is patient with us, and He is forgiving. We must not take advantage of God's forgiving nature and test the limits of His patience. The spawn of evil must be stopped now, before it is too late, before it changes us forever, before God has no other choice but to punish us, to annihilate us."

There was a long silence. Nobody in the room talked, even among themselves. As if they feared God's hand of judgment right there in the very room.

What is this bullshit? Francis shook his head and took a look at Jessie, who only showed a deep concern in her face.

"Inside the depths of Babel hide these beings known as the b'nai Elohim, sons of God, or beings that are believed to be fallen angels. But they are servants of Satan, sent to deceive us, to mislead us from our true destiny. And we must act as judgment of God, the hand of God, to smite them, cast them to oblivion, before they destroy our very humanity.

"In Jeremiah 10:10, 'At His wrath the earth shall tremble, and the nation shall not be able to abide His threatening. Thus then shall you say to them, the gods that have not made heaven and earth, let them perish from earth and from under heaven.'"

Andy went on to read another passage from the Bible, one from the Old Testament. It was about the people who were building the Tower of Babel. They tried to reach the heavens, to reach God, and were finally punished by a communication problem created by God. When everyone suddenly spoke another tongue, they could not understand each other and were forced to abandon the project and scatter among the world.

Francis knew the story well as many legends and fantasies drew reference from this story. He wondered if it was a blatant message to the people here, that God was going to punish the people in Babel for trying to reach godhood and He was probably going to decimate the human race. It was hard to believe that people would actually listen to such gibberish, but Francis knew never to underestimate the gullibility of religious fanatics.

Damnation, Francis realized that he was in an AGTC meeting, and those sitting next to him might yet be terrorists. He shuddered and then shot a furtive glance at Jessie, who also looked over at him and nodded slightly with confirmation, as if she knew what he was thinking. Francis thought that she must be struggling to decide whether these misguided people were doing the right thing, and if they belonged behind bars or the throne of the highest commencement in heaven. Babel definitely deserved to be destroyed, for what they had done to him, for what they had done to others. But were these people justified to do what they had done? And did they have the power to fight? And how many so-called terrorists sitting around them were victims of Babel, host of this parasitic power?

While Andy continued the story of the tower, Francis closed his eyes as he suddenly experienced an overpowering feeling of nausea. His mind drifted. With uncontrollable dizziness, his mind sailed across an unending ocean of darkness, and he started to see a myriad of random images like a collection of unsorted slides being flashed through in an incredible speed. He concentrated to sort out the images, and he saw images of Michelle, alive, and naked, thrashing and squirming in bed as if she was copulating with an unseen force. Francis shook his head and tried to shut the images away, but could not. It was like someone had hacked into his brain, gaining control of it and forcing him to dream while he was awake. A few more flashes and he saw Michelle again, this time as the drifting phantom, who was strangling an unrecognizable young woman. And as he remembered how it felt to have the essence of someone else's life and power flowing through his veins, and he felt himself secretly longing for those moments, he trembled.

Opening his eyes, he stared upwards at the ceiling, trying to shut off the images. Feeling deeply ashamed of having unclean thoughts in a holy place, he saw what seemed to be petals of a pink flower drifting across the ceiling, sailing across on the current of an unseen summer wind. Shaking his head, he concluded that he must be hallucinating. He looked at Andy who was still reciting, yet he could not hear the words. Francis only craved for his dream, so intensely that it subdued him, holding him entranced.

Jessie turned towards him, with a big droplet of sweat on her forehead. "Are you okay?" she whispered. "You look a little pale."

"I…" Francis struggled to find his own voice. "I think I need to step out for a minute for some air." He stood up, staggering towards the door, trying to be as inconspicuous as possible.

It was warm outside, as opposed to the chilling air-conditioned room inside. But instantly he felt invigorated, and was in better control of himself again. The thoughts had left him. The invasion of his mind came to a stop. Letting out a deep breath, he found a seat on one of the benches surrounding the church compound.

A few other people also walked out of the room, their faces distraught as if the world had ended in front of them just a moment ago. Jessie was among the last to leave the room, and she seated herself next to him. Her lips parted, but she said nothing.

"You couldn't stand it either?" Francis broke the silence.

"Right, I saw…" she shook her head. "I dreamed…"

"You don't have to tell me." He wasn't planning to share his own private urges.

She nodded. "There's something in that room."

"You didn't happen to see pink flower petals flying in the air, did you?"

"What?"

"A Pillar, probably."

"In there?"

"Why not?"

"It's a church!"

"Sure, the Bible said no Pillar power tapping in church."

"But why?"

He did not know. But someone had forced them to face their own inner desires, perhaps as a trial of sort.

"It's for weeding out the ones who do not feel strongly in the cause, in God." It was Andy who answered, and next to him stood a black man with glasses. "This is Doctor Bill Lindsay. He's the one who stirred the air, so to say, and make you dream. And he has worked under the Pillar Project in Babel."

He shook their hands as they introduced themselves. "I must apologize for the intrusion to your mind. There are new comers to the fellowship every week, as members are encouraged to bring others. I do this as a test to make sure that only the faithful ones that strongly believe in our cause will stay, thus to make sure that no one would betray us in the future."

"So we failed your test?" Jessie asked sourly.

"Ah, you were not meant to be tested," Andy interjected. "I wanted both of you to come not because I wanted you to join our cause, but to see and understand what I'm working towards. Bill and I are the only ones working inside Babel, therefore it is of the utmost importance that Babel does not doubt our loyalty. Otherwise everything we have worked for would be for naught."

Andy was asking for their understanding, and perhaps for Francis' forgiveness. Francis understood why Andy had done what he did in Mammoth, but he could not relate to it and could ever forgive him, or trust him. He had murdered innocents to prove his loyalty to Babel, and he would do it again. Serving a greater cause did not excuse him, or justify him, from doing wrong. Francis did not care how God thought about it, but he himself did not like it one bit.

"What do you hope to accomplish?" Jessie asked, dedicated to prying for answers.

"Stopping the Pillar Project, and ultimately the destruction of Babel."

"How are you going to accomplish that?" Jessie continued her bombardment of questions.

"I'm only creating a diversion here and perhaps an effort to hinder Babel's progress. But the real plan…" He paused, as if he needed time to weigh the importance of mankind's fate with the information he was going to divulge. "Now it's neither the time nor place to discuss this matter. In time…"

"And what do you expect us to do?"

"Only to forget what you have seen tonight, that is all I ask." That, Francis could do. He already did not want to remember. "I have one question. Do either of you know about Project Lilitu."

The scientist shook his head.

"I only know of it," Andy answered. "To tell you the truth, it's something that involves you. That's all I know."

It did not make sense, Francis thought. The information was right there in the computer system, which was probably wiped out now. He could not believe that neither of them had seen it. Yet they did not seem to be lying. Perhaps it was something about himself that he absolutely could not know, something that would change the course of everything. He decided not to pursue it further. "How many people have they done this to?"

"You mean how many have been made into…" said the scientist reluctantly. "Hosts?"

Francis nodded.

"We do not know." Bill sighed. "After the early phase of the experiment, after the drug has been stabilized, all the scientists involved were converted. It was to keep our mouth shut and remain loyal. Some of us did not make it, naturally. And the rest of us, our survival depended on our loyalty. None of us had access to the pills, and none of us could make it on our own. Even though some of us tried to escape the grasp of Babel, none escaped alive." A pained, deeply troubled face surfaced as he paused to let out a breath of air. "Then they started on selected employees, and perhaps even outside people that were willing to pay for power, and maybe people whom Babel wanted to control. Perhaps the government, the police, and the bureau are already under Babel's control. It would not be hard to accomplish, as Babel has already created a group of elite assassins, a group consisting of very powerful gifted who complete important tasks for Babel. That is one reason why so many people were subjected to the drug, because they wanted to find the most powerful of Pillars."

"Anyhow, we must go back to attend the rest of the meeting," Andy said. "We'll talk again, soon."

After the two men left, they headed back to the car. Jessie was unusually silent, and Francis wondered if what she had dreamed had impacted her just as much as it did him. He himself felt a forlorn disparity, about the salvation of his own soul. Never had he believed in any other moral codes than his own, and he had abided by them until now. No matter how he tried to hide it, how he tried to cover it with other emotions, his humanity was forever changed. He was no longer the Francis Seto he once was. He was now something different, something evil. Project Lilitu, he conjectured, was about his humanity hanging on the scale.

CHAPTER TWENTY-SEVEN

The previous night they had parted early after the fellowship. Francis felt that he should have told her about his problem, she was a good listener, making him communicate in a way that he had never dreamed possible. She connected with him and made his world feel real. However he did not know what to say. He could not bring himself to say that he despised his cursed power, hated himself, and loathed the dark soul he now possessed. He did not think she'd understand, and did not want her to despise him. In addition to that, she seemed plagued by an insurmountable trouble. Perhaps, she too, experienced a shocking dark side to her soul.

Once again he had dreamed powerful dreams – dreams that stirred his desire like a single droplet of water in an unending desert, dreams that made him wake up panting, sweating, shuddering, and wanting more. Leaving his bed, he stood in the shower, not knowing for how long he needed to wash himself clean. It seemed like an eternity was not enough.

The phone rang, forcing him to end his cleansing ritual. Andy needed Jessie's phone number, saying that he wanted to make sure that she was not going to involve the police in what she had seen last night. Francis knew she was not going to. And if she were, probably no amount of talk would convince her otherwise. After all she was a strong willed woman. Nevertheless he gave it to his manager, now murderer, and secret religious leader of an uprising. He did not know whether to admire him, or hate him.

He decided to go back to work. Not that he had to, not that Andy told him to. It was the only thing to do to calm himself, as he could no longer find solace in his imaginary worlds.

His damaged computers were replaced. Since all of his projects resided on a remote server, his work was not hindered.

Andy had already dropped him a few emails about directions for improvements on his current projects. They had made a habit of not communicating verbally when it came to assigning work because emails were easily tracked and could be read over and over again for clarity.

It was odd that he did not feel disgusted at working inside the corporation that changed him. Hating Babel was an undeniable concept that had tattooed itself to his mind, but being inside Babel was another different idea entirely. He did not detest the dull metal cubicles of this office, nor the towering buildings, nor the recreational facilities. Everything there gave him an eerie sense of belonging, like he was home. Perhaps what Andy said was true, they were all drawn to this place with their fate intertwined to this nexus of power, the root of all evil, like moths drawn to a flame.

The hours passed by. It was already evening when Kyle paid him a surprise visit and asked if he wanted to go get a drink.

"Sure, I could use one. How did you know I was here anyway?"

"Pure luck, I guess. I had something to finish off and I just decided to see if anyone was around."

They settled at one of the tables in the corner of the Ravens, far from any crowd. Francis ordered a Bailey's, which he had taken a liking to ever since Jessie introduced it to him, plus some barbecued wings. He was famished. Kyle ordered a Gin and Tonic.

"So, how are you holding up?" Kyle started.

It took a while before he understood the question. "I'm surviving."

"Good." The waitress came with the drinks and the food. Francis quickly took a bite. He could not believe he was so engrossed in work that he had totally ignored his stomach. "You got any questions?"

Actually he had too many, and would not know where to begin. "Andy. You know about everything that he did?"

Kyle nodded, taking a sip from his glass. "I do. Even though morally I do not approve of everything that he has done, he's admirable in his ambition. And perhaps he's the one that will give us an opportunity to topple…" He paused to search for a word to replace Babel, "our oppressor."

"What's his real plan?"

"That's for him to reveal. The fact is that I do not know. When the time comes, he's going to reveal it. And I know it's going to involve us. He had told me that the uprising is only going to be a diversion, for us to strike at the heart of Babel."

How is that going to be done? Where is the heart of this international, multibillion corporation? Kyle probably had no idea either. So he decided not to pursue the matter any further. "So how did you get involved, how did you end up here?"

"That's a long story. Something happened in my life, and I almost lost the will to live. I found out about this job soon after, and it was almost as if it was meant for me. I was the only agent in the…" He lowered his voice to a whisper, "Bureau that was not on a case at the time and had extensive computer experience. It was perfect so I volunteered, knowing the danger involved. However, I don't know what I'm doing anymore." He sighed. "They changed me. And the more I worked here, the more I felt like I belonged here. I still report back to headquarters to my supervisor. But they've only told me to stay put and gather as much information as possible. It sounded like nothing but an excuse to tell me to stay here and not bother them with calls. I don't even know who in the Bureau I can trust anymore."

"So how high does this thing go?"

"Higher than you can ever imagine, Francis." Kyle's eyes darted around furtively behind his wire-framed glasses. "Why do you think nobody is investigating the many disappearances Babel had orchestrated? Why do you think the Bureau hasn't done anything constructive except interfere with police work? Why do you think your lady friend in the LAPD is on vacation? And why do you think Mammoth PD hasn't bothered you any further?"

He got the picture, he thought. "So they must know about you?"

"Of course they know." Kyle smiled a desperate smile. "But knowing that it is a trap is already halfway out of it."

But not if they know that you know, then you're right where you started.

"As for why they have not eliminated me, because they don't see me as a threat. As a matter of fact, I'm still useful to them."

"Something doesn't add up," Francis observed. "You said you've been the one emailing me. But how did you know where the Tormentor was going?"

"You're very shrewd, young man. I was just going to get to that." He gulped down the rest of his drink. "Informing you about where to go was my task. Someone instructed me to send a message to you, telling you where to track down the Tormentor. As you have guessed, that someone probably manipulated the Tormentor's whereabouts."

"So I was sent there to either kill or be killed."

"Yes, as a trial of sort."

"For what? Who's playing these games?" To his surprise, he did not feel the slightest sign of agitation.

"Getting to the bottom of that, I presume, would be winning half of the game."

"What about me hacking into the system? Was that part of some instructions also?"

"That you did on your own, and I tried my best to help you stay alive. But who's not to say that they have baited you with information and you've acted the way they wanted you to. But the important thing is that you're alive now, and you already know more than you know before, you're one step closer to beating your enemy."

And who is the enemy? "So I presume you don't know anything about Project Lilitu?"

"You probably know as much as I. There was never any information about the project in the database. I only know that you are what they called Lilitu, because of your unique ability. You know that you have the power to destroy other Pillars and merge them with yourself. You can potentially become the most powerful Pillar in the world. You are the one they're afraid of. You are the one with the power to destroy them."

Francis did not want to be the most powerful Pillar in the world. He just wanted to rid himself of his curse and salvage his soul. What he wanted to do was to fight his urge to devour other Pillars, because he was afraid of what he was going to become. He decided to change the subject. "You called your power Cow, is that right?"

"Cao, short for chaos and order. She has the ability to manipulate the space between particles, thus changing the state of matters from liquid to gas to solid, of course within possible parameters."

Like him, Kyle had referred to his power as a real person. "The little girl, was she someone you knew?"

"Yes," he said, with a deep sadness in his eyes. Francis thought perhaps he had touched on a subject that was too personal. "She has the image of my daughter who passed away."

Was that the incident Kyle mentioned earlier about losing his will to continue living? Francis decided it was not his place to pry, and he did not really want to know anyway.

"What about you? Is Lilitu the image of someone you knew?"

"I prefer to call her Michelle, an old acquaintance that passed away."

"We have something in common then. Both of our Pillars are images of someone we once held dear in our memories. Not all gifted have that privilege."

It wasn't as much a privilege as perhaps a haunting facade. "How many hosts are there?"

"You prefer to use the word hosts–"

"Because I don't see it as a gift." But as a parasitic entity that was perhaps feeding on his humanity.

"Right, nobody except them know how many of us there are. But I'm sure the number is finite and not as many as one would think. After all Babel needs to keep track and control all its subjects, within a tight grasp. One bad seed like the Tormentor could create havoc in the world and create unnecessarily attention. That's just my guess, anyway." Kyle took a quick glance at his watch. "Look, I have to go."

"It's alright. I'll take care of the bill." Francis interrupted Kyle's reaching for his wallet. "I was thinking of maybe staying here for another drink."

"Okay, thank you." He stood up and extended his hand to Francis. "It's been a pleasure talking to you. Try to stay sober."

*　　　*　　　*　　　*

Jessie spent her Saturday morning in frustration. The thought of the previous night, the fellowship, had made her tremble. She had dreamed when she was awake, and she had seen things that she did not wish to see.

She was trapped in a dark closet, like the way she was trapped when she was a child. Then a man pulled her out, a man who was nothing more than a shadow, someone whose face she could not see. Yet this man felt real, and he touched her, in every way to give her the most pleasure. She was nowhere, and everywhere, aimlessly floating among darkness. Then there was a blinding flash, and she was somewhere else in a light. She was holding a baby in her arms, a newborn baby with almost no hair on its head. It was a girl, and she had big expressive eyes. Jessie felt a sense of fulfillment and joy when she looked at her and knew that the baby was hers. A hand, a man's hand was massaging her back, and the other had brushed her hair with adoration. She felt the desperate need to turn around to see the identity of this man. Yet when she turned, all she saw was a hollow shadow like a faceless ghost. It frightened her, and she had left the fellowship.

Her reckoning in the church had made her feel ashamed of herself. She had always thought that her one mission in the world was justice. The one person who had violated her and murdered her father had fled justice. And she had vowed, in front of her father's grave, that she would not let any criminals escape justice when she could help it. Somewhere deep inside, she had often wanted the one person who murdered her father to surface again, to commit a crime one more time so that she could have her vengeance. But he never did. In time the memory of this person who had forever scarred her drifted away and became locked in the depths of her subconscious.

That was not what she dreamed in the church, not avenging her father, not justice for herself. She wanted a man to love her, to build a family with her. That moment when she was held she had forgotten about everything that she stood for, wanted to forget everything that she fought for. She was just a weak little girl waiting for someone to depend on, waiting to be loved. And she hated the desire embedded deep in her heart. Love had done nothing but made her weak. It almost destroyed her during her college years. It made her forget her mission in life, her vow to her father. She needed to be strong now. She needed to avenge her late partner, and everyone who died because of Babel. Because only in seeing justice would her father see peace.

She wondered about what she really wanted in life, whether the downfall of Babel would bring her peace, whether she was using Francis to get to an ultimate evil or she was just enjoying his company.

The thoughts were making her head explode. What does it matter anyway? Maybe inside I'm just a weak little girl who needs to be loved more than anyone else. But I still have a tough armor protecting me. And I will do whatever that feels right.

Wondering about what Francis saw in the church, Jessie remembered he had turned deadly pale and had to struggle to find his way out of the room. But she was too troubled by her own dreams to ask him what he saw. She was sure that he was not going to tell her though, as she herself did not know how to tell him. She just hoped that he was not as troubled as she was. But she wanted to talk to him.

She called but nobody answered the phone. As she was wondering where he was, her phone rang. She had hoped that it was Francis but instead it was a voice that sounded oddly familiar. It was his manager, Andy Roach.

"How did you get this number?"

"Francis gave it to me. I told him I had to talk to you."

About what? "I'm listening."

"Look, can we perhaps meet somewhere and talk."

"What?"

"Do you have any dinner plans tonight?"

"What about Francis?"

"I just called him and he's not home. Did you make plans with him?"

"No, not exactly."

"Perhaps it's best if I can meet you alone anyway. Francis seems a bit agitated when he sees me."

"Not without good reason."

"I understand, and I apologize." He sounded regretful. "I was just hoping that we could be friends."

"Fine, fine, fine." She sighed and decided that it wouldn't hurt to have dinner with him. She could possibly find out more about Babel and his plans, which could be beneficial to Francis and her in the long run. Besides, she had thought him pretty attractive, not to mention quite charming and intimidating during his public speech. Then she reminded herself to not trust him, not just because he had killed two innocent men, but because Francis didn't. "OK, Mi Piace, seven-thirty."

"I know where it is."

"And it's not a date," she told him.

"Of course."

When she put down the phone, she suddenly felt guilty. She was doing something behind Francis' back. Because she had gotten an impression that Francis disliked and distrusted his manager very much so, she felt like breaking a trust of friendship just talking to Andy, let alone dining with him. But then she told herself that it was for their benefit. Knowing the true intent behind Andy's machination would help in their struggle against Babel. And they needed all the advantage they could have at the moment.

*   *   *   *

Jessie put on something young and plain. And thought about why she thought of clothing as young or old, and concluded that she must be getting old. When one was young, clothes did not have age, they were just clothes. She shook her head. Age should be the last thing she needed to worry about, for that was something she had absolutely no control over. She stared at herself in the full-length mirror, until she was satisfied that she looked just right – plain yet not unattractive.

She was three minutes early. However he had already gotten a table, which happened to be the same table where she had eaten with Francis.

"Wine?" he asked as she seated herself.

"Nah, not really a wine person." What she needed was coffee. "I'm ready to order, by the way."

"Don't have to look at the menu, huh?"
"Not really."

"You come here a lot?"

"Look, is there something you wanted to talk about?" She was irritated, not being civil. Maybe it was to cover up the guilt she felt earlier.

"Let's just order first." Ignoring her attempted rudeness, he smiled. He was wearing a dressy blue long sleeved shirt, which refined the outlines of his broad shoulders. His features were deeply chiseled like an ancient sculpture, his jaw square in an appealing way, his blue eyes penetratingly dark like the deep end of the ocean, and he moved with an arrogant bearing that was not non-pleasing to the eyes. She had not studied his features extensively the previous day, and now she had to admit that he was even more attractive than she had thought. She met his gaze and had to look away, a bit embarrassed.

"I just wanted to ask you what you thought of the fellowship," he said, after the waiter left with their order.

She looked around at the few occupied tables surrounding them and lowered her voice to an audible whisper. "You guys are terrorists, with God's permission or not. And I can't believe I'm having this conversation with you at this moment."

"But you are, therefore you see some redeeming qualities in me."

"So what do you want from me, really?"

"Actually I want your understanding and compassion. And I want the same thing from Francis, but I don't think I can have a conversation with him in friendly terms, not yet anyway. But you can. And I want both of you to help me in my cause. The only way to defeat Babel is us working together."

"You know I'm not going to participate in any illegal or terrorist activity. It's hard enough that I don't expose you, or arrest you."

"Oh you are not going to do that. You have nothing to gain from it." He was sure, and he was right, in a disturbingly sort of way. "You know that nobody was hurt during the fire."

Before she wanted to say something, he continued, "And yet I killed two innocent people, right? Do you think I'm evil, detective?"

The waiter came with their dishes, and most importantly, her coffee.

"I'm not qualified to be the judge of that," she answered after the waiter left. "Just because you preach Christianity and fight as an enemy of evil doesn't make you good. But no, I don't see the madness in you as I have seen in some killers. You don't kill for pleasure, but you will for the things you believe in." And he would kill her, if Babel asked him to prove his loyalty, or if she stood in the way of his religious uprising. Suddenly she felt her heart pounding in a violent rhythm.

"You're a fair judge of character." He smiled. It was a gentle smile, but it did not calm her heart one bit. "Francis' prejudice against me, to the truth, I suspect, is not just because of the way I deceived him back in Mammoth. My Pillar, for some odd reason, signified something that he's afraid of, is that true?"

Francis had told her briefly about the gift his father had given him when he was a child. Even though she suspected it was hallucination perhaps due to a childhood fear, she had understood him perfectly. That was his weakness. He had confided in her, trusted her, so she was not going to give him away. "It's not like that. But the truth is nobody likes clowns, especially scary looking ones with a face like the devil."

He nodded, accepting her simple explanation. "I do admit, Joker has his fearful side. However one must not judge a book by its cover–"

I hope I never would. So just like Francis, he had named his Pillar entity and treated it like a person. She thought it was a bit unsettling.

"The truth is that Joker is really an angel in disguise. I saw him first when I was a teenager, and I thought I was haunted by a boogieman. When I learned to control him, I had become a healer. That's when I started believing in God, because He has given me a unique gift to repair the broken and heal the sick. After college and a few working years, I came to know of this corporation felt the shadow loomed behind it. I knew it was my destiny to work here, to cleanse this place of the taint of evil."

How noble of him, Jessie said to herself. She had to admit that he had a very charismatic quality, that of a natural leader. His intoxicating smile and powerful voice could ensorcel his audience. "So you're saying your coming to work in Babel is pure coincidence?"

"Ah, but there are no coincidences. Fate is what has drawn me to this place. It was the path that God laid for me."

Faith was such a mysterious concept people who believed it sometimes seemed insane in others' eyes. But some had told her that those who had faith was always enveloped in joy and purpose and would never find themselves lost in life. She had always wondered if it was real or an illusion. "Has it ever occurred to you that you might have been a product of an early experiment of Babel?"

"That is entirely possible. But whether it's a genetic mutation from birth, or experimental human intervention. It is God's gift and message to me, that I must use this gift to help mankind."

Faith answers everything, that's what you get when you talk with religious fanatics. "Okay, so how many have these permanent abilities?"

"I've always thought that I was the only other one, until I met Francis."

"The only other one?"

"The person who created Babel," he said, lowering his voice to a barely audible volume. "Enoch Jeremy Bel. He is the one who directs project Pillar, he is the mastermind behind all the evil schemes Babel has committed, and he is the one who wants to control the world."

"How can you be so sure?" And don't tell me God told you so.

"I'm sure because I have talked to him, and I know. Project Pillar's beginning has to be based on a prototype. He could not have invented how to change the genetic codes of the human brain just by whim and accident. He was that prototype. And I know his ambition. He wants to change humankind. And he wants to attain godhood. He's our one true enemy." An intense hate was radiating from his blue eyes, and his fist was clenched.

He seemed to have been truthful about everything that he had said. She had told herself that just because he claimed to be a man of God, and just because he was distractingly attractive, she should hear everything he said with a strong sense of doubt. But she believed him.

"So what's your plan? An assassination attempt?"

He sighed, looking a bit lost. "I haven't finalized a solid plan yet. But whatever we're going to do, we can only pray that we will not die trying. Enoch Bel possibly possesses the most powerful Pillar in the world, and nobody knows his true ability, not to mention that he has the command of a group of elites that is equally foreboding."

"But you're not afraid, right?"

"Oh I am afraid, but not for my own life. But because the fate of mankind depends on our success, I'm afraid it's just too heavy a burden for me to uphold. Therefore I need others to carry this burden with me. Mostly you, and Francis."

"Me? What do you need me for? I don't have any special powers."

"I see the determination and courage in your eyes, and we need that very much to defeat our enemies."

"That's just a pretty way of saying 'I need you to convince Francis, but tag along if you like'."

"No, no, it's not like that. You are as valuable as anyone else, gifted or not."

"Can we eat now?"

"Of course, the food is getting cold." He closed his eyes to deliver a solemn, silent prayer before he started his meal.

During and after the meal, they had not mentioned the sensitive subject of Babel anymore. Jessie found out that they had gone to the same university, albeit different years. At length they had discussed college life. After that her enmity and distrust of him seemed to have dissolved. He proved to be like any other guy except that he was charming and a marvelous conversationalist. He had told her how in college he had struggled not to draw attention to himself.

He commented that if one looked hard enough, one would be amazed to see how many things in the world were actually broken, and needed fixing, though he could not fix broken hearts.

They each paid for their own share of the meal, as she insisted. After dinner they took a walk on the quaint downtown streets of Brea.

"Why do you keep trailing behind me? You are not staring at my ass, are you?"

"No, no," he chuckled. "I was just thinking, I'm sorry. I did not mean to be rude. But now that you mention it, it's not unpleasant to the eyes."

She saw an image of herself going bright red. And she decided to just leave it at that. "Look, I should get back."

"Sure, I understand. Thank you for coming out here and listen to me babble."

She gave him a smile, bid him farewell, and returned to her car. When she sat in her car, she found that her heart was pounding. She was intrigued and intimidated. And she did not know if it was a good, or a bad thing.

CHAPTER TWENTY-EIGHT

"Babel Cydonia is almost nearing its final stage, a giant pyramid structures that sits in the industrial area of Everett, Washington. Here are a few words from the president of Babel Corps, Doctor Enoch Bel."

"Why a pyramid, Doctor Bel?"

"It's always been a childhood dream, to build something so massive, and to build something that's such a defining representation of the glorious accomplishment of human civilization."

"What is the pyramid going to be used for?"

"It'll be a number of things. It'll be offices, labs, and an indoor theme park that is going to be opened to the public, and it's going to be my home."

"So when do you think the public will get to see the inside of it?"

"Probably another six months to a year."

"I can hardly wait. Thanks for your time, Doctor Bel."

"No problem."

"Here's Shannon O'Donald of channel—"

Francis took his eyes off the big projection TV then. After his third glass he was feeling giddy and oblivious to his surroundings. Most importantly he forgot what he needed to think about. Perhaps that was what he wanted, the urge to just lay down and not think about anything at all. The place was getting considerably more packed as the night got deeper. He felt strangely relaxed.

A woman stood up from her table, walked towards his, and seated herself across him. "Are you alright?"

Francis nodded. There was something familiar about the face, but he couldn't place it in his blank mind.

"You wouldn't mind if I sit here, do you? It's awfully lonely drinking by myself." She was dark-skinned, Hispanic, very beautiful, with dark curly hair that poured down her shoulders like a mane of a lioness. She was business attired, with a dark shirt he couldn't tell whether blue or black in the faint lighting and a skirt of perhaps a lighter color.

"You do remember me, don't you?" She pouted in a sensual way.

He remembered seeing her lips before. He frantically searched his mind and after what seemed a long moment of memory plundering, he found his answer. She was the woman who interviewed him. No, he corrected himself. She was the one who spoke to him and supposedly made him feel comfortable before his interview. And he faintly remembered seeing her the last time he was here.

"Sophie?"

"Yes," she smiled at his recollection. "And you are Francis, if I remember right."

He gave a nod of confirmation.

"Boy, you look a lot more grown up than I last saw you at the interview. I mean that in a good way, of course," she added after seeing his grimace. "More mature and confident."

It was less than a year ago. Francis thought she was just making conversation – conversation that he did not care to have. "It must be the light."

She gave out a short giggle.

It's not meant to be funny.

"So how's work treating you? You like it here?"

"Yeah, it's not bad."

"So how come you are here drinking alone?"

If it's any of your business, isn't that what bars are for? "I came with a friend after work, but he left earlier. I just felt like staying for a while, to relax a bit."

"It is very relaxing here. I come all the time, usually on weekdays though."

"You look like you just got off work. I didn't think that HR has to work weekends." He observed, and started wondering why he was talking to this woman instead of telling her to shut up and leave him alone. Sure she was a pretty thing to look at, but he was not exactly in the mood to gawk at women at the moment. Maybe he was drunk; no, he was just buzzed. Or maybe it was Jessie's influence that made him communicate with people.

"Not usually. But I got a lot of paperwork to do, and I haven't been quite productive earlier this week."

"Oh, why is that?" To the truth, he was not really interested. He just did not want to rudely leave the threads of conversation hanging.

She ordered a drink before telling him. She mentioned her failed relationships, and it continued to work-related problems and difficulties with friends. She said that some of her girlfriends thought of her as too promiscuous and aggressive. Guys she dated either cheated on her or felt insecure about their relationships.

The way she had poured out her heart he felt like being at the other end of a confession booth, or psychotherapy. Even though her life seemed a mess, compared to his problems it felt like a droplet of water in an ocean. He did not exactly felt sorry for her, first of all because he did not know her, and secondly because it seemed that she had brought all her problems to herself. She would have been free of restraint if she too denounced the world like he did. People could not hurt you anymore if you simply did not care. Yet he thought better than to give such advice.

For each three drinks she ordered, he had one. He thought that he should not drink anymore, for he did not know his own tolerance. Yet he ordered drink after drink anyway. Because it felt impolite to make her do all the drinking by herself, not to mention she was already doing most of the talking. He sipped his drink slowly though, not wanting to get drunk.

She was becoming incoherent and even unfocused as she had more. He had to stop her from ordering more before she slumped back like a half-dead animal. When he looked at the watch it was already past one o'clock. He went over to her, trying to shake her to her senses.

"Hey, where do you live? Let me give you a ride home."

"Don't... don't wanna go," she murmured. "Your place... back to your place."

He sighed. "Can you even walk?"

She gave more than a few dramatic nods with her eyes half opened, leering at him with lunacy. He pulled her up after taking care of the bill. She seemed to be able to walk, staggering left and right like a boat sail amidst a storm.

Francis put one of her arms over his shoulder, letting her lean on him for support as he walked back to the parking lot. While wondering what sort of unnecessarily mischief he had gotten himself into, the gardenlike smell of her hair, one side of her firm breasts brushing against his arm, he felt himself a little bit aroused. It was a feeling he had missed, welcomed, and even treasured. Because it was human, much more human than the sensations he felt when the succubus did her work. And he needed more than anything to be reminded that he was still human.

Back at the apartment he guided her to his bed, and she fell down limp and asleep instantly. He felt a sense of déjà vu and remembered he had almost done the identical thing a few days back when he carried Jessie back from the ordeal with the Tormentor. It was only a few days ago, but it felt like years. A lot had happened since then. He shrugged. After taking her shoes off, he tried to shuffle Sophie into a more comfortable position. As he tugged at her waist, she moaned. One of her hands flung towards him and grabbed his arm, pulling him to her. When he staggered, almost crushed into her, he propped himself up with one elbow and his face was less than an inch away from her sensual, inviting lips. There was a very long moment of weakness, of struggle. Then he pulled himself up, out of her reach. Although he was in desperate need to prove himself human, taking advantage of a drunk woman was not the human thing to do, he thought. Thankfully she did not insist, her hand let go and her half-closed eyes shut themselves again. He stood up and covered her with a blanket.

He felt dizzy then, as if a spell suddenly came over him. He knew he had a little bit too much to drink. Even though he had managed to drive home safely, he was not used to heavy alcohol intake and he felt so buzzed that his head was almost exploding. He knew he was walking a thin line between sober and drunk. Either way he was dead tired, so tumbling onto his couch seemed the only sensible thing to do. He closed his eyes, emerging into darkness.

*   *   *   *

Bright light spread before him when he opened his eyes, and he realized he was lying on his back, looking up at the ceiling of some institutional room, all insulated tiles and easy-clean surfaces.

Hospital. How did I get here?

Trying to remember what had happened, Francis could only faintly recalled who he was. His memory felt so uncomfortably distant, like a close friend suddenly becoming a total stranger.

Looking around at the room, he saw white walls, and a bouquet of flowers on the cupboard at the end of his bed. He was definitely in a hospital, even wearing some sort of patient's robe.

He heard the sound of a door opening. A nurse walked in. She was young, Asian, and her uniform looked strange. Different from his recollection of what nurses wore when he was last in a hospital, even different from what he saw on TV. Yet her attire told him that she was definitely a nurse.

The nurse looked at him and he saw momentary shock in her eyes, as if she had not expected to see him awake. She turned back into the corridor and called out for someone.

The nurse was speaking Cantonese. Perhaps he wasn't in the United States, that's why the nurse's uniform looked different.

A man with a white coat came in. He was short and stocky with thick glasses.

"I'm Doctor Woo." He said with a smile that was meant to be comforting. Francis thought it was not doing much for him.

"Where am I?" he asked, in Cantonese.

"This is Queen Mary Hospital." He knew of the place. Not where exactly, but he knew it was somewhere in Hong Kong.

"What am I doing here?"

"You've had a bad accident."

"I mean what am I doing in Hong Kong?"

"What do you mean?" the doctor said, looking confused for a moment. "You live here, Mr. Seto. You have suffered some severe head injuries, and it might have affected your memory. But let me assure you that it's only temporary. In time everything will come back to you. What's the last thing you remember?"

It was strange that anyone called him by his last name. Francis thought about the question, but nothing came to mind. "I'm not quite sure. How long have I been here?"

"You were in a coma, Mr. Seto–"

"Please, just Francis." The formality was clearly getting on his nerves.

"As I was saying, you've been in a coma for almost up to a month and a half now. We didn't know when you were going to wake up, but it's good that you finally did. We've notified your wife, she's on her way right now."

"What?" He wasn't sure if he heard it right. "My wife?"

"Yes, she's on her way."

"What day is this?"

"October 10th."

"The year?"

"2006."

Oh my God. The last thing he remembered was the year 2001. And it was summer, and he remembered he was in a lot of trouble. He was fighting against something. He didn't know what. He couldn't place it. Everything felt like a distant dream. He said nothing to the doctor, only managed a few faint nods.

The doctor assured that he was all right and told him to get some rest, as if he hadn't had enough already. When he left, Francis raised his hand and stared at the wedding band on his finger. It was plain, just like anybody else's ring, but on his finger it felt like a distinctly foreign object. He did not remember putting it on there, it felt alien. It was something that did not belong.

He heard footsteps, the clicking noise made by high heels. Right after the door opened, he was caught in an embrace before he had a chance to look at who it was.

"Oh, my love. You're all right." The smell of her was familiar. He looked up and he knew that he recognized her. Her skin was lighter than he remembered, but it was still tanned a healthy brown. Her hair was straighter and longer, and curled in natural waves. Her eyes were dark and intelligent. The thing that stood out most was her lips, which seemed to be in an eternal pout, yet sensual beyond measure. She was more beautiful than he remembered.

"Sophie?" He spoke English, so that's what he'd figure that was the language they communicated to each other with, despite they were in Hong Kong. "I... I..." He didn't know what to tell her really. So he just held her close to him, brushing her hair with his hand. It felt good to have someone to hold on to.

"How are you feeling?" she whispered, caressing his ear with her warm breath.

"Good, and I really need to get away from this bed."

"The doctor told me you have amnesia."

"Yeah, I seem to be missing a good chunk of five years, maybe even more."

"At least you still remember my name." She stared into his eyes and smiled. "Oh I missed you so much." She gave him a few soft kisses on the lips.

But I don't really remember who you are. Yet he just held her there and kissed her back, as passionately as could. He did not really care if he really knew this woman, or if he loved this woman. He was sure in time he would remember. And he could feel this woman's love and care towards him, which made him feel so invigorated, so full of life, and it was a feeling that he remembered that he'd hold on to for the rest of his life.

A knock on the door interrupted their moment. Doctor Woo came in. Sophie asked if Francis could leave right away. The doctor replied that there were a few documents to sign and he needed to schedule a checkup and an appointment for therapy with his amnesia, but he could go home. The doctor's English was not very fluent, but it was understandable.

Sophie brought him a change of clothing, a somewhat formal-looking shirt and khakis. He felt weird putting a shirt on, as if he had not done so in ages. He had remembered himself not to be a shirt person, but he realized that it was because of the lapses from his amnesia.

"Is there a mirror?" he asked after everything was done and the doctor said he was ready to go.

"In the bathroom," Sophie said. "Why, you look fine."

He saw that he had put on more mass than he last remembered. Yet instead of being slim, he had gained muscle. He felt more confident, as if he could walk around naked and be proud. He stared at himself in the mirror. His hair was longer, and he might have looked older. He was still the same Francis Seto.

A driver in an E-class Mercedes was waiting for them at the front entrance to the hospital. On the way home he watched the city of Hong Kong from the window. Not much had changed from the time he had remembered – the crowds, the towering buildings, the traffic, and everywhere you went you were still in a metropolitan. He had too many questions he wanted to ask his wife, but he did not know where to begin. He found out that he was the CTO of Babel Hong Kong. Three years ago they moved here when the Hong Kong division of the corporation was started. They married four years ago and had an eleven month old daughter named Jessica. He asked about the accident and she told him that he was driving by himself and a truck ran a red light and hit him, totaling the car.

"Do you remember where we met?" Sophie asked, her hands grasping his tightly.

"I think so. I was still in college, it was during the interview."

"And I thought you were really cute. Of course I did not have any jurisdiction whether you get hired or not. I just sorted out the resumes and talked to each of you about the company. Who knew we would be here today?" She leaned her head on his shoulder. "Do you remember the first time we dated?"

"I think we met again in the bar." He tried to remember what happened afterwards, but he couldn't. For a moment his head ached.

"Are you okay?"

"Yes, I'm fine. I just can't remember anything afterwards. My head hurts if I tried to think about it."

"Don't think too hard then, honey. It'll come back to you. Yes, we met at the Ravens and you took me back to your place because I was really drunk. You were a real gentleman, didn't even lay a hand on me. In the morning, I wouldn't let you get away. We made love all day and then fell in love with each other."

One of her hands had moved down to his crotch, massaging him. He was already aroused, and she made him yearn against his trousers.

"We're going to go home. And we'll make love," she murmured with a determined sparkle in her eyes. "When you relive the good old times, everything will come back to you."

They owned an apartment, or flat, as the British called it, which was the penthouse of a tall residential building on the hills, just overlooking the financial district – Central and the Victoria harbor. Land was expensive in Hong Kong, and scarcely anyone owned houses like in the States. Their apartment was already considered extremely extravagant compared to the majority of the middle class.

The interior of their apartment was beautiful – the living room with a wall-sized tilted glass window just overlooking the harbor had paintings and tapestries, adorned like something out of the Victorian era. While the dining room was more in the flavor of ancient Chinese design, with handcrafted statues, Chinese calligraphy, and wooden furniture, he had no recollection of how the idea of the interior design developed, but it was brilliant and he loved it.

The first thing he wanted to check on was his daughter. It wasn't a very huge apartment so he went into one of the three rooms and found her in a cradle. An older Chinese woman, dressed as a maid, was with her. She nodded at his presence and left the room hurriedly, as if her presence in some way offended him. He reached down the cradle and touched his daughter's face, which was warm to the touch. She was light-skinned like him, with only a small patch of black hair. She was beautiful, innocent, and very much asleep. He bet that she had her mother's eyes.

He walked into the bedroom, which was not large but comfortable. The design was modern, and much plainer than the living room. He surmised that was what he'd have wanted because he was not sure if he was comfortable sleeping in a bedroom out of the Victorian era or one of the dynasties from ancient China.

He went into the adjoining bathroom and prepared for a shower. Taking off his clothes, he took a good look at himself on the mirror. He was still lean but muscular, as he had suspected. His biceps were twice as thick as he had remembered and he even had a faint outline of six packs on his stomach. Everything about him was physically so different, as if he was a in a stranger's body. Yet he wore the same face and when he looked into his own copper eyes he saw only himself.

When the hot water splashed upon him he remembered someone he knew back in the days when he was still in the States, a woman. It was someone important to him, someone that had made a difference in his life. He couldn't recall who it was. It remained a shadow that lurked in the depths of his torn mind. Whoever it was, he wondered how she was doing now, and wondered if he still kept in contact with her. If only he could figure out whom it was.

The doubts were instantly erased when he came out of the shower and saw Sophie waiting for him. She was still quite fully clothed, the fabric of the dress covering the swell of her bosom. Yet his throat was dry and he was fully aroused.

He kissed her, undressing her gently, yet with urgent passion. Not only was she beautiful, she was the mother of their child and the woman who he loved and was spending the rest of his life with. His heart pounded, as if he was going to make love with her the first time and did not know what it was going to be like. That was true in a way, and the anticipation of it was exhilarating.

He lifted her onto the sink, and she took hold of him and guided him inside her. Then he began moving, circling his hips, first slowly and gently. Gradually speeding up, he soon grinded against her. She gripped his arms. As her moans became louder, he sensed them peaking. As if attempting to hasten the culmination of her own pleasure, she wrapped her legs around him and thrust back in return. That greedy desire made him explode. He spent himself inside her, spurting until he felt his loins emptied. She held him tight against her as she shook and shrieked with gratification.

Later as he lay in bed, staring at the white ceiling, with his wife in his arms, he thought about his life. He had gained fame, fortune, and family. He didn't know how he advanced to the position of CTO being so young, he did not know how he won the heart of such a beautiful woman. He had everything that one would have wanted. He wondered what happened to things of his past – books, games, imaginary worlds. Did he not need those things anymore? Were they but a distance past forever buried in a grave which spawned his grownup life? What had happened during the period of five years? And what had made him forget about it, if it was the happiest of his life? Could amnesia be so strangely selective? Yet, he wondered, if he was content about this life. The perfection of it troubled him.

When Sophie was asleep, he decided to see his daughter. He wanted to see her eyes. When he was in the child's room, he noticed something. There was an oil painting hanging on the far end of the room. Depicted was a clown with an evil looking face embracing a small Asian woman with short hair, who looked oddly familiar. It looked like the clown was about to kiss the woman, who showed a mixture of terror and anticipation in her eyes. The clown, though, sent a chill down his spine. He remembered his old childhood fear, and the existence of a more recent event that triggered his fear. He couldn't place it, as if his memories about certain things had been blurred and his mind fractured into pieces that could not connect with each other.

There was something wrong with the apartment; in fact there was something wrong with the whole world of 2006. He knew because he would not put a painting of a clown up anywhere in his home, much less his daughter's room. He had been in the middle of a battle five years ago, a battle he did not want to fight yet had been drawn into. And he was still in the middle of it.

He went back to Sophie. Shaking her awake, he planned to confront her.

"Who are you?" He grabbed her arms and sat atop her, pinning her down on the bed.

"What are you talking about, my love? You're hurting me."

"Who are you? They sent you, didn't they?"

"I don't know what you're talking about. You are not yourself, you need rest. Just go to sleep and you'll be fine tomorrow."

"No, there was no accident. This is not real." There was doubt in his mind, if he was doing the right thing or not. He was not sure, but he went ahead anyway. His hands went to her neck, his thumbs on the fragile flesh of her throat. He strangled her.

She opened her mouth, but made no sound. He felt her pulse quickening, thumping against his fingers. Everything seemed so real to him and he thought that maybe he made a mistake. As he squeezed her bare throat, he felt her struggle cease, her life slipping away. Just when he was beginning to feel sorry for her, her skin was turning a metallic color. Her eyes became dark voids without pupils, and her hair became as orange as the sun. She pushed him away with an enormous strength and sat up on the bed, laughing like a lunatic.

"Francis Seto, you are a fool to not stay in the future where you can live happily ever after. Instead you choose to break the curse. Know that you have not won. Now I will take you to your past. That's where you shall be broken."

Things shifted around him as he was in the middle of the vortex. His apartment was torn apart like a sheet of paper and blackness enveloped him. He floated in the darkness like an astronaut drifting in space without propulsion to move him forward.

Light slipped in and tore away the darkness, he found himself in a familiar room. The metallic woman who had resembled Sophie stood beside him. She showed no desire to fight or kill him. As she said, she was there to show him something. What he did not know.

But his memory had come back to him. He knew it was still the summer of 2001, and he had taken Sophie back to his apartment. She must have faked her drunken condition, in order to draw him into her trap. He did not know what kind of power she had, but he suspected that the android like thing standing next to him was her Pillar. If she wanted to attack him, she could have caught him off guard anytime. Maybe she was not capable of physical attack. That was why she had chosen the path of mental assault.

He looked away from the metallic entity, towards a large bed in the middle of a bedroom. A naked man was on the bed, his attention focused on the woman under him. Her legs were locked around his hips, his buttocks bunched and released to the rhythm of his movements. Francis turned away, embarrassed.

"Go ahead and have a closer look." The android's voice was crisp, clear, and still sounded like Sophie's, yet now with a taint of being mechanical. "They can't see you. We're only here as observers, visiting the hidden depths of your memory."

My memory? He went closer. The moans of the woman disturbed him, making him feel like a peeping tom. He recognized her. It was Michelle, not the phantom he had seen, but alive. The man on top of her was none other than himself. The shock sent him stumbling backwards. This was the night in Mammoth, spring of 1998.

"Let me take you to the morning," the mechanical version of Sophie said, snapping her finger.

Once again everything spun around them. When things stabilized and he could feel the solid floor with his feet, he saw the sunshine through the closed curtains. The couple drawn together by fate, or perhaps accident, lay in each other's arms, talking quietly to each other.

They talked about school and classes. Francis had remembered everything that was said, to the very word. Sophie's Pillar was not lying to him, this was real in some way, or it had been. Now he was but an invisible observer to his own act, drifting in a space and time that was antediluvian.

"So what are we going to do from now on?" Francis of the past asked.

"What do you mean?" Michelle said snuggling next to him.

"I mean, how are we going to see each other?"

She gave off a soft laugh. "Francis, I don't even know you."

"But you said you loved me last night." Wait a minute, this conversation never happened. It was not the way he remembered it.

"Of course I did, we were making love. People making love say that to each other all the time."

"And you didn't mean it?"

"How can I possibly love you? I don't even know you."

"And you don't plan to get to know me?"

"Look." She turned his face to look at her. He trembled. "I wanted to fuck last night. I have that craving from time to time when I don't have a boyfriend. And I'm not looking for one right now. I was at the bar last night, and you happened to be there. I saw you looking at me. I felt you wanting me. I found you attractive, so I decided to have you for the night. There's really nothing more to it than a simple one night stand. If you want to fuck me now again, we can. But it'll be the last time."

As she was reaching over to kiss him, he pushed her away and stood up, an angry scowl on his face. That was what he'd imagine himself looking when he found that Sam had betrayed him back in high school.

I don't remember any of this, none of this happened.

She leaned over, trying to reach him with her hand. A small wind kicked up, a localized gust that swirled about the room. That wind picked up speed and soon became an unseen force so powerful that even now, standing there as an oblivious observer to his own memory, Francis felt it.

This force threw Michelle backward, pinning her against the wall behind the bed. Francis from the past now stared at the scene with his mouth agape, not knowing what had happened, not knowing what to do.

Francis the observer looked towards Michelle, who was magically stuck on the wall. Her mouth was wide open, as if she was screaming, but there was no sound. Her face was becoming pale, and there were red marks on her throat. There were marks of unseen fingers. There were marks of an invisible strangler.

A short moment later the wind died and the limp body of Michelle dropped onto the bed with a loud thump. Francis from the past had retreated to a corner, his face distorted with terror.

Then he found himself checking Michelle's body. She was dead. He stood there for a long moment, murmuring to himself, trying to figure out what to do. After he got dressed, he picked up her dress and scattered underwear from the floor. Then he dressed her like someone dressing a mannequin.

Francis turned away, sick of his own act. "I did not do this, this is not real."

"Oh yes, you did." He saw a smile of victory behind Sophie's mechanical face, even though her mouth did not even twitch. "Now, let's fast forward to the next scene."

Everything once again shifted and he found himself floating in midair. Looking down he saw himself dragging the body into the car. In the bird's eye view he watched himself drive off. He watched the car slowly climbing up the tight canyon. There was the truck coming down in the opposite lane with the speed of a diving eagle, much too fast for a heavy vehicle in a steep incline with a particularly tight maneuverable space. Everything was almost identical to the way he remembered it, except now that he was looking at events in a third person's point of view.

Francis in this strange version of the past was not trying to avoid the head on collision. He seemed to have welcomed it, plunging ahead to the oncoming truck. However at the last minute, the wheel was turned, and the car spun away like a whirlwind. It went off the rocky cliff in a gust of sand, tumbling down the slope like a snowball. Francis closed his eyes, looking away from the horrid scene of the accident. "This is not how it happened. She was alive when we were still in the car. I did not kill her. You think you can show me a false past and try to break me? It's not that easy."

The void of Sophie's eyes stared at him, judging him. She was smiling in victory, yet her mechanical face showed no emotion. "I constructed the future from your desires, and I made the past from your memories. I have only showed you truth."

But I have done none of those things. Have I?

"Your inner power awakened when you became angry, and you killed her. Yet you lied to yourself, clouding your own memories. You have succeeded in fooling yourself, but you cannot fool me. I can find every hidden secret within your mind."

No I will not listen to you. To question myself I have admitted defeat. I have murdered no one.

The android moved her hand, as if preparing to smite him. Suddenly her hands went to her head, clutching it as if it was about to explode. She screamed a bone-rattling wail that was bordering on madness.

Everything shifted once again, this time dramatically dizzier.

He was back on his couch in his own room. He looked up and saw Sophie standing there looking down at him. Her eyes were transfixed in a moment of shock and despair. A trail of blood ran down one side of her nose. He looked up and saw a bullet hole on her forehead, a deep dark aperture that ended her life. She took one step back and doubled backwards like a fallen chess piece.

He turned around and saw the angel that had come to his rescue – Jessie.

CHAPTER TWENTY-NINE

"What are we going to do with the body?" He stared at Sophie, lying lifeless on the ground. The only indication of life there ever existed within her was the blood still dripping from her head wound.

"We're going to dispose of it."

"We're not going to call the cops?"

"Francis, I am the cops. Besides, what are you going to say to them? Do you have any garbage bags?"

He went to get it. "Jessie, you are so calm." And he was shaking, panicking like a child who broke his parents' rules waiting to be punished.

"I've seen many deaths before, remember? And don't worry about this. Nobody is going to file a missing person's report. Babel has it all covered, she probably wont even be ID-ed if she was found." They shoved the body into the bag and tried their best to clean up the blood. Is this my second time moving a dead body? The mere thought of it occupied his mind with dread.

"How did you know I was in trouble anyway?"

"I called at two and nobody answered. I knew you weren't going to be out that late so I came to check on you, in case you were in trouble." She stared up from what they were doing and gave him a reassuring smile. "Your door wasn't locked. But I would have broken it down if I had to. Then I saw her standing there, and I knew she was doing something to you. I told her to move away, but she wouldn't listen to me. So I had to shoot her. What did she do to you?"

He told her briefly, skipping all the details. He didn't tell her about Michelle. The hallway and garage were both empty thankfully and they moved the body without detection from curious neighbors. He popped the trunk to his Honda and shoved the body in like authentic garbage.

Jessie directed him to a garbage dumpster out of town in a deserted miniature shopping mall. They flung the body over and heard the thump as it hit the bottom. It was gone then, forever out of their sight.

"Francis," she brushed close until she was only inches away from him. Her gaze held his. "Are you alright?"

He felt his heart beating irregularly fast. "Yes." He had to look away.

Her hand brushed against his. He tried to flinch away but she clasped it in hers. Despite the warm weather, his hand was stone cold. But hers was like a heater that gave him warmth.

"You're cold."

"A little bit."

"Look at me, Francis."

He did and saw the sparkle in her dark eyes. He had often seen the strength and determination in her eyes. He had not thought of her as beautiful but she held an attractive composure about her, in a tomboyish sort of way.

She kissed him, a soft friendly peck on the lips at first and then intensely with a passionate hunger. When she pulled away and again looked him in the eyes, he didn't know what to say. He only felt a sense of euphoria washed over him.

"Let's get away from all this, put everything behind us."

"What about Babel?"

"Just for a few days, that's all I ask. We can deal with things when we come back."

He nodded. She had suggested what he wanted the most, to get away from everything. To forget about his curse, to forget about Babel hunting him down, to forget about Babel trying to destroy the world, to forget about what he had done and what he was becoming. He didn't need to deal with any of it.

"Where are we going?" he asked when they got back into the car.

"Let's go to Vegas. That's the closest place we can get to in a car."

"I have a confession to make," he said as he pulled the car onto the northbound freeway 57. He needed to get it out of him before he could forget about everything and live a few days of normal life.

He told her about the alternate reality he saw when Sophie made him revisit his past. He told her about how he had murdered Michelle.

"I don't believe a word of it." Her hand went to his, gripping it with reassurance. "When I looked into your eyes, I don't see a killer. And this is what I'm paid to do. I look into peoples' eyes and I find the killer in them. You have to trust yourself, trust the way you remembered it. Don't let them get to you."

"Thank you, Jessie." Yet, he was not sure if she was right. She had put too much faith in his character, which he no longer trusted.

When they got onto the eastbound freeway 10, Francis thought of something that bothered him.

"Why are we taking my car?"

"What?"

"You heard me. You said you were—"

"Claustrophobic," she interrupted. "You don't trust me, Francis?"

"It's not that." He didn't know what's real and what's not. "So why?"

"How much bigger do you think the interior of a SUV is anyway?"

She had a point. There wasn't much difference when he thought about it. The inside of a Honda Accord was not exactly tight. "Why are you claustrophobic?"

"I ... I prefer not to talk about that, really. Francis, why are you interrogating me? Is it because I kissed you, and you don't think you're in the real world? You're not dreaming, Francis. You are in the real world and... I'm in love with you."

Why are you in love with me? "Just one more question." But he was not going to ask the one he wanted to ask. "Which detective grade are you?"

"What? What kind of question is that?"

"You don't know?"

"Of course I know."

"Then answer me."

For a brief moment she was thoughtful. Then she answered. "Second."

None of this was real. He wasn't sure of course, just like he wasn't sure about the truth of the incident with Michelle. There was only one way to find out.

From the back seat, Michelle reached forward, wrapping her arm around Jessie's neck, hand touching elbow in a lock.

"What are you doing?"

"What am I doing? I haven't done anything yet. You messed up, Sophie. You're not supposed to be able to see anything." When he was sure, he gave the mental command for Michelle to attack her.

"You can't harm me, this is still my world–" That was obviously a lie. She struggled, her legs frantically kicking the glove compartment.

The next moment he was not in his car, he was on his couch, the same place he had found himself earlier. Sophie was directly in front of him, where before she had been shot in an altered reality, then struggling against her attacker from behind, she kicked and she screamed like a helpless child. Where is her Pillar? Why isn't she defending herself?

Francis commanded Michelle to loosen her grip, while still holding Sophie in the same locked position. Michelle complied with reluctance, yet her ghastly face displayed no emotion. Francis couldn't help but shiver with the coldness that zapped through his body. He wondered if he had really killed Michelle in the past.

"What are you doing? Kill me, and be done with it." Sophie glowered at him.

"Why aren't you defending yourself? Where's your Pillar?"

"It only works in REM sleep. Even then it won't be able to attack you."

"Then what does it do?"

"Why? Just kill me."

"Humor me."

"It traps you in your dream state forever. Then your body in real life will die, lacking nourishment."

"It's like the Christmas Carol. The future, the past, and the present."

"But you're not Scrooge. You should have stayed in there. Now you'll die in another's hands, and I guarantee you, it'll be much more painful than the grave I have prepared for you–" She struggled, and Michelle tightened her grip.

Take it easy, don't hurt her, yet. "Why?"

"Why what?"

"Why do they want me dead?"

"How am I supposed to know? I do what they tell me, to stay alive."

"They send you the pills. And they tell you to do things on email." It wasn't a question, but an observation. She neither confirmed nor denied it.

"Kill me, please. Just kill me."

And that was tempting. Michelle could feel the sweet essence of life flowing in her veins. He could feel it, and he wanted it very much. He wasn't physically aroused. But somewhere in his mind he had developed an urge to feed on other hosts, especially when they were so close, only inches away. He presumed that's how vampires felt when they were within grasps of flesh and blood, if there were such monstrosity as vampires. He shook his head, trying to remember who he was, why he was here. He was not going to become the demon Babel's making him. He needed to rid himself of the curse, and killing and taking what's not his would only taint his soul even further. He had already embarked upon a journey blacker than tar; he needed to turn back now before it was too late.

He commanded Michelle to release her. For a moment he thought he saw, or felt, a glowing spark of defiance from the phantom's eyes. It was the reluctance of a starving predator releasing an easy prey. But she had already released the woman.

Sophie fell onto her kneels gasping for air. When she looked up, there were tears in her eyes. "Why? Why are you letting me go?"

"You are a victim, just like I am. Maybe you tried to trap me inside some virtual reality world until I die. But you didn't really try to harm me, not physically anyway. I'm not going to kill an unarmed woman who can't even protect herself."

"You have no idea what they're going to do to me."

Maybe they were going to give her some fake pills that will send her down to the depths of hell, maybe they would send an assassin after her and torture her to death, maybe… but it was not going to be blood on his hands, he couldn't live with it anymore. "Just go away, leave me alone. And don't ever come back again."

She staggered towards the door, half limping and half crawling, looking like a senile old woman with only a bit of strength clinging to what little life she had. When she closed the door, Francis remembered he had forgotten to ask her an important question. He needed her to tell him the version of the past he saw was false.

When he rushed to the door, a near-piercing shriek which reached a level of madness originated from just outside the door. Just one thin wooden panel away he could feel the trepidation that transpired. When he opened the door he saw nothing, the noise had long ceased, only faintly echoing in his mind, terrorizing him. He looked down the hallway into the shadows and he saw not a single movement. Someone had gotten to her where he now stood. He didn't know how. There was no body, no blood, no anything, as if someone just erased her the moment she stepped out of his apartment. If there were someone that powerful watching over what he did and they wanted him dead, why didn't they just erase him also? He couldn't help but wondered. Just who was he supposed to be?

*   *   *   *

Jessie jerked awake panting, as if she had just walked through hell and back. She only faintly remembered what she had dreamed. There was the mysterious man without a face making love to her, and it felt so real. She remembered trying many times to see his face, just like the visions in the fellowship, she could not grasp the solid outline of his face. It was like a blur on a tampered film, or simply a shadow, a void that did not yet come into existence. And at the end of her dream of pleasure came the terror that chilled her even now. The man who was holding her close to him abruptly became something else, a sinister being wearing the face of a circus clown. Only his eyes were red and his teeth sharp like the jaws of a shark. His grip was strong, and it felt real. She felt her arms being torn away from her body. She had looked into those red eyes that hid behind the semi-human facade. And they had laughed at her timidity and helplessness with a condescending malevolence, like a predator toying with its prey.

She sat up on her bed, still shaking from the aftermath of her dream. The flashing alarm clock told her that it was a little past five in the morning. She looked out the window at the glooming darkness in anticipation of dawn. A neighboring dog bayed, creating a disturbing cacophony, an un-conducted orchestra of barking and wailing that was neither random nor planned, but seemed an urgent message informing her that the animals, too, felt that a predator was lurking in the shadows cast by her dream, and they were just as terrified as she was. She felt like she was being watched by something she could not see.

The thought gave her little consolation. The last thing she needed was unnecessary paranoia. Questions dashed through her mind. The few knocks at the door made her jump.

"Jess, are you alright?" It was Mark sticking his head in after pushing the door ajar.

"Come in, what are you doing up? It's late. Or should I say early." She illuminated the room with a warming blast as she pushed the switch on the lamp sitting on her nightstand. The warmth was not so much physical but ethereal, something that glowed within her, pushing the fear away.

"I heard you scream so I decided to check on you."

"Did I scream?" She didn't think she had but she wasn't sure now. But Mark's nod confirmed it. "I don't remember closing the door. Did you?" She had never had a habit of closing the door. Unless she was dressing or undressing, she almost always left the door fully opened, even when she slept.

There was never anything too private that she had to do in her room without being seen, it was a way of her expressing she never wanted to be shut off from her family. But living away all these years she was like a hermit in her family's eyes, especially her parents. She was back now, and she had made sure that her door was always opened.

"I closed it a little earlier."

She was confused and made sure that was clearly expressed on her face.

"Well, you didn't just scream. Earlier you woke me up–"

"What? Was I talking in my dreams? What did I say?"

Mark looked at the floor, a little embarrassed. He didn't have to say it and she knew what kind of noises she was making. "How loud?"

"Quite."

"I didn't wake them up, did I?" She was referring to the folks. Mark's room was right next to hers, and she understood that the wooden walls were as bad at insulating sound as thin air. Her room was the farthest away from her parents, and she hoped that she wasn't loud enough.

"That's why I shut the door for you. So I don't think they woke up."

"Thanks, Markie."

"You know, when I first heard it, I almost thought that you had brought someone home. But then I figured you would have closed the door."

"Don't be ridiculous, Mark."

"That's what I thought."

"It felt so real."

"You need to get laid, sis."

"And I can't believe we're having this conversation." She was quite embarrassed at this point, feeling almost lightheaded. And her little brother's blatant ridicule was only making it worse. He was right though, that's what she probably needed. It's been so long sometimes she didn't even remember how it felt to sleep in someone's arms.

"I'm a grown up now, Jess. If you want to talk about it, I'm here." There was a mischievous grin on his face, the same one he always had over the years when he found a chance to make fun of her.

"I'm not really in the mood of sexual discussion, not with my little brother at least. But I want to ask you one thing though. Have you ever had such a dream that felt so real?"

"Sexual?"

She glowered at him. "I'm serious, Mark."

"Alright, I had enough fun teasing you already."

"Then tell me something useful."

"I've never had such a dream. But I've read about such things. When dreams feel real, that means there're powerful forces at work. That, or you've been visited by a incubus."

She sighed, and readied herself for another of Mark's cryptic lectures of the paranormal.

"Dreams are often just subconscious mumble jumbles, but when a dream crosses into reality, it is a sign that it is prophetic. Premonition of your subconscious mind, that's what it was. It is a sign, a warning. You are doing something very important and dangerous that involves powerful forces. The dream is telling you something, perhaps that you're going to get laid very soon. We should celebrate, I'll go get the champagne bottle."

"You're enjoying this, aren't you?"

"Of course, wouldn't have it any other way."

"Thanks, Mark. I think I'll think about it some more on my own."

"No details?"

"Not in a million year."

She told him to leave the door opened when he left. Then she stared at the darkness waiting outside the curtains, reluctant to turn the light off. She thought about her dream, the vision she saw in the church, and about Andy's speech at the fellowship. She and Francis had involved themselves in a religious war somehow. And she was afraid, afraid even more than when she chased after the Tormentor. It was now because of her understanding of Babel, what it was doing to mankind, and her own helplessness that made her dream these nightmares. Babel was trying to frighten her, trying to make her give up, but she had already made up her mind. She was going to convince Francis to fight alongside Andy, even though he did not trust him. But they had a common enemy, an alliance would strengthen them. Thoughts were over-flooding her mind.

Why am I doing this? Is it because of the guilt I don't want to face myself with knowing the truth to only walk away? Do I seek the justice that I so long and live for, and maybe in doing so I can redeem everyone that's been wronged, even myself? Or is it the ultimate darkness, like the criminal minds, that I find so appealing and it is attracting me like a magnet? Can I not walk away because it's a crime to do so, or is it because I can't stand to lose this one connection between him and I? Francis, such an enigma, I feel that you won't be able to continue to fight without me, yet I can do nothing to help you. Yet I care about what happens, and I wonder about how this story will end. But why?

When Jessie finally slept, she didn't get up until late in the morning. There was a phone call for her, and she was quite surprised that it was Francis. His voice sounded a bit distraught on the phone. When she asked him what was wrong, he said that he would tell her when he saw her. It wasn't like him to be so secretive. He either said what he could say and kept his mouth shut for things he wasn't going to reveal. She had promised lunch with her family and then helping out Mark at the bookstore. It wasn't really so much as helping than just accompanying her little brother at the quiet store. So she told him to look for her there in the afternoon.

Francis came in around a little past four while she was inventorying the books in the back. He was still distant and troubled. Yet he managed a brief smile when he saw her.

Only having a few more rows on the shelf to inventory, she let Mark entertain Francis. Her brother had told her that he really liked Francis, not just because he was a faithful customer who didn't mind coming into the quaint little store while there were countless modern stores just around the corner, but... actually she didn't really know. Sometimes there wasn't a reason when someone liked someone. Mark had said that Francis was not very talkative and he had often just responded to questions with a one-word answer, yet he did not think of Francis as unfriendly; maybe he was just uncomfortable talking to strangers. When she had first met him, she had thought that people stayed strangers around him. She was right, because he was someone who erected unseen barriers around himself. He had admitted so himself. Yet the more she knew him, she had felt that wall around him slowly dissolving.

For a while she watched him talk with her brother. Despite his troubled look, he was surprisingly friendly and chatty. She thought that he had changed and gave an inward smile. Perhaps seeing him become more human was more satisfying than being the hand of justice.

They went to the Starbucks a few blocks away and sat down on one of the outside seats with their ice-cold cappuccino and mocha. Then Francis began recounting the incident from the night before. He talked to her about Kyle and than meeting Sophie in the bar.

She was a little bit uncomfortable when he said that he had brought this strange woman home because she was too drunk to go anywhere on her own. And she scowled at him, with wrinkled forehead, thinking that maybe making him become friendlier wasn't such a good idea after all. Then she questioned herself why she'd care about what he did with the woman, it wasn't her place to pry at another's private life.

He noticed her disapproval and quickly explained that he just left her there on the bed without doing anything further, saying so with an urgent vehemence. She didn't know whether to smile or continue scowling at him. She was probably doing both at the same time.

He continued the story about waking up in the future with amnesia. It sounded quite unbelievable, but she didn't doubt his words at all. Not only did his troubled eyes convey that he could not be saying anything else but the truth, but also she was ready to believe anything after the she had known the involvement of Babel. They were gods, and they had the power to do whatever they wanted.

Francis was skipping details in his recounting, she could tell because he hesitated when he had got to some parts of the story. She thought that it might be embarrassing and private so she did not try to pry, just sat and listened like one of the children surrounding good old grandma for a fairy tale. Occasionally she asked him to repeat things in detail. It was a bit too strange for her to take in all at once, and she had regretted not being able to let Mark know about this, he would have been more than fascinated.

She felt an uneasy chill spreading within her when he told her about the picture of the clown holding someone that remotely resembled her. She wondered if she should tell him about her dream but decided against it at the end, as it was too embarrassing and it would serve no purpose. Plus she would probably have given him more cause for anxiety than he already possessed.

To Jessie, he looked more afraid than shameful when he described his sojourn in the past. Since he took a long time to find the right words to say, she made sure that she was not pushing him, but letting him go at his own pace. She knew that it was something that wasn't easy to talk about, for anyone and especially for him.

She listened carefully as he described watching himself kill Michelle as sort of an awakening of his mysterious power. Then the view of him dragging the body to the car and the accident, which in the reconstructed past was more deliberate than accidental. At the last minute he pulled the steering wheel, avoiding the direct head-on collision. As a result of the skid, as he had really remembered it, Michelle's body, unprotected by a seatbelt, was thrown out of the window while he was knocked unconscious in the driver seat.

He was silent for a long time after that.

"That's not the way you remembered it, right?" He had told her about that night, although not the details, but he did not kill her, somehow she was sure of that.

He shook his head.

"But you're not sure?"

"I… I don't know what to think anymore. I can't even trust my own memory. I might have done it and blocked it out of my memory. I don't know."

"You think you can just do something and repress the memory? It's not that easy." She too, had things in her memory that she wanted to block out forever. But it wasn't that simple to rewrite the past. Life wasn't a movie script.

"I… " He avoided her gaze and turned his head to a few skaters that flashed by.

"You may be imaginative, but you're not that good. It was a trap designed to make you feel guilty, make you lose the will to live, to fight. That's just what they want. You don't need to doubt yourself."

She moved to sit somewhere close to him thinking that the closeness would comfort him. Yet when he turned back toward her he appeared to involuntary flinch, as if for a moment he was afraid of the closeness. She tilted a few inches away towards the edge of the small table.

"Let me tell you the rest of the story," he said, leaning closer. A gesture of apology for his flinching?

Sometimes she wondered if she read too much into people's body language. People probably had little idiosyncratic movements. But she read them nevertheless, maybe because she found a deeper meaning in doing so. Even though on most occasions she wasn't right, she never really stopped analyzing people's actions. Maybe in some way trying to understand other people she understood herself a little better. I really think way too much, she concluded.

"Wait, let me tell you something first." As much as she wanted to hear the rest of the story, she was seeing way too much guilt on Francis' face, a lot more than he deserved. He still doubted himself, she was sure. As for why he could not trust his own memory she did not know, but he should be able to trust his own action. He wasn't a cold-blooded killer. If he were, his conscience wouldn't be devouring him, based on something that probably wasn't true at all. She wasn't always right about killers, but she was sure about him. There was too much to worry about, other than something he did or did not do in the past. It was her job to wipe his guilt away; it was the least she could do for her friend. "Have you ever heard of postmortem lividity?"

There was a spark of recognition in his eyes, but he shook his head.

"It's something that's quite often encountered in homicide cases. When the human heart ceases to pump blood through the body, blood settles in the lower half of the body, depending on the position. Over time a bruising effect is created on the skin. When the body is moved, the bruising remains in the original position because the blood has coagulated. Later the bruising effect becomes apparent and can be easily spotted by the naked eye. It doesn't take a coroner to recognize a moved body. An experienced homicide detective can identify it in the blink of an eye."

"What you're saying—"

"Is that nobody gets away from murder. Well, that's not true," she corrected herself. "People do get away. But it's not easy and certainly not an amateur like you, that is if you were a killer. Even if you didn't leave strangulation marks on her neck, which is very unlikely, the coroner, if not the detective, could still easily tell that the body had been moved. Not to mention cause of death, asphyxiation is very different than simply crushing her head in a car accident. And don't tell me there's been a conspiracy to cover up your little murder. You know what? Let's say even if you did it. What does it matter? It's already in the past. What are you going to do? You're going kill yourself and atone for your sin? You can do nothing but to move forward in life. You don't live for the past, but the future. So stop looking back and question yourself. Remember it as the dear memory you've always remembered."

Jessie didn't interrupt the next few moments of silence, reckoning that Francis needed time to digest all that she said. Actually even she was surprised at how rational she was in that verbatim speech.

"I think I know what you mean," Francis said finally looking up.

Although there was still unease on his face, he seemed a little less distraught. He now looked like someone exhausted at the end of a struggle instead of someone who was battling constant pain.

"Thanks, Jessie. Though I still need to think about it more, I don't think I would have ever thought it through without you."

That was probably one of the nicest things he had ever said. "You're welcome. Now tell me the rest of the story."

He then continued on talking about the last phony reality his assassin took him to, when it was her that came to his rescue.

"I did what?" she interrupted when he mentioned both of them discarding the body into the trash dump.

"You–"

"Yeah, I heard you the first time. But that's so unreal. I would never do that. First of all, I'd never have shot someone in the head, not someone unarmed." She thought about it, and actually she wasn't sure. If she was really there, she might have shot the intruder the same way, especially if she knew that the intruder was a host. She couldn't see Pillars. And fighting against invisible entities was extremely dangerous.

"But you were so real. I had no reason to doubt you. You even wrinkled your nose like you always did."

"What? I most absolutely do not wrinkle my nose."

"You just did."

She reached for her nose as if her hand was going to hold it down.

And when he grinned broadly, she scowled at him. Even though she was a bit relieved at seeing his mood improve, she was a bit irritated at him playing a joke on her.

He then changed the subject and told her about the plan to go to Vegas and to get away from everything. Hearing him recount the details didn't make much, but she couldn't blame him. If she were in his shoes, she might not have questioned reality also. As he continued, she felt that he was hiding specific details from her, yet she thought better than to question him. After all, if the phony version of reality was molded from the depths of his mind, it was definitely shaped after his every hidden desire, designed to contain him in a false reality so he could escape and forget about his problems. She was sure that there were things that he should just keep to himself, but then she couldn't help but wonder what things he had dreamed about that involved her. It was tempting for her simply to brush it away and not know. Yet she could not bring herself to interrogate him about the details he had skipped, maybe one day he would tell her.

"I wouldn't have said that either," she objected when he told her about their conversation about him and Michelle in the false past. The whole idea was giving her a headache. "Actually the old me would have said that, looking into your eyes and not seeing a killer in you. That's right, I don't. But I was wrong when I looked into Mary's eyes. All I saw was a sad, lonely girl and I completely missed the presence of the cruel Tormentor. Ever since then, I make sure that I was not going to totally rely on my own judgment."

"So now when you look into my eyes, you're not sure?"

She held his gaze for a long moment. "I am sure that you didn't kill her. But I wouldn't have said that as my argument, because it has nothing to do with looking into your eyes. You know, it's a lot of bullshit if I tell you I can look into your eyes and tell you you're not a killer while you have lived with yourself for over twenty years and you don't know." She noticed she had raised her voice and a few wandering pedestrians suddenly looked over. "I'm sorry, I didn't mean to raise my voice. I just—"

"Actually I'm the one who should apologize. You're right, it doesn't matter if I've done it or not. I should trust myself, and I should just live for the future, and not the past."

She didn't know why she was suddenly angry at him, which wasn't like her at all. She rarely got mad at anyone. Maybe she just really wanted him to understand why it was so important to not dwell in the past. Silently she let him resume his narrative. He first suspected things to be not right while he realized that the counterfeit Jessie didn't insist on taking her car. She understood that, because she would have preferred to take the SUV, especially while she had to spend four hours in it on a trip to Las Vegas. She then silently applauded at his shrewdness when he told her he had asked about the detective grading system.

"You know, she was actually right. I was promoted just a few months ago."

"Lucky guess. But she took too long to think about it."

"How did you think of something like that to ask?"

"It just came up. I've read it somewhere and I always wondered about it, but never had the chance to ask you. How many grades are there anyway?"

"Well, technically three, but a lieutenant is sort of like a grade four."

He then told her how he had use Michelle to confirm the false reality, and seemed embarrassed to say that he attacked her even though it wasn't really her.

Jessie realized that he had already tried to subdue her twice, even though the second time it was only an image of her. Maybe she trusted him so much because she had put her life in his hands while he had the power to take it. Then he chose to preserve it, had even saved her life when she was a total stranger. Though she could not use those facts as proof that he did not murder Michelle in the past, it was proof enough that even if he did, to her it did not matter.

Then the long twisting tale of multiple realities came to an end when he told her that he let Sophie go, and she screamed and disappeared outside his door. He was afraid that she was not alive anymore.

"I'm proud of you, Francis. Even though she might not be alive anyway, but you did not take her life when she was at your mercy."

"I wanted to take her life, when Michelle held her neck in her hands. It wasn't right. She was as much a victim as I was, and in the real world she couldn't even defend herself. I fought the urge so I could let her go. I'm not sure I can do this again."

"It takes a lot of strength to fight your urges. In the future you might kill again, if only in self-defense, or you might not. As long as you know that you've been right and you can live with yourself, that's the most important thing."

"But how long is this going to continue? Do I have to live in fear everyday, either to kill or be killed?"

She couldn't answer him, and it pained her to not be able to do so. Someday it was going to end. She was going to make sure of that. Now she could only change the subject. "I talked to Andy yesterday."

He didn't look surprised. "What did he say?"

She told him briefly about what he had said concerning his plans with Babel. She did not tell Francis that she met with Andy, but led him to believe they talked on the phone. It wasn't exactly a lie, just not mentioning all the truth.

"Enoch Bel," he repeated after her in a whisper, as if saying a demon's name would risk the chance of summoning it to the world, as some legends would say. "The man who started it all. It's strange but I don't know if I should feel angry or afraid at the mention of his name. But what can we do?"

"Knowing your enemy is the first step of winning the battle."

He sighed with overwhelming anxiety. "You know, part of me, a big part of me actually, wants to go back to that altered reality that I saw yesterday. There I could perhaps hide away from my cursed fate at this crossroads where I must face either destruction or an impossible confrontation with power almost as great as God's."

"It's that small part of Francis that I'm really proud of. And you won't be alone. I'll be by your side, and there'll be others."

CHAPTER THIRTY

The next day Francis went to work as usual, feeling like an ordinary human being. His unanswered questions remained a mystery. He could do nothing to solve the mystery about himself, the mystery about Babel, and the mystery about Michelle. He was back to the life of a lonely automaton, mindlessly going about the repetition of day-to-day life without a purpose. For a moment it seemed that the events that had transpired, things that had been set into motion, whatever they were, were but a fleeting dream.

It was difficult to stop thinking about whether he had murdered Michelle, and what he was becoming, carrying the accursed power known as Pillar. In a way he had become an angel of death, a taker of life. Somewhere in the depths of his mind, he was churning with disgust. In the darkness of chaotic thoughts, Jessie had led him into the light, telling him that he had to look forward instead of back at the uncertain past. He had to trust his own memories and treasure them, he didn't have to live in guilt and self-blame. Instead he should look ahead to the future his own hands were going to create.

He thought back to the day when he thought Michelle was a haunting spirit. Even now when he knew that she was nothing but a projection of his mind, he was not sure what she really was. Maybe she was the guardian angel who came to warn him against danger, protect him from evil, and save him against the grasps of Babel. Yet she was also an instrument of the experiments of Babel. She was Lilith, instrument of desire, seducer of men, taker of life, stealer of souls, and embodiment of pure evil.

Perhaps there was no distinction of good and evil in the real world, a gigantic chessboard pitching evil against evil. Maybe it took evil to fight evil. Or maybe evil was but a disguise of good. They had viewed Babel as the ultimate evil, but perhaps Babel saw itself as salvation to the human race. Perhaps somewhere in the future timeline of earth, humans needed this genetically enhanced ability to face an apocalypse that would wipe out the human race. Then looking back in history one would not dispute that Babel was on the side of good, fighting for the best interest of the survival of the human race.

He had thought Andy evil, a cold-blooded murderer, the host of the devil-guised death clown who would have injected him with the drug and killed him without remorse, if he didn't prove to already be a capable host. Yet Andy had seen himself to be the representative of God, leading men to fight against the oppression of genetic engineering. And in disguise of the face that emanated an aura of death, the clown was some sort of healer. It even saved his life when he fought the Tormentor. Francis wondered if Andy was a holy man doing God's will, a terrorist using religion to plot unlawful destruction, an angel wearing the skin of a demon, or a killer lurking in a priest's robe.

The real world had no line between good and evil. People only fought for what they believed in. He didn't know he believed in – only that Babel was trying to kill him and he had to stay alive. And whoever tried to take his life was his enemy. That was the sole reason to fight. He didn't really care about justice, about unethical genetic engineering, evolution of the human race, or about who was trying to be God and rule the world. He did not feel the need for vengeance. As long as he was left alone and could continue a normal life, he didn't care about the existence of his Pillar power – Michelle. He did not want to be forced into situations where he had to take another life. But he did not want to be the executioner, he did not want the position of power to judge another's sin with life and death, that was fate's job and he wanted no part of it. He did not need to see the blood on his hands, to feel the shame of guilt, and to taste the essence of life flowing between his veins, no matter how good it felt. He just wanted to be left alone. It was ironic that when he had his simple life, he hated it and tried to escape from it every chance that he had. Now as his simple life turned into a dark twisting adventure, he yearned to return to it. Yet he knew once he returned to it, he would not feel content and would seek refuge and escape from the mundane repetitive lonely life. Perhaps he was doing all the wrong things in his life.

That night Andy called. It was a conference call with Jessie and Kyle on the other lines. He said that Enoch Bel would be present in a meeting on Wednesday night. He had planned a distraction of some sort, a disturbance by his church group. During the distraction, the four of them were to get to the penthouse of the administrative building, Enoch's residence in Los Angeles. It seemed that open confrontation was the only plan Andy had in mind, with no subtlety involved. It wasn't much of a plan, Francis thought. But he had already agreed to it. Even though he did not really care about the truth of Babel's plan, he wanted some answers about himself. He had objected to Jessie's being part of the so-called secret operation, even though it was for her that he had agreed to his part. He didn't want anything happening to her, as she was not a host and she couldn't protect herself against things she couldn't see. He knew the fruitlessness of his objection, and also he respected her decision. Yet he could not face himself for not trying to stop her from going. But part of him wanted her to be there, because her presence would give him strength, and definition, something he needed to stay in control.

*　　　*　　　*　　　*

Wednesday night came a lot faster than Jessie had wanted. She was anxious when she parked at the guest area of the parking lot and started her march towards the rendezvous point. She had no idea what was going to happen tonight. But she guessed that something important was going to happen – perhaps Francis would find the truth about himself, and perhaps they would all perish at the hands of evil. She was not afraid, because she had already committed herself to the cause. She was not doing it only for herself, but she was doing it for Francis, her father, Terry, and everyone who suffered at the hands of Babel.

Even though it was well past eight o'clock, the Babel compound seemed unusually crowded. Just outside the fountain area in the center of the five tall towers, a throng had gathered holding up signposts and yelling, "God forbids genetic engineering." They kept repeating themselves in mindless chanting which gave her an impression that they had been enslaved by their faith, as if repeating the same lines over and over again would be atonement for the sins of mankind. She wondered if that was the distraction Andy had promised to provide for their operation. If it was, the only benefit so far was to irritate her as she endured the torment of that chanting all the way from the parking lot to the front of the administrative tower.

When she passed by the genetic research tower, a group of people in white lab coats rushed out of the building. Even though it was rather late, it seemed unlikely that so many people were rushing from work at the same time. Out of curiosity, she stopped a young woman and asked her what was going on.

"There's been a bomb threat," she said pausing to catch her breath. "This is not the first time. But none of the previous threats were authentic. But still we had to evacuate the building as soon as possible, just in case. Those religious zealots over there, they should keep their opinion to themselves. Believe it or not, some of us got work to do and kids to feed. Are these people going to make God feed my kids?"

The woman seemed a little ticked off with the interruption to her tasks, as if not finishing her work tonight would get her fired. Jessie wondered who the zealot really was, probably both groups were. She just hoped that the two groups of people would not confront each other; especially when it came to the matter of career and religion, it was usually a dangerous mob situation. Angry crowds did not react rationally, even if they were scientists and Christians.

It was a cruel idea for a distraction if it was Andy's plan to instigate a mob fight, but she was not here to judge what was right and what needed to be done. She was here only for one reason.

She wasn't late but they were already there waiting for her. There was a deep expression of concern on Francis' face. It could be just her imagination but he seemed to have lit up a bit when he saw her. Yet he was as silent as a mute. Andy's face betrayed no sort of anxiety whatsoever, and she even detected a slight hint of amusement, probably an eagerness to see his own plan come into fruition. The third man was not as tall and imposing as Andy. He was bald in a stylish way, possibly in his late thirties but no less tough looking. The wire-framed glasses did not cloud the careful calculating intelligence that gleamed from his eyes. She had never met him because she had been unconscious the previous time he was around. He was Kyle, the undercover agent. He had that shrewd observing look about him that Jessie had seen in so many agents. He shook her hand with a firm grip and introduced himself.

"What's with the bomb threat?" she directed her question towards Andy.

"Because I don't want anyone to get hurt."

"What?"

"You heard me."

"You put a bomb in there?"

"Not me specifically, and not just one bomb. A few scattered across designated floors which are involved with Project Pillars. The bombs are not very strong. They will not cause any structural damage to the building, but they will wreak havoc on the equipment and storage, and mainly computers and experiments."

She sighed and didn't offer any negative comments, even though she wanted to. She was not here to judge what's wrong and right. Andy was a terrorist after all. The things he did perhaps were wrong in the law's eyes, but still admirable.

"So why do you need them?" She pointed at the throng.

"For show mainly. And they want to witness the hammer of God."

"Hammer my ass. You're exposing them to unnecessary danger. When the cops get here–"

"Don't worry. They'll be gone by then. Look, detective, if you're done with your interrogation, we'll get on with it."

"Sorry," she muttered, but she wasn't really. People didn't need to get hurt.

"Okay," Andy looked towards the top of the tower, as if he could see what was going on in that room which was almost as far away as the clouds. "Thirty-fifth floor. That's where our man is. In about three minutes, the bombs are going to explode. Then security will be coming out to look at the crisis. Then we can sneak in. I've already got the access card for the elevator to the penthouse."

"And what are we doing specifically?" Jessie already knew the answer, but she needed a confirmation.

"Barge in and eliminate our target. And try to stay behind and out of our way. None of us know what kind of power he's capable of, yet he knows the extent of each of our power even better than us ourselves. If there are no guards, then it's four against one. We have a good chance."

Prior to the decision about this operation, she had discussed with Andy at length about whether this operation was a good idea. They even argued, quite heatedly on the phone. He had not told her about the bombs, but nevertheless she did not feel an assassination attempt was the right way to solve a problem. Removing a president would not stop a country from functioning, unless you removed the whole government. Yet he had insisted that Project Pillar would fall apart once Enoch Bel was no longer there to lead it, and everything would come into place afterwards. She did not really agree but she could not offer any other alternative ideas. Not only was he as strong-minded and stubborn as she was, he seemed to have waited years for this day, as if it was a day of revelation. She knew that he could have carried out his plan anytime, today was not the only sacred day that the founder of Babel was going to be vulnerable. But today was the first opportunity that came up since Francis was ready to fight. He seemed to have been the extra weight Andy's been waiting for all these years that tipped the balance of their chance of winning against their opponent. Jessie was sure that her being there didn't really matter, as long as Francis was willing to fight alongside. Francis had not objected to the plan, nor did he sound excited about it. He was like a prisoner with a death sentence walking towards his own inevitable fate. Neither thrilled nor frightened, he only expressed a forlorn anxiety as if he was still regretful about life and what little he had done. We're not here to die, she told herself. We're here to do what's right.

A sly smile of victory touched Andy's lips as he looked up from his watch. There was a distant crackle and then series of thunder as the chain reaction of bombs detonated. The fire lid up the sky like a flash, and shards of broken glass window rained like sparkles of stardust. There was nothing beautiful about the scene. It was the aftermath of pure destruction.

Security guards and crowds alike stared upward at the spectacle in silent awe. Andy motioned them to go in. Past the now empty reception desks, they reached the lobby with the clusters of elevators. Andy slid the access card on the panel at the innermost elevator, the one which Jessie suspected would take them straight to their destination.

While they waited, Francis had put a reassuring hand on her shoulder. Yet she could feel that he needed as much reassurance as she did. She nodded and told him that it'd be okay.

When the elevator opened, Andy motioned for them to go in first. A painting at the back of the elevator wall captured Jessie's undivided attention for a moment – a tower with ancient designs standing in an open field reached up the sky. The top of the tower could not be seen, only covered by clouds – The Tower of Babel.

She felt Francis' presence next to her. When she turned around, the elevator was empty except Francis and her. No sign of Andy and Kyle. Yet she felt the metal cage going upward. The indicator on top of the door quickly turned to eleven, and then twelve. Panic washed over her.

"Francis, where's Andy and Kyle?"

He turned towards her from the painting and studied the interior of the elevator. "I don't know."

"Did you see them come in?"

"Not specifically. But I heard and felt them come in. I was busy checking out the painting."

"Damn." Where could they have gone?

"It looks like we've been attacked," he said calmly. "Let's just wait and see what happens."

She looked up at the indicator and watched the light went from twenty all the way to thirty-four… then thirty-five lit up.

The elevator didn't stop. And it showed no sign of stopping. The speed of its upward motion did not change, but it was still going up. The light on the indicator remained on thirty-five.

"How many floors are there?" she asked.

"Thirty-five," Francis said. "You can see the tower from outside. There's a limit to how high up it goes. This is not possible."

She took a look at the painting behind them, and couldn't help but felt a coldness spreading all over her spine. She looked up and noticed the ceiling for the second time. She wasn't sure but it seemed to be crushing down upon her. Leaning at the corner, she felt overwhelmed by vertigo and nausea.

"Michelle's not strong enough to pry anything open in here—" He stopped the mumbling and looked towards her. "What's wrong?"

He put his hand on her forehead. "You're sweating."

"The ceiling—"

"What about it?" He then covered her eyelids with his hand. "Don't look at it."

She didn't have to. She could feel it crushing her. The Darkness. Her leg buckled, giving out strength. She felt herself falling.

He caught her and held her close to him. That moment she felt the warmth flowing from him to her. It comforted her.

"I'll get us out of here," he whispered a promise to her and she felt the warm air lingering on her earlobes.

She had never felt so close to anyone. In his arms she found the strength to not give in to her fear. She clutched on to that pillar that stood between the ground and the crushing sky.

"How long has it been?" She was too afraid to open her eyes.

"Almost ten minutes."

"Is the elevator getting smaller?"

For a moment he didn't answer her, then with much reluctance he did. "Yes."

So it wasn't just her.

There was the clang of metal banging against metal all around her, and she felt Francis' breath quickening.

"What's happening?"

"Don't worry, it's just Michelle."

When the activity stopped, the only noise in the elevator was the tingling sound of its upward motion, and the beating of Francis' heart. He had given up.

"Is this what you're most afraid of?"

She never thought about it this way. But when she did, she realized that it was her worst fear. "Yes."

"I think someone's trying to use your fear to kill both of us."

"I'm sorry, Francis."

"No, it's not your fault. If it's not you, it could have been me. And it might have been even worse. You never told me about your claustrophobia. Why don't you tell me now?"

*   *   *   *

She was twelve. No, it first started when she was eleven. She had no mother then, only lived with Mark and her father, who was a police officer in Irvine. To watch over them when he was on duty, Father hired a babysitter, whom he had met because she had called in for an attempted break-in once. Their usual babysitter decided to move out of town. Her name was Beth, and she was a nice pretty blond lady in her late twenties. She had a telemarketing job, and all she needed to do was call people from home. Beth would pick her up after school and take Jessie to her place. Mark usually came with her because he got off school earlier than she did. For weeks she was satisfied with the new arrangement. Beth wasn't as talkative as the last baby-sitter because most of the time she was busy on the phone, but she also let them do whatever they wanted and baked them cookies in the afternoon.

Everything was okay until her new boyfriend came along. Beth called him Johnny, a biker with too many tattoos on his arm. He was nice to them at first but he wasn't nice to Beth. Whenever he came over he wouldn't let Beth continue her job on the phone. They would go into a room to have sex. Jessie was an adolescent than and she was fascinated with the idea of sex, just like any other kids. She would listen to them outside the locked door. Beth usually sounded happy for only ten minutes and then she would cry and begged him to stop. He was beating her. Beth had told them how much she loved Johnny, but from the bruises on her face Jessie knew that she couldn't love him as much as she was afraid of him.

She listened everyday, sometimes even on weekends when Father was on duty. Mark, just a little kid, was always in his own little world, playing video games or watching TV, and he never noticed anything. She, on the other hand, even found photos which Johnny kept in a drawer, photos of his naked girlfriend. He liked taking pictures, and it seemed he enjoyed doing so even during their sexual act.

One day Johnny didn't beat his girlfriend right after sex and came out for drink, surprising Jessie at the door.

"You little bastard, you like listening, huh?" He grabbed her hair and pulled her inside the room, locking her into a dark closet. It was the first time she experienced the tight darkness. Beth was screaming outside, begging him to leave her alone. But he only beat her, even more severely this time. The only thing Jessie could do was to tremble in the dark closet.

When she got back into the light, Johnny told her if she were to tell anyone, he would hurt Mark. And she specifically was not to tell her father. If she did he would be very angry and people would die. She believed him and kept his mouth shut. From that day on, Johnny would lock her inside the closet while he and his reluctant girlfriend had sex. She could do nothing but tremble and listen, and let the darkness crushed her.

Things didn't stop there. One day Johnny opened the closet just after sex and he was still naked. She tried to turn away, but he made her look at him.

"Look at me, you little bitch." Then he made her kneel in front of his limp penis. "Give me a blowjob, and no biting."

She didn't even know what that was, but he taught her. He said it was like sucking a lollipop. His hands were around her neck at first and he told her if she did anything wrong, he would strangle and kill her. Horrified, she did what she was told. He made her suck and lick it until it was large and hard again. And it never ended until he made her swallow his ejaculation. The first time she almost choked when the glue-like liquid unexpectedly exploded down her throat, but after that she learned to be ready for it.

That went on every day for months. He would pull her out from the dark closet and made her kneel in front of him. Sometimes he reached down and squeezed her bottom while he was excited but he never touched her anywhere else. Sometimes he took pictures of her while she was doing it. Every day she feared going to Beth's place, she feared getting locked into the closet when Johnny came, and she feared getting pulled out of the closet. And she didn't tell anyone because Johnny had threatened to kill her father.

Father eventually found out. She didn't remember the details, but she expected that he saw a change in her. When he found out about the photos, he broke into Beth's place one night and stole them. With the evidence at hand Johnny was taken into police custody and eventually he ended up in jail.

She didn't really find out until much later, when it was already too late, that Johnny was quite a smart man and had studied law in prison. He appealed after a year, and the court listened to his case. Apparently the law enabled him to make the appeal on basis of illegally obtained evidence. Father, although a police officer, did not have a search warrant when he took the evidence. He was much too angry at the time to think about the consequences. Jessie understood that, however the mistake had caused him his life. It was ironic how the law protected criminals. Johnny was released after serving two years in prison and he came back that night and stabbed Father to death in his bed. She had only heard him scream and then found him dead in a pool of blood. The police found Johnny's fingerprints in the room. Nobody saw Johnny after that.

*   *   *   *

She cried while Francis brushed her hair, his lips brushing softly against her forehead.

"It's okay, nobody will ever hurt you like that again."

She didn't stop crying. Somewhere deep in her mind she had always remembered the exact details of what happened to her. But she had long chosen to not tell anyone about it – not Terry, not Mark, not even her new loving parents. Now revisiting the events put a blade churning in her stomach.

"You know what?" he said softly. "You don't really have to be claustrophobic. You're not so much afraid of the dark closet, as you're afraid of what Johnny did to you afterwards. Your mind subconsciously gave you claustrophobia, so that you had no need to revisit the dread that event caused."

He was right.

When she finally had the courage to open her eyes, she looked into his. The tears had clouded her vision but for the first time she saw the compassion within the sorrow from his brown eyes. She was no longer afraid. That moment seemed suspended in time, and she didn't even feel the horrid motion of the elevator's horrid ongoing motion. She only felt the warmth from him and the incessant pounding of his heart.

He reached downward.

She reached upward.

When there were only inches between their lips, she felt the elevator door opened, bathing the dark cage with an overwhelming beam of bright light

"Let's go." He had released her.

A young brunette in a business suit sat behind a reception desk in front of large ornate wooden double doors. "Doctor Bel is waiting for you."

The others were nowhere to be seen.

Jessie had a firm grip on her gun and hid it behind her. She wasn't sure she could really shoot straight at anything. She was trembling from an ominous power that she felt emanating from that room before her, a power so overwhelming it threatened her very existence. She held on to her gun for temporary comfort more than protection.

The secretary opened the door for them and ushered them in, closing it behind them. Jessie found herself in a giant room with wooden panels and an unused fireplace. Behind the couches and coffee table which made up the meeting lounge corner, a large desk sat in the middle of the room. A man in a dark suit with his back toward them stood before the tall glass windows, staring at the night sky.

"Francis Shun Seto, Detective Jessie Hiroko Ishimine, welcome to my humble abode." His voice was deep, with a slight European accent.

Francis gave her a quick bemused look; his mouth silently traced the word: Hiroko?

It wasn't the time and place for a middle name discussion.

The man turned around to look at them. He was smaller than Andy, but still tall and imposing. His face was bearded, and his head with white hair sat low on his wide shoulders. He looked to be well into his late fifties. Jessie thought that she must have seen him on TV before but she couldn't recall. Even though he had the belly of a man who ate well, he was still muscular. His blue eyes were set deeply beneath his brows, but they glinted with prideful intelligence. He had the air of someone who easily instilled fear into people's hearts.

"What have you done with the others?" Francis demanded.

"I'm afraid they're going to be late. It looks like you're on your own." His tone showed amusement.

"What is Project Lilitu?"

"Who gave you permission to barge in here and demand answers from me? You have not yet earned your right for your answers. There's only one thing I can tell you, Francis Seto. You need to fulfill your destiny."

"What is my destiny?"

"In time it will reveal itself. To defeat me in combat is one of the many things you have to do. But now you're not strong enough."

"What if I choose not to?"

He laughed – a disdainful, scornful laugh. "You think you can choose? Free will is but an illusion. Puny human beings lead their lives following the thin threads of fate. There is never a choice. Each man embarks on a journey to fulfill his individual destiny. Some walks towards destruction, and some towards salvation. A man is not complete without his destiny."

"What are you talking about?"

"The next time you meet me, you'll be ready to accept your fate. I'll leave something for you to find me with. Until then."

The next moment he was gone, vanished into thin air.

Francis stared at something in his hand, a horrified expression on his face. It was a torn black and white photograph. There was a woman's face on it. She was smiling and very beautiful, leaning against the person next to her. That person had been torn from the photograph.

"How did you get that?"

"I don't know. It was just in my hand."

"Well, who is it on the photo?"

He didn't say anything for a long moment, as if he needed to summon the courage to mutter the next few words.

"It's my mother."

CHAPTER THIRTY-ONE

Why did Enoch Bel have a picture of my mother? Is it a message that he's going to kill her? Why is it torn? Who's the person next to her? Not only did he not get any answers coming here, he now had more perplexing questions.

Andy and Kyle strode in with a lost expression on their face as if they'd been through a trial which took their souls.

"Where were you guys?" Jessie asked them.

"We were trapped." Andy gave a quick glance to Kyle while he caught his breath. "And Kyle got us out. Where's Bel?"

"Gone," Jessie answered.

"What do you mean gone?"

"He just disappeared," Francis added. "He left this in my hand."

"Damnation," Andy cursed and reluctantly took a look at the torn photograph in his hand. Suddenly his face lit up. "That's for me."

"What do you mean it's for you?" Francis flinched while Andy tried to take it from his hand.

"It's Francis' mother in the picture." Jessie stepped between them, blocking Andy's advances.

"That doesn't change the fact that I need it to track down our enemy—"

"Come over here, guys. Hurry up," Kyle was at the far end of the room, standing in front of the tall glass window panes. "Something's wrong."

Francis looked down from the thirty-fifth floor and saw the group of people who looked only a little bigger than the size of ants, gathered around the central fountain.

"What? What's wrong?" Andy asked impatiently. The moment his words came out, a bright light sizzled where the crowd stood. A fire swept over the tiny figures. Silently, they watched each of the tiny people burned into cinders.

"No!" Andy fell to the floor on his knees, fists clenched and knuckles white. He hammered the floor with his fists like a mad man.

For the first time Francis saw tears in his manager's eyes. He didn't really care about any of those people from church, but he felt his mood turning sour. They didn't deserve to die like that.

"How did you know?" Jessie's voice was barely audible when she turned to Kyle.

"Something just felt wrong when I looked down. I don't know how to explain it."

"I got them killed." Andy finally pulled himself up and leaned against the desk in the center of the room as if he were ill.

"But why?" Jessie questioned with a grimace.

"It's a message to us saying that those who stand against him will perish." A hateful anger burned in his blue eyes, decimating all traces of tears he had a moment ago. "He'll pay for his crime."

When Francis' eyes met his, their gazes interlocked. In that moment all that enmity he had against Andy dissipated, and was replaced by a mutual understanding that they must work together to defeat their common enemy. Francis held out his hand with the torn photograph.

Slowly Andy took it and stared at it with a newfound fascination. "She's a beautiful woman."

"Why? Why does Enoch have my mother's photograph?"

"I believe I can answer your question. But this is not the time and place to discuss the matter." Andy handed the photograph back to him. "Hang on to it with your dear life. It's the only key for us to locate Bel's whereabouts. We need to get out of here. Let's find a place to sit down and plan our next move, somewhere far away from here."

The silence on the way down was unbearable, yet none of them issued any word at all. They were all solemn and grim, as if that attitude made up for what happened to those unfortunate people. Francis exchanged a glance with Jessie, and he saw a dreadful sorrow in her eyes he had never seen before. She had seen death more than he did and he had thought her accustomed to it. Yet now she looked like someone who just lost a member of her family. Maybe she wasn't as strong as she looked.

The charcoaled bodies were piled in front of the fountain, a necropolis of black rocks. Andy stood in front of the dead and murmured a solemn prayer to hopefully grant them the peace they deserved. The sound of sirens in a distance was getting closer. Francis turned away from the dead, bile lingering in his throat. He wondered where God was when these people, His Children, needed Him the most.

Andy named a place for them to meet, a sports bar at the edge of town. And said he wanted to stay a while and watch over those who had sacrificed themselves.

Kyle hurried off in another direction to his car which was parked on the street.

Silently, Francis and Jessie walked towards the parking lot. Francis wanted to say something to her, perhaps to offer comfort. But he didn't know what to say. When his hand brushed hers, he couldn't help but steal a glance in her direction. She looked down on the floor as if she was a ranger looking for tracks in the wilderness. However, her face was calm and pristine, no longer reflecting the horror they had just witnessed. When she looked up, he looked past her towards the horizon. He didn't know why he was being so furtive about staring into her eyes; he almost wanted to slap himself.

"Hey, let's just go in my car." There was an I'm-okay sort of smile on her face.

"But..."

"We'll come back afterwards for yours."

"How about I drive?"

"Nah, I'll drive. Old habits die hard."

"Are you alright?"

"I feel like a new person, after being in the elevator, after telling you everything. I've never told anyone, well except my father who's dead, and of course I had to tell my story in court, but that's it. I hid it somewhere deep in my heart. I didn't really forget it, but I chose not to recall it."

Francis thought he was the only one who kept things to himself. He had never expected her to have such forbidden secrets. He felt sorry for her having to grow up with the shadow of what happened. He wasn't fond of his own childhood memories, but after hearing hers he felt ashamed to even try to hide his own. It had probably taken a great deal of determination and courage for her to grow up unscathed and into a successful woman. He was proud of her.

"It's funny that I've always told you how good it feels to let go of all your feelings and just say it out loud. I couldn't do it myself."

"That wasn't something easy to say, even if our lives depended upon it."

"For a while I hated the person who murdered my father, abused me, and took my life away from me. Mark and I drifted from foster home to foster home until we found the right parents but I'm glad we did. There was so much hate in me. All I thought about was plotting revenge. Love from my new parents changed me. They treated me like their own daughter and I felt like I had a family again. That hate went away and I chose to not dwell on what really happened to me. Claustrophobia was my mind's defense against dread, a forged key that locked away my past. When I went to college I wanted to understand the minds of killers, but I never really did. Some say they were born with the instinct, and some say they were made into who they were. Maybe if I weren't loved at the end, the darkness would have consumed me, I would have turned into one—"

"I don't believe that."

"Don't put too much faith in me." The alarm of her car gave the signal beep of deactivation and they climbed into it before she continued. "And maybe evil just exists in the world. There's good, and there's evil. There's you and me, and there's Babel."

Don't put too much faith in me, Francis thought. I'm not sure which end of the spectrum I'm standing at just yet.

"Sometimes I wondered why I became a cop. Perhaps I wanted to know the father who I never had the chance to really know; perhaps I wanted to help the unfortunates like I once was and make sure those who did it really answer for it; perhaps I thought that little that I could do I could make a difference in this world."

"You can." He thought that she made a difference in his already. "So you never thought about catching that one guy who destroyed you life?"

She sighed. "What's the point really? He's gone for good. Sometimes I hoped that in some way he had answered for what he'd done in life, perhaps an untimely death, or maybe a lifetime of guilt. Anyway, I wasn't going to waste my life chasing after a phantom. You know what, Francis? I've made up my mind. I'm going to quit Homicide."

"What?"

"I think I'm meant to do something else. I don't know what yet, really. Just something that has to do with abused kids, or even pedophiles. I feel like a new person. After revisiting every detail in my past, and understanding it. I know becoming a cop to catch serial killers isn't what I want to do in life anymore."

"Maybe you shouldn't go on this Babel hunt." Francis understood something also. He wasn't doing this for her. He was doing it for himself – not just to figure out who he really was, but what he wanted to do in the future. Perhaps Enoch was right, he had a destiny to fulfill. He didn't like the idea of agreeing with his enemy, but something boiled like liquid gold in his heart. For the first time, he felt alive in this world; he felt that he was here for a purpose. He didn't know what yet, but the journey towards the Tower of Babel was what he needed to take part in to figure it out. And at the top of that tower, Enoch Bel awaited him.

"Maybe you shouldn't either." Her voice suddenly severed his thoughts like a sharp blade. "How about taking up that offer of going to Vegas for a few days, to get away from everything?"

Although not in this reality, she did ask him before. That was what he most wanted in his mind, to get away from everything. But that was then, now everything was different. "No, I can't. I need to do this."

For a long moment she didn't say anything. It wasn't until she parked the car that she turned towards him with an affectionate smile. "You've grown up, Francis. You're not running away anymore."

Watching that one dimple softly lighting up the darkness and the confusion that clouded him like a thick cloak, he had found out how much he was attached to her and how much he had depended on her. He needed courage more than that of fighting the unknown Pillars of Babel to let her go. "Don't come with me this time. It's not what you're supposed to do anymore."

"Don't be silly. Nobody tells me what I'm supposed to do or not. I saw those people burn to death today, watching them like God from heaven, and I couldn't do anything about it. I told myself, this is going to be my last case. What do you say, partner?"

"We might not survive this."

"Then it's my job to make sure you don't get yourself killed."

"Alright, you got a deal. Let's not keep the others waiting anymore."

The sports bar Andy recommended was a quiet joint at the corner of a local shopping mall. A few lonely patrons were scattered along the bar, holding their beer mugs and watching the TV screen behind the bar counter. Andy and Kyle were already there in the back with their own mugs. They simply nodded when they sat down and didn't question their delay.

They ordered snacks and a few more beers. None of them had dinner yet but Francis suspected no one had an appetite. He certainly felt no craving for food, not even snacks.

Andy motioned for them to watch the ten o'clock news on TV. "Today at approximately nine-twenty p.m., twenty-eight people committed suicide in front of the headquarters of Bel and Biological Engineering Laboratories in Newport Beach. They burned themselves to death, a religious message to the public that God does not condone genetic engineering. A series of bombs went off in the research tower earlier, but nobody was harmed as a bomb threat was carried out prior to the detonations. The police are still investigating whether the two incidents are related and are now questioning witnesses to the mass suicide. We'll interrupt normal programs to bring you more coverage to this tragedy as we get more information. This is Shannon O'Donald of Channel Thirteen Eye Witness News—"

Andy's fists thundering on the wooden table alerted the few dozing patrons. The bartender scowled at their table, but said nothing and soon continued drying glasses. "They didn't need to die."

"It's not your fault," Jessie said.

Silence returned when the food and drinks arrived. Each of them drank like travelers crossing a desert but none of them touched the food as if it was sacred, or poisoned.

"Kyle," Andy said, breaking the silence. "I need you to get me a tracer. A light one and it has to work across far distances."

"What for?" The man raised his eyebrows and questioned.

"The photograph... I need to attach the tracer onto it. When I restore the picture, the smaller part will reattach with the larger piece, then we'll know where he is. I assume that Bel's still carrying the rest of the photograph with him. That's what he had in mind for us to locate him."

Francis took it out of his pocket and stared into the eyes of his young mother. "Is that why he left it in my hands?" His heart pounded like drums in a concert. Why is Mother involved?

"That, and a message for you. Who do you think the person next to your mother is?"

Francis shook his head. He had no idea.

"Enoch Bel himself, twenty-four years ago."

Twenty-four years ago? Francis started to tremble. Jessie had put a hand on his lap, yet it didn't stop him from shuddering like the ground near an erupting volcano.

"Enoch's my—"

"Father." Andy finished the sentence for him.

And the truth struck Francis and shocked him like a lightning bolt. Enoch was Jean-Pierre.

"How long have you known?"

"I suspected after the incident at Mammoth. You and I are the only ones born with the power, other than Bel."

"I'm born with it? And you're…"

"I'm also his son."

Francis didn't want to believe it, but he could find nothing to deny the truth with. Andy was his half-brother. And they were all here, at Babel, for a reason.

"My mother was a dancer, no, a prostitute, in Mexico and that's where she met him. She died not too long after my birth and I lived with my uncle in Florida ever since. I never knew Enoch until joining Babel, which was an accident for me but I'm sure it was Enoch's plan all along. He told me of my lineage, but I couldn't accept him as my father. I wanted to leave the company then, but I also knew that I needed to be there. I saw the evil brooding in Babel and I wanted to put a stop to it. I didn't join Bel's cause right away. I faked interest for him to divulge information and then told him to just leave me alone while I decided. He told me his plan would take a long time into fruition and I could take my time. I used this time to plan my resistance against him.

"The time came sooner than I expected when my loyalty needed to be on trial. That's what I did in Mammoth." Andy's eyes were downcast, avoiding Francis' gaze. "Yet I've been played a fool. Not only did he know that I was the one who consorted to start the fire at the labs, he knew of my intention all along. It was all a game to him, to see how far I would go to prove my loyalty, which meant nothing to neither of us, because it's just a charade. There wasn't anything that he didn't know. He used me to awake your powers. And he also knew you would fight against him, that we would join forces. We did everything that he planned. Yet, there's nothing else that we can do. We're just little pieces on a chessboard waiting for an omnipotent power to plan the next move. People's lives are nothing but his toys. My faith is the only thing left in me, the only thing Bel couldn't take away. I pray every night for strength and courage, to see this to the end. Only that I don't even know what end this is going to lead us…"

"We're going to find out." Francis surprised even himself when he spoke. For the first time in his life he felt the need to do something.

The group disbanded shortly after, each shocked to learn the truth about Francis and Andy's lineage. They planned to reconvene at the same place the next evening to plan their next move.

Francis thought about calling his mother after he got home. Yet he didn't know what he was going to say. He wasn't going to tell her than he was at war with his biological father. His being born to this world was not entirely her fault. She had someone who loved her now and he doubted that she could really tell him anything about Enoch that he didn't already know. He didn't really need to get her involved and make her worry about him.

Everything that happened today and the truth that he found out bore down at him like a tidal wave. Yet he had felt an epiphany, a moment when questions and answers coalesced into a new truth, a truth that gave meaning to his life.

CHAPTER THIRTY-TWO

When Jessie got to the bar the next day, it was no more crowded than the previous night. Kyle was the only one there, focused on the laptop computer in front of him. While she announced herself, the man looked startled for a brief moment

"Hey, you're early."

"Old habits," she offered him a smile, and realized that it was the first time they really spoken to each other. "So, what are you doing?"

"I'm setting up the connection for the tracer system," He was connecting a line from his cell phone to the laptop. "The whole system is actually running off a server in the federal building in Westwood. But I'm going to remotely connect to it via VPN so I can run it from here."

"What's a VPN?"

"Oh, sorry. I always forget that I'm not talking to a techie." He wasn't looking at her while he talked. His eyes were intent on the computer screen before him.

Jessie often wondered how people talked and worked at the same time. When she worked on a computer, she needed undivided attention, and she bet that what she did on a computer was much simpler than what Kyle was doing.

"VPN is a virtual private network," he answered.

It still didn't make much more sense to her than before, but she decided to let it go. It didn't really matter.

"It's a little slow and probably not going to be as real-time as it should be, but it'll suffice."

Jessie only smiled and looked towards the flashing television, letting the man go about his work without having to explain to her what he was doing.

Francis and Andy soon arrived together. She surmised that they probably came together after work. She wondered if Francis was finally getting along with his manager, now half brother. He had told her before that he distrusted Andy and she wondered if that enmity had finally dissolved by understanding they must work side by side to face the threats of Babel, if not already melted by the bond of bad blood that intertwined their destinies together. She didn't really expect them to acknowledge each other as brothers, but it would be great if they at least could be friends.

The three men gathered around the computer like bees on honey, totally ignoring her existence. Men! She sighed. When it came to electronic toys, men gave their undivided attention. She often wondered which was more captivating, a naked woman, or electronic toys they had never seen before. She suspected it was the latter that would last longer in capturing their attention span.

She was glad of the first sign of harmony between them. Last time they fought in the racquetball court like archenemies intent on tearing each other's throats out. Now they were like two little boys, they were still fighting, but they were fighting to be the first to play with a new toy. She watched them in an absolute fascination.

The two looked like they were from opposite ends of the galaxy, difficult to believe that they shared a father. Andy was tanned, muscular, and had a commanding presence about him. He had the charisma of a natural leader, and his blue eyes glowed with a confidence. Francis was pale and slender, and one really had to know him to notice his presence. His brown eyes showed determination now instead of sorrow. Francis had changed, she thought. He no longer looked like the lost college freshmen trying to locate the lecture hall, no longer was the child that ran away from his problems; he was now a grown-up man who was willing to face and battle with his own fate. They were both attractive. While Andy's western face was wild, daring and manly, Francis' Asian look was more conservatively charming and boyish. Francis had told her that his mother was a newscaster and journalist who often appeared on TV. She had seen her picture and she was stunningly beautiful, even in black and white. She doubted if Andy's mother were any less attractive.

It was ironic that the two Pillars, a term she was still not very comfortable with, phantoms that were the projections of the mind, powerful entities that she could not see, also seemed like the complete opposite of each other. She remembered the clown from her dream, the mere thought of it made her tremble. And even from Francis' description of it, it had the appearance of something spawned out of absolute terror. Yet its ability was almost angelic, a power that healed and restored. Francis' Pillar, the image of Michelle, someone she had never seen but didn't doubt her beauty, with the face of an angel. Yet she was a succubus that could steal and devour a man's soul. They were opposite sides of the same coin. Perhaps it was their cooperation that will destroy the root of evil, the root of their own evil.

Francis looked up from the computer screen with a guilty face. Perhaps he felt bad for ignoring her. "Hey, Jessie. Would you be so kind to order us some food and beer? Anything will be fine. We're still watching Kyle set up the system."

Maybe not, she corrected herself. The guilty face was but bait for slavery. The men played and the women served. She rolled her eyes and grunted a yes, nevertheless.

When Kyle finished, Andy took the small black device with a flashing light from him and used some sort of super glue to attach the tracker to the corner of the photograph. Then he blew at it until he looked satisfied that the two were not coming apart easily.

"Is everything ready?" Andy specifically directed the question to the agent. "There's no turning back."

"Let me double check." He took the device from him and studied it intently like a piece of art. "Yeah, looks ready."

"Alright, let's do it outside then," Andy suggested and the four of them walked to the entrance of the sports bar. Jessie envisioned the phantom of the devil-faced clown standing before them and touching the piece of photograph. The mere thought of it did not bring her much comfort.

She watched the miniature device with the face of Francis' mother lifted up from Andy's hand like a magician's performance. For a short moment it remained stationary in mid air, as if deciding which direction to go. And then it was gone, straight behind her like a bullet escaping from the confines of the barrel.

She felt like she had just participated in a ritual, perhaps a declaration of war, a determination to hunt down the man Enoch Bel, whose existence threatened the very nature of the human race. The four stood there in a mute acknowledging silence, an understanding that they were now comrades in arms, partners that were going to journey to the end together, watch each other's back, and probably die in each others arms, if it came to that.

When they were back at the table, Jessie joined in at monitoring the LCD display. On the screen a map of the United States was displayed. The windowed display redrew itself every few seconds or so, and Jessie surmised that's what Kyle meant by not being totally real time. A red blinking dot traveled up the California coast like a bug jumping towards the top of the computer monitor, shown in an animated film sort of way, because of the constant refreshing. Only if scaled to real size of the world, the red dot was moving up in an incredibly unbelievable speed.

"Absolutely fucking incredible," Kyle exclaimed, and then flashed her a guilty glance. "Pardon my language, Ma'am. It's moving faster than missiles. I think it's almost at the speed of sound, if not faster."

"I don't think it's quite that fast," Andy observed. The dot was now beyond the California border. They watched and waited in silence as the little red bug jumped into Washington State from Oregon, traveling northbound like a determined rocket. Shortly north of Seattle, the red dot stopped moving and just blinked, like a flashing eyeball taunting them. Was that where they would meet their demise?

"Everett," Kyle observed. Jessie guessed that was the name of the small city on the northern outskirt of Seattle.

"The pyramid, Babel Cydonia," Andy added. "He's waiting for us there."

"What is this Babel Cydonia?" she asked them.

"A new building that's not completely finished yet," Kyle answered with a grim face. "Bel's plan was to move some of the West Coast operation there from the Newport office. Supposedly the new building is not populated. Nobody's seen the inside. The outside looks like a giant –"

"Pyramid." She remembered it from somewhere. "I think I might have seen it on TV."

"We're going there tomorrow then." Andy spoke with urgency, as if it was an inexorable fact and not a mere suggestion.

"I'll get us plane tickets." Kyle nodded. "Everyone leaves me your full name, as it appears in your passport. I'll try to find the earliest available flight there. And don't forget your phone numbers. I'll call to confirm."

She stole a glance to Francis and saw the fiery blaze in his eyes as he stared at the computer screen. She saw a myriad of emotions in him – anger, confusion, and hope. She wondered what she could do to console him.

He looked up at her with a stretched smile, a mute acknowledgement of her concern.

When their brief meeting adjourned, she went home with anticipation, excitement, and fear. She had made up her mind that it was going to be her last confrontation between good and evil. Although she figured that she was never going to leave criminal investigation totally behind, it was the last time she was going to walk bravely into the crossfire between angels and demons. After overcoming her childhood fears, she understood that she no longer needed to fight those who vowed to take others' life, but to help those in need like she once was as a child. She was not going to become a social worker or anything remotely close to that, but perhaps she could use her education and experience to help solve cases and rescue children from pedophiles. She wasn't afraid to think back to that few months of abuse and to determine that others who were like her needed her. Many men got away with what Johnny did, and many children were damaged. She didn't see what happened in the past as something to blame. She no longer hated that man for abusing her, for the vengeful act of murdering her father, and not even for the crooked way that the law let him walk. Events came together in her life to lead her towards her mission.

Her last case, as she had called the last confrontation with Babel, perhaps not so much as a case but a desperate war which lingered on the boundary of hopelessness, was not something that she pledged to do in front of all the deaths she had seen. The newfound determination in Francis' eyes, a purpose to find answers, a fortitude to seek redemption, and an insurmountable willpower to extinguish an overwhelming evil – it was like looking into her own eyes of her past, the girl who became a weapon to fight evil in order to look for answers, not knowing that the answers lied hidden in herself all along. Francis, just like her, needed to embark upon that journey to unlock the mysteries of his past, his identity, and his future. She felt a great need to accompany him in that quest, a strange sensation almost like a mother needing to watch her toddler's first step.

Jessie wasn't sure what kind of feelings she had for this young man whom she had known less than two weeks but felt that she had known him all her life. Not sure if it was love, she certainly did not have the heart-pounding crush on him as she had on other men, and she never thought of them as getting romantically involved. It was some sort of maternal love, or that of siblings, like between her and Mark, something that lay at a deeper level, held together by the strongest bond of friendship she had ever felt in her life. He was someone that she was sure bore no ill will towards her, someone she absolutely trusted with her life.

Walking into Enoch Bel's penthouse office at the top of the Babel tower was only a prelude to the sense of foreboding and unease. She had the dreadful feeling that none of them may come back alive. The only thing that they could do was to know that they were on the side of justice and it must prevail at the end, something that in the past she had often told herself when she was in desperate situations. It was nothing but a ludicrous ideology, but sometimes that slim hope was all one could hold on to and it made the difference.

She looked at things in her room and wondered if it was going to be the last time she was going to be here. She took out her diary and wrote her thoughts down word for word, treating it like an important record of her existence.

The phone startled her and she immediately picked it up. Kyle on the other line confirmed their departure to Seattle on United Shuttle the following day at noon. Apparently no return flight was booked, none of them really knew if they were going to return or not.

She packed a change of clothing and some toiletries and felt the sudden need to talk with her family. She didn't want to think of it as a farewell but just in case anything was to happen to her, she shook her head and didn't really want to think about it.

"Mom," she called, finding her in the living room watching TV. She was alone and Jessie was glad. If she could approach each of her family members on a one-on-one conversation, she would avoid getting emotionally ganged up. "Can we talk?"

"Of course, dear." Her mother's hair was already white, but she didn't really look old. Mom turned down the volume of the TV and looked over with a warm smile, the same smile that greeted Jessie the first day they had met as foster parent and child, a smile with such sincerity that won her over despite her distrust and doubt at the world.

"I'm getting away for a few days," she told her mother.

"Oh, where to?"

"Seattle, I think." She wasn't really sure if hell was the next stop after.

"With a man?"

"Well, not really." She knew that explaining wasn't going to be a breeze. "It's sort of unofficial police business."

"I thought you're on vacation?"

"Technically yes, that's why it's unofficial. I'm taking some matters into my own hands."

"You look troubled, dear."

It was often hard to hide emotions from one's parents, and Jessie probably had the words extremely distraught written on her forehead anyway.

"It's going to be dangerous, isn't it?"

"More than anything I've ever faced," she admitted reluctantly. "But it's something I have to do."

"Well, you're a grown up now. I know if you've made up your mind on something, nothing's going to change it."

The next thing Jessie was going to say was even harder, and she had to take a deep breath before continuing. "Mom, just in case I don't come back."

That moment they looked into each other's eyes and a wave of emotions flooded her eyes. "Don't be silly, girl."

"Just, in case. My diary," she said swallowing and then blinking her eyes to make the wetness go away. "I want you to read it. The first drawer on the nightstand."

Her mother gave a solemn nod. "But it won't come to that, dear. You promise me you'll come back here and let me see you get married and have kids of your own."

"I can promise to come back here. But I'm not so sure about the latter." They both let out a soft giggle and then held each other in a tight embrace.

"Mom, tell me what's love." She didn't know what she was thinking, but she wanted to ask that.

"You mean like the way that I love you?"

She sighed with a grimace. "You know what I mean."

"Haven't we had this conversation many times before?"

"Well it's time to hear it again."

"Are you in love, dear?"

"Mom!" she protested. "Not really."

"Not really?" Mother eyed her with a pair of nonbeliever's eyes which reminded her of the way she looked at suspects, and sometimes witnesses. "It's either yes or no."

"I was the one asking questions."

"Alright, I'm just teasing. Love ..." She took a moment to think about it. "It's about complementing each other; it's about becoming someone so completely that you can't live without each other; it's about knowing the worst things about the one you love, yet embracing and cherishing them. Your father, he doesn't say very much and sometimes he gives some very awful comments. He's stubborn and sometimes rude like an ox. He's not romantic or funny and he certainly is not rich." She glanced around furtively to check for eavesdroppers. "But when we're together it's the best thing that ever happened to me. When I look at him, I saw the adoration and care in his eyes and that's all that matters. His quietness gives me peace. The stupid things he says, although not funny, makes me laugh nevertheless. His stubbornness makes me feel a joy of accomplishment when I make him see that my way is right. And I love him, not despite all the bad traits he has, but because of them, because of who he is, it is someone I can't live without. And that's my take on love."

"Mom." Tears filled Jessie's eyes again, hearing the same words she had heard years before. "I so envy you."

"Someday you'll find your own true love. You're still a little girl. I didn't find your dad until I was thirty-five. And always remember, love is never the same for everyone. There's never a universal definition for love. When it comes down to the basics, it's all about happiness. As long as you're happy—"

"I know." She hugged her mother again, even tighter than before, as if she was never going to see her again.

Next she spoke to her father. He was a man of few words and a nod often spoke great lengths. Yet he had shown a deep concern and saying goodbye wasn't any easier than speaking to her mother.

Finally there was Mark, not only someone she grew up looking after and loved like a child of her own, but the closest of friends. During their chaotic childhood, she had nothing to cling on to except the hope to find a loving home for Mark so he could grow up avoiding the shadows that marred her. When he was no longer a child and the gap between their ages became less significant, they had confided in each other and became the best of friends. It was difficult thinking that she was not going to see him again.

For a long time they talked. She didn't say anything about Babel even though he was eager to know. She had planned to tell him when she came back, or he could find out from her diary if it came to that. They just talked about everyday life and nostalgic old times. Joy and satisfaction coursed through her. She was proud of him, proud of how he had turned out, and perhaps a little proud of her own role as a sister that had watched over him. He didn't get exceptional grades like she did, but he also didn't end up with the wrong crowd and almost drop out of college like she did. She was never going to be finished watching over him, but she was through worrying about him. He was mature enough to choose his way. And now she could walk her own path without regret.

Francis had called her later in the night to ask if she wanted to go to the airport together since they lived close by. It wasn't like him to be so prone to details yet he was not the same person that she had met two weeks ago. She wasn't either. Both of them had seen things that made them learn more about themselves, and made them grow. A person never stopped growing until the day he died. She hoped that she would never have to stop growing up.

She tried to go to bed reasonably early, around twelve. But she couldn't sleep. The mixture of dread and excitement pounded at her like drums in a cacophonous orchestra. She ended up adding more entries to her dairy and revisiting some fond ones from the old days. Exhausted she fell into a deep slumber shortly after four.

The next morning Francis arrived at ten. She was barely ready then, just out of the shower with her hair dripping wet. She had switched off the alarm clock by accident, and only had a little less than twenty minutes to get ready. Telling herself that she wasn't on a pleasure romantic trip, she decided that she didn't really have to be presentable. And then she corrected herself that she was always presentable, despite not having time to get ready.

She gave her last mental checklist a look to make sure she had her passport, wallet and badge, guns and ammo, and everything else she had stuffed into the traveling bag. Francis didn't have to wait long.

Talking to Francis had become more and more comfortable since the first day they had met. He was still a quiet fellow, and she liked it the way he was; some people found solitude in silence. The important thing was he now paid attention. He was a good listener, and little things that he said often had more profound meanings than he gave credit for. And most importantly, the silence was not awkward between them. Being in the force had taught her that the best of partners were not the ones who always had something to talk about, but to know when to be silent and feel utterly comfortable in the silence. Francis had become a good partner.

John Wayne Orange County Airport was only a quarter hour drive away, situated at the edge of Newport Beach, not far from the Babel buildings. It was considerably smaller than LAX, the main airport for Los Angeles, but it was far from being deserted. The silicon valley of LA, Orange County, was busy with its own air traffic. Consultants and other businessmen who traveled day in and out to get to work populated the ticket counters and the hallways like working ants.

They didn't have to wait long before Kyle and Andy came to the United Shuttle counter. Each of them had dressed casually with T-shirts, polo shirts, jeans and khakis. Standing in the midst of the suit-wearing crowd, they looked like a group of tourists. The fact that they didn't know what was going to happen on their trip ironically matched the way they looked.

None of them had any sizable luggage. Kyle had brought his laptop computer with him, saying that it would be a good source of information if they happened to need it. After getting their boarding passes with confirmed seats, they marched towards the gate with grim determination.

Both Kyle and Jessie had the authority to bypass the metal detectors with their badges so they could enter with their firearms, but perfunctorily their luggage still went through the X-ray sensor.

"Where's my laptop?" Kyle said impatiently, while he waited for the leather case to come out of the sluggish dark tunnel of the sensory machine. The rest of them were already at the other side of the checkpoint, the entrance point to the boarding gates. Handheld luggage of various sizes from the people who stood in line behind them had already been spit out by the machine, yet there was no sign of Kyle's leather case.

He confronted one of the security officers and demanded the whereabouts of his portable computer.

"Sir, are you sure you put it in here?"

"Yes, of course. She saw me put it in." He referred to Jessie. "Her bag was right after mine. And she picked it up right after. I saw no sign of mine."

"You sure?" The guard eyed him with suspicion, in spite of knowing that he was a federal agent. "You sure nobody else picked it up?"

"I'm been watching the whole time. I'm telling you, it didn't come out."

"That's not possible."

"Well, the impossible just happened," he said glowering at the guard. "Let me speak to your supervisor."

The guard reluctantly walked away, red-faced, to a telephone behind the machine.

"It's just a laptop, Kyle," Andy hissed softly right next to the agent's ear. "Don't worry too much about it if you don't get it back. The Bureau will get you another one."

"I have a lot of personal things in it, and I thought we might need it later on."

"That can't be helped. You should have backed it up. And I don't think we'll really need it anyway."

"But… how?"

"It's just a guess, but I think we might have been attacked."

"Pillars?"

Andy put a finger to his lips and motioned the agitated agent to be quiet while the security guard engaging in a conversation with his newly arrived supervisor gestured towards them. "We'll wait for you at the gate."

"You think we might have been attacked?" Francis asked, after they were a few paces from the checkpoint.

"It's possible. You don't see things disappearing from airport security checkpoints everyday." Andy's answer was bemused, but not without certain truth. "Bel is going to try to eliminate us before we get to him. I'm sure of that. It's all part of a big game that we have no choice but to play. Be on guard at all times, and be afraid. Fear will make you cautious, and caution will save your life."

"Are you sure we should be getting on a plane at all?" Jessie couldn't imagine what would happen if a supernatural war was started in the middle of the sky. "A plane is not exactly the ideal place to get into a fight."

"There really is no ideal place to start a fight," Andy looked forward at the disembarking passengers at their designated gate, his handsome face for a while lost in deep thoughts. It reminded her of Francis when his mind wandered. Despite their many differences, that expression was similar.

"We have already chosen to be here. Let's make the most of it."

When they found empty seats to wait for the boarding announcement, Kyle returned with a defeated expression that seemed to say I give up. He didn't make any additional comments or complaints. All of them had already expected that his lost goods were not recoverable. The only questions now were that when the enemy was going to attack again, what kind of power their enemy had, and where this assassin was hiding.

Jessie glanced around furtively, trying to study each person in the waiting area. It was hopeless. Any of them could be an enemy watching their every move, waiting for the best chance to strike. Be it the man in a suit reading his newspaper sitting right across her, or the woman in a business suit who kept tugging at her short black skirt and glancing around to see if any men was watching her display of seductive legs, or even the kid at the far end of the aisle whose only interest was the Gameboy he was holding. She certainly hoped Babel did not stoop so low as to use kids as experiment subjects against them. Danger was not only at every corner, but in the very air that they breathed.

Having expected this before coming on to this trip, she didn't have any second thoughts now. She was reasonably safe because her three companions were the most powerful of hosts. Francis had explained to her what each of them could do. Kyle could change the state of matters with a blink of an eye. Andy's Pillar had superior strength and speed and was also gifted with the power to heal. Lastly Francis' Michelle who wielded a blade like a seasoned samurai, had also stolen part of Tormentor's power, a degrading cell death to those she touched, and she was a constant growing Pillar who knew no limits of power, only the number of souls she devoured. Maybe it was because of Francis' influence, she had thought of Michelle as a separate entity to Francis. And maybe she saw the evil core of the succubus as something entirely different from Francis' kind soul, a way of saying that she did not want to hold the deaths the succubus had caused to Francis' account, even though none of the victims of the she-demon had deserved to live. Noticing how far her thoughts had digressed, she told herself that she was in good hands, plus she was good enough to defend herself.

Andy's voice interrupted her thoughts. "Understanding and knowing the true limits of our enemies' power would be the first step to victory," he warned them, as if he had anticipated the very danger in the air. "Ignorance will be our defeat. The first step is not to fight, but to be aware of, to comprehend the powers of our true enemy. And always remember this: we'll never win the war unless we understand what Enoch Bel's power is."

"And that means," Kyle added in a whisper. "Everyone we come across that's trying to kill us, if we can avoid taking their lives. We'll do so and try to find out from them what kind of power Enoch's Pillar holds. Even though I doubt any of his mere underlings would know, we can't let the chance that the closest of Enoch's guard would have that knowledge slip out of our hands."

Andy nodded in absolute agreement, a small smile formed on his regal face. "He wants to play a game with us. We'll use that very game against him."

They had a plan, of a sort. It was time to board the plane. The ultimate battle of good and evil was drawing near, and they seemed to have the odds working against them. Their enemy knew them like an open book, yet they knew nothing about what they were coming up against. Jessie's heart raced and the adrenaline rushed through her like liquid gold. She couldn't help but tremble with a dreadful exhilaration.

CHAPTER THIRTY-THREE

Having not been on a plane for more than a handful of times, Jessie was itchy about flying, because she had been claustrophobic. She didn't like elevators either, but she's never been inside one for more than five minutes. Of course the time she was in one longer than that had turned out to cure her phobia. Now she felt uneasy because she knew they were going to be attacked. And on the United 737 forty thousand feet above the air wasn't a comfortable place to be, anticipating an ambush.

Jessie looked around the cabin, and felt an uneasy draft on her neck. The flight attendant just made her last round, giving a final check to passengers' buckles as the aircraft taxied out to the end of the runway. They were in the middle of the airplane, economy class. Next to her Francis had put his seat in the upright position, an air of nervous silence hung around him.

She looked back at the two guys behind her through the thin gap between Francis' and her seat. Kyle stared out through the window, his glasses sparkled in the sunlight, hiding his expression. Andy looked the opposite way, one of his shoulders leaning out of his seat as if the space was too tight for him. Her eyes focused on his finely chiseled features. Just before she was going to look away, his ocean-blue gaze landed on her. She was caught like a child through a peep hole, and she felt even more embarrassed when his mouth twitched into a smile. She looked away back to Francis, who was still staring at the back of the seat before him with an oblivious face. She wondered what he was thinking.

The engine sounds amplified. The airliner started moving. She felt the sensation of being thrown backwards, and soon the floor was coming up under her feet. The body of the aircraft followed the nose into the sky, and they were on the way to Seattle.

There was a tap on her shoulder. Kyle leaned over from the back with a manila envelope in his hand.

"I thought you two should take a look at this."

"What is it?" she asked, taking the yellow envelope.

"Something the Bureau cooked up, the file on Bel."

She opened it and skimmed through it. There were two photographs. One was taken recently, the other probably in his early forties with fewer lines on his gaunt face. The man had powerful features, not as handsome as Andy's but with the same commanding presence. His eyes were not as penetrating, but looked as if they were made to hide deep secrets – lonely, with sorrowful depths, sort of like Francis when she thought about it. She didn't really have a chance to study the man when she met him because her fear was clouding her senses, so she took the time to study the pictures now.

He was born in 1949 in Nigeria, Africa. His father, David Baal (she noted the inconsistency of the family name), worked in the French embassy in Nigeria and had Egyptian blood. His mother was a daughter of a rich French family in the textile industry which operated across central Africa. Both parents passed away when he was eight in a plane crash which he miraculously survived. He was then brought up by his uncle from his mother's side who resided in London. As a child prodigy, he attended Oxford University at age thirteen and completed his first undergraduate degree in Chemistry, at age fifteen. He then moved to the United States, changing his family name to Bel, and attended medical school in Harvard, became a brain surgeon, but later quit his residency to go back to school, earning his doctorates in biochemistry, molecular biology and neurology. He won his first Nobel Prize in biochemistry when he was forty-one, a theory dealing with ATP consumption. The company, Bel And Biological Engineering Laboratories, was founded two years later when Enoch Bel quit his research and teaching at the university and became a successful entrepreneur in the blooming biotech industries. When he was fifty, he won his second Nobel

Prize with his breakthrough research in the permanent genetic cure of Cystic Fibrosis. This time Enoch Bel and the growing young company B.A.B.E.L. took full credit of the successful discovery. Investors poured in from all over the world and the company quickly grew tenfold in just a year, becoming a multinational multi-billion dollar corporation.

That was the success life story of Enoch Bel. Not the usual confidential files from the Bureau with vicious criminal records.

"Baal," Francis murmured. He said the strange word in a daunting way.

"What about it?" She couldn't place where she have heard the word.

"In mythology Baal is an evil god," Francis explained.

She wished she could have asked Mark, who was the true expert in folklore and occult religion.

"In the Bible," Andy's voice startled her. "Baal is short for Beelzebub – demons, the devil, antichrist, and pure evil."

"Just a name. Egyptian or Arabic, right?"

"Then why change it?" Andy added, proving his point. "Francis and I are children of the Antichrist, spawn of evil. We must challenge our birthright and let God show us the light. We must use that light to purge the world of darkness, the darkness that flows in our very veins."

That was melodiously poetic, if not a little unrealistic, she admitted. "Francis Baal,"

He glared at her, protesting. "Please don't call me that."

"Sounds ominous, doesn't it?"

"Gives me the creeps, Hiro."

"Alright, be nice. No name calling."

"You got a deal."

"And it's Hiroko, not Hiro."

"I like Hiro."

"Suit yourself. You're not going to say it anyway."

A little over half an hour after flight, when she was on the way back from the restroom, she felt a skewering sense of wrongness. The aircraft tilted to the left side. Her feeling of wrongness that pricked at her skin like a teasing sharp blade wasn't about the skewed plane. She surveyed the people that had seated before her. They seemed somehow different after the five-minute sojourn in the bathroom. When she went back to her seat, Francis' eyes were closed, his head tilted, leaning on the window side of the cabin. There was something different about him. She couldn't identify the difference at first, but after a moment she noticed that his boyish face became even younger. It was the same face, yet it was devoid of the maturity he had when she met him.

"What's wrong?" Andy was still sipping at his drink.

Jessie studied him. He looked the same.

She didn't answer him and looked over to Kyle. The man's arm was folded, head lowered in a grim concentration. He looked younger, without the lines of middle age.

"Anything wrong with me?" Jessie asked.

"You look just fine." Andy said it in a way that bordered on sexual harassment. She let that go, wondering if the joke really made her feel better or worse.

"No, seriously. Look at Kyle."

He did. "Oh, shit." That got everyone's attention. "But you look the same."

"So do you." But why? She glanced around the cabin at other passengers, but there was no way that she could tell if they looked any different.

Because none of their faces had been noticed before and there was nothing to compare with.

"I feel..." Kyle studied his own hands, marveling at it. "This is so strange, I feel invigorated in a way. Younger."

"What about me?" Francis asked her.

He was even considerably younger now. He was a little frailer than she last remembered him, and he looked like he would have a few years back. "You look younger."

"But I still remember why I am here," he said. "It's not like we went back in time."

"Yet it looks like biologically you guys are going backwards in time," Andy observed. "I think we're under the influence of a very powerful Pillar, something that has a wide attack range. We need to find and terminate the host."

She wasn't listening to him, but wondering why Francis and Kyle had been changed but not Andy and her. The key to solving the mystery was to know the rules. Assuming that the whole airplane was under the same influence of this power, and Andy was unaffected. Was it because of the drink in his hands? Perhaps the humidity? No, a drink didn't have that much water in it, plus he had already drained his glass, the only thing remaining was two blocks of ice cubes. What about herself? She was a woman, that's all she could think of. The two things didn't connect.

A shrill scream from a woman came from the back of the cabin. She un-holstered her Smith & Wesson, holding it steady with both hands. Her sudden motion shocked everyone in the cabin and they looked at her wide-eyed, thinking her a terrorist hijacking the plane.

"What the hell are you doing?" Kyle grunted.

"LAPD," Jessie managed something close to a roar, getting everyone's attention. "Investigating possible terrorist activity on the plane. Nobody moves. Nobody makes a sound." The woman in the back ignored her warning, screaming like an afflicted patient in an asylum.

"I'll come along and guard your back," Andy said behind her.

"Bring the glass."

"Excuse me?"

"Just bring it."

"Yes, ma'am."

*   *   *   *

Francis stared at his own hands. They were the same hands, yet he looked at them as if they were different. Michelle, he called out to her, to the power that was within him. What was inside a moment ago was now replaced by an empty void. She was no longer with him. She no longer guarded him. He had thought of her as a curse, and he wanted to find a way to get rid of her before. But now he felt empty, vulnerable, without her at his side. And he almost felt like he needed to apologize to her for ever trying to wish her away. He knew why Michelle was gone, because his body had gone back in time. Still technically, or biologically, he had the power since birth, but it did not wake itself until Andy's Pillar triggered it. He was now completely defenseless.

Kyle was standing in the aisle and he gestured for Francis to follow him.

"We are going to check the front while they check the back," the FBI agent said. He looked younger. He was still bald though, the shiny surface of his scalp glowered under the cabin lights.

"I've been bald for a while, it's something done by choice." Francis felt instantly embarrassed for looking at his bald spot. "Cao is gone."

It took him a while before he realized that Kyle was referring to his Pillar, the image of his little girl. There was an unspeakable sentiment and sadness in his eyes. Francis wondered how personal the man had viewed his own Pillar.

"Mine's gone too." And he'd always thought getting rid of it was going to be something worth celebrating, it was hardly that.

With Kyle leading, they walked forward at a slow pace. And that turned into a run when screams came from the front of the plane. Francis guessed something happened in the first class cabin.

There was nobody there. No passengers, no stewardess, not even the seats. The first class cabin was an empty room like a staging ground for a Hollywood movie.

Kyle held him back and pointed. Francis saw some sort of distortion in the emptiness. Something was in the middle of the room, floating. He couldn't really see it, but he could feel it. And looking through that thing at the back wall, to the front of the airplane, straight lines became slightly undulating, like looking through heat waves in a desert. Something stood between them and the head of the plane, and that same thing totally erased everything in the first class cabin like they never existed.

Both of them backed away. Francis cursed at his loss of power, and his lost perception. If Michelle were here, he would know what he was up against.

"There's more than one of them." Kyle's observation brought no additional comfort.

Francis' shirt was loose. He was shrinking. He was probably nothing more than a teenager now. He wondered what would happen to them at the end. Turning back into a fetus? Reverse Meiosis. Back into egg and sperm and then cease to exist. He looked back at the unaware passengers, thankfully there were all businessmen, and none as young as him. Yet he had remembered seeing a boy in the waiting area. That meant he wasn't going to be the first becoming a fetus, the thought horrified him.

He backed away another step, out of the restroom and preparation area that separated first class and economy class. Before them, an unseen force was digesting the plane. Behind them, a more malevolent force was trying to take them back in time, except their mother's womb was not here to save them. And anyone before them could be an enemy.

Only one thing was clear. Even backwards, the clock was ticking. They were running out of time.

*   *   *   *

She tried to look into everyone's eyes when she slowly marched towards the end of the plane, with Andy trailing behind her with the glass in his hand. The ice cubes rocked against the glass like marbles in a child's hand. Everyone appeared full of dreadful fear as she marched past them pointing her weapon forward. She wondered if that fear was a reflection of hers.

Through a few standing passengers and stewardess, Jessie reached the woman in the back sitting on an aisle seat holding a baby in her arms. There were tears and madness in her eyes. The infant in her hand was naked, quietly sucking on his thumb looking innocent and lost. He was no more than a few months old. The seat next to the woman was empty, only with a few articles of children clothing scattered like a messy corner of her closet.

When she saw the flashing Gameboy screen next to a small wrinkled T-shirt, she understood. She remembered the little boy she had seen earlier before boarding the plane. Because of his age, the reverse aging process was much more noticeable than adults like herself. That was why the mother screamed earlier, and was now helplessly clinging onto her child. In a few minutes, maybe, the little boy was going to turn back into…. She didn't really want to think about it.

"Tell me what's happening to my child." The woman ignored the gun, but looked at Jessie as a desperate pleading mother.

"Can you reverse the process?" she asked Andy behind her.

"I'm trying," he let out a short exasperated breath. "But no. He's not damaged, it's just going backwards in time. I can't do anything about it. The only way we can help the baby is to eliminate the host."

She looked at him. He was younger, with a delicate, unlined face. The power was finally affecting him, and she was sure it was affecting her also. She felt the subtle change in herself.

What was the link between him and her? What was the link between the glass he was holding and her? If she couldn't solve the riddle the baby would die, and at the end they would all return to where they came from, sperm and egg, cells, nothingness. It was desperation that suddenly made it all click together.

"Put the ice cubes on the baby," she told Andy. "It'll perhaps halt the process, if I'm right."

As Andy proceeded as she instructed, she started walking back towards the front, while she searched her memory to find the clue. She had remembered seeing a glass of ice cubes somewhere. If she was right and her assailant was a man, he would be subjected to the same rules of the game. He would have a glass of ice cubes. The connection between her and the ice cubes was temperature. Their enemy was attacking based on body temperature. Someone who had a higher body temperature was more susceptible to the attack. A woman had a slightly lower body temperature, and so did a man who was chewing ice.

She found him – a man in a business suit just like any others with dark hair and a mustache. He held a glass filled with ice cubes. She pointed the barrel of her gun straight at him. He glared back at her without fear. She hesitated.

Throughout her career she had never shot someone unarmed, unprovoked. She had to make that choice now, and she had no time to waste. He could be upon her any moment now. The physical manifestation of his Pillar could kill her in a second. She was as vulnerable as a sheep in a fox's den. A moment of hesitation would have cost not only her life, but perhaps everyone else's life on the airplane. She wagered that he was not an innocent man.

She fired, just before she felt something powerful knock the wind out of her.

*   *   *   *

Francis saw the distortion taking form before his eyes. It was a ball as black as tar, a miniature black hole. Just like the phenomenon he saw in space movies, this black hole before him was sucking everything in its path into its void. An emptiness that was boundless and limitless, the black hole would devour them without remorse.

"We're getting back to normal," Kyle said. "Andy and Jessie must have finished one of the assailants. Now it's our turn to stop this madness."

He was back to his normal age. He once again felt the familiar power within him. He felt a gravity-like force pulling him towards the blackness. He backed away another step. The black hole was advancing, and people were going to die.

"I have an idea," Kyle said, looking up at the ceiling of the cabin. "Francis, get ready to sprint forward as quick as possible."

Glancing up, Francis took a while before understanding what Kyle planned. Cao, the little girl in the purple dress, Kyle's Pillar, hung inverted right above them like a spider crawling along a horizontal support beam. The same physical laws of nature did not seem to apply to Kyle's Pillar as it had to him.

She was changing the structure of the plastic panels above them. He saw the plastic panel bubbled and oozed like the surface of a swamp. When the cloudy liquid started dripping down, it looked like he was in a cave with inverted icicles waiting to fall and crush him any moment.

He heard the screams behind him as other passengers noticed the phenomenon. Through the plastic hole and the electronic wires beyond the panel, there was the metal casing, the outer layer of the plane. On the other side, the sky, with currents going backward at four hundred miles per hour, would provide a horrible death to those who were jettisoned. He glanced at the slowly approaching mass of blackness, a more horrible fate awaited those who were unfortunate to be drawn inside.

A loud pang and he felt the currents moving. The newly constructed hole above them was trying to suck them out of the airplane. Cao was gone then, no longer clinging above them like an agile ape. The black sphere, now crumbled like a squashed soccer ball, was the next to be flushed outside by the sudden displacement of air.

Francis looked forward, the coast was clear. Braving the updraft of current, he launched himself in a dash of madness, using Michelle's limited strength to propel him like a rocket. He was out of the danger zone and now in the empty first class cabin which was hauntingly quiet.

Before him was the cockpit. Whoever sent out the black hole was beyond the door, he was sure of it. He kicked the door open.

The copilot was missing. He had never been in a cockpit but he knew there were supposed to be two pilots. A woman turned her chair around, and looked back at him in surprise. He had never seen any female pilots, even though he knew that the career was not exclusive to men. Her white collared shirt confirmed her identity. She was young and attractive, but she was also an enemy. Her fright confirmed it as Michelle descended upon her like an angel of death.

"No," she screamed before the long fingers went for her throat. "We'll all die—" Her voice was then muffled by the nails digging deeply into her carotid artery. Blood gushed out of her throat, trailing down Michelle's hands. He thought about letting her go just like he had let Sophie go, but she was trying to decimate everyone on her own plane. She did not deserve to live.

"Why?" He looked into her eyes as he felt her life slowly drifting away. "Why all the innocent people on the plane?"

He felt a strong pull behind him. The edge of the black hole was but inches away. It was back. It was trying to suck him away to oblivion. It was her last defense.

He felt the essence of life, the essence of her soul flowed into him as he gave a violent tremble of ecstasy. It was a new height of sensation, something infinitely more powerful and alluring than what he felt the previous time.

He felt her windpipe crush in Michelle's hand. He stared at her dead eyes, still staring at him widely. The force waiting to devour him had dissipated. That was what it came down to – the basic rules of nature, to either feed or be devoured. He was only doing it to save himself, to save other innocent people on this plane. He had done nothing wrong. Yet, he wondered why he felt so guilty about the ecstasy that was flowing through him like an accursed drug.

Slumping to the floor of the cockpit, Francis was immobile as the power coursed through him like wild currents of an electric charge. His senses ran wild, chasing the current like thunder after lightning. His limbs were numb, and he felt nothing except the thrill that surged through him like successive waves of an orgasm. Each time he took someone else's life, the sensation increased at least ten fold.

Darkness enveloped him.

*   *   *   *

Jessie tried her best to drag Francis out of the cockpit. The shoulder she had hit when she fell ached. Even though Andy repaired it right after the impact, her shoulder still felt like it had shattered into little pieces. She knew it was only psychological, she was only remembering the pain instead of feeling it. She told herself that Francis needed her now.

The plane dipped to the side and she was thrown off balance. Taking a deep breath, she staggered out of the cockpit with Francis slumped against her.

The aircraft was losing altitude. Even though Andy and Kyle had patched the hole they drilled earlier, the plane had been blown off course, and there were no pilots left to steer the staggering, plummeting bird of steel.

Emergency oxygen masks fell from the overhead compartments. People were panicking, screaming, yelling at each other. There was nothing Jessie could do to calm them. She had saved them from an earlier death, yet she was helpless to save them from this plunging destruction.

She got to the emergency exit, and out the window she saw the blue ocean below her. It felt like to her that the blue sea was but inches away. There were probably still a couple thousand feet above the surface, but in the next few minutes they would be at the bottom.

Andy turned away from the window and folded his arm. With a face calmer than the sea, he smiled when he saw the concern on her face. "Don't worry, Kyle will get us out of here."

Francis, are you afraid of death? She shook him, trying to wake him up, but to no avail. What happened to you?

"What are we going to do, officer?" A woman whose face was full of worries and fright asked her.

"Just go back to your seat and calm those around you. It's going to be okay," Jessie lied.

Kyle came to them from the first class cabin and the way he shook his head indicated that he had no idea how to control the airplane, even though earlier he told them that he had limited helicopter piloting experiences. They were running out of time. In the matter of minutes they would plunge into the ocean.

"Alright, we'll have to go with plan B." Kyle had told them to wait at the emergency exit earlier, if he failed to seize control of the airplane.

Jessie wondered what plan B entailed. "And what is that?"

"We're going to jump," Kyle answered with a straight face.

"You're not serious."

"Dead serious. Don't worry, it's going to be alright."

"What about—" she was going to ask about the rest of the passengers on the plane. But suddenly, as Kyle took the unconscious Francis, Andy's hand gripped her arm and pulled her towards him. The plane was plunging nearly vertically. The emergency exit door before her became distorted; oozing, melting, and bubbling like hot liquid. Andy pressed her against the now rubber-like wall. Being pressed up against his rock hard body and immersed in something like a mud bath, her situation for the moment was vaguely erotic. A gust of wind blew behind her, she heard the loud rumbling of the aircraft's engine and felt herself tumbling down to whatever lay below. Behind her the cacophony of screams and wails was like an orchestra of death. Closing her eyes and hearing her heart thump, she heard something hit water with an exploding splash.

Jessie opened her eyes, and saw Andy gazing down at her. He smiled charmingly and told her they were safe. She twisted her leg a little bit trying to get to a more comfortable position and felt her kneecap softly brushing against his groin. She felt him get hard and she turned her face away, embarrassed. She was not offended, but only swallowed.

"I'm sorry." He rolled away from her.

She let out a short breath. With her hands, she felt the rubber-like substance under her. They were floating on top of something Kyle had created out of the emergency exit door from the plane. She looked over at Francis, who was in Kyle's arms and finally stirring. They made it. They were safe.

A short distance away from them she saw flames erupt like blistering fireballs. Only the tail and one side of the wing were visible above the surface of the ocean, and they were rapidly sinking. Jessie struggled to stand up but Andy gripped her arm and pulled her down. "There's nothing we can do for them anymore. May God watch over them in heaven."

"But..." She didn't really know what she wanted to say. She only closed her eyes and let a drop of tear run down her face.

CHAPTER THIRTY-FOUR

Francis mutely watched the remnant of the aircraft disappearing. He didn't really know what to think anymore. A moment ago before he passed out, he was caught up in the guilt of killing an enemy, enjoyment he felt from taking her life. Now a whole plane of bystanders lost their lives in front of him, innocent people, but he felt numb about their deaths. He felt sorry, but it wasn't his fault, he wasn't responsible. He was only trying to stay alive.

He looked over at Jessie. She had the same numb expression on her face, except for the tears sliding slowly down the curve of her cheeks, glistening in the sunlight. He reached over planning to wipe them away with the back of his hand, but she already did so herself and only nodded at him.

"So how do we get out of here?" After marveling at the half liquid steel he was sitting on, Francis looked over at the shore. It was visible. He guessed that was perhaps a mile away, perhaps less. "Do we swim?"

"No, we walk."

Francis had thought of it as a joke but Kyle's straight face told him that he wasn't trying to be funny.

Cao was jumping up and down, and wherever she touched the water, it turned into ice. Kyle walked first, trailing behind his Pillar, Jessie looked skeptical and took a long time examining the thickness of the icy plates they were stepping on. She knocked at it with the heel of her boot. Cao looked back at them with a bemused face. Apparently if they were too far behind, the ice was going to turn back into water.

As Jessie started her walk across the ocean, Francis touched the bridge of ice out of curiosity. It wasn't cold. "How come it's not cold?" he asked Kyle.

"Cao doesn't change temperature," Kyle explained as they carefully walked across the sea. Francis bet if someone were watching them from the shore, they would be freaked out entirely. "She changes the distance between particles. What you see as ice is not really ice, but solid H2O. That's why it's not cold. Just like metal and plastic, she melted them and wrapped it around us but they're not hot as they would have been in their natural state."

It made a strange sort of sense, Francis thought. Not just temperature, pressure could affect the forces between particles. That's why in places with high pressure, water would turn into ice above its natural melting point. But this was the first time he saw solid water in room picture, not to mention liquid metal that felt like a waterbed. The power of Pillars could not really be rationalized by conventional rules of physics.

"So, what do you see when you look at something?"

"What do you mean?" Kyle looked a bit lost with his question.

Francis thought he needed to rephrase it. "I mean, do you see particles when you look at something?" He assumed that the agent would have to see individual particles in order to manipulate them. He couldn't imagine how someone would view life seeing every single particle in an everyday object.

"Nope, Cao does. I don't specifically. Is that right, Cao?"

The little girl nodded happily as she sauntered ahead.

"She's a type C Pillar, isn't she?" He finally began to understand.

"Yes," Kyle confirmed. "She has a personality. She doesn't do everything that I tell her to, but most of the time she's a good girl. At night sometimes I have to tell her bedtime stories, so that the next day she'll have a good temper."

Jessie leaned over and whispered, "This is just way weird."

"Yes," Francis whispered back. "You know, there are some Chinese stories about people keeping ghosts of children as pets. They do things for you and you have to feed them sweets. If you forget to feed them they turn on you. I almost see a similarity here."

"Yikes, you're giving me goose bumps." She said rubbing at her arms.

"Francis ..." she said slowly and softly, and he thought he was detecting a trace of affection.

"Yes?"

"Oh, nothing. Never mind."

Perhaps the wind had blown the affection away. Or perhaps it was just his feeling stressful. And perhaps... he wondered how many chances he would have in his life walking across Pacific Ocean, well perhaps not all the way across, just a little part. But somehow it felt special in a strange sort of way. He wondered if she felt the same way. Damn, what the hell is happening to me?

He looked behind him. Andy trailed at the back where the ice was almost dissolving. The man was unusually quiet, and he lowered his head while he met Francis' gaze. It wasn't like him to be shying away from eye contact. Francis thought that was his specialty. Somewhere deep down his heart he still distrusted Andy, perhaps it was the clown. His fear of that particular clown was a much deeper terror than Jessie's claustrophobia. And he knew exactly why he was afraid of it. As a child he had been terrified of his father's gift, and both the doll and Andy's Pillar wore the same devilish face. He wished what he saw in his childhood was but an illusion, but he knew it was true – a memory branded deeply in his mind.

When they got to the shore, Kyle was exhausted and almost collapsed on the beach. It must have taken him a lot of energy to construct the icy bridge. Luckily they had arrived at an unoccupied beach and encountered no swimmers or surfers.

Francis had no idea where they were, but an educated guess would be somewhere north of San Francisco, according to the flight path.

While they rested, Andy suggested that they should hitchhike north and then try to find a car rental place so they could drive the rest of the way. Apparently reaching their destination by flight was way too dangerous. If they were going to jeopardize anyone's life, it better be just their own.

They were only a few minutes from the highway after climbing a steep incline off the shore. Andy resumed his leadership role. He instructed Jessie to target a vehicle on the highway, preferably a truck or something that had the capacity for all four of them, for hitchhiking while the rest of them waited a distance back. She was a girl, so it was going to be easier to stop someone, plus she had a badge, the ticket to get them on board easily.

It only took her five minutes to stop a small pick-up. The driver was a middle-age man going up to Oregon after visiting a friend in San Francisco. Since they had picked a car at random, Francis thought that the driver being an assassin sent from Babel was a slim chance. However, he wasn't sure how long it would take for those who wanted them dead to pick up their trail. He was ready for them this time.

Sitting at the back of a pick-up truck wasn't an ideal way of traveling. It was dangerously uncomfortable, and not even legal, Francis thought. The wind cut his face and the sun bore down on them like an inferno. The only thing that stood against him and the road, which was going by at eighty miles per hour, was a fragile wooden fence. Not to mention he had to sit cross-legged and his legs felt numb.

"We're twenty miles from Point Reyes Station," Andy observed. "On the Pacific Coast Highway."

"Where's that?"

"A little north of San Francisco, still a good two hundred miles away from the Oregon border."

"When do you think we'll get to Seattle?"

"Let me see," Andy stared at the opposing traffic that flashed by like rockets. "It takes around thirty hours of straight driving from LA to Seattle. We're about seven hours from LA. Today is Friday, we're going to get there Sunday latest, assuming that we don't get slowed down too much on the way."

*　　*　　*　　*

She was the only one sitting in the front. Even though Jessie preferred to be in the back, it would seem rude to abandon the driver. While the music from KISS FM station hummed softly in the background, the man was quite chatty, talking about his family. She listened, nodded, and briefly concurred with him when he asked for her opinion, but she wasn't really paying attention.

She wanted to be in the back with them. But she wasn't sure if she wanted to see Francis, or Andy. Something had happened between Andy and her. She had felt it. She had felt herself drawn to him. Something pulled her to him like opposite poles of a magnet. Andy reminded her of Terry, the cool-headedness, the leadership-like charisma, the same way he looked at her. That was not the reason why her heart jumped every time she gazed into his eyes. There was darkness behind his beauty, behind his strength, behind his faith. And she was drawn to that mystifying darkness like a moth drawn to a flame. Inner demons, that's what darkness was about, and the ongoing struggle with them. Why am I drawn to darkness? Is that why I came to this journey? And I thought I came to watch over Francis.

Yet Francis, she had never felt more at ease when she was in his presence. It was a friendship so special and dear to her. The two half brothers were opposite sides of the same coin, and she liked the coin. She liked how comfortable and safe she felt in Francis' arms, and she also liked how dangerous and intriguingly erotic to be in Andy's. But a spinning coin would only land on one side.

She understood the vision she saw in church now. She had wanted someone, someone she could be madly in love with. She was in love with evil before, with finding the roots of it, with extinguishing it. Now she was here because of her desire to love one of the two men she came here with.

In her head she saw the coin spinning...

She felt like she was going mad.

Her reverie was interrupted when the driver told her that he was taking a break at the rest area a mile ahead. She grunted to acknowledge his decisions. He was the captain and she was just a guest. The ship would dock at his command. And she might as well use the restroom.

There were a lot of 18-wheelers parked at the rest area and the small pick-up they were in was like a sailboat parking alongside an armada. Truck drivers lingered around the area, talking, laughing, and munching on snacks. None looked to be in a rush to leave the place to resume their work. They were the same as white-collars, reluctant to come back to the office after their lunch break.

Francis was the first to head to the restroom while their driver headed in the opposite direction to the snack area. Kyle and Andy both jumped off the back of the pickup truck, stretching their arms and legs.

Jessie stole a glance towards Francis as she followed him towards the restrooms. She wondered what he was thinking.

The lady's room was a mess. A strong stench of urine and whatever else made her gag. The toilets were filthy, and she would rather die than have to sit on one of them. She didn't have an urgent need anyway. So she only went to the sink to wash her hands and brushed her hair back into place.

She had never been gladder to be out of the restroom. Walking over to the outside of the men's room, she waited for Francis to come out and wondered if the men's room was as bad as the one she's just been to.

A noise came from the restroom. A shattering of glass, she surmised a mirror being broken.

"Francis, are you alright?" She stuck her head around the wall, but her view was blocked. She thought she would wait at least a few seconds for response before recklessly barging in. She was not concerned about embarrassment but her inability to help and the possibility of endangering him further if under attack.

Then she heard hurried footsteps. Francis emerged from behind the wall and stared at her with a terrified expression.

"What happened?" she asked.

He continued staring at her without saying anything.

"Shit," his eyes suddenly widened and one of his hands grabbed her jaw, turning her head slightly to the side with almost enough force to break her neck. "Don't look at me."

After releasing her, he stepped behind her with his back touching hers.

"What's happening?" She tried her best to resist the urge to not look at him.

*   *   *   *

Francis splashed water onto his face and stared into the mirror. He had done the same thing on the way up to Berkeley in a roadside restroom when he was on his quest to find out about Michelle. Now it felt like a continuation of the same trip. This time he was here to understand his own identity.

He was no longer afraid of seeing the ghastly face of Michelle behind him. She was part of him. Things had happened so fast. Two weeks ago he was a loner who rejected life and escaped towards fantasy. Now he had a friend, he could be the grandson of the devil, he had a half brother he never knew about, he was a freak with weird powers, yet he had never felt more alive. He was doing something, whatever it was.

He saw something stir behind him, and felt a trickle of fear.

Turning around to study the empty restroom, he saw nothing that was out of the ordinary.

Francis turned back to look at the reflection on the mirror. Like a spider, something was crawling along the wall behind him. It was a humanoid, someone wrapped in filthy rags like a street bum, his face indiscernible.

He turned around again. Nothing.

Looking back at the mirror, he saw the approaching man was now standing upright. A long knife in his hand, the man held it backhanded liked a skilled assassin.

He turned around. Nobody stood behind him.

In the reflection, the approaching man was only a few paces away.

Instantly, Michelle guarded him, standing between him and his virtual assailant, but only in the reflection of the stained restroom mirror. The act of her appearance was instinctual, a command that was involuntary, which required no more thought than a simple reflex. In the real world she stood between him and nothing.

Francis issued a mental command to attack. She only stirred, her face showed confusion. She didn't know what to attack. He stared at the reflection and swore. The knife slashed down at him. That split second he tried his best to avoid the flashing blade. It caught his shoulder, he felt blood drawn, a sharp pain zapped through him like electricity through a conductor.

Attack, attack the mirror.

With the blade in hand, she stabbed it onto the mirror like a pin to a cardboard, nailing the reflection of the mysterious goon. The impact spider-webbed the mirror, making the reflection on it almost indiscernible. The impact did nothing to hamper the assailant, who was now moving towards Francis' reflection with the predatory finesse of a spider with its prey caught in the web.

Michelle's second stroke shattered the mirror. Francis watched them fall onto the floor like snowflakes. He heard Jessie's voice from outside and saw images of his terrified self on the floor.

There were too many reflections. He didn't know where his enemy was. He had made his situation worse than before, and his shoulder burned with a searing pain.

He ran out of the restroom.

When he saw Jessie's face, relief washed over him instantly

There was something in her eyes. She opened her mouth and words came out but he did not pay attention to it. He saw himself on the convex of her dark brown pupils.

Reflection.

A figure was reaching for his throat in the reflection.

His hand went for her jaw and he managed to turn her head aside just in time. He hated it every time he had to be rough on her, but the opportunities seemed to always be showing up, and this time she was even fully conscious to feel his rough treatment.

He stood behind her then, his back touching hers.

"What's happening?" she managed in a soft, but alarmed voice.

"I'm under attack."

"Pillar?"

"Yes."

"Why can't I look at you?"

"The reflection on your eyes." Francis glanced around to make sure he saw no other reflective surfaces. Thankfully nobody else was around. "The enemy Pillar only exists inside the reflection. I cannot see it in the real world. Yet it can hurt my reflection, and it hurts me."

"And you saw it in my eyes?" She sounded dubious, like a psychiatrist listening to her patient's ravings.

"Damn," he muttered when he noticed someone approached. He was wearing a pair of wide-framed sunglasses.

"Do you have the time?" the man asked.

Francis saw it then, he saw it clearly in the reflection on the man's shades. It was too late. He saw himself being slashed open.

$$* \qquad * \qquad * \qquad *$$

She had neither time to digest what Francis had just told her, nor to scream when she felt Francis slipping away from behind her and slumped to the ground. She turned and saw a pool of blood under his body.

Be calm, be calm. She told herself repeatedly. She pointed her Smith & Wesson at the intruder and backed away from Francis' body.

"Turn around and face the wall," she ordered the man. "LAPD."

The man did as he was told. "What, what did I do?"

"Face the wall," she repeated. "If you turn back and look at me, I'll shoot."

She backed away another step, making sure she was close enough to be able to keep her mark contained and far enough just in case if the man was a host. She remembered the rules, the farther away the Pillar was from the host, the weaker it became. She took a moment to think over what Francis had told her. If what he said was true and he was attacked by the reflection, then…

"What do you want with me, Officer? I didn't do nothing." He was now hugging the brick wall of the restroom nervously. "Can I see some ID?"

"Fucking shut up, and don't you turn around," Jessie warned. The man before them wore a baseball cap, tank top and dirty jeans. He was a typical truck driver. If what Francis said were true, the man before her could just be an innocent bystander. Someone else could be attacking them in a remote location. Yet that person in front of them could also be an enemy. She couldn't take the chance to let him go, but she could not shoot someone innocent. Francis lay limp on the ground drenched in his own blood. Is he still alive?

Andy could save him. But her companions were too far away. And too many other people were around. It wasn't wise to attract unnecessarily attention. She would risk being attacked if eyes stared at her. Yet she couldn't go get help and leave Francis alone. If he was still alive she needed to keep the enemy away from him. He must still be alive.

"What do you fucking want with me? I'm going to call my lawyer," the man complained.

"Fuck you, asshole. Just shut up." She wished she still had her cell phone to call Kyle. The only thing she could do now was to wait for them to check on Francis and her. Hopefully they would sense that something was wrong if their bathroom trip took too long. She hoped that Andy was going to get here in time.

She took another step backward, an involuntary one. She felt something wrong instantly. Glancing back she saw a pond of water behind her. Before stepping quickly away she felt a slashing impact on her back. She clenched her teeth. It wasn't a deep cut. And she realized she just experienced what Francis had told her. She couldn't see Pillars, but she was just attacked by a Pillar bound to a reflection. That also meant that the Pillar could not attack her in reality.

Hurry up, guys.

A group of people was approaching. She would be vulnerable again. Something was not right with the man spread before her. He was too calm for someone who had seen a man knifed in front of him by an invisible force. Her gaze landed on his left wrist. A watch, he had a watch, yet he had asked the time. He was the enemy. Yet she told herself that she could be wrong. She needed to make sure.

"Why did you ask for the time?"

"Because I fucking want to know what time it is. Since when is it a crime to—"

"And what's the watch on your wrist for?" She interrupted him.

"It ain't fucking working. Cheap shit my wife gave me for—"
"Why don't you take it off and throw it over here." She had a plan. If the man was lying, then he was the enemy and she could shoot him. But… "No, on second thought, hold on to it." She realized that a watch had a reflective surface. She almost set a trap for herself.

From the right side she saw a group of people approaching, all truckers she presumed. She moved to the left, while keeping a vigilant eye on the ground she was stepping on and the barrel of her pistol pointing straight at her mark's back.

Someone called her name behind her. It was Andy, thank God. She resisted the urge to look but knew he was behind a pine tree.

Jessie expected to be attacked any moment, and she could only trust that Andy could save her fast enough. When the anticipated attacks didn't come, she sighed with relief, only to realize that in any minute the approaching crowd would be upon them, upon Francis, and it would be all over.

She told Andy their predicament.

"Another world inside mirrors and reflections? That's not possible," he said.

"Never mind what's possible and not," She felt a bit agitated. It wasn't a time for scientific debate. "Go save Francis."

"We have to move cautiously." He then told her to move slowly towards Francis' body without looking at it.

Suddenly she realized her mark wasn't there against the restroom walls anymore, he had joined the truckers on the right. They were almost upon them.

"Light," Andy said suddenly.

"What?"

"Our enemy is light. What we see in a mirror is the way our eyes interpret light that reflects back to us. If our assailant attacks us through a reflection, that means he's hiding in the path of the light. If I can find where he hides, than I should be able to finish him off."

Jessie kept her eyes focused on the distant horizon as she and Andy approached Francis' body. "How's Francis?"

"I can't save him yet. I can't risk looking at him. Since he's hurt I don't think I'm fast enough to restore him before he's marred fatally."

"Damnation," she muttered while she watched the trucker who she suspected earlier pointing at their direction. The truckers were about ten good paces away. She wondered how close and clear their reflections had to be in order for Andy and her to be attacked. She was going to find out very soon.

"I have a plan," Andy said slowly, without the usual confidence he carried in his voice.

"Well, spit it out now. We haven't gotten much time." Eight paces.

"Draw their attention."

"Excuse me?"

"Make sure everyone's eyes fall on you, and you only."

Six paces.

There was only one way to do that. She swore, before she reached up and took off her tank top, and then unhooked her bra, letting it slide off her shoulders. Her breasts were bare. I am never going to do this, ever, again.

The men gawked, every single one of them, leering at her speechless like hungry animals.

Andy crept up on them from the side, kicking at the ground and sand went into one of the men's eyes, his hands abruptly covered his face. A second later that man crumbled to the ground like a melting snowman. Andy's plan had succeeded, even though she did not totally understand how he attacked something in the path of light.

Jessie got dressed quickly, couldn't help but feeling naughty and embarrassed. It was nice when a girl got attention, but too much was too much. She had to use her gun and badge to keep the commotion down, and the men away from her.

Francis got up after Andy healed him. His shirt was drenched with blood. Yet he was whole.

Jessie burrowed into his chest, hugging him in joy. She got his blood spluttered all over her too but she was just glad that he was alive. When she let go, she saw Andy watching her. She detected a hint of jealousy in his eyes.

Kyle joined them then after hearing a brief version of their story he went to appease the crowd with his Bureau credentials and to call an ambulance for the fallen man. Andy suggested that they get out of the scene as fast as possible, to avoid confrontation with local law enforcement.

$$* \qquad * \qquad * \qquad *$$

Francis stared at the pool of his own blood.

"How are you feeling?" Andy asked in a concerned but slightly bemused tone.

"Light-headed."

"You lost a lot of blood."

"The blood doesn't go back to my body," he observed.

"No, once you lose it, it's not yours anymore."

"Thanks." He was reluctant to say it, but he said it anyway. The clown had touched him again and healed him. Yet the thought of the vile creature touching him turned his stomach. If only he could choose death.

Andy said nothing. He only walked away.

CHAPTER THIRTY-FIVE

A few hours northward and the four reached Scotia, a town built by the Pacific Lumber Company on the banks of the Eel River midway between the coast and the Humboldt Redwoods.

It was a quaint small town with two huge mills and ten blocks of white houses. After spotting an Avis car rental she asked the driver to drop them off. Thanking the man, they went to the receptionist desk. At first the obese lady behind the counter was reluctant to serve them seeing their bloodstained clothes. And of course a flash of her badge changed her mind.

By the time they left with a spacious metallic Toyota Avalon and a few cross-state maps the sky was already dark. Jessie thought it was a good idea to go shop for supplies, including a change of clothes.

They stopped at Target, where they could get everything in a relative short time. That included traveling luggage bags, clothes, toiletries and even a few bags of snacks.

Andy suggested staying at the town for the night and they agreed. They were all exhausted and needed their energy replenished. Going towards the unknown in the dark was not preferable.

From the recommendations of the Target staff, they headed towards the Scotia Inn, a rustic favorite of tourists, just a block away from the famous town museum.

The inn was only half full. Although none of them were really worried about cost, they have decided to stay together in two adjoining rooms. That way they could watch each other's back if the omnipotent Babel decided to murder them in their sleep.

She chose a room with Francis, thinking that it was the natural choice. She didn't know Kyle, and she refused to let her thoughts linger on Andy.

When she prepared to take a shower, Francis told her that he was going to wait for her down at the hotel restaurant with Kyle. He said he needed something to munch on, as he was feeling rather weak from his earlier blood donation.

Jessie took her time in the shower. Water washed over her, washed away the dry blood, cleansed her spiritually, and achromatized the deaths she had witnessed. She didn't come out of it a new person, but at least she felt invigorated.

When she was finished drying herself and putting a clean shirt on, she headed out of the room and thought she would check if anyone was next door before heading down to the restaurant.

The door opened after a few knocks.

Andy only had a towel wrapped around his lower torso. She averted her gaze, embarrassed. But he pulled her inside nevertheless and pressed her against him where she had nowhere to turn.

She stared at his muscles, still glistening from the moisture, his finely chiseled face and his ocean blue eyes. They explored each other's eyes for a long moment with hunger and longing. Her throat was dry, so dry that it was almost hurting.

He was so close that she could feel his breath quickening.

When he pressed his lips to hers, her lips parted; she let the passion take over her and submitted to his deep determined kiss.

Her hands were all over his body, so were his. She untied the knot and let the towel drop to the floor. He was long, large, and beautiful. Unbuttoning her flannel shirt, she left her breasts bare. She turned away from him and let her shirt fall to the floor. She felt him watching her, wanting her. Her heart pounded.

"You're hurt," he said softly. She felt his hand touching her wound in the back, and she flinched. Warmth flew from his touch, and she felt the wounds closing. He touched her at the same spot again, now the only thing she felt was excitement.

"I want you." It was neither a confession nor a request. It was more like a demand waiting to be fulfilled.

"I know." It wasn't an answer. It was more like an acknowledgement to a command. From behind, he cupped her breasts and kissed her ears and neck; his shaft, now long and hard, pressed against her jeans.

From gently tracing the outline of her left nipple, he suddenly pinched and twisted it. Her knees shaking with helpless eroticism; the need of being hurt, being taken, overwhelmed her with sheer pleasure.

His right hand went deep into the front of her jeans. She trembled.

Pulling her away from the wall he threw her roughly onto the bed. Her blood raced.

He mounted her, his penis pressing against her flat stomach. His hands on the nape of her bare neck, he choked her. It felt like heaven colliding with hell. The darkness in his eyes, she saw it clearly now. He was succumbing to its raw power. She was succumbing to that power also. She wanted to completely surrender. When she started to have difficulty to breathe, he released her and came down on her kissing her, breathing hot air into her. She loved the way he overpowered her, she loved the way he hurt her. Nails dug onto his back, legs wrapped around his buttocks, she wanted so much to just lose herself in wild copulation. It was the act of lovemaking, the act of the creation of life that could wash away the deaths that had brushed against her.

A sense of guilt suddenly sluiced over her. She thought about Francis, and her act of pure lust felt as mortified as being walked in by her parents. It was wrong, but she longed for it. It hurt, but she adored it. She just wanted her mind to stop functioning for that moment and let her senses take over, but she kept thinking about Francis. In some odd way she felt guilty betraying him.

She pushed Andy away, and he did not force himself on her any longer. He just rolled away without saying anything. She sat up, found her shirt and started buttoning.

"I'm sorry, I can't do this," she told him.

He didn't say anything.

She just walked away.

She found the restaurant downstairs. Francis and Kyle were seated in a quiet corner. When Kyle saw her, he started pouring beer from a pitcher into an empty glass. Francis avoided her gaze. She didn't think anything of it at first. It might have been coincidental. Sometimes Francis avoided eye contact. He had done it so frequently when he first knew her. But lately he hadn't. Every time he had looked at her he seemed to have spoken great lengths with his eyes.

Look at me, Francis. Tell me I've been wrong. Look at me and make me feel warm with your friendship.

He didn't look at her. As if he knew she had betrayed him, as if he had seen what she had done. That wasn't possible. Succumbing to darkness, she surrendered to lust. She was human. She made mistakes. It wasn't like she was in some way bound to Francis.

Andy arrived at the scene. She couldn't look at him. And he said nothing as he sat down. It was going to be an awkward dinner.

Kyle was the only one talking. He didn't ask any of them the reason for the tension, he just resumed his monologue as if nothing was wrong.

Francis was the first to leave, saying that he needed sleep.

Andy was the second, saying that he had lost his appetite.

"Don't you dare walk out on me, young lady," Kyle said, like a father to a daughter, with a sense of command, yet full of warmth.

She had lifted the heels of her boots, but she put them back.

"I'm an old man."

"No, you're not."

"I am. And I watch you three like watching over children. We've embarked on a dark journey. Frankly, I don't know if any of us would come out of this alive. It's only reasonable that you have turned to each other for hope and support. I may not know any of you very well, but I do know what's going on. I've seen the way you look at each other. It reminded me so much of my youth." She wondered if he was talking about Francis or Andy, probably both.

"But you're not old."

"Don't change the subject."

"Francis saw, didn't he?"

"Naturally," he said nodding, a little amused. "He said he was going up to check on you. He came down and didn't say one word afterwards. I pretty much knew what happened then."

"Nothing really happened."

He looked at her without saying anything.

It wasn't true. She had crossed the line. Feeling ashamed, she averted her eyes and focused on the pitcher before her.

Damn it.

"I'm drawn to darkness," she confessed.

"We all are. It's knowing what's shame, knowing what's wrong, and knowing what's guilt that ultimately lead us onto the straight path."

It wasn't that simple.

"You want to be left alone?"

"Actually, stay. Don't talk to me, but just sit there." It seemed a lot to ask for. "I feel like shit."

"Why do you think you feel like shit?"

"I thought you weren't talking to me."

"I don't strike any deals with the emotionally unstable."

"I feel much better now."

"Either I go, or I stay and talk."

"Do whatever you want."

"Answer my question then."

"Why do I feel like shit?" she repeated for her own sake. "Because I do."

"Gosh, you talk like a five-year old."

"I'm ashamed."

"Why are you ashamed?"

She felt like she was being interrogated. "I'm ashamed of my guilt."

"Next, you're going to tell me you're guilty of your shame."

"Read me like an open book."

"That's circular reasoning."

"No, that's the void of reasoning. Gosh, Kyle. You're a harsh man."

"Age does that to a person."

Grimacing and pressing her hand to her temple, she said, "I don't know. Because I'm drawn to evil. Because I'm drawn to power." She wanted to say abuse, but thought better of it.

"So everyone succumbs to their urges once in a while. You're not a saint. Why should you be any different?"

She said nothing.

"Let me tell you why," he continued. "You feel ashamed of yourself because you've hurt someone you love. You have wronged him, you have betrayed him, and in betraying him you betrayed yourself. You feel tainted, you feel that you're not his equal any longer, or perhaps you're no longer superior to him."

She shook her head, and felt the tears welling up.

"He looks up to you."

"It's not true." I'm nothing. I don't deserve it.

"And you care about the way he looks up to you."

"I'm a selfish bitch."

"You may be that, but who isn't? Nobody loves another person just for the other person. We all care and love because we want something in return."

"I don't love him."

"Are you so sure?"

"And he doesn't love me."

"Then why do both of you look like the world has just fallen apart?"

She didn't know how to answer that.

Frowning, he said, "Why did you come on this journey?"

She could not answer that either.

"Do you want justice? I thought that only exists in stories. Are you drawn to the darkness? Telling yourself that would make you feel better? I think you're here because of Francis. And he's here because of you."

"He's not here because of me."

"I have seen Francis the first day when he came to Babel. He had never asked me anything other than technical questions. He never once ate outside of his desk. I had never seen joy or sorrow on his face. To me he simply didn't care about anything. Do you think he really gives a damn about stopping his own father's plan of madness? Do you think his world would be any different if Babel ruled it? Sure, he tells himself that he's going to confront Enoch Bel to find his own identity, to cleanse his own blood, to conquer his own destiny. What do you think they really mean to him?"

"What are you trying to say? You're not saying he's doing this for me?"

"No, he's doing this for himself, to prove his own self-worth. But it is because of you that he cares. He wants to be worthy in your eyes."

"This is not true," she said burrowing her face in her palms. "He doesn't love me."

"He doesn't know that he loves you. Let me tell you why I came on this journey. A few years back I lost everyone I loved in a car accident. I have no idea why I survived. I stopped believing in God. He tormented me by sparing my life. I took this assignment then, knowing that it was either suicide or completely fruitless. I was just a puppet whose strings were pulled by both sides. The bureau was long bought out and infiltrated. Babel knew about me and didn't care about my existence. To them I wasn't even a nuisance. I made my reports every other week knowing that nobody reads them. I started just sending the same file every time and nobody rebuked me for it. Life was devoid of meaning.

"Babel then started to convert some of the employees they saw as potential test subjects, or pawns that they could utilize in the future. Babel had absolute control over us, because we needed to receive the drug to stay alive, and they made sure we were mindlessly loyal. They didn't even care about my charade. I got two salaries, from both Babel and the government and I was well off. But money didn't mean anything to me. After I became a host, I saw my daughter again, I'm sure Francis told you that. I called her Cao. She isn't like any other Pillars. She has a mind of her own, a sentient entity. She is part of me, yet something else entirely. She is real. I loved again. My life was once again filled with meaning. It is the best gift I could ever ask for.

"Cao is not my daughter. I know that. But I see her as the love I had, and the love I still have, for my daughter. It's an illusion but that's all I can cling on to. All illusions end at some point. This is my journey to the end. Cao knows that, and she wants to be here, to fight the devouring darkness, to craft the end to the story of my life."

"You came here to die." She said it, not knowing whether she was for or against his ultimatum. He made it sound so inevitable that she couldn't argue with it.

"Yes, and I want to die a hero. Perhaps that's the chance God gave me. I started believing again when I saw Cao. And when I met Andy I knew the journey I was going to embark on. As an agent I was never really on the field, always supporting behind a desk, behind computer equipment. Now it was my chance to do something real. I don't really care who wins at the end, good or evil. I care that I've tried my best doing something I think is right."

After listening to his anecdote she still felt terrible, but to a lesser degree.

"Thanks."

"I'm just trying my best to make sure we stay in one piece. Now you try your best to figure out what you want."

She wasn't really sure what she wanted.

"You know, I don't really like the bureau," she told him.

"No cops ever do. We take your cases from you and show you how the real job is done."

"But you're alright. And you're wrong. This is not the end. This is just the beginning." She felt better, but she was still haunted, torn apart, ashamed and alone. He wants to be worthy in my eyes. Was I so blind by my urges that I couldn't even see that?

When she went back to the room, it was enveloped in darkness. She turned the bathroom light on and it gave her enough light to find her way in the room. Francis lay motionless in his bed, appearing to be asleep.

"Francis," she called but there was no response. She changed into the pajamas she just bought and got into her own bed. "Francis, say something."

She knew he was awake. She knew he couldn't fall asleep. She knew he was ignoring her on purpose. It was tearing her apart.

"Francis, I'm sorry." Only the still silence of the night listened and accepted her apology. "Whatever you saw me do tonight, I didn't mean to…" she took a deep breath before continuing. "I didn't mean to hurt you. I just ended up hurting myself. I don't really know what came over me. I don't love Andy. I …" She didn't really know how to continue.

"Francis, say something. Tell me you understand. Tell me you'll forgive me." Tell me you love me.

There was only silence, and darkness.

Tears ran down her cheeks.

*   *   *   *

It was like high school again. What Francis saw was breaking him from inside out. He knew now that to him she was more than a friend. He cared about her. He felt lonely again, and the loneliness ripped at him like a saw tearing away his sanity bit by bit.

He lay there staring at the darkness. When he felt her come into the room, talking to him, he couldn't really hear her. He felt numb and oblivious. He wanted to cry but couldn't.

She didn't need him. Strong and alive, beautiful and compassionate, independent and flawless, she didn't need him. He was a loser, an introvert, someone without purpose, without dream, someone who preferred fantasy than reality, someone who despised himself, someone who killed, took and rejoiced and hated himself for it. He had no self-worth. He didn't deserve friendship and care. She deserved better things and was right to turn to other men.

It was inevitable fate.

It seemed pointless to be on this journey now. Nobody cared enough to judge him. Why should he care enough to judge himself? Why should he duel with Babel? He didn't hate his father like Andy did. He didn't need to represent goodness. He was just trying to stay alive.

He thought he was doing something for himself, finding his own identity. But he felt crushed. And he didn't care anymore. He wasn't even curious about Babel's plan or Project Lilitu any longer. He had already lost the will to fight. Tomorrow life would go on. He just wouldn't be living his.

The night went on in sleepless punishment. By morning he was functioning like an automaton. He thought he passed by Jessie while going to the bathroom but he neither looked nor talked to her. He would see the journey to the end, because he was already too deep into it. No longer caring about respect, self-worth, survival or who he really was and why he was here, he just went on along with the natural flow made up by the threads of fate.

CHAPTER THIRTY-SIX

They left shortly after seven in the morning after a brief breakfast at the hotel cafe. Andy reckoned that they should utilize the sunlight as much as possible and not travel in the dark to avoid unnecessary danger. Francis didn't really pay attention to the conversation at the table, but it seemed none of them were in a chatty mode.

Jessie had a sour face – the most bitter that he had ever seen. He wondered why he still noticed. Maybe he cared, maybe he didn't. Either way it did not matter anymore. She didn't need him. She never really did.

He had offered to drive. If he put all his attention on the road, he didn't really need to think about anything else and he wouldn't have to worry about the awkward silence.

They bid farewell to the Californian border and entered the state of Oregon shortly after nine. The interstate 101 went past rockbound coast, ancient forests, innumerable towns and villages and rarely lost sight of the Pacific Ocean. Tourists said that everywhere in the States looked the same. It was only a partial truth. While each town they passed through weren't distinctly different from one another, a slight difference of sceneries could be spotted crossing into Oregon from California. The southern state of California was a desert where vegetation was scarce but the northern part of the golden state and Oregon were full of places where the timber boom went bust. Instead of the plain trailers and stucco bungalows throughout the south, beautiful forests and rustic towns with history surrounded them.

The beautiful scenery of costal Oregon didn't do much to alleviate Francis' mood however. He no longer felt like being on a road trip. He no longer had friends. It only felt like an inevitable run to the end.

He saw her in the rearview mirror while she stared bleakly at the blue ocean. Somewhere inside he yearned for things to be different. But life was out of his control. Fate often had a cruel sense of humor. He told himself not to care. To not care, he would not feel pain. To not covet companionship, he would not feel lonely. To not ask for anything, he would not feel the unfairness in life.

A little past two in the afternoon they reached the town of Florence. There they decided to take their break and look for a place to eat lunch. As they passed the Siuslaw River Bridge towards the north of Florence, they found the old town along the north bank of the river. Looking like a Victorian town in Europe, old town Florence was a graceful place filled with interesting boutiques and galleries. Francis thought that it was the kind of place that made Oregon much more pristine and beautiful than the desolate California.

Francis parked at one of the meter's parking on Bay Street and they started walking towards the shore.

Even though the summer sun was an ablaze fireball bearing down at them, the gentle sea breeze brushing by felt refreshing. Perhaps it was the shore, or perhaps it was Oregon, or a little of both, but it felt more like spring than summer.

As they walked past various Victorian boutiques and gift shops, Francis suddenly noticed there were quite a number of gnats in the air. At first he thought it was his imagination, as he knew that sometimes weary eyes would see black dots darting here and there in the corners. However when he felt the little black dots brushed by and his skin tingled he knew they were real. Both Andy and Kyle were brushing their hands in front of them.

"What's wrong?" Jessie asked. Francis felt a sudden jolt inside as he heard her voice. He felt like he hadn't heard it in a long time. She'd probably tried to talk to him last night and even this morning, but his mind couldn't register the voice he heard. Now that he heard her voice again, he recognized the sweet melodious familiarity that made him shudder with an overwhelming sadness. He shook his head and tried to brush the thoughts away.

"Damn flies," Kyle said in annoyance.

"What flies?"

"What do you mean what flies? They're all around us."

"I don't see anything." She put her hand up, feeling the air. "I kind of feel something."

"But you don't see anything," Andy observed.

"Nope, I don't."

"Damn it."

It took Francis a while to register why Andy had cursed. As they all stopped and surveyed their surroundings, Francis looked up and something caught his attention. On the third floor of a three-story building across the way at the end of the street, a twinkle of light sparkled in a window, bright like a star in the night.

Jessie was looking up at it too.

"You see it?" Francis said.

Jessie looked towards him, a moment of shock registered on her face. "You haven't said anything to me all day."

"I know. But do you see it?"

"Yes." She looked up again.

"What is it?"

"A reflection. If it's not someone trying to message us, then it's probably a positioned sniper."

"You're kidding, right?" As soon as he said that, he heard the sound of gunfire. She was right.

The four of them ducked.

Glass shattered behind them. It was the window of a gallery.

Dropping to the ground, they leaned upon the side of an old Dodge parked in front of the store. From that angle the sniper could not have a direct shot at them.

"I can't believe Bel is using a sniper on us." Kyle said. There was no more gunfire.

"Whatever works, I guess. There's still the matter of the gnats." Andy turned towards the building behind them, while still protected behind the car.

Another sound of gunfire.

The sniper was just scaring them and wasting bullets. They were safe in their position. Francis was sure of that.

He saw the bullet come. He had never imagined himself being able to see the path of a bullet. But it rippled through the air just as he had seen in the movies. Michelle's perception had grown. The bullet arrowed past them and should have landed somewhere behind the window of the boutique, but he saw the bullet turn and angle its way towards him.

Like a guided missile it came at him. He never even thought about exactly how to react, only knowing that he must do something about it. Michelle was already there and took one step away from him swinging the blade in her hand like an expert samurai. An arc of blackness was drawn across the air. Where the blade touched the bullet the next moment it was no longer there, as if it never came that way.

"The insects are Pillars," Andy warned. "Someone deployed them here to deflect the bullets."

That's why Jessie couldn't see them. That's why the bullet could turn.

Two more gunshots followed.

He watched the bullets dashing among the black dots around them. He felt like he was in a giant pinball machine. Michelle could stop one bullet coming at him if she had enough time to react. But he knew that he could not stop the multiple shots that bounced across the air as if they were alive.

Both Kyle and Andy had their Pillars in front of them, defending them like loyal soldiers. The clown was frantically punching the bullets that flew his way. Cao was jumping here and there gleefully as if she was in a kindergarten playground. Apparently she hadn't learned how to spell fear. Jessie was nowhere to be seen.

The thought distracted Francis; he saw a bullet came right for his throat. In the next moment there was only a splatter like splashed glue on his skin. It stung more than it hurt.

"Thanks, Cao," he said. The liquefying of the bullets saved his life.

"Pay attention, Francis," Kyle warned.

He heeded the warning now. Michelle batted the bullets away like a pro-baseball player hitting homeruns.

For a moment the gunfire ceased.

"Where's Jessie?"

"She ran off," Andy answered, as he was trying to catch his rapid breath. "Probably towards where the sniper is hiding."

"Damn it. Doesn't she know better to not go places where we can't protect her?"

Kyle's scream next to him sent chills down his spine. The agent was being pulled into the ground under the car like it was quicksand, by a skeletal hand emerging from the depths of earth.

Extending his hand Francis tried to save Kyle from drowning into the shadowy depths. But the momentum was so strong it was also pulling Francis down. He saw Kyle's head submerge into the ground, as if another world existed beyond the stone of the pavement. He didn't want to let go but he had to. Flinching from the shadow, he realized that he had stepped out into the open. The sniper could now take a clear shot at him. Yet he rather risked that, than to be pulled downward into the terrifying unknown.

No shots came. Cao had disappeared. Kyle was nowhere to be seen.

He felt eyes watching him and things moving around him. He looked at the shadow cast by the car. His eyes traced it towards a light pole, a shadow bridge from the side of the street to where he stood. Something was moving towards him. Feeling his hair go up on the back of his neck, he took a glimpse behind him and saw something emerge from the ground.

Under a hood he saw a menacing skeletal face that held him entranced. He felt the grip on his arms and the ground under him dissolving and soon he sank into it. Michelle stood one pace away from him. She was also sinking.

Attack, he told her silently. Her blade bit madly into the cloak of the skeletal creature behind him. Nothing happened. The creature ignored the stab like the brush of a feather. Waist-deep in the pond of darkness, he felt nothing under him. The thought of drowning in the shadowy unknown was petrifying.

The devil-faced clown strode from the front of the car to where the light pole stood. It grabbed the long pole and then with a snap, broke it in half. Quickly, it turned around and threw the top half of the pole towards him. The spear-like shaft arced towards him, spinning in the air like a deadly boomerang. Francis caught it with his bare hand, for a while thinking that the clown was almost going to kill him instead of helping him.

"Save Kyle and get rid of that thing. I'll go help Jessie," Andy yelled.

Francis looked towards him and nodded. That moment he felt the strong pull of the light pole and found himself sailing across the air in an incredible speed. While the pole was whole again, the impact dropped Francis painfully on the ground. He understood it now. Restoration, just like restoring his mother's picture, Andy could make something whole again, a joining of two broken pieces with an incredible force no matter how far they're apart. And that force was much stronger than the pull from the depths of darkness.

In a distance, Andy ran off and disappeared into the building on the other side of the street. Francis sat bather in the bright sunlight. The skeletal creature stood two paces away watching him like a mute statue. It was standing in the shadow cast by the roof of the shop. It couldn't cross over to him. It abhorred sunlight. What happens if I pull it into sunlight?

Since physical attack was futile, it seemed the only possible way. He looked up at the bright sun and then back at the creature that reeked of death and darkness. He was momentarily safe now. However, if Kyle was still alive, Francis wondered how long he could hold on. He needed to think of a strategy fast.

Rising, he surveyed his surroundings, trying to think of a plan. Two albatrosses leisurely sailed by. The creature had disappeared. Where did it go? He saw the shadow of the two birds floating across the tarred surface of the street and he suddenly understood and cursed.

He ran as fast as he could

As long as the shadows of the albatrosses did not come into contact with his own, he was safe.

When he stopped to catch his breath, the two birds had already passed him. He looked back at his own shadow. Nothing lurked there.

He took another step forward and suddenly realized that he had stepped into another shadowed zone – a long shadow cast by a tall tree at the corner of the pavement.

There it had him. Its skeletal grip on his ankle pulled him down. He fell and the solid ground was at once turning into the muddy devouring darkness. He was sinking. Now there was no one around to save him.

The tree. If only he could take down the tree. Michelle was sinking now. She couldn't reach it. The actual tree was at least eight feet away from him. He struggled, trying to crawl away from the whirlpool of darkness. But the more he struggled, the faster he went in. Just like quicksand, it was a deathtrap. He stared at the skeletal face that now emerged from oblivion. Francis swore that it was grinning at him.

You haven't won yet, bastard.

He found what he was looking for. Michelle found what he wanted her to find – the roots of the tree.

Apoptosis, cell degradation, the power of the Tormentor.

The trunk of the tree turned a charcoal color, and then pieces started to fall off. It shattered into tiny insignificant pieces. The warmth of sunlight bathed him. He found himself upon solid ground once more. The skeletal creature smoked and steamed, like a vampire exposed in sunlight. It tried to crawl away. Michelle had pinned it to the pavement. Its strength soon disappeared along with the darkness, and became a helpless doll struggling futilely in the baptism of the glorious sun.

The creature slumped to the ground, eventually even its cloak liquefied and evaporated. No sign of its existence remained. Francis just sat in the sunlight and let out a long exhausted breath. A few passerby tourists eyed him suspiciously, but none bothered to affront him with concern. He wondered where Kyle had ended up. And he wondered if Jessie was all right.

*   *   *   *

Jessie ran as fast as she had ever run. She never doubted that she would get shot at but when she reached the other side of the street unscathed, she was glad. She thought maybe their enemy was more intent on taking down her gifted companions and thus ignored her existence. He would be sorry. The double doors to the apartment complex were opened and she hurried inside. Quickly she located the stairs and started her winding way upward. She remembered where the sniper was, the second room from the left on the third floor.

She drew her revolver, clicked off the safety and put her back against the wall while she approached room 303. The door was slightly ajar. Crouching low, she kicked the door opened and pointed the barrel of her gun inside.

Gunfire responded.

She quickly got out of the way, leaning her back on the wall right next to the apartment door. She didn't really get a good look at the assailant. She only knew that the sniper now was responding with a handgun, possibly semi-automatic from the sound of it.

There were two more shots.

Pain shot through her as the bullets brushed her kneecap and her thigh. Her jeans were scorched and she bled.

He couldn't have gotten her from this angle.

The damn flies, they were here. But she couldn't see them.

She was greatly disadvantaged and she wasn't going to fight an unfair battle. Clenching her teeth, she ran down the hall just before another two shots were fired. She turned the corner and saw a young girl going into her apartment. She didn't look any older than fifteen, and she was frightened when she saw her gun.

"Police Officer," Jessie told her. "Can I use your apartment?" She felt footsteps behind her around the corner. If the girl didn't comply, she thought she was going to use force.

But she didn't have to; the girl nodded.

She showed her badge when she got in the apartment, but the girl hardly glanced at it.

"I'll just hide out for a few minutes," Jessie assured her and sat down on one of the chairs around a small wooden dining table.

The girl said nothing. Was she a mute?

She put her left hand on the wooden table and she leaned back a little to relax. She didn't really know how to confront her enemy outside. But hopefully she had bought enough time for Francis and the gang to retaliate. The girl had walked up next to her on the other side of the small table but Jessie didn't pay attention to her.

When the flash came, it was already too late. The blade of the dagger came down and pinned her hand to the wooden table. Blood spurted and pain shot through her like a violent strike of lightning. She found herself screaming, her other hand squeezed off three shots, but the girl already disappeared, probably into one of the rooms of the apartment. The whole left side of her body was numb, no longer feeling the pain. She couldn't move. She didn't dare to move.

She pointed the barrel of her gun straight at where the young girl disappeared. She clenched her teeth and waited.

There was gunfire outside and then silence. She didn't know how long she had waited. She became accustomed to the pain already, as if it was part of her.

A mad wailing came from the rooms. For a long moment it went on without respite, then it ceased and silence returned.

Then she heard her name being called; she didn't know who it was. She called back. The door opened and Andy stormed in. She glanced to her left, signaling him that there was still possible danger about the premises. Cautiously he stepped into the rooms and disappeared from her sight.

When he came out, he shook his head. "Nobody inside. I think whoever it is Francis must have taken care of him. There are some mutilated bodies inside though. I'm assuming they're the original inhabitants of this apartment."

She heard sirens.

He approached her and kneeled in front of her, putting his hands on her knees.

She clenched her teeth and glanced towards her bloody hand.

"I know," Andy admitted. His blue eyes were gazing into hers. "You're hurt. You want me to save you. But just listen to me first." There was some sort of madness in his eyes, the same madness she brought out in him the previous night, the same madness that had aroused her badly and drenched her in a lunatic craving. His hand went to her cheek touching her, wiping the tears from her face.

"God made you such a fine specimen. So alive, so beautiful, so brave." His hand went from her cheek to her neck and down to her left breast, where he gave it a soft squeeze. She struggled, and realized she was pinned to table. The pain blinded her.

"Don't touch me, you bastard. I'm going to shoot you."

"The mere sight of you excites me and fills me with madness. Makes me forget why I am here, makes me want to abandon everything I believe in. And I just want to hurt you and take you. In your eyes I can see how much you loved the way I hurt you."

She shook her head. "It's all a mistake, I didn't mean to lead you on. Now let go of me."

"Sure you didn't. You made me sin. You made me forget God. You're a little devil." There was madness in his tone, nevertheless he released her from his touch..

"Damn it. What the hell is wrong with you?" She wondered if there was a second personality hidden behind his goodness and faith.

"We'll see. We'll see at the end which side you stand on." He stood up, leaned over, and put his hand over the hilt of the dagger that had nailed her hand on the table. When he twisted it, she screamed with agony. When he yanked it out of her hand, the mere sight of the dark wound almost made her faint.

The next moment she felt the warmth of healing flowed through her. She looked at her hand and it was unscathed. She touched the left palm with her right hand, expected to feel pain but there was none.

"Thanks," she muttered.

The man had turned his back with his head lowered as if he was ashamed at what he just did.

At the end which side I stand on? What does that mean?

"The sniper?" She tried to change the subject.

"I took care of him. Look, I'm sorry." His gaze for a moment fell on her eyes and then he averted them again. "I become not myself from time to time when I see you."

"Don't worry about it," she lied.

"No, I should be able to control myself."

Control what? The darkness? The evil? "I'm the one who should apologize. I was wrong to lead you on last night."

"Let's just get out of here."

Last night she had wanted him so much. Now she was afraid of him. She was also afraid of losing Francis, if she hadn't lost him already. She had felt an indescribably overwhelming joy when he had first spoken to her today, even though it wasn't something personal. But his mere words had charged her with life and energy. The absence of them voided her of meaning. She needed his friendship as much as she needed the very oxygen in the air. In the two weeks she had known him, she had not realized how much she had grown accustomed to the very core of his being. And the pain of abandonment of that friendship had hurt her more than the dagger through her palm.

CHAPTER THIRTY-SEVEN

The cop instinct inside her told her to look at the bodies inside the room but she decided against it. The killer was apprehended, one way or the other. There wasn't anything she could do.

Francis and Kyle were waiting downstairs. While Francis looked on edge, Kyle looked frightened as if he had been through hell and back. They hurried back towards the car while a few local cops across the street investigated the scene outside the gallery with the broken glass. Jessie wondered if anything was ever going to get resolved.

They had forgotten about their empty stomachs. Francis resumed the driver seat and took them out of the town as quick as possible. Kyle recounted and described the dark void he was dragged into by the creature that walked the shadows. He said that he was able to breathe in that darkness, but he felt the air becoming very thin. He would have been dead if they didn't save him in time. When Kyle was finished, Andy recounted his brief duel with the sniper. In close range the sniper wasn't his equal at all, because the strange Pillar gnats were technically harmless. When Andy asked Francis what happened, he admitted that he had destroyed the shadow creature out of sheer luck. His tale was briefer than Cliff Notes summary.

The young girl who stabbed her was so young, not any older than fifteen years judging by her appearance. Jessie felt enraged and wondered if what she had traded for her power.

They only stopped to get some snacks at the gas station and rode northward nonstop towards the border of Washington and Oregon. No other surprise attacks came after the incident at Florence. When the sky turned dark, they stopped at Tillamook, a town where cows outnumbered people by at least two to one. Sprawled over lush grasslands at the southern end of Tillamook Bay, the town was still a hundred or so miles away from the Washington border. They were close to their destination, possibly just slightly more than half a day away.

They stopped at a quiet local inn, and Francis requested his own room. When she objected, he didn't give much of an explanation but remained silent.

They had country-style cooking for dinner at a small restaurant across from the inn. Only Kyle and Andy participated in a conversation. They were talking about how to react to possible threats and the concern about the mystery of Enoch Bel's power. Jessie didn't really pay attention. It didn't really matter to her.

After Francis made his exit like a silent phantom, she gently knocked on his door. "Francis, open the door. I want to talk to you."

There was no response.

"Damn it, I know you're in there." She clenched her fist and pounded like a crazy woman until her knuckles hurt.

There was no response.

"Fine, I'm just going to sit out here all night." She made sure it was loud enough to be heard. Then she sat down, legs folded, leaning against the wooden door and just stared forward at the empty hallway. A warm breeze brushed her face but she shivered.

Lost in chaotic thoughts and confusing frustration, mental and physical exhaustion claimed her and she found herself dozing off. Her head dipped and her eyelids grew heavy. Then there was just darkness, empty darkness like a void.

When her eyes opened, she found herself leaning against something and a warm blanket covered her shoulders. There was the gentle rhythm of his breath and the warmth of his proximity. He was sitting next to her in the hallway, legs folded like a monk and her head was on his shoulder. It was so comfortable even though she was now conscious she didn't want to give that away, afraid that the slightest of movements and the quietest of words would tumble and melt everything away like a fleeting dream.

"You're such a silly girl," he reprimanded softly, with affection. So he knew she was awake, must have felt the shifts and movements of her head.

She didn't say anything and for a moment just snuggled her head against his shoulder until she found the most comfortable position. She had thought him a bit scrawny before but his shoulder was far from bony. There were enough muscles on it to function as a pillow, albeit not a comfortable one.

"Your head's sort of heavy."

"Have you forgiven me?" she asked.

"What's there to forgive? I should be asking for your forgiveness. I threw away everything you taught me. I didn't know how to deal with a situation. I am the same stupid Francis I was when I met you. I wanted to be shut out from the world, thinking that solitude gave me comfort. But—"

"Hush…" she interrupted. "You're dealing with it now, just like you're dealing with Babel."

"I'm not really dealing with Babel. I came here because I wanted to… for … I…" He stuttered and couldn't continue. "Never mind."

"You're dealing with me now."

"I couldn't stop."

"Why?"

"Because you're my friend."

Just that?

"And you never stopped being a friend. I just thought…"

"Thought what?"

"Never mind."

"That word again."

"You don't like that word?"

"Not particularly. Because it stands for 'I'm too chicken to tell you the truth.' It's very irresponsible."

"I am chicken."

"I know, and irresponsible."

"Gee, that helps."

"But I like you for just who you are. You don't have to prove anything to me. You don't have to be who you're not."

"What if I say let's forget about all this heroic stuff and just go back to LA?"

"Then let's go."

For a moment he didn't say anything, as if he was really considering the possibility. "I can't."

"I know. You're really not that irresponsible. But you're still chicken."

"I'm scared shitless."

"The worst that can happen is death."

"There are worse things than death."

"Oh, like what?"

"Never mind."

"There's that again."

"Why don't we go inside?"

"I thought you'd never ask. My butt hurts."

"Really? I'll take a look at it."

"Not a chance."

One queen-sized bed was inside. They both sat on the opposite edge, and a long moment of silence followed.

"You know, I don't really care about Andy." She had meant to say love, but that word evaded her. She couldn't bring herself to deny something she didn't understand.

He took another dreadfully long moment to digest what she had told him. And she suddenly felt afraid that he was shutting her off again.

"What happened was…" She swallowed and thought of how to say it. "Just some sort of raw animal hunger. It was stupid."

"You don't really have to tell me."

"Friends tell each other things."

"You're free to love anyone you want."

There's that word again. "I don't love him."

"He's not such a bad guy. Maybe I misjudged him. He's much more than I ever will be."

"Don't be absurd. Each person is different. There's never more of one person than another. You are jealous, aren't you?"

There was another long period of silence. "It's my first time having a real friend. I couldn't bear the loneliness… when I was in high school. I thought I had a friend, actually I thought I had two." He told her about Rosa and Sam, and it made her heart ache listening to the tale. He had thought what transpired between Andy and her the same event happening again.

"You didn't lose me, and you never will."

"I was so stupid."

"Everyone makes mistake. We both did. But friends tolerate each other's mistakes. That's what friends do." She crawled inside the blanket and settled herself only inches away from him.

He tried to move away, but he was already at the edge of the bed.

"Don't worry, I won't bite."

Then as if the final barrier between them broke down, they comfortably snuggled against each other like children fending off the coldness of the night. The closeness of their bodies gave her a sense of calmness. It wasn't anything sexual. She just felt safe and peaceful. It was an amazing feeling.

"Your hair smells really nice."

"It's not turning you on, is it?"

"Not like that," he said with an embarrassed cough. "Sort of smells like Mom's hair."

"Great, I remind you of your mother."

"No, it's not like that either. I've never felt this way all these years I'm away from home. But I sort of miss her. Even though she doesn't really care about me…"

She thought that Francis' mother probably cared about him a great deal, but in her own way. Yet she didn't say anything.

"But somewhere inside me I want her to be there tomorrow. It'd be like a family reunion. But then I don't want her to watch us slaughter each other."

"You're not going to slaughter each other."

"Yes, we are. I know it."

"I'll still see you after tomorrow." I have to.

He said nothing.

And she felt a tear run down her cheek from the corner of her eye. She didn't know if that was for breaking down his barrier one more time and connecting with him, or the bad premonition she's feeling at the moment. It was both.

Jessie wished that they could just lie in bed like that for the rest of eternity and tomorrow would never come. She was suddenly thinking about God. If He existed, she told herself, He must have a hand in the upcoming confrontation between light and darkness. Perhaps it was too much asking for the particular moment to be suspended in eternity, especially for a nonbeliever. She prayed, for the first time in her life, for Francis' safety.

CHAPTER THIRTY-EIGHT

They woke up and got ready before dawn the next morning. During breakfast Andy further explained the route to Seattle. He explained that they had been taking a short detour towards their final destination instead of the optimal route. His reasoning was that the route was not as easily anticipated. Yet the previous day they had been ambushed all the same. Francis wondered if there existed a way to Babel Cydonia without confrontation.

He resumed the driving despite the objections. He had felt a lot better today but he preferred to be the driver because he was still not in the mood for chattering.

Last night he had finally realized that he had reacted wrongly towards Jessie's act. Reaction was the enemy, he still remembered what Michelle's roommate at Berkeley told him. But reaction was a human response. Perhaps one who did not react would become one with God, as she said. He was only human and he had felt betrayed and lost and devoid of hope after witnessing Jessie in his half brother's arm. He still cared about her and he could feel that she was also hurt by the way that he had shut her out because she too cared about him. Perhaps after knowing her, he realized that he had lost the ability to truly be detached from the world. Things still happened around him and emotion flowed like the very currents of air. Feeling and seeing them, he felt changed by them. Was it a curse, or a blessing?

He had cherished the friendship Jessie offered. Not really knowing if he was in love with her or not, he had hoped that she loved him, like in the alternate version of reality Sophie showed him. Then maybe he would know then if he really loved her. He knew he was being selfish and he was trying to claim something that didn't really exist between them, which wasn't really fair to her. It was true that he went on this journey because he wanted to impress her, wanted to be worthy of her. And it broke him down that she would love someone else instead of him. Now he understood that even if she couldn't love him, she could still be his friend. And in this lonely world, he desperately needed that friendship. Nobody had given him that until now.

As he drove northward on Highway 101 in the barely dawning light, he noticed a black car in the rearview mirror. He thought nothing of it at first, but when the trailing vehicle matched his speed and changed lanes according to his movement it became suspicious.

"I think we're being followed."

The others looked.

It looked like a Ford Mustang but it was a lot bulkier. There seemed to be a thick layer of steel coating the exterior of the car, making the sports car looked like an armored tank, yet it seemed no less versatile in its speed. When it was closely trailing them, Francis tried to look at the driver. But the windows were shaded.

The black Mustang rammed into them like a raging bull.

Francis stomped on the gas pedal.

"Be careful, Francis," Jessie warned.

He was now going a hundred miles per hour and had the feeling that the wind had lifted the car, which was gliding forward without touching the ground. The Mustang followed closely without respite.

"What the heck are you doing?" Andy asked when the window on Jessie's side in the back rolled down. Then she leaned outside with her gun drawn and started firing at the car behind them.

After a few shots, Francis saw the Mustang slowing down and then skidding to the side. She had popped one of the front tires.

It was a good chance to lose his opponent. He accelerated and soon the Mustang disappeared in the rearview mirror.

"Nice shot," Kyle commented.

"Should take him a while to fix that tire," Jessie said.

"Or not," Francis said as she saw it come from the left lane with the speed of a thunderbolt. The next moment the mysterious car was going beside them at a hundred and five miles per hour. Francis glanced at his left side and saw only a dark shadow. But he sensed that the driver was looking back at him through the shaded window. It was a challenge of a racer, carried with an ominous animosity of a ruthless killer. He felt a reluctant chill spreading from his spine. But he also felt the adrenaline pour through him like hot lava.

In the corner of his eye, he saw the devil-faced clown appearing in between the two speeding vehicles. There he landed countless punches on the side of the Mustang like a boxer gone berserk. Francis saw the exterior of the car wrinkling after Andy's ferocious attack, but the next moment it was as smooth as new, even the windows did not have one scratch on them.

"You're not restoring the car while you hit it, right?" Kyle said dubiously.

"Don't be absurd," Andy muttered angrily.

"Then whoever it is he has the same ability as you do."

"It's not like that. Notice the exterior of the Mustang? The extra layer of coating, or should I say armor, makes it as strong as titanium. Joker has a hard time penetrating it. And it seems the armor is healing itself."

"You think the car itself is a Pillar?" Kyle sounded a bit awe-struck.

"Or just the armor on top of it," Andy explained. And meanwhile Francis was going forward in a hundred and ten per mile. He had never driven so fast in his life. And the mysterious car next to him showed no sign of relenting. "Jessie, can you see the strange armor on the car?"

"Yes."

"Then that means it is not a Pillar ability."

"It still could be," Kyle said.

"How so?"

"Remember the document from the project? It stated that it is possible for a Pillar to have enough physical manifestation to appear to ordinary human beings. I think Babel had once tested on a host who could construct a whole building as a Pillar and normal vision could detect it. So it is possible that whoever this driver is, the armor over the car has enough physical power for Jessie to be able to see it."

"That is not good news," Andy commented with a dreadful sarcasm, "but at least we're not facing two attackers at the same time."

A truck was ahead of them and Francis started slowing down, hoping the car next to him would have no time to react. Then they could just stop and lose the tail entirely. But the driver only matched their speed and stayed paralleled like a parasite.

The Mustang closed the distance between them until it was only inches away from the side of their Avalon. The side mirror shattered and broke away. Francis held on to the steering wheel with all his strength and braced for the impact. The contact made the car tremble and he was losing control of the steering wheel. The car skidded towards the right.

He didn't realize it but he went off on an exit ramp, an exit for a town called Seaside. Slowing down, he took a right in the crossroad and slowly crawled forward. Their pursuer was nowhere in sight. The mirror on the left had reattached itself.

"I've repaired the damage on the car," Andy said softly, still alert and worried.

"Lucky we didn't go off a cliff instead," Kyle said.

"That wouldn't have killed us. I can fix us up in no time even if we went off a cliff."

"Still, I'd rather not go off a cliff."

Francis had a bad feeling. Their entrance into Seaside was forced. It seemed that the Mustang had pushed them into a trap. He looked around. They were in what seemed to be a downtown area with shops and restaurants. He had turned left when exiting a northbound freeway and it meant that he was now heading west. That meant little to him though. He thought that he should make a U-turn and go back to the freeway as soon as possible.

When he passed a cross street, he saw the same black car again. It was now trailing them from a distance. Compared to the ferocity just a few minutes ago, their pursuer was now watching them casually like a predator.

"Watch out!" Kyle next to him exclaimed.

When he looked forward, he saw a figure walking right in front. What's he doing walking in the middle of the street? Kyle's hand came to the wheel and pulled it before Francis could react. He heard the skid of the tires as the car spun uncontrollably to the right. He stomped on the brakes and the car slid forward sideways. The person crossing the street was unscathed and passed by the window like a phantom. Strangely that was no sudden reaction. He simply walked forward as if nothing had happened. Francis then felt the thundering impact at the back of the car. Someone rammed into them. It was the black Mustang.

The impact lifted them. The air bags exploded. Francis felt the car spin through the air. He was hanging upside down. The seatbelt choked him, and his chest hurt. The whiteness of the air bag covered his face, and he felt the impact as the car crashed into the ground. Then darkness claimed him.

*   *   *   *

Jessie opened her eyes. She felt like she's been beaten by a baseball bat. The car was upside down. Francis and Andy was both unconscious. Kyle was nowhere to be seen. She kicked the door open and crawled outside. The agent was a couple feet away flat on the ground, face down. She looked back towards the Avalon. The windshield had shattered. She wanted to check on Kyle, but she also wanted to pull Francis and Andy out of the car. An inverted car might explode if there was a gas leak. She wasn't sure.

When she decided that she couldn't take the chance and was going to go for the two still in the car, she saw the black mustang, which had returned from giving them a lift. It wasn't heading towards their wreckage. It was going for Kyle, who lay helplessly in the middle of the road.

She ran. She had never run faster in her life. Lifting Kyle by the collar of his shirt, she discovered that he was too heavy for her to simply lift out of harm's way. The Black Death was only a few feet away now coming towards them like a charging bull. She dragged with all her strength. It was too close. The wheels brushed his shoes. She watched the black car disappear down the street. Then she heard the screeching of tire against the tar of the street. It was making a quick U-turn.

She looked down at Kyle, and saw a trail of blood down his forehead and a large crack on his glasses. Thank God the lens were plastic, otherwise it would have been ugly. She gave him a quick shove and he stirred.

"You okay?"

"Yes." He eyes were half-closed as if he just woke up from a long night.

"Can you run? You're going to need to in a few seconds."

"Shit."

They got up and watched the car come their way again.

"The river." Kyle pointed forward and they dashed for it.

When she reached the riverbank she dove into the murky depths. As she surfaced, she saw the bottom of the black mustang right above her in the air. Then it landed with a gigantic and thunderous splash like a killer whale's dive. Not knowing how deep the water was, Jessie knew she couldn't stand on the bottom so she kept paddling. Drawing her Smith & Wesson out to keep it above the surface, she had a feeling that she was going to need it very soon but she couldn't do anything about her backup revolver.

Kyle emerged from the water and told her to climb on the ice platform he created. After he climbed out, he pulled her upward onto the almost plastic-like floating ice.

A dark burly man climbed up from the now rapidly sinking Mustang and stood on top of the roof. For a while he observed them with amusement and gloated with a vicious smile, like a pedophile watching children in a cage.

Jessie held her gun with both hands and aimed. When she looked at the man again, he was different. He was now covered in black steel and as if he had just grown two feet, he stood like a giant in some sort of metal clothing which was a cross between a bodysuit and armor from medieval times. No skin was shown between the joints or where the neck was. It covered him entirely, even his face and his eyes. She fired two shots – one head, one chest. They both bounced off harmlessly.

"Interesting," Kyle exclaimed. "He seemed to have removed the armor of the car and put it on himself."

It was too late for her to really see the state of the vehicle, now only the roof was above the surface. She wondered how heavy the steel really was. She wondered if he could float.

"Make an ice bridge for him," she told Kyle.

"What?"

"When he takes the bait, I want you to deactivate that part of the bridge and make him fall. You can do that, can you?"

"Yes, Cao can do that." He always insisted on referring to his Pillar as a totally separate individual. She didn't really want to argue over technicalities.

"Wait for my signal." She saw the ice bridge extend towards their assailant and wondered where Cao was. Sometimes she wished she had the power to see the cute innocent little girl float around in the battlefield like it was a playground. On second thought, she didn't really want to see it. Some things were better left for imagination.

The armored man looked at the icy bridge. His helmeted head pointed downwards. He lifted one of his legs and tested the integrity of the ice bridge. It supported him, but he was hesitant to go on.

When the man seemed to look up at them, Jessie used her index finger to gesture him forward while her other hand pointed the gun straight at him. She was issuing a challenge and he was going to take it just like any other man with a big ego. "Come on, big fellow."

She was right. He did and started marching towards them.

"Now!"

Kyle murmured something silently, perhaps issuing a command to Cao.

Where the armored man stood, the ice became water again. He staggered and fell.

Jessie dove into the water and watched the tin man sink. She didn't know if he really reached the bottom in the murky water but he started climbing up with ease as if the steel covering his body weighed nothing at all. She cursed. The man followed them into the water because he knew that he could still defeat them there. There has to be a way. She watched the air bubbles coming from the armor and she tried to think of her next plan.

Both the man and she went back on top of the ice platform. Kyle created more ice behind them and they started backing towards the brick walls of the riverbank.

The man stopped his march and was suddenly punching at the air wildly like a man trying to smack an annoying fly circling around him.

"What's happening?" she asked.

"Cao is attacking," Kyle said with a concerned tone. "She's no good at physical combat, but at least she's fast and she can avoid his punches."

"Can you not change the structure of his armor?" She knew he had probably tried that because a veteran like him didn't need her to tell him how to use his own Pillar. But she just had to make sure.

"That's the first thing I tried. It's no use. It's not really steel, not made up of particles. It's pure concentrated energy. That's what Pillars are."

She fired another shot at her enemy. There was no effect.

"It's no use. That thing is probably tougher than titanium."

And she'd bet that thing could crush both of their skulls in the matter of seconds if it got close to them. She thought back to when she was in the water watching the armored man. She remembered bubbles coming from his back, somewhere below the neck along the spinal cord. That's where he breathed. There must be a hole there big enough for a bullet to pass through. "I have a plan," she whispered to Kyle and then asked him if he could do what she was going to ask him to do.

"It's possible. I'll ask Cao to try it."

"Good." The man was now only six paces from them.

She fired a shot deliberately into the water right next to the man's foot. As she predicted his helmeted head looked downward, curious at what she was shooting at. She immediate fired another shot past his neck. She had asked Kyle to use Cao to redirect her bullet into the place where the man breathed. She got the idea from the last battle with the sniper. Cao was fast and she could probably do the same.

When the armored figure look up again, it seemed stunned. He took a step backwards and toppled to the side. As he fell, the armor faded away. Then he just floated lifelessly on the river in a pool of dark red blood.

*   *   *   *

When Francis opened his eyes, he was lying flat on the ground. Andy stood on top of him, glaring down at him with his cold blue gaze.

"Nice driving," he said coldly.

"I did my best." He got up and wondered if he was hurt at all. He wouldn't know because Andy would have fixed him up. He didn't feel hurt. "Where are the others?"

"I don't know. They were missing when I woke up. Bumped my head on the roof of the car."

Francis looked around when he heard footsteps and he saw people approaching. It was only shortly after dawn, awfully strange to have so many people wandering on the street. Something was wrong with them though – they staggered from side to side as they walked as if they couldn't find their balance. Their skin was so white that it was almost a grayish color of death. When they got closer, he saw that their eyes were out of focus.

"Zombies," Andy warned.

He felt like he was in the middle of the movie Night of the Living Dead. Except that it was dawn, but the righteousness of the sunlight did not help diminish the dreadful evil lingering in the air.

The clown appeared before Andy and took a few steps forward to confront one of the approaching zombies. When the clown's fist touched the zombie, there was an explosion and chunks of dead flesh were launched into the air like a gore fest. The clown disappeared. Francis looked towards Andy. He was unscathed, except for the deep fear on his face.

"Lucky I pulled him back just when I suspected something was wrong." Andy let out a breath of relief. "It seems they're all armed with explosives."

Three of the undead were before them. And another two were staggering close behind. The wreckage blocked any escape westward towards what seemed to be a river. They had no choice but to head east.

Francis had a bad feeling about it all. It seemed that they were being lured into a cascade of traps, first the exit from the freeway, now they were separated from their companions. The convenient escape path was the prelude to a death trap orchestrated by their enemy. But they had no choice but to take it, hoping that in knowing that it was a trap they had a chance of survival.

When they reached the intersection they turned left. There a homeless woman sat on top of a stack of rags. She was busy sewing what seemed to be a black garment made of a few separate pieces of wool. Her eyes were closed and she appeared to be blind.

"Please... please spare me some change."

Francis felt his heart jumped when the woman spoke. From the almost empty cup with only a few pennies and dimes, Francis looked towards the back of where the woman sat. There was a pile of dead rats. Some were beheaded and some skinned. He felt bile rising to his throat as he smelled the stench of rotten death.

Andy dropped something into the cup and made a tinkling sound. "Old Lady, you have to get out of here. It's dangerous."

"Oh nonsense, I've been here almost five years now. And I have all these rations with me. Rat-ions, get it?" Then she indulged herself in a mad laughter.

"Never mind her," Francis urged him to move on as he saw two of the zombies turned the corner.

They went a few paces along the smaller street and saw another group of the living dead ahead of them. They were trapped.

"Here." Andy's clown broke down a door to a condo on the side of the street and they dashed inside. Then Andy quickly repaired the door behind them.

"Anyone?" Andy yelled but nobody answered. The room was a mess. Dust and spider webs covered the place.

Francis wasn't surprised if nobody lived here. After checking to make sure that the door was secure, they got behind the window and observed the movement of the zombies outside, who were patrolling from one end of the street to the other aimlessly. For the moment they seemed safe.

"We need to figure out what kind of ability our enemy has," Andy suggested.

"Animation of the dead. Putting explosives inside bodies," Francis answered nonchalantly.

"I mean other than that, how do the zombies track us? Their eyes look unfocused."

"Rats."

"What?"

Francis pointed at the rat that was crawling towards them from the back. It was a big rat, as big as someone's foot. There was something wrong with the way it moved, just like the way those living dead moved outside. Devoid of life, it was a zombie.

They both managed to jump out of the way as the staggering dead rat reached where they stood a moment ago. The explosion was small but it managed to shake the walls and shattered the windows. Another rat was already coming from the doorway towards the back of the room.

Michelle positioned herself between them, blade in hand readied to strike.

"What are you doing?" Andy barked. "You touch that thing and you're dead."

"I know what I'm doing," Francis assured him.

With a sweep of the blade, Michelle drew an arc across the air. And the darkness trailing behind the blade consumed the dead rat entirely, wiping away its existence. That was the new ability he took from the pilot who assaulted them on the plane with the dark hole.

"Neat," Andy commented. "But we can't keep defending forever. Attack is the best defense." He took out a lighter. With a spark, the flickering flame danced in his hand. The next zombie rat that strode into the room headed towards him.

So the undead went towards the heat source. Michelle took out another rat with a clean strike.

"Here is the plan." Andy opened his palm revealing a half of a quarter.

"What is it?"

"Two fifths of a quarter."

"Why that precise?"

"Because I gave the other piece to the old lady."

"She's…"

"Examine the rat closely."

Francis did as he suggested and saw lines on the back as if the rat had been sewn back into one piece. He understood what Andy wanted to do. With that less-than-half of a quarter he could take out the old woman with her own bomb.

"The question is putting the quarter into the rat. That takes precise surgery." Andy jumped back as the rat closed in. "And you're going to do it. I can sew up the rat afterwards."

Michelle wiped the rat totally away from existence. Another came. Like cannon fodder, they came one after one relentlessly.

Francis concentrated and made sure Michelle's blade this time only brushed the top of the rat and not wiping away the whole thing. He clenched his teeth as he watched the precision of her surgical incision. While Andy continued backing away with his flickering lighter, the clown reached down and inserted the less-than-half quarter into the rat's body. When the opening sealed itself, the rat was lifted off the floor. Its four short legs pawed at the thin air as if it was swimming through the currents. Then like a rocket the rat flew out of the window and disappeared off to the side. In a distant they heard the explosion and a shrill scream. No more rats came afterwards.

They looked out the window – the zombies were now lying lifelessly on the street. They had won their battle.

"I can't believe they killed that many people just trying to trap us." Francis shook his head and sighed, as they walked through the bodies.

"That's why we need to destroy Babel." Andy lowered his head and offered a brief solemn prayer to his Lord.

They passed by where the sinister old woman was, now only a pile of unrecognizable flesh and blood, and turned the corner back onto Broadway Street. When they got back to the wreckage site, the others were still nowhere in sight. Francis couldn't help but worry, his heart feeling heavier by the second.

"I'm going to fix the car."

When Andy touched the wrecked vehicle, out of the corner of Francis' eyes he saw a spark at the point of contact, then a blazing red fireball. Francis dropped to the floor and covered his head, avoiding the debris. Andy was thrown a few feet backwards and was lying on the ground with his arms spread as if he was welcoming something from the heavens.

Francis pulled himself up after determining that it was safe to do so. He checked on Andy's now blackened body. There was still a pulse. He was unconscious, but alive. Francis knew that the explosion would have killed a normal person, but Andy must have reacted and protected himself with his Pillar when he sensed something was wrong. Francis looked around and only saw lifeless bodies lying around them. An enemy was still lurking in the vicinity. The explosives they encountered were the very same that they had faced just moments ago. They had miscalculated. They had assumed that the one who animated the dead and supplied the explosives was the very same person. They were wrong. Whoever armed with the supernatural explosives was still out there, lurking and waiting, and he was already successful in eliminating the healer in their party. Jessie and Kyle was nowhere to be found. He hoped that they were still alive. But he was alone now.

Carefully he stepped away from Andy's body. If he acted as if Andy were dead, then the assassin would have no reason to doubt that the man could have survived such a destructive explosion. Francis was the target now, and he needed to make sure he stayed alive until Andy could wake up. Offense was the best defense. If he could find out where their ambusher was hiding, then he had a better chance of not getting surprised. In his mind, he gave a quick analysis of their enemy. The bombs could not move. They must be placed. Without the assistance of the zombies, the assailant would not be able to do any remote bombardments if he didn't come into contact with anything. As he was not attacked at the moment, their assailant was neither physically powerful, nor remotely controlling his Pillar. He looked down at the bodies scattered around him, what if one of them was not really a dead body? He wouldn't know until he came into contact with them, and if he did he could be trapped in an explosion. It seemed better to just stand there and wait, but he preferred to be in the offensive. Standing there in the middle of a war zone was like waiting for one's demise.

He ordered Michelle to use her new ability. He had already given it a name – Void Blade. With that she could cut open the dead bodies around him without directly coming into contact with them. He started his surgical work of gore on the scattered flesh directly in front of him. There was no blood at the severing wound and he wondered what was really inside those bodies. He wondered if the strange woman drained all the water from the dead, and if multiple parts of her Pillar hid inside the bodies and manipulated them like a puppeteer. The mere thought turned his stomach.

When Francis heard a few gunshots in a distance, hope returned to him. He didn't know for sure but he knew that was Jessie. She was probably still alive and now fighting on her own, perhaps with Kyle. He wondered just how many different hosts had ambushed them. There were three at least counting the mysterious driver of the black mustang. Francis clenched his fist in anger, his knuckles turning white.

Then he felt someone grab his foot. He turned and saw one of the bodies – no, it was a man who had crawled up behind him and grabbed his right foot. Then he felt it, a rush of heat, something, something he couldn't describe, a strange feeling, entered him where the man's fingertips came into contact. Something foreign had violated his very body. The man got up. He had dark eyes and long black hair, and wore a vicious smirk. Then Francis knew that the man had put a Pillar bomb on him.

The man dashed to the right and started to run. Francis followed. His opponent must be able to detonate his own bomb. And that meant the man needed to get out of the explosion range so he wouldn't get hurt himself. As long as Francis trailed his assailant closely he would be safe. However it would be instant death if he got outrun. He hoped that he wouldn't trip before his stamina gave out.

The man was fast. He looked as if he had a frail physique but he ran like a marathon runner. Francis himself wasn't slow, but he found no way to gain any distance. He was two big steps behind and he had stayed that way for an entire block. The man turned a corner and Francis followed closely like a puppet which had no choice but to mimic the master's movement. He was now three steps away. The surprise turn made him stagger and slow down to adjust his direction. Francis wondered how far it would take for the bomb to detonate without harming its master – four steps? Or perhaps five? He had no luck on closing on his opponent. If he didn't do something soon, he was going to die a gruesome death.

When he was still running for his life, a sudden idea came to him. Even though the man was out of Michelle's reach, she could take out the existing space between them by her Void Blade. He wasn't sure if he understood the theory behind it, but he knew that it was going to work. He couldn't cancel the entire space between them so that he would catch the man, but when he took out where the space where the path of the blade sweep by, the tip of Michelle's sword, which was now just out of reach, could come into contact with the man. Then he could bestow the power of Apoptosis upon him and that would surely slow him down.

Satisfied with the plan, he commanded Michelle to attack. It was as he anticipated. When the dark arc she drew in the air disappeared, Michelle was brought one step closer to the fleeing target, as if she had miraculously pulled the man back with some sort of magnetic power. The tip of her blade, like a venomous snake, bit onto the man's shoulders. Blood drenched his clothes.

At first the man had no intention of slowing down, but when his arm started to darken, he slowed his step to stare at his oozing arm in horror.

Francis wondered how much it hurt. He had once been touched by the Tormentor the same way and he thought he was going to die for sure. It already seemed an eternity ago but that he could not easily forget that night. The clown had saved him and he thought he had met an angel from hell. The man in front of him must be terrified. He shook his head. It wasn't the time to empathize with the enemy. Francis knew that he would be killed the instant the bomb detonated.

The blade had disappeared from Michelle's hand. He always wondered where it really went. With her bare hands she caught the man around the throat and lifted him off the ground. Francis never knew that she had that much strength in her. She must have grown more powerful throughout the course of their incessant battles.

The man's feet dangled helplessly in the air like a lynched victim. His bloodshot eyes stared into Michelle's with a dreadful terror beyond measure. He wanted to scream but could not. Francis felt the quickening pulse, the blood pumping through his victim. They all had that same horrified face. He was judgment and he took what they did not deserve to have – their blood, their power, their life, their essence, and their soul. That power overwhelmed him once more like a tidal wave and drenched him in an ocean of ecstasy.

CHAPTER THIRTY-NINE

When he opened his eyes, he found himself lying on the back seat of a car, with his head on Jessie's lap. One of her hands was on his heaving chest, she looked down at him.

"Hey," she greeted with a sweet smile. Her hair was still wet and she had to hook it back behind one of her ears so that it didn't cover her face. Though she looked like she's just been through a watery hell, her beauty had really transcended physical splendor. She could fall through a garbage dump and he'd still find her lively and attractive.

"Hey yourself." There was something maternal about the position they were now in. It was warm and comfortable.

"You've been out for a while," she told him.

"Different car?" He noticed the interior.

"Yeah, we're in a Volvo. The rental was totally incinerated."

"Stole it?"

"Yeah, Andy did."

"You let him do that? What kind of a detective are you?"

"If it pleases you, I can take him into custody after we get through all this." She smiled again and leaned even closer, one of her hands brushed his hair. "Are you alright?"

"I'm fine. Just one of those blackouts again after I…" He didn't really know how to term his act. "So, what about you? What happened? Your hair is wet, but your clothes are not."

"Do I have to answer those questions in that specific order, Sherlock?"

"Not really."

"Kyle fixed my clothes. He took out the moisture, but I didn't really want him to mess with my hair."

He laughed.

"Other than that I'm fine." She then told him about their confrontation with the driver of the black Mustang. He then filled her in with his side of the story.

"Where are we now?"

"If you get up and look, you'd find out."

"You don't mind if I stay like this for a while, do you? It's so comfortable."

"Your head is kinda heavy though. Yeah well, we're going west on Highway 12. We'll get back on 5 North soon and we'll be on our way straight to Everett."

"We're in Washington already? How long have I blacked out?"

"An hour or so."

He normally did not lose consciousness for that long, or not at all. Perhaps her lap, or just her being there next to him, was too comfortable and he was just asleep, trying to recover from the stressful exhaustion of this journey. He wished that he could just stay like that for the rest of eternity. He knew that the worst of their journey was not over, but had just begun. Things they had been through were only a prelude to their final nightmare. Not until today had he realized the magnitude of power Babel held in its hands. Combining the forces of the most powerful of Pillar hosts could wipe out any armies and cities in an instant. If Enoch Bel really wanted to destroy them, he could have. Perhaps he was only toying with them.

They stopped by McDonald's to get a quick lunch on the way to Seattle. The weather in the north had turned significantly cooler. Even under the summer sun, the air was comfortably lukewarm.

"I have a really bad feeling about the whole thing," Jessie whispered when they were getting closer to Seattle.

"I know," Francis concurred. "So do I. But it's something I have to face."

"We," she corrected him. "It's something we have to face."

"Okay." He understood what she meant though. Friends faced difficulties together. That was friendship, and camaraderie. And right now he needed her support more than ever.

"I just wished all these terrible things never happened."

"Mr. Choi losing his horse."

"Huh?" Her face showed clear bewilderment.

"It's an old Chinese saying."

"Tell me."

"Do I have to? It's embarrassing."

"Who says?"

"Well, it's a parody about when something happens, you never know whether it turns out to be good or bad, until the very end." Only, what is the very end? "My mother told me the story when I was small, when I barely even understood anything. I'm not sure if I got it accurately. But the story is about a well-loved horse breeder in a community somewhere in ancient China. His name is Choi, if you haven't guessed already. One day, his favorite horse ran off from his establishment. It was a beautiful black horse. Em, no, maybe it was a white horse... with black patches on the–"

She arched an un-approving eyebrow.

"Never mind. Just trying to have some fun telling a story. Anyway, Choi was quite depressed losing his favorite horse. And the community was concerned about him. I guess there wasn't much entertainment back then and people found joy in gossip, which probably is still true nowadays, to some certain extent. Ah, I'm digressing again. Anyway, back to the story. People were superstitious, they believed in bad omens. They thought the mere incident of the runaway horse was bad luck for the Choi family. However, on the next day there was a surprise turn of event. Choi's horse came back, and it even brought a group of wild, but purebred horses with it. Choi was ecstatic because of his love of horses and having his favorite one back and not only that, but a sudden increase in wealth. He started to train the wild herd immediately. The community was also happy about the news, and totally changed their mind about the dark omens.

"Choi's son took a liking to one of the new horses and he spent his days training it. However, the wild horses were untamed and dangerous, and Choi's son ended up falling off and breaking his leg. So the community went back to talking about bad luck for the family. A few days passed when Choi's now cripple son spent his days at home recovering, the emperor's imperial soldiers came into town and brought an imperial indict to summon all able men to join the army to fight a war against the invading northern forces. Choi was already too old to be a soldier but his son was of the right age. If only he were not crippled, he would have been sent to the front. After the families in the community lost their loving husbands and sons to the army, they were depressed about the uncertain fates of their loved ones. So the community concluded that Choi was very lucky because of his runaway horse he got to keep his loving son at home and not losing him in the war. But Choi only said, 'What's the luck in that? I was hoping that my son would do something great with his life, like serving his country and truly growing up to be a man. Now he has missed his chance. Bad omens indeed.'"

There was a long moment of silence when she digested the story. Then her eyes lit up with some sort of enlightenment, "That was beautiful."

"The expression really means that you never really know. Bad things can bring good outcomes, and good outcomes can come with bad consequences, and the results are just open to how we interpret it. If none of this happened, we'd have never met and become friends. I'd have never found out my own identity, I'd never be sure of myself and care about the things around me. We might all die here today. But at least we'd have lived our lives and have nothing to regret." He couldn't believe he just said all that. Only a couple weeks ago not only would he not have the courage to say something that he believed in, he simply would not have believed in anything about life.

"You know, you could be a professional story teller."

"You mean one of those old men who sit in the corner of the park and tell children their lifelong experiences. Thanks, but no thanks."

She gave a mischievous chuckle and it soon turned into a laugh.

He laughed too, and for a moment forgot even why he was laughing. He realized perhaps it was their last true moment of joy.

Past the metropolitan area of Seattle, an engaging combination of scenic beauty and high-tech panache, was the small suburban area of Edmonds and finally Everett, still a thoroughly blue-collar place and heavy industry center with a feeling of a much greater distance from Seattle's high-tech flash than the half-hour it actually was. Where I-5 crossed Hwy-2 was their final destination. The pyramid known as Babel Cydonia stood menacingly tall under the afternoon sun. Francis stared at the massive structure and experienced a rush of adrenaline mixed with terror flowing through him. It was the place where he would face his final test – a test of courage and the faith of his own humanity.

They drove through an unguarded opening in the construction fence; through seemingly miles of unending, un-landscaped, muddy grounds; and past what seemed to be a Sphinx in the middle of construction with an unrecognizable face. Finally they reached the base of the dark pyramid. It almost looked like the Luxor – the Las Vegas casino modeled after a pyramid, but that was only a miniature model of a real one. The one before them was as large and impressive as one sat in the middle of an Egyptian desert. Only, the one before them with walls made of dark opal panes looked like something descended from the future, and carried with it a darkness that towered over them like an omnipotent oppressor.

The entrance was a double glass door that led into a long, wide hallway dimly illuminated by flickering florescent light. The place seemed more like a spook-house then a high-tech corporation. At the end of the long hallway was another double glass door, on it a sign said, "When you enter this room, do not say the forbidden word 'Hot'."

Beyond the threshold was a gigantic room with wooden beams and a ceiling higher than that of a cathedral. There were shelves surrounding them. On the shelves dolls stared at them with their lifeless eyes as if they wanted to convey a desperate message – they didn't want to be a collector's item. Some of them were terribly lifelike as if they could once have been human; some were just clumps of asparagus. Some looked like evil scarecrows and some were dressed in delicate Victorian clothing appearing as dashing as a doll could possibly be. And they all stared with the empty, soulless doll eyes, each telling a tortured tale.

"I have seen the dolls before," Jessie spoke softly, as if she was afraid that the miniature mannequins would hear her. "In a nightmare."

Francis didn't really know what to say. Despite the warm, choking air in the room, he felt cold.

"So what happens if we say the word hot?" The moment Kyle said that, Francis saw a sparkle of blue light surrounding him. Then he was no longer there. On the ground there was a small figure. Jessie picked it up and held it close to her. It was a doll with Kyle's face on it. Even the clothing was identical. It was Kyle. Except now that he was no longer human and he only stared without a simple trace of the life he once held.

"Now, I would be very careful with that doll."

They heard a squeaking noise ahead of them as a tall black leather chair spun around. On it sat a young Asian woman in a business suit. She was not unattractive, had an arrogant composure about her that was downright offensive.

"I wouldn't put a scratch on it if you want to have any hopes of getting him back alive."

"What do you want?" Andy said was on the verge on an outburst. The clown's fist was already just inches away from the woman's face. Francis had got to admit that Andy was much more of a veteran that he was, for he had not even gotten over the shock to properly react.

"It's not wise to threaten me." She curled her lips in a smile, showing not even a small trace of uncertainty or fear. "I'm your last obstacle, so to say, before your eventual meeting with Doctor Bel. But I doubt that you'll ever get there. See, you have already entered my playground. In here you cannot hurt me, you can only follow the rules of the game."

"What game?" Andy asked, with no less anger in his voice. The clown struggled seemingly to test its ability to strike the woman down. It seemed to only shiver and was not able to make a real offensive move against her.

"The rule was written on the front door." She leaned back and crossed her legs. Her skirt was short, designed to display her long, pale, and flawless legs. "If you can refrain from saying the forbidden word for the whole hour, I'll bring you to your final destination, where Doctor Bel will personally deal with you."

"How do we get Kyle back?"

"Very simple. You get me to break the rules. Then Kyle will come back right away, and you don't even have to wait the whole hour."

Andy's fist was clenched, his knuckles white. The devil-faced clown was nowhere to be seen.

"Why don't you relax and have a seat?" She pointed at the couch before her. "You have exactly fifty-seven minutes, thirty-six seconds to kill."

They did so. Jessie clutched the Kyle doll closely to her chest as if letting go of it was going to end his life. There were a few minutes of silence when they just stared at each other, like they were masters at the opposite sides of a chessboard, gazing into each other's eyes to look for a weakness and clue to defeat each other.

"Staying quiet would not help you," the woman said. "You'll never get me to say the word this way and you never get your friend back."

"What's with the heat in here?" Francis didn't really notice the discrepancy in the air until Andy mentioned it. It was chokingly hot. There was a sudden blue shimmer of light, and Andy was no longer there.

"Heat is not a forbidden word." When Jessie opened her mouth, Francis had tried to stop her but he was too late. The blue sparkles of defeat whirled around them and where they sat a moment ago only three limp dolls lay scattered on the couch.

"Damn it," Francis muttered softly, reluctant to touch and study the vile reincarnation of his companions.

The woman in front of him gave out a few gloating giggles. "Oh, I must have forgotten to mention that any derivative or conjugation of the forbidden word is also forbidden. I had assumed the meaning was implied." Her head thrown back and her giggles turned into laughter. Then she composed herself and brushed her long dark her back into place with her fingers. "I guess it's just you and me, honey. Oh I have forgotten to introduce myself. I'm Heather."

Francis said nothing, his mind churning and he was trying his best to calm his own rage.

"What a rude young man. Never mind, I already know who you are."

"This game is too simple. I want to change the rules."

"Of course, I'm here but to serve. Anything you want, I'm game."

Yes, he was hoping she'd say that. He knew that neither of them was going to say the word or any conjugation of the word for the remaining hour and he was just going to face Enoch Bel by himself. No, he would not have that. Four of them came here and he wasn't going anywhere until all four of them were able to advance. He needed to save them. He needed to save Jessie. And not just her, he needed to save Kyle and Andy because they were comrades. Not having a plan how to defeat the woman before him, he was only going to try his best.

"OK, for the next fifty minutes," He began making it up as he went along. "I want the forbidden word to switch to forbidden letters."

"What do you have in mind?"

"The five vowels."

"All of them?"

He nodded.

"You do know that all words are composed with vowels." And it meant that they couldn't say anything at all. No, he needed leverage on it if he was going to have any slim chance of winning.

"First we'll start with A," Francis added, improvising without an ultimate plan in mind. "For each increment of ten minutes we'll add the next vowel, E, and then the rest."

"That is very interesting," She smiled a small evil grin. "I accept your challenge." She stared at her wristwatch. Francis stared at his own – it was Four-thirty nine in the afternoon. "Now."

It meant that he had until five-thirty to defeat her, and the chance of saying anything will gradually decrease. He needed to talk to bait her to break the rules, and he better got it done in the next ten minutes. He knew that she was much better at the game than he was. And the only leverage he had over her was that he was desperate to get his companions back. Losing was not an option.

She switched the way she crossed her legs, Francis looked away. Maybe in other circumstances he would have found her sexually attractive, but now he only felt offended by her vile nature and her challenging, demeaning gaze.

"Do you find me," she tilted her head and stared at him curiously, "hot?"

She had said the former forbidden word deliberately. Francis knew that, it was a challenge. "No."

"Fifty minutes is very long."

"Indeed." He had to be careful. Before he said something, he needed to spell it out first, and he needed to see those letters in his head. He could do that. When it came to imagination he was without peers. He could process and display in his mind anything that he was thinking of, almost like a movie, if only he could stay calm enough.

"It's so torturing to not be…" she paused for a while to search for her words. "Expressing myself to the degree I desire."

"I see that you," he almost said "almost" but refrained, his mind displaying the next array of words he wanted to say. "More or less got stumped."

"Roughly." She switched her legs again. And the mere act of it was getting quite annoying. "This is more fun that I ever thought possible."

"I'm delighted that you're enjoying yourself. These dolls," Francis spoke slowly. "Your victims?"

"Of course." She nodded with pride. "I'm... one collector." Francis noticed that she almost said 'a collector', but she was good. It was not going to be easy winning the game.

"You follow Enoch not..." He had to avoid the word "because" but found no replacements for it, so he decided to skip it entirely. "He didn't force you to do this with the pills."

"I would've done it despite. I love power. I enjoy suffering. I enjoy even more dressing the dolls."

"You're disgusting."

"Why, such nice complements. The strong survives, the feeble dies. That's how the world functions."

"Such pitiful excuses for the vile things you do."

"Lecturing me will not help you win." She looked at the wristwatch. "Just few more minutes and our nice... colloquy will be much more limited."

"Bitch," he muttered.

"You will not benefit from rudeness. Why don't you be one good boy and just sit there quietly for the next forty minutes?"

She was already getting better at the game. She no longer stumbled. That meant getting her to choke on her own words was getting harder any passing seconds. He needed another set of tactics.

He ordered Michelle to circle around them. Hopefully her ghostly presence would somehow make his opponent nervous, and thus giving him more confidence.

Heather's eyes had followed Michelle's movement. Her countenance betrayed neither fear nor concern. Yet she was curious at whatever mischief he was planning. He couldn't attack her directly, that he already knew. The embedded set of rules inside this space of a room prohibited him from taking any offensive action against her, it was almost like the universal law that men needed to breathe oxygen to stay alive. But that didn't mean that he couldn't attack something else.

He gave the mental command for Michelle to go up to one of the shelves with the dolls and then chopped it in half with her blade. The result wasn't pretty. Dolls dropped like a mudslide and scattered across the floor.

The woman before him scowled. "That will get you nowhere."

Francis gave himself one point for getting her angry. She cared about her collection. And he had the leverage to make her angry, probably not enough for her to stumble on her own words. But it was a start. And he also proved something else. He could harm her indirectly.

Heather turned her head and tried to search for Michelle. But she wasn't there. Francis had already called her back.

"Where is she?" she demanded.

"Oh, I don't know," he lied. "I don't possess much control over her."

"Wretched lying son-of…." She didn't say the rest of it and instead looked down at her watch. "Thirty seconds before the next vowel."

"Your clock is wrong."

"Huh?"

"Well, it is. Yours is one minute too fast. Here, see mine." He threw her his watch.

She caught it in mid air and before she started to look at it, her face darkened. Her hands were darkening too. Soon they would be oozing as it spread all over her body.

"How does it feel?"

"You…" She stared at him in horror.

"Yes, it's one bomb. And it just exploded." His new ability had awakened just in time. It was almost too coincidental to be true. But whatever power he took from the last battle, he could now place a virtual unseen bomb on any object. And the explosion of the bomb caused an outbreak of the virus, that tormenting power which caused cell to degrade – Apoptosis.

"Killing me won't cure your friends." She stared at her oozing hands, terrified. "Stop it, stop it now."

"I don't know how."

"Stop it, please. I don't want to die. I'll bring your friends back."

"You won't need to. You just broke your own rules three times."

A blue light surrounded her and then the next moment in her seat was just a little fragile doll. Francis went over and picked it up. It was a beautiful doll, with lush black hair and sparkling eyes that was a little bit too lively for its own good. When he turned around his companions were back to normal. They stared at their own hands, amazed to have them back. He had never felt more delighted to see them there.

Francis took a step back and then threw the doll to the other side of the room with all his strength. While it arched across the air, there was another blue glitter surrounding it. A figure dropped to the floor.

"Ouch," Heather said, struggling up from the ground. "Almost broke my back."

"You." Francis clenched his fist and readied himself to fight her again.

"You can't trap me with my own power. Once my Pillar is trapped it will reverse the process by itself. Anyway, you have won. I will now take you to Doctor Bel."

"What about those other dolls?" Francis pointed at the surrounding lifeless spectators.

"Once someone becomes a doll for a time, he stays dead. Killing me won't bring them back."

"You deserve to die." How many dolls were in the room? How many people had died in her hands? Thousands? Tens of thousands?

"Oh?" she said, amused.

But it was already over. Only the last battle awaited him, his father awaited him, and his destiny awaited him.

CHAPTER FORTY

They waited for the elevator to come down. The number on the indicator screen started at thirty-six. Francis couldn't help but wonder how gigantic the inside of the pyramid actually was. And they willingly walked into a maze of desolation, a trap that they might never free themselves from.

"Bel's power," Andy said after being silent for a long period of time. "What is it?"

"Nobody knows," Heather answered noncommittally. "Or nobody ever lives to find out."

"If you're lying. Then I'll–"

"You'll what? What reason do I have to lie at this point? You'll all find out what true horror means when you meet Doctor Bel. That I can assure you."

"May God have pity on your soul."

"Yeah, fuck you."

The elevator door opened. Reluctantly each of them stepped in. Jessie was holding on to his arm and standing close to him. She was shaking. Francis swore that he'd never seen her so afraid, not even when they were in the elevator that other time during an attack. Her terror was bitter, astringent and just extremely cold.

Despite the old-age interior design of the elevator, it only took a short moment to reach the thirty-sixth floor. Heather led them into another long hallway which spiraled and zigzagged through confusing routes and finally arriving at a thick double door lavishly decorated with golden carvings. Francis saw mythical beings from Egyptian folklore depicted in what seemed a vividly epic battle – warriors holding spears with heads of animals, winged mammals and godly warriors wielding thunder bolts in their hands. He paused and admired the lifelike craftsmanship displayed before his eyes. Their reluctant guide didn't have to inform them, but they all knew that the room before them was their ultimate and final destination.

Heather reached for the latch and flinched back, as if she had sensed a terrible, gnawing cold on the other side of the door. The same dirty cold that Francis and each of his companions were feeling at that very moment.

Her hesitation did not last long. After taking a deep breath, she reached for the latch once more. Francis watched her push the folded door inward, then his eyes sprinted to the other side of the threshold. He saw a figure standing holding the edge of the door. It was Heather, with an expression of shock on her face. Her mouth opened, and a trail of blood ran from the corner of her lips. Francis lowered his gaze and saw the bloody mess. Where her stomach once was, now blood and entrails were pouring down from her open wound. Terror swam through Francis' veins and the dirty coldness he felt a moment ago became a destructive blizzard. He could feel that every stand of hair on his body was standing up on its own. A moment ago she was opening the door for them. The next she was already inside, killed as if someone had just thrust a spear through her abdomen, and she didn't even have the time to scream. He saw only shock in her eyes before she slumped lifelessly down to the floor, a bloody pool before them.

"What the hell just happened?" Kyle said, his eyes narrowing.

"Whatever it is, it's too dangerous for us to face right now without knowing what it is that just attacked us," Andy backed away from the doorway trying to sound as calm as possible. But he was only trying. "We need another plan."

"And you better come up with one right away," Kyle followed up. "It could be anyone of us next."

"We run."

"I'm not running," Francis felt a bit agitated when he heard that. He didn't come here all this way to just cower away at the last minute.

"Listen to me," Kyle said as he put a firm hand on his shoulder. "Andy's right. We need to get away right now, just temporarily, and fight back when we have a better chance."

Francis shook his head but reluctantly followed his companions' footsteps away from the room where the golden battle took place. He didn't agree on the strategy of escape, but he knew he didn't have a chance fighting by himself either. They had come here together, and they were going to leave together.

Footsteps came after them, an ominous presence tracking them in the winding passages. When he felt the presence almost upon him, Francis turned around but saw nothing. When his focus turned back towards what was ahead of him, he found that he was alone.

An arm snatched him and pulled him into a side doorway. His heart almost burst with startling fright, even to find out it was only Kyle. They were on top of what seemed to be a staircase leading downward and they were alone.

"Where are the others?"

"I don't know. I wasn't paying attention."

"You mean, they're just gone? How could this happen?"

"Yeah, turned a corner and I couldn't see them anymore. I was busy looking for a place to make our last stand. I found it."

"Where?"

"Below us." Kyle started down the stairs.

He wasn't even going to bother asking the details, he just had to trust the FBI agent. Hopefully he knew what he was doing. "But what about them?"

"Hopefully they'll catch up in time. Then they will be able to surprise Enoch Bel in a pincer attack"

It wasn't much of a plan. But they didn't really have time to sit down in a meeting to hash it out. "How do you know Enoch is after us first and not them?" Francis had never run downstairs so fast before, taking two to three steps at a time. He wasn't afraid of falling though. He was more afraid at the horrible presence that hunted them.

"We are easier prey."

"Thanks for the confidence."

"No, think about it. We can't heal ourselves. Andy can." The winding staircase spiraled downwards like a snake reaching from the heavens to the ground. "It makes sense that Bel would choose to pick us off first. And besides, I can feel that he's coming after us."

Kyle was right. Bel was right behind them, Francis was sure of that.

A sudden exit took them into a large room – a room that looked an indoor theme park. Its ceiling was of the color of a morning blue sky and its walls painted with sceneries from a desert paradise and from afar they were not walls at all, but distant images. The indoor environment carried the theme of a desert. And from a distance they heard the sound of a waterfall. They were in an oasis.

Francis continued trailing behind Kyle, couldn't help but marvel at the surrounding sight, and wondered what the place was for. All the things he had been through and witnessed these few weeks he had learned that nothing was impossible. And the improbable often happened, when you least suspected it.

When the indoor pond and waterfall came into view, Francis almost understood why Kyle had chosen this place. He was looking for the source of water, just like one of those diving rods that nomads used. Francis didn't really know what Kyle had in mind. But he knew the man had a purpose and a plan because he had run forward with a hard determination that wasn't driven by either fright or panic.

Francis followed the leap into the water. It was only knee deep and the depth did not increase when they went towards the waterfall in the back. About ten paces from the shore Kyle climbed onto an artificial rock that was like a floating platform. Francis did the same.

"Cao, it's time to do your magic." Francis watched the little girl joyfully dance on the water around them as if she was performing a ritual.

"What is she doing?" Francis asked.

"Booby trapping the very air around us."

"How?"

"Making a hydrogen bomb."

Francis never really liked organic chemistry and he certainly did not know how a hydrogen bomb worked. But breaking down the $H2O$ around them created a plentiful supply of hydrogen. That's why Kyle was looking for the highest concentration of water in the building. There was something about nuclear fission, β radiation, and the right amount of hydrogen atoms that would make deadly explosions. As long as it was effective and was going to save their asses, he didn't need to know how it worked.

A figure in an imposing black suit stopped at the shore, meticulously surveying them. It was Enoch Bel. "Boys, you can run, but you cannot hide." His deep voice penetrated their thin defenses and struck an agonizing fear into Francis' heart. The battle had just begun but Francis felt like he had already lost it.

"Stay close to me," Kyle murmured.

Enoch extended a hand before him testing the air suspiciously. "Very nice job, Agent Gideon. You should get a trophy for your work. But this will not stop me."

Francis saw the shadow behind Enoch then. A large humanoid form with muscular limbs, almost naked except for the loincloth at its waist. It's head was that of a wolf – a mythical figure, perhaps a god, the very same one that was depicted on the golden battlefield in the room upstairs. There was something very terrifying about the wolf-man hybrid, something that Francis couldn't place right away which wasn't quite right. The next moment Francis found out why. The wolf's head spun 180 degrees clockwise and revealed another face equally vicious behind it, that of a bird, to be more precise, a falcon – with a large deadly beak and shrewd eyes that gleamed with an ominous red, the same horrifying crimson evil he had seen from the clown. There was a sparkle in the pair of eyes and it was so bright that for a moment the whole room was enveloped in a flash. Then Bel and the bird creature no longer stood at that place at the shore. They had vanished in mid air.

Francis saw and felt the explosion around him as the very air crackled like unseen fireworks. He searched for Enoch's figure but to his horror, saw Kyle lifted off the ground. The creature, now switched back into the face of the wolf, had its fist and total length of its right arm through Kyle's stomach, holding him up like a bloody pipe. Enoch stood only a pace behind with his arms folded, his expression that of utter bemusement.

Francis took a step backward and saw Kyle's blood poured down like the waterfall behind them, except it was dark red and with it flowed with Kyle's life. Kyle turned his head and looked at him, a moment of shock as if he didn't know what had hit him – the same expression Francis had seen when Heather was butchered before them. Then that shock turned into sadness as a drop of tear trailed from the corner of his eye.

"Time, Francis, Time."

"What?"

"Time is your enemy…" He then closed his eyes and left a smile on his face – a smile of contentment, he then passed away.

"No…" Francis backed away into the water. His own tears blurred his vision. He couldn't believe it but Kyle was dead, right before his eyes. One second he was there, and the next he was dead. How was it possible? Time … what did it mean?

"A pity, my son." The wolf creature dropped the lifeless body onto the rock and Enoch Bel spoke with a triumphant grin. "Is this man worth your tears? Or are you crying because you're so afraid of me?"

"Don't call me your son." Francis kept backing away and thinking. Time was his enemy. How? One moment Bel was standing there, and the next moment he killed Kyle. The hydrogen bombs, Enoch had passed through all of them because they exploded, but he was unscathed. If he could not perceive the time of Enoch's passage, neither did Kyle nor the hydrogen bombs. Because time had been frozen. The eyes of the eagle head had the power to control time. If that was true, he was truly doomed. How could he fight against time?

Enoch laughed. "Who do you think you are, Francis Baal, mankind's savior? You are my seed, my very own offspring. Evil and domination and murder flow in your veins just like mine."

"No," Francis shook his head. He knew he wasn't like his father.

"Do you know why you are here this particular night?" he continued, not waiting for an answer, "because you can't deny your own destiny. You are here tonight because it's been long written in the stars, not because you want and choose to be here. Do you know why this place, Babel Cydonia is built? Just like the ancient pyramids in Egypt, they were modeled after the structures built on Mars. You did not know that, did you? Tonight is a special night. It is when Babel Cydonia faces directly the Cydonian structure on Mars. It is when the ascension begins."

Mars? Ascension? What the hell is he talking about?

"Have you finally figured out what Project Lilitu is?"

Francis shook his head. He hadn't even thought about it anymore after he had decided to come here.

"You are Project Lilitu. The perfect killing machine, the strongest Pillar of all, or rather I should say, the potential to become the strongest Pillar, once you had fused enough of your victims within you. You were born to devour others, you were born to take what's rightfully yours."

Francis felt a strong headache like acid tearing away his brain tissues. He dropped down to his knees and clutched painfully at his head.

"Yes, the truth shall free your soul," Bel said. Francis didn't want to hear anymore, but he couldn't find the strength to tell his father to stop. "Project Pillars. Do you know why it exists? It's not for controlling human beings, wreaking havoc amongst society, and manipulating government officials. We don't really need to do any of that. It's just a front. Project Pillars was created as a plan to feed you victims, yes you. The others were nothing but bottom of the food chain. Why did you think I sent assassins to hunt you down? Of course they could have killed you. Then you would have become unfit to become the antichrist. But haven't you always wondered why you so often narrowly escaped your plight? Because I wanted you to. Because the main reason was to feed you, to make you more powerful, to awake your true destiny."

"The antichrist?" What did that have to do with him?

"Yes, didn't you know? You are the antichrist." Enoch laughed a mad laughter. "And what, you thought you were on a sacred mission to destroy evil?

Don't be naive. You are the very representation of what you came to fight…
evil."

"No, this is not true." Francis desperately looked around for Andy.
Where was he? Where was Jessie? He needed them, to come here and save him.

"Who are you looking for? Your brother is not going to come. He used
you, just like I used him. He's using you to get to me, and I used him to bring
you here safely. Without your help he wouldn't stand a chance against me. But
who he wants to finally destroy is you, not me. Now he waits quietly for the
outcome of this battle."

"I will not fight," Francis declared.

"Hah, you think it's a choice? You were never born to choose. I can
easily wrench the title of the antichrist from you. There's much I still want to
destroy in this world."

"No, I don't want to be the antichrist."

"Then be prepared to give it up."

*   *   *   *

Andy had a strong grip on her arm. She wanted to free herself but
couldn't. Francis and Kyle were gone. She didn't know where she was, until she
saw the golden door and Heather's body again she knew they had circled
around. "We made a big circle."

"I know." He pulled her into the room, and she averted her face when
they had to step over the pool of blood and the body.

"Let go of me, you're hurting me."

He did and she found herself in a lavish living room under what
seemed to be the top part of the pyramid, a dome made of dark opal glass
panels. Through the shaded glass she saw the setting sun outside the top of the
pyramid. The room they were in was not as large as the reception area but it was

still the size of a small lecture hall, with its own spiral staircase going up to a loft. She was in the center of a vortex, where energy flowed and concentrated, ready to explode.

"You knew where you were going, didn't you?"

"Of course, I've been here before," he answered. "A few months back, most of the rooms were still in construction then."

"What are we doing here?"

"We wait."

"And you pick such a nice time to be eloquent."

"Francis will be fine."

"What exactly are we waiting for?"

"The outcome of the battle. Have a seat," he pointed towards the couch. "It'll be a while."

"I don't want to fucking sit."

"There's no need to get edgy."

"Why are we here, and not there, wherever they are."

"Because it is Francis' fight. Not yours. Not mine."

"Bull shit. Why did we come here then?"

"I came to destroy the antichrist."

"And waiting here helps a lot obviously." What the heck was wrong with him? She was enraged. She needed to be where Francis was. He needed her help.

"The antichrist will come."

"I'm leaving."

"Oh, you're not."

Jessie drew her Smith & Wesson and pointed the barrel at him, at the same time backing away until she was sure that Andy could not reach her with his Pillar. "Try to stop me."

"Oh I will. You're making a big mistake."

She backed away more, and he rushed her. She fired, and saw the bullet stopped inches before his face, before dropping harmlessly to the ground. Unseen hands lifted her by her shoulders and slammed her to the wall, knocking the wind out of her.

She choked and dropped her gun. Her whole body stung painfully, and she wished so much that she could fight back in some way. "Why…"

"Nothing good comes out from siding with evil."

"What are you talking about?"

"You don't get it, do you? Francis is evil. Francis is the antichrist."

"You're mad."

He told her then, the truth about Project Lilitu and Project Pillars. The truth struck her like a lightning bolt. She felt paralyzed and helpless.

"You used us."

"Yes, I needed Francis to finish Bel off. Only he can do it. And then I'll finish off the antichrist. Babel will be no more. There will be no more Pillars and hosts in the world. I'll even take my own life to make sure of that. Mankind will be saved."

"This is what you call saving mankind? Killing your own brother, leaving your friend out there to die. Lying to all of us…"

"I'm doing this for God, and for men. How can you understand, you don't even have faith."

"Fuck you and your filthy faith."

"That's alright. I've got enough faith for the both of us. When you are watched over by God, you see the world differently. You think differently. You make sacrifices for the ultimate good. Maybe in your eyes I am loathsome, maybe in the world's eyes I am despicable. It doesn't matter. What matters is I am doing this for the love of God." There was only madness in his blue eyes. The madness, the darkness, had finally consumed him. "Let me ask you one final question. Which side are you on? Good, or evil?"

"Neither." She spat on the floor before him. "I side with Francis, because he's my friend. It doesn't matter who he really is. I don't abandon and betray friends." And besides, she knew that Francis was incapable of evil. She had seen it in his eyes, and she had seen it in his soul. She knew him. He might be the antichrist or whatever monster the crazy people from Babel wanted him to be but she knew that there was only gentleness in his brown eyes, whenever it was not covered by his sorrowful loneliness. He didn't have the soul of a murderer, and he certainly did not have the soul of an evil figurehead. He was her friend.

"Those who stand against God will burn in hell." He gave her a hard kick in the stomach and her head spun. She clenched her teeth and endured the pain. She thought about Francis. And she thought about how they were going to get through this. Together they would. They had to.

CHAPTER FORTY-ONE

Enoch Bel had that same penetrating blue gaze that Andy had – disturbingly powerful eyes that reached right into one's soul, seized it, and never let go. They stared at each other for a long period of silence, a session of foreplay before their death match, a serene period when strength and weaknesses were measured, when hate against each other was justified. Still, Francis had felt no hate against the father who had abandoned him. He only felt pity. There was more to life than just power and domination, he had learned about that now. He didn't really know Enoch, but he knew that his father was as lonely as he himself ever was. Wealth and power maybe bought loyalty and fear, but it could never buy friendship, love, and happiness.

Yet he had to fight, perhaps it was true that he had no choice but to fight his father this day. He did not believe himself to be the antichrist. God and religion and the devil had nothing to do with what transpired here today. He was just facing a mad man who was trying to destroy the world, destroy humanity. And Francis was the last obstacle that stood between his father and his lunatic plan. And he wasn't here for either good or evil, he was here fighting for himself. And he was going to be reborn.

Kyle had sacrificed himself to unravel the mystery of Bel's power. Francis wanted so much to grieve for him. He hadn't known the man for long, but he would have been proud to call him a friend. Francis knew that the man had fulfilled his destiny. Now he could be with his wife and child in the heavens. And Cao was gone, as he no longer needed the illusion of his daughter to keep him alive. He could be with the real her now. To not let Kyle's death be in vain, and to prove his own worth, and to be able to rescue Jessie and get away from this wretched place, he vowed to defeat his father.

Francis pondered how he could fight against time. There was a weakness and limitation to each Pillar. He knew that from all the battles which he had been drawn into before this. Perhaps the Project Pillars was nothing but a training program, even a feeding program, designed to make him capable and strong, but that too was the only thing that could save him now. Time only stopped when the falcon's eyes sparkled. Whenever he faced the wolf, he was safe. How long Enoch needed to rest in between time-freezing sessions was an unknown. Francis knew that the power could not be used continuously or otherwise they would have been long dead, even after Heather was killed. How long did time freeze when Enoch used his power was also an unknown. Francis guessed five seconds, from the ten paces his father took to murder Kyle. There were too many questions he needed answers for. But there was no time...

The battle had begun. The wolf creature dashed in and Michelle met it head-on, her blade drawn and ready. If it were him a few weeks ago when he first learned of Michelle's power he would have been slaughtered in the close hand-to-hand combat, now although she was not as physically strong as the wolf creature she matched the quick speed. She was tough. Francis remembered the brief few seconds he fought with Andy's clown in the racquetball court. Then the clown's punches were like flashes of light, impossible to block and avoid. The wolf man was as fast as the clown, and now Michelle dodged the blows with ease.

Francis noticed one thing. Bel was always not more than two steps behind his own Pillar and he appeared to be concentrating. It meant he was a Type A host, one who had absolute control over his Pillar yet he needed to issue every command and reacted to every single minute detail himself. And his range was limited. Then Francis had an advantage. He could be much farther away from Michelle and he did not need to concentrate on the battle. Michelle reacted to situations adaptively when it came to close combat, he couldn't have done it better himself. Slowly he backed away, if the maximum range between

Michelle and him hadn't changed over the time of her growth, he could be quite far away from the battle, at least a good fifteen paces. Then when the time came, he could get away from the time-freezing spell, provided its area was limited as he presumed. Running and keeping himself alive was not a winning strategy, he needed a way to defeat his opponent.

After a flurry of violent blows, Michelle saw an opening and a piercing strike caught the side of the wolf creature's ribs. It cringed and jumped back out of reach, surprised but not seriously hurt. The only way Francis could ensure his victory was by apoptosis, if only Michelle could touch Bel's real body directly. On the other hand, if he was caught in the stationary time, Enoch would win. They were both walking between a thin line of life and death, and that was how soldiers on the battlefield felt. Yet he couldn't easily tag Enoch with his power, however it was much easier for Enoch to kill him in the drift of time.

That moment of hesitation was all Enoch needed. The wolf's head spun and in its place the falcon now stared ominously at him, making him feel like a puny rat waiting to be devoured by a diving falcon from the sky. Instantly he called Michelle back. He saw the image of Michelle disperse and he saw the light from the falcon's crimson eyes. He was still too close. He knew that. If he were caught in the drift of stationary time, he would be dead before realizing it.

Francis made Michelle stand behind him holding on to him. Her hand with the blade swung at the air behind him. He had done the same when he was trying to catch the opponent who inserted a bomb into him earlier today. Hopefully the space that the path of the sword canceled out would take him far enough away. Feeling himself thrown backwards like a violent recoil from a bazooka, Francis made himself concentrate on what surrounded him as he traveled backwards. If he was not far away enough to escape time, perhaps he was far away enough for Enoch to avoid being able to reach him before time flowed normally again. That meant in any second Enoch would be a lot closer than before, it was almost like teleportation.

He was right. Even before his feet had a firm stand on the ground, the wolf creature was before him. He was still whole, he wasn't dead yet. That meant his plan had worked. An inhuman fist aimed mercilessly at his stomach. There was a loud clang and he felt his whole body shake from the impact. Michelle was there just in time to block the blow with the blade held backhanded like a dagger, her other hand supported the blunt side of the sword so that the strong impact did not throw her backwards too much.

The wolf creature staggered, a thin layer of dust swarmed around them like a prelude to a tornado. Bel moaned in agony as Francis saw the blood drip down from his fist. Now it was his chance, his one chance before the time froze again.

Michelle launched a series of mad assaults at her surprised opponent. Francis slipped his watch off his wrist, the one thing that was going to save his life twice. He wrapped the mechanical thing around his fist, and he circled around to where Enoch stood. He knew that Enoch was not going to sense his approach, concentrated on Michelle's assault. With the distraction of the pain and perhaps even calculating the time he needed before his next time-manipulation spell, he was well occupied.

Francis was now behind them, watching the fight from two directions. He saw what Michelle perceived, and he also saw from where his real body stood. The head of the falcon lay limp behind the wolf's, the red gaze gone from its eyes. For a moment he thought the empty eye sockets watched him, discovering his plan of sneaking from behind. But they were only limp, lifeless and empty.

Francis silently approached from behind and drove his fist onto Enoch's back. He felt the outburst of the unseen air as the explosion began. He had tagged his watch with an apoptosis bomb and upon impact the disease was spreading like an outbreak of an epidemic. He didn't really know if he himself would be affected but he was right that his own power could not harm himself.

Enoch fell down to his knees, his eyes bloodshot and staring forward in a mixture of awe and horror. The wolf man also ceased attacking and stood motionless before them like a finely crafted statue. "Well done, my son. I'm proud of you. Take me now, take the power that enables you to rule the world."

"No," Francis shook his head.

"You need it to face your brother."

"No, I don't. I don't need your filthy power."

He laughed as he watched his hands turn charcoal black. "You still don't get it, do you? You think you have a choice? You are the leader of men. You're the antichrist. You will jumpstart mankind's next step of evolution. You will cleanse this land and begin anew. You will take my power. You have no choice, absolutely no choice."

"No…" Francis screamed when he saw Michelle slipped her hands around the man's neck. He commanded her to back off. But she didn't listen to him. It was too late to even ponder the nature of her disobedience. She was already drawn to the victim like a newborn drawn to the breasts. She was a succubus, and he was the taker of souls. The power shot through him like a short-circuited drug. He trembled and flowed in a space that was eternity and he knew that he was one step away from being complete. Or was it one step away from totally losing himself? Darkness devoured him and he was one with darkness.

*   *   *   *

"You're a damn hypocrite, you know that?" Jessie grunted in pain. A few kicks and her whole body became sore. If only she could fight back, if only she was not so weak and helpless.

"You wouldn't understand."

She understood completely. The darkness within him had finally consumed him. "What about your followers, the ones from the fellowship?" She couldn't even remember the name of the church. "They died because of you. Doesn't that mean anything to you? Don't you want revenge?"

"Don't speak evil to me, you little bitch. Revenge means nothing to me, they died serving God. They were necessarily sacrifices in the grand scheme."

"You're nothing but evil hiding behind the excuse of God." Either she kept talking until Francis came or she could attempt to confuse him enough to the point of mental breakdown. It was a long shot either way but if she distanced herself, she was sure she could outrun him. "You kill because you enjoy it. Inside you're just the same as your father."

"He is not my father." There was a flash of anger in his eyes.

Was her psychoanalysis working? She understood well that it could backfire on her. He could get angry enough to beat her to death. But she wasn't afraid of death. She wanted to get to Francis.

"And we are nothing alike. What do you think, a few psychology classes at Stanford and a few years catching serial killers you think you understand everything, don't you? The real world is not that simple. It's not always about black and white." He was calmed immediately.

The only thing she accomplished was staling. She hoped that Francis could take care of himself, and she hoped that he didn't have to kill his own father.

"I was born knowing my true destiny, as the antithesis of the antichrist."

Who in the world uses the word antithesis? But she said nothing.

"I am the fist of God. I am here to destroy the antichrist. It doesn't matter what I go through to get that accomplished. I am willing to take the guise of darkness, even embrace darkness, and understand darkness, to eventually destroy it."

"Bullshit."

"Like I said, you wouldn't understand, because you have already sold your soul to the devil. You are tainted."

She sighed, and wondered if God really sent the person in front of her to fight against evil. If it was so, she pitied the world. She closed her eyes and for the first time in her life, she silently prayed and asked for Francis' safety. It seemed selfish to ask for something so personal as an atheist. But if only there were a chance that God really existed, and if he were listening, she needed a little divine power to help her.

"I'll give you one chance," Andy said, interrupting her thoughts.

When she opened her eyes, she saw that he was holding a metal box. After pressing a red button on the bottom of the metal casing, the box opened and a cloud of steam burst out. A second look told her that it wasn't steam, but cold air. It was a mini-refrigerator, designed probably to keep DNA and protein alike alive. Inside there was a syringe.

She instantly knew what he was planning, and she shook her head, desperately. No, this is not happening.

"Haven't you always wondered if you were a host, what kind of powers you would have?"

"It has not once crossed my mind." And that was the absolute truth. She had only pitied those who were changed by Babel. Even though they had gain power, they had lost part of their humanity becoming slaves to their own greed and Babel's utter domination.

"Well, it has crossed mine many times." He grinned menacingly, showing a flash of teeth at the corner of his mouth. "Always wondered what kind of power a lively and brave woman like you would wield at her hands. Would you be able to rival my Pillar?"

She shook her head. She didn't want any of it. "I thought you wanted to get rid of all the Pillars in the world. Why are you doing this?"

"You've sold your soul to the devil already, what does it matter?"

He was mad, she concluded. He was really mad because his eyes gleamed with lunacy.

"You want to help Francis, you want to fight back. I'm giving you that chance right now. It's up to you whether you would survive the drug or not, or should I say, it's up to God. The only thing I will promise you is that I will end your pain quickly."

That was no way getting out of it. "Give it to me then." She got up and took a step forward until she was bravely standing just less than a pace away from him.

"No, I'll do it for you."

"I want to do it myself." She challenged him. I have to get my hands on that syringe.

For a long moment they stared at each other. She saw the darkness in his eyes so horrible that it disgusted her but she did not falter. She had been attracted to him. What the hell was I thinking?

He handed the syringe to her, which she gripped so tightly that she was afraid it was going to shatter in her hands. Andy pointed to her bare arm. But she knew that probably anywhere would work.

Her gaze was in a continual lock with his. She needed an opening, a moment when his guard was down. She found something under her feet, probably something broken during the struggle, and kicked it behind her. His stare trailed the sudden sound, and she knew that was the right moment. She lunged herself at him and went for his heart. She missed but still was able to stick the needle into his chest. She felt unseen hands choking her from behind. She almost couldn't breathe but with a slight push she managed to empty everything in the syringe into him. She was thrown backwards and hit something, experiencing the painful shock of bones breaking. Then she was lifted up, a hand slapped her, and sharp nails drew blood from her face.

"Bitch, you'll pay for this."

She closed her eyes. "Francis, Francis."

*   *   *   *

In the darkness, he heard his name being called. He searched frantically for the source of that sound and crawled towards it. But the darkness was eternal. He kept on crawling and he knew that there must be a way out eventually. If he just kept on going …

"Francis," he heard it again. And for a moment there was light. Where there was light, there was hope. He kept going.

Then he opened his eyes to see Enoch Bels dried up corpse lying next to him. A mixture of bile and his lunch reached his throat, which almost choked him, but he swallowed, leaving a sour taste in his mouth. He felt weak and his head spun, as well as satisfied and disgusted. The satisfaction disgusted him.

There was one thing he needed to get from his father. In the pocket of Bel's jacket he found the photograph – this time the whole one, with a younger version of Enoch holding his mother lovingly. Seeing the whole photograph made him realize how happy her mother was, how happy they both were. He shoved the photo into his pocket.

It wasn't over.

Jessie, where was she? Was she the one calling him? She needed him.

He didn't know how he'd know but he knew where she was, as if he had become clairvoyant.

Quickly he went through the door and up the stairs to the top floor. As he navigated the winding passageways as if he had lived there all his life, his strength returned and he felt like a new person.

Entering the golden doorway, he saw Jessie slumped on the couch, either asleep or unconscious. There was dry blood on her shirt and her face, fresh blood on her hands. There were dark patches on the brown couch, no doubt soaked with her blood. He took a closer look and saw blood coming out from her lacerated wrist. He clenched his fist.

Andy stared motionlessly at the transparent dome, the pinnacle of the pyramid, his hands clasped behind him as if he was calmly marveling at the setting sun. The sky was in a deep orange – the last moment of light before darkness.

"I see that you have gotten rid of our father," Andy said with an amused tone. "Sunset up here is beautiful, isn't it?"

"What have you done to her?"

"Oh, I beat her up, I healed her, and I beat her up again. She deserved every bit of it because she's a whore. And then I decided to make a small cut to her artery. With every moment that passes, her life is slipping by. I'd say she has about ten minutes left. Actually, make that nine."

"Why?" He only saw a blinding white light of fury. The anger building up inside him was ready for a violent outburst. He had never felt so furious in his life.

"Because she's your little whore. And she poked me with that fucking needle. What did she think she could do? Give me a brain tumor? It doesn't work that way, I'm already gifted."

Francis didn't know what he was talking about. He couldn't see anything in his eyes except the blinding white light. And his knuckles hurt from clenching his fist so tight.

"Antichrist, you're afraid of me, aren't you? I've always been better than you, and I always will be better than you. I beat you in racquetball, I beat you in the arcade, I beat you in career, I beat you to taking your little whore to bed, and I beat you in combat. You're inferior. I was born to strike fear into your very core. I know how much you're afraid of Joker, and I know how much you're afraid of me. Tell you what, if you can take my power than you can save your little whore."

"Stop calling her a whore."

"She's what she is."

"And I'm not afraid of you."

"Oh?" He laughed. "Prove it, you little worm."

Sam, in high school, had called him a little worm. But he was not a little worm. He had been a worm, hiding in a hole in the ground, afraid to face the world and its problems, afraid to face emotions, afraid to deal with people. He no longer wanted to be a worm. He was part of this world. And this world was part of him.

Yet he was still afraid of the devil-faced clown. And it was his last trial to overcome that fear. Michelle's normal acrobatic-like agility and swiftness were affected by his fear, and she became slowed and burdened. The very sight of the clown sent chills down his spine and froze the air around him. She took hits which normally she wouldn't have taken, and Francis clenched in pain as each punch of the clown shocked him like a bolt from the heavens.

The two ethereal phantoms danced around each other. Michelle forever on the defensive, dodging, ducking, parrying lightening-fast blows. The clown pressed his offensive, intimidating her like a predator toying with its prey.

"You can't hurt me, Antichrist." And Francis knew that he was right. The clown could immediately seal up all the wounds Michelle inflicted and none of his peripheral powers were effective against him, as if the whole existence of the clown was meant to be a weapon for his demise. He felt useless and incompetent before the clown, and those ominous crimson eyes stared into his soul, devouring him. The clown reeked of an unholy air of death, and he was as afraid of it as when he saw it in Mammoth, and when he saw it as a child.

He shook his head. Jessie needed him. He didn't have time to be afraid. Jessie overcame her phobia. He could overcome his own too.

Michelle took two direct blows to the chest and the impact threw him two steps backward. Sharp pain sizzled through his body when he breathed.

Time, time was on his side now. He suddenly realized that. He held his father's power. If only he could use it. He saw another punch coming, and he kept thinking about time. And suddenly everything seemed to slow down and he saw the path of the clown's punch ahead of time. He was observing his surroundings in two different time frames, and he saw what was happening now and what was happening in the future. It was only a few seconds into the future, but in that timeframe only he and Michelle could move. That gave him time to order Michelle to circle around the clown and Andy before time flowed normally again.

The clown's punch caught only thin air and Michelle successfully made a deep cut into Andy's back, a wound that would normally kill a person but in this case was quickly patched up as if no trace of it had ever occurred. Even the open shirt sewed itself up, only traces of blood remained. Andy had said once blood left the body it was an outside substance. And that meant Jessie could die if she lost too much blood before he could get her healed. He needed to hurry.

Andy and the clown both jumped back a distance away, reassessing the situation. "You took the power, didn't you?"

Francis didn't answer him. The rules had been changed. Time did not become frozen. He didn't know what it was. When he first took the swordsman's power in Babel's parking lot, he changed the claymore into a katana. When he took Tormentor's power, it was reduced to the cell degradation omitting the entropic degradation effect. When he took the power of the black hole he changed it into a space-erasing ability of Michelle's sword strike. When he took the power of bomb creation he adapted it like a viral outburst of Apoptosis. When he took Enoch's time freezing ability, what became of it? To be able to defeat the foe before him right now he needed to understand the extent of his own power.

"You were here and then you were gone, and I don't even remember punching you." Andy grinned, as if he finally found joy in the one-sided combat. "This is getting interesting, isn't it? Did you freeze time?"

"You knew of Enoch Bel's power, didn't you?"

"Naturally."

"Yet you pretend you didn't."

He laughed. "I pretended a lot of things. But I did it to make sure of your downfall, evil of all evil. I did it for God and for the human race. You wouldn't understand because you were born to destroy life."

It wasn't true. He wasn't born to destroy the human race. And life was precious. His brother was mad.

"Why didn't you just stab your sword into my heart if you had time frozen, because you couldn't."

He was right. Time was not frozen. He could not attack someone during that period like Enoch did with his frozen time. If only he could figure out what that ability was. Yet he had the upper hand now. He didn't fully understand his ability and neither did Andy. He had an advantage.

This time it was his turn to press the offensive. And when the clown counterattacked, he used his new ability again. He thought about time and saw the path of the clown's attack. He made Michelle move to the clown's side and as time flowed normally again she caught him in a downward thrust, which was quickly healed again.

Yet Francis understood a little bit more about his power. Whenever he used the power, time still flowed. Yet only he could perceive the time in between the presence and the future. And whoever affected by the power was not able to experience that time.

Francis saw a glimpse of recognition and enlightenment in Andy's eyes and he knew that his brother also understood his power. The clown turned its back to Francis and raised its hands to strike at Andy. Blood dripped from Andy's wrist, but he only grinned in a frenzied triumph. "I understand now, Francis. Come again, I'll destroy you."

Time was pseudo-frozen again and Michelle circled around the devil-faced clown. And when time flowed and Michelle was posed for the attack Joker turned and elbowed her in the face. The impact threw Francis to the ground and broke his nose. He ignored the pain and got up again.

"You want to know how I did it?" Andy pointed at the pool of blood dripping from his own wrist. "I kept mp eyes on the droplets of blood. I know what you did with time. You erased it. Every time I only experienced the outcome of my action but not what happened in between. So I kept my eyes on each single drop of blood from my wrist. When the pool of blood increased I knew you have used your power. You have lost."

"Oh really?" Francis used his power again and this time he did not make Michelle get close enough for Joker to counterattack. And watched the devil-faced clown wildly dashing here and there to escape the attacks which never came. Francis knew that he still had the upper hand, despite both of their understanding of the limitations to his new power. Andy only had a glimpse of a moment to counteract his attack after finding out time had been tampered with using his blood meter. But Francis was the one who held the advantage to constantly be on the offensive.

The fight was suddenly interrupted when Andy dropped to the floor on his knees, both his hands clutched at his head and wailed, "You little bitch, what have you done to my head!"

Francis took the moment to manipulate time, and he staggered. This time he couldn't see the future. He saw the pool of blood below Andy's wrist getting smaller and smaller, and blood flowing backwards into Andy's wound. It was like watching a videotape of a waterfall in reverse. Michelle for a moment was out of control and moving backwards to where she started. And Francis saw three explosive punches landing onto her chest. He felt his own ribcage shatter and he was thrown flat onto the floor. He saw the darkening pinnacle of the pyramid. The sky had already darkened. The stars were laughing at his failure.

Andy stood over him, his hand still clutching at his forehead. A trail of blood ran down his face. "I can feel the neurons jumping in my brain. How ironic, isn't it? What the little whore did to me end up saving me—"

"Don't call her a whore," Francis muttered.

"What did you say? Anyway, how does it feel to see the time you erased being restored again. It was like a miracle, God's miracle. God won today, and the devil lost. It was a glorious battle."

"Save Jessie, she has nothing to do with this." That was his last breath, before it hurt too much to breathe.

"Oh no. She has sold her soul to the devil. She deserves to burn in hell."

Andy slumped down to the floor again and screamed. His face a contorted rictus of agonizing terror as both his hands were clutching his temples so tightly that he looked like he was trying to keep his head from exploding. Francis saw the empty syringe on the floor and understood. Andy had defeated him. But Jessie and he together had won the battle. Andy had brought the drug P.I.L.L.A.R. with him and somehow Jessie had used it on him. Francis didn't really know what the drug did to people who were already born with the necessarily genes. It didn't matter. This was his chance.

He knew it was going to be the last time when Michelle's hand reached his brother's throat. The nails dug deep into Andy's flesh and blood. He felt the carotid artery thrashed and the heart pumped. He felt the life flowing through Michelle's fingers to the very core of his being.

I'm doing this to save Jessie, he told himself. I'm not doing this for joy and pleasure. Yet the exploding ecstasy came, blinding and crippling him. His ribs and injuries healed as the sensation enveloped him. He crawled towards her, without submitting to the overwhelming darkness. She was so close and yet so far away. Yet he went on because she needed him. Please, God. Don't let her die.

Then he saw Michelle walking over to Jessie. Her hands brushed her bloody wrist and he saw the wound seal itself. He no longer saw what Michelle saw, and as he looked up at her, he knew he had lost the connection with his Pillar. She was no longer his power. She was something else.

She wore the same face and the same dress but she looked more alive, more human. And what was translucent before now replaced by substance. Her smile assured him that Jessie was safe. And she looked just like when he had met her that day in Mammoth – beautiful, glorious and very much alive. Her skin started glowing, a white blinding light. And he saw the feathered wings unfold behind her. Sparkles of light danced and she was an angel that shone with graceful regality. Francis wondered if he was experiencing afterlife.

Her feet were inches from the ground and she glided towards him. He took the extended hand – soft and warm just like a human being, and let her pulled him up. He felt himself instantly imbibed with strength.

"Michelle?"

"That is the name of the one who belonged to the past, your memory. I am Lilith," she said her name with a certain authority. "Or in Hebrew I am known as Lilitu."

"But you look—"

"Yes, you have shaped me in the image of the one known as Michelle."

"Why am I talking to you, aren't you part of me? My Pillar?"

"Yes, I used to be. But now I am the guide."

The guide?

"And I'll guide you through the steps towards your ascension, your apotheosis."

"Ascension? Apotheosis?"

"Yes, you are the Antichrist."

"I am?"

"As it has written in the scripture. You are the spawn of the dragon released from the prison of earth, you are the Antichrist."

"What am I supposed to do?"

"To ascend to your throne and guide the human race towards the next evolution. To prepare and to behold, to steer and to rule."

"Am I not an evil being who will destroy the human race?"

She smiled, as if she was ridiculing him. "You will cleanse the world. Death, annihilation, life and birth are but parts of an inevitable cycle, a wheel that turns until the end of time. Choose now, Antichrist."

"Choose?"

"Choose to forsake your duty and remain in this world. Or choose to embark on a new journey for the evolution of the human race."

"I get to choose?"

"Of course, everyone in this world chooses their path. And you are not excluded from that privilege. The power to choose is what makes you human. And before becoming the One Who Watches, you are still human and you will choose. Take my hand, and you will embark on your new journey, and this world will change. Humans will change. Humans will be ready—"

"Ready for what?"

"For what is to come."

"Are you saying that if I don't do this, human beings will not be ready for what is to come?"

"I am only the guide. I do not foresee the future. I do not predict the uncertainty. You are the one who steers the destiny of Earth. You will choose the path."

"If I don't take your hand?"

"Then you go back to being a normal human being. The human race will not undertake the next step of evolution right away. Earth will be as is."

There he was, at the fork road of his destiny. For the first time he could choose. No, he had always chosen. He had chosen to come here with his freewill. Nobody had made him climb the Tower of Babel. Nobody had made him confront an evil darker than the night. He chose to come. Francis didn't really know what would happen to this world if he chose to embark on his ascension. He just knew that it wasn't something evil. The world wasn't going to be destroyed, as he was but helping the human race embark on its next step. It sounded like the right thing to do. To leave this world behind him, just like he always had when he went on a journey of his imagination. There wasn't much in this world that he was going to really miss. His family probably wouldn't have noticed if he was gone. His friends... he hardly had any friends. He turned back and saw the slumped figure of Jessie, who was still unconscious. He walked over to her, kneeled down, and gave her a kiss on her cheek. She was his one true friend. She had taught him how beautiful this world really was. And he was really going to miss her.

"Goodbye," he murmured, and felt a tear ran slowly down the side of his face. He felt the pain in his heart and soul then. Not only was she his best friend, she was who he loved with all his heart.

*   *   *   *

Jessie had heard the conversation between Francis and Michelle. Struggling to open her eyes, she wanted so much to tell him that she was awake but failed to even stir. She heard his goodbye and felt the warm kiss on her cheek. She wanted so much to stop him from going wherever he was going. But she couldn't, like a tormented soul trapped inside an inert body. She prayed and prayed for God to release her so that she could tell him her words – about how she really felt.

The footsteps were father and farther away.

When she prayed for the last time, her prayer was answered.

Opening her eyes, a bright light blinded her. She saw Michelle for the first time – an angelic being whose regal beauty was so intimidating that for a moment she was stunned. Then she focused on the back of the man before her, gathering her strength to get up and run towards him.

Catching him in an embrace from the back, she clasped her arms around him. "Francis, don't go."

"I... I have to go. It's my destiny."

"What about me… you're going to leave me all alone in this world."

"You'll never be alone. I'll always remember you."

"I…" She gathered her breath. "I love you."

For a moment he didn't say anything, his head only tilted a little bit backwards. If only she could look him in the eyes. But she had already said what she really wanted to say. She had finally realized that he was the one that she loved and wanted to love for the rest of her life. She had probably known that for a long time but failed to really grasp the idea and admit it. Until today, until at the last moment of losing him, then she knew how precious he was to her.

"You don't mean that. It's a cruel thing to say to try to save the human race—"

"To hell with the human race. I mean every word I said from the bottom of my heart and you know it. You were so different the first time I met you. I watched you grow up, from this withdrawn quiet boy to this brave responsible man who finally understood how to make friends and care about people and enjoy the beautiful things in this world. It's that change in you that makes me feel whole. I was not very different from you. I went after killers seeking justice and I started to forget the real purpose of life and I didn't even remember why I was afraid of darkness and why I was drawn to it and why I wanted to destroy it and days just slipped by and I… It was seeing the joy in your eyes you've never had before you met me, that made me feel the joy I have never felt myself. And in your eyes I see how beautiful and perfect you see me as, which I'm not, but it makes me feel like I'm in heaven."

He turned around then and put a finger on her lips. His brown eyes were filling up with tears. They were not tears of weakness or sadness, but tears of love and caring and the evidence of a man so moved by what he had just witnessed the only way to express his emotions was through weeping.

"But you're that beautiful and perfect, and I love you more than I love my own life, and I can't believe I just said that." He smiled genuinely and he was really very handsome, a quality that glowed from within him, something that would never wither away. "You give meaning to my life and when you are with me everything glows. You make me want to look forward to a bright future and before being there, enjoy every last little moments around me. I finally understand what love is, and when I saw you close to somebody else it just tore me apart, and when you were in danger, something churned in my stomach constantly reminding me that your safety meant more to me than my own life. You are the best thing that happened to me. If I have to choose between you and godhood, I don't even have to think twice—"

She knew exactly what he meant before he finished the sentence and she shut him up by kissing him. This time the kiss lingered, devoid of any divine interruption. Silently she thanked God for that.

The kiss felt like it lasted an eternity. Under the blessing of the full moon at the pinnacle of Babel Cydonia, the couple held each other in an embrace, realizing how lucky they were to finally find each other.

"That was a lot better than the first time."

"What first time?" She pinched him on the face.

"Ouch!" He chuckled. "Remember the first day when we met for really the first time, I thanked you when you were walking out the door for building me a bridge and you said it's always been there."

"How can I ever forget? And I know what you found on the other side."

He had found her, and he no longer had to pace back and forth between loneliness and wondering about what's real and what's not.

And she just realized, he had saved her life so many times she had lost count. "You're my hero, Francis," she told him.

"And you're my Hiro." It took her a while to get it, and she couldn't stop giggling after that.

The angelic entity known as Lilith had long disappeared without a trace, in her place only a pillar of sparkling light stood. That night the residents of Everett saw the pillar of light reaching from the top of Babel Cydonia towards the heavens. It was neither the light of man's path towards godhood nor the sign of the world's destruction, but a blessing for a new couple. Francis' heart had chosen the Earth because finally he had learned how to love. There a long journey had drawn to an end but it was only the beginning of a journey entirely new.

Epilogue

Entry: March 31st 2004

It's been almost three years since I found the time to pick up this pen and open my diary to write again. I was too happy and content just living my life. Yet today I felt the urge to write my thoughts down again, mainly to have something to remember myself by when I grow old. However I doubt that I'll ever forget what happened.

I'm five months pregnant by the way. We're having a daughter, and I'm naming her Michelle. But let me get back to the beginning, or the end, whichever you call it. After the incident at Everett that was the end of Babel Corps. The remnants of the company merged with others in the biotech industry and that was the last I ever heard of the word Babel. The government had covered up most of the things that happened, and nobody really knew what happened to the Pillar research data. Either everything was destroyed in the fire or someone buried the research somewhere. There weren't any more supernatural disturbances in the world, or at least the ones directly related to Project Pillars anyway.

Francis left information technology then and started his writing career, due to Mark's and my suggestion and support. Well, let me correct myself, he didn't really leave the IT altogether because he and Mark started a small online community about folklores and legends. It was a big success for a small venture, although they didn't really earn a lot out of it (the internet boom was already over by then). What they earned was satisfaction that the community, no matter how small it was, loved it and words spread quickly. The little money Francis earned on the website was enough to finance him for his writing. I told him I could support him, but you know how stubborn men are. They're all against that idea, for some reason. I was offered a job at the Bureau (I think they did that to shut me up about Babel) and I worked as a profiler at the child crime division ever since. It was something I was meant to do, just like Francis knew that he was really meant to write – to finally have somewhere to put down all his imagination, to finally be able to share with the world. I, on the other hand helped those who were abused and I did everything I could to stop it from happening. Well, most of the time at work I spent it behind a desk reading cases and analyzing files. Francis didn't want me being in the field again, being so dangerous and all. Well not until that time… but let me save that for another entry.

Francis and I were married six months after the incident at Babel. I never knew he could be so sweet. The way he proposed to me I just melted like chocolate over fire. Even though when we held each other that night at the top of Babel Cydonia, I knew I was going to be with him forever, hay what man will give up godhood for love? But it was still a sight to see him propose to me. On our honeymoon we went everywhere. We went to Japan and stayed in Tokyo and Osaka. It was a country that felt absolutely foreign, yet familiar to me. Then we were in Hong Kong and I even got along with Francis' parents. They are really very nice, although a bit cold. Of course they are not as nice as my parents, even Francis admitted so, but the relationships between his parents and him improved drastically after I showed up. Well, I made Francis connect with people, that's my specialty. His mother never really got the truth out of us, about Enoch Bel and Babel. We didn't want to spoil her brief memories of love with the darkness we went through, but I always suspected that she knew something more than she admitted. Maybe it was a woman's intuition. Mark and Francis became good friends, not best friends because Francis is still my best friend. That would never change. But they are similar in a lot of ways and I always hope that someday Mark would find someone like Francis did.

After being together with Francis, I finally realized what Mother meant about love. For me its definition is a little different than hers. It probably is for everyone because love is such a mysterious and wonderful thing everyone has to experience in his own way. But to me, true love is knowing that someone's there for you even when you've faced the worst of times. It's the feeling that even when you fall from a cliff you'd always know that someone's there waiting to catch you at the bottom, no matter what. With someone you love you not only share and spend the time of joy together, but you share the pain. Sometimes you have to go through the worst of times to really know who loves you. So for those of us who reach a painful time in life, there's always much more to look forward to. Life is like a roller-coaster ride. There're the ups and there're the downs. You never know what you'll find at the bottom, if you find someone who's willing to ride to the bottom with you, it's almost as good as being at the top. You never know when Mr. Choi lost his horse what's going to happen next and whether you should celebrate or sulk. Just make the best out of the presence and look forward to the future and make sure you are sharing it with someone you care about.

Two years after the fall of Babel, Francis finally found a publisher for his first novel. It was a retelling of the very same magical tale we all faced together, of course with all the real names and places changed. He won a first novel award. To the truth I had found his writing style crude and Mark did a lot of editing work to make it passable. I was a little bit surprised that he won an award but I was very happy for him because he told his tale not by the writing, but by his heart. Steven King once said he has a heart of a little boy and he keeps it in a jar by his bed. Well, Francis has a heart of a little boy also but I am always holding it right next to mine. (Gosh that just sounded really corny, didn't it? But who cares, I'm the only one who's going to read this anyway)

Mark became an editor and writer for a magazine but had yet to write his own book. He hadn't really changed and always wondered about the what-ifs. What if Francis really embarked on that journey? Other than my sure misery, who knows what would have happened? Would the human race have really changed? I guess those questions are better left unanswered. My brother, the whirlwind of weird ideas, has one interesting theory though. What if the human race were meant to evolve, to be ready for an evitable threat that lingered closely on the horizon, did my love for Francis doomed the human race then? I don't really feel guilty though. The human race, my happiness, what's more important? I'm just kidding though. There are things that you just can't be weighing on a balance. And not to mention, the adaptive and courageous species known as the human race will just find another way to deal with whatever this imaginary threat is. Perhaps Francis had steered the world towards a different path than the one that was originally planned. But he was free to choose. There was no right or wrong, black or white. There was only the path of a brighter future, the one he believed in. Human beings no longer needed Pillars, we become pillars for each other. It is through the support of each others that we get through life.

I never saw Michelle after that. Neither did Francis. What was the link between the real Michelle and the entity Lilith? Was Michelle really just a figment of Francis' memory? Or was she a guardian angel who protected Francis against the darkness that tried to devour him? The answers to those questions stayed as mysteries too, just like "Are there ghosts" or "Is there a God?" Francis and I still haven't gotten around to going to church yet. But how can we really deny the existence of a higher being, someone who really watches over us? Sometimes we get together and pray, and we pray for those who died for their own cause, like Enoch Bel, Andy, Kyle, those people at the church, the innocents whose life were scorched and extinguished by the senseless battles, Terry and even the Tormentor Mary – whose soul was once consumed with hate and fear and is now finally released.

Oh, did I ever mention that I grew my hair long after that? Francis never said anything but I know he loved it. (And no, I'm not trying to look like Michelle, but I can't deny that there was an inspiration factor involved.)

To say we live happily ever after... Well, that's only an ending in fairy tales. Our life has just begun. Remember what I said earlier that I was back in the field of that one time because... well that's an adventure that almost took us apart. But love gave us the courage to face even the darkest of darkness just like what we have gone through with Babel. But now, that's a story to be told another time. Until then...

ABOUT THE AUTHOR

Fabian Chung is an amateur software engineer, part-time writer, professional dreamer who occasionally dabbles in project management and game design. He resides in Los Angeles and currently working on his next novel which may or may not be part of the ongoing Pillars series and also the next blockbuster video game. Please visit his blog at jetfable.blog.com and the website at www.JetFable.com.